Rogue

Karen Lynch

ISBN: 0692516794
ISBN-13:978-0692516799

Cover Designer: Nikos Lima

To John Beattie

If I had a flower for every time I thought of you… I could walk through my garden forever. – Alfred Lord Tennyson

ACKNOWLEDGEMENTS

First, I want to thank my family and friends for their love and support and their belief in me. Next, I have to thank my readers for giving my books a chance and going on this amazing journey with me. You are the reason I write. I also have to thank my editor, Kelly, my beta readers, and my very talented cover artist, Nikos. Thank you to Rana Hillis for giving me the name for Draegan the demon, one of the more interesting demons in this book. Finally, I want to send a special thank you to my PA, Sara Meadows, and the dedicated and wonderful readers who run the Mohiri group: Jeff, Rana, Sara, Jeannie and Shannon (who loves Nikolas as much as I do).

CHAPTER 1

"OH MY GOD! I can't believe I let you talk me into this."

"M-me?" I wobbled on stiff legs toward the dilapidated building that used to be the Butler Falls lumber mill. My wet clothes hung heavily on me, and the cold wind was an icy lash across my face. If my teeth chattered any harder they would surely break. "You're the one wh-who insisted on coming along."

Jordan huffed as she caught up to me in three long strides, her short blond hair flattened wetly against her head. She passed me and pushed open the wooden door, which groaned loudly on its rusty hinges. By the time I entered the building she had shed her wet coat and pulled a small flashlight from the plastic bag she carried. She set the flashlight down on an overturned wooden barrel and began stripping off her clothes.

Shivering violently, I pulled off my own wet clothes. My numb fingers fumbled with the button of my jeans for thirty seconds before it finally came undone. Down to my bra and panties, I ripped open the plastic bag I had tucked inside my coat and pulled out dry clothes and sneakers. My breath fogged the air around me as I struggled to pull the jeans up my damp legs, and I nearly fell over from the effort.

Jordan swung her flashlight in my direction, momentarily blinding me. "You said you could keep us warm in the river, but you forgot to mention that I'd freeze my ass off when we got here."

I sighed when my thick sweater settled over my body. It wasn't as warm as a coat, but it was a vast improvement over wet clothes. I slipped on my dry socks and sneakers before I straightened up to answer her. "I said I could get us down the river, and here we are. Okay, I forgot one tiny detail. You have to admit it was a brilliant plan."

"Bloody genius." I couldn't see her face behind the flashlight, but I knew she was wearing her signature smirk. "If we don't die from exposure, this will go down as the most awesome getaway *ever*! I still can't believe what you did back there. Or that we just rode that crazy river all the way to town and we're still alive to talk about it. They'll be talking about this one for years."

"You know me, wild and unpredictable." I picked up my plastic bag, which still contained a folded blue T-shirt, and tucked it into the waistband of my jeans under my sweater. From an inside pocket of my wet coat I pulled my sheathed silver dagger, which I also tucked inside my jeans. I didn't have to ask Jordan if she had weapons on her. She probably wore a knife to bed.

"I'm starting to believe you're capable of anything." She lowered the flashlight. "Do you think they know we're gone?"

I wrung the water from my ponytail and started for the door. "Yes – or they will soon enough. And you know the first place they'll look is town. We need to get a move on before he... they get here."

Jordan followed me outside. "I wouldn't want to be anywhere near Nikolas when he realizes you gave him the slip. He's going to lose it. I'm telling you now, if he catches up with us, I'm using you for a shield. He'll be too focused on you to start raging at me."

"Wow, what a friend." I blew on my hands and rubbed them together before tucking them under my arms. Why hadn't I thought to bring a pair of gloves? And a cap? Peering through the darkness, I saw the faint outline of a road to my left, and I started jogging in that direction.

Jordan ran beside me. "I happen to have a strong survival instinct, which is why you asked me to come with you."

A laugh burst from me. "I didn't ask you. You blackmailed me, remember?"

"I merely pointed out that you might have cool powers but you can't fight for shit, and you'll need someone with my skills out here."

"You also said you'd tell Nikolas what I was planning if I didn't let you come."

She coughed. "Um, I wouldn't really have done that. I just didn't want to stay there with you gone and Liv..."

"I know." We fell silent, neither of us ready to talk about Olivia. I'd known Olivia for only month, but her death had affected me deeply. I knew Jordan was grieving the loss of her friend even though she kept it inside.

The road was dark and the night was quiet except for the sound of our breath and our feet slapping the pavement. After five minutes, it felt like my hair was frozen to my scalp, but at least the exercise was warming the rest of my body. It was another five minutes before we hit the main road. Fear of being out in the open made us quicken our pace, and I was panting heavily by the time we reached the farmhouse belonging to the only person I knew in Butler Falls.

Jordan rang the doorbell and Derek Mason opened it to stare at us with wide eyes. "What happened to you two?" He ushered us inside and the wave of heat made my cold face tingle. "Where are your coats, and why is your hair wet?"

"Long story." Jordan walked over to stand in front of the blazing fire in the living room. "I thought your friend Wes was going to be here."

"He'll be here at six. It's only quarter 'til." Derek looked from Jordan to me like he wasn't quite sure what to make of us. "You girls must be freezing. Do you want a blanket or something hot to drink? I can make some hot chocolate or tea."

I gave him a grateful smile. "Hot chocolate would be awesome. And I wouldn't mind a hair dryer if you have one."

"Sure. There's one in the bathroom at the end of the hall upstairs. I'll put the kettle on." Derek was a great host. I'd met him at a party here two weeks ago, and he had gone out of his way to make us feel at home. Of course, that was before his best friends showed up as newly-made vampires and tried to kill us. Thank God, Derek didn't remember any of that. The Mohiri healers had used a drug to modify his memories, and he thought his bruises were from falling from the loft while giving Jordan and me a tour of the barn. I had no idea what story Tristan had come up with to account for Derek's missing friends.

Within five minutes, Jordan and I were cradling mugs of steaming hot chocolate, and I was warm for the first time since I'd left the river. We sat in the living room where Jordan and Derek kept up a steady conversation, while I watched the clock and waited for Derek's friend to arrive.

At five minutes after six, a knock came at the door, and I was so jittery I nearly spilled hot chocolate over me. A tall blond man in his early twenties let himself in. I recognized him from the party. Derek reintroduced us to Wes, and we wasted no time in getting down to business.

"You got the money I transferred this morning?" Jordan asked Wes.

"I did, thanks." He reached inside his coat and pulled out some folded papers. "Here's the title and registration. I filled the tank and checked the oil. She's good to go."

"Perfect." I stood and carried my mug to the kitchen. "Thanks for taking care of this on such short notice, Wes. And thanks for the hot chocolate, Derek."

Derek followed me. "You seem to be in a hurry. Is everything okay?"

I rinsed my cup and faced him. He looked genuinely concerned, and I tried to think of something to reassure him.

Jordan answered for me. "We're supposed to meet some friends in Boise tonight." The dazzling smile she turned on Derek made him forget whatever he was going to say, and he merely nodded instead. I hid my smile. Jordan was lethal in more ways than one.

Wes laughed. "Something tells me Boise better watch out."

"You have no idea." Jordan grinned and held up her hand. "Keys?"

He pulled a set from his pocket and handed them to her. "You do know how to drive a stick, right?"

She rolled her eyes. "Who doesn't?"

I decided to keep silent on that subject.

Derek and Wes accompanied us outside where an older model white Ford Escort sat in the driveway. We thanked both men. Then I hurried to the car, hoping the heater worked well. Damn, it was cold outside tonight.

"Hold on a sec." Derek ran inside and returned a minute later with two fleece jackets. "Here, take these before you freeze to death."

I refused them because I doubted we'd be able to return them anytime soon, but he waved it off. "My mother keeps buying them for me, and I have more than I'll ever use," he argued.

"Thanks." I pulled on one of the jackets and handed the other to Jordan. We slid into the front seats, waved to Derek and Wes, and pulled away.

"And we're off!" Jordan let out a whoop and gave me a wide smile. "Next stop, Boise."

"Let's get out of town first and then we can celebrate." I glanced around, expecting to feel a telltale brush against my mind at any second. Butler Falls was only five miles from Westhorne, and it wouldn't take Nikolas long to get mobile and come after us. This was my only shot at leaving. If they caught me now, there would be no second chance. Nikolas would make sure of that.

Jordan and I were tense as we sped through town as fast as we could go without drawing attention to us. At one point, a dark SUV appeared behind us, and my heart leaped into my throat until the vehicle turned into a grocery store parking lot. By the time we reached the highway exit, my stomach was tied in painful knots and Jordan's knuckles were white from clenching the steering wheel. We both released audible sighs when we merged onto the highway and picked up speed.

After we put a few miles behind us, Jordan began fiddling with the radio, and I turned up the heater to warm my cold feet. I missed my boots, but they had been too bulky to fit inside my coat with my change of clothes. Someone definitely would have noticed and our getaway would have been over before it had even started.

I still couldn't believe we had pulled it off. Westhorne was going to be in an uproar when they realized Jordan and I were gone. I'd left letters explaining why I was leaving, though I didn't expect them to placate the people who read them.

Nate had been through so much lately, and he was going to be very upset when he heard what I'd done. But I was doing this for him and everyone else I cared about. None of us was safe as long as the Master was alive. Our only connection to him was Madeline, and I was sure I could find her with David's help. I wouldn't be here if I didn't believe that.

Nate wasn't the only one who would be upset. An ache settled in my chest when I thought about Nikolas. Already, I missed him and I wondered how long it would be before I saw him again. In the back of my mind, a sad voice whispered, *Solmi*. My Mori couldn't understand why we were leaving Nikolas and his Mori behind. For once, I had no words of comfort for it.

I pictured Nikolas's reaction when he discovered I was gone. I hadn't talked to him since we had argued about his plans to take me away and hide me from the Master. He'd come to my room twice, but I wouldn't open the door even though it had been so hard to feel him nearby and not go to him. Nikolas was astute, and he would have known I was planning something as soon as he'd seen my face.

He'd left me alone after that, but he'd made it clear that he knew me a little better than I'd accused him of. When I'd left my room to go to the menagerie, Niall and Seamus had materialized beside me and accompanied me there. They hadn't left my side when I'd taken Hugo and Woolf out, though I could tell they were nervous around the hellhounds. On my way back to the main building we were met by Chris who took over babysitting duty. Nikolas might have been giving me space, but he hadn't been taking any chances either.

Did he know I was gone? Had he already found the letter I'd left in his apartment? He was going to be furious. He wouldn't agree with my reasons, but I'd had to try to explain them anyway, and to make sure he knew my leaving had nothing to do with our bond. If I'd believed I could have convinced him to work with me on this, I would have chosen that option in a heartbeat. But I'd seen his face when he said he was going to take me away, and there would be no compromising with him. Not on this.

"Ah, hell!"

"What is it?" My head whipped around, expecting to see a pair of headlights closing in on us.

"I forgot my damn sword."

I stared at Jordan, willing my heart to settle back into a normal rhythm. "Your sword?"

"Yeah." She let out a mournful sigh. "I'll never find one as good as mine."

"Jordan, we barely snuck away as it is. If anyone had seen you carrying a sword, they would have known something was up."

"I know, but I still hate leaving it behind."

"We'll find you a new one." I looked around. "How close are we?"

"About twenty minutes. I may have broken the speed limit a little."

Soon the lights of Boise appeared in the distance, and before I knew it,

Jordan was maneuvering the car through the busy city streets. She handled the car well for someone who had spent most of her life at a Mohiri stronghold. When I mentioned it, she smiled and said it was easy to get the boys in Butler Falls to let you drive their cars.

After half a dozen wrong turns and a stop at a 7-Eleven for gas and directions, we finally reached our destination. Jordan pulled up in front of St. John's Cathedral, and I waved wildly at the two figures standing by the large door at the top of the steps. They jogged over to the car, and Jordan popped the trunk so they could stow away their large backpacks.

Roland climbed in behind me and rubbed his hands against his thighs. "What took you so long? We nearly froze our asses off."

I turned in my seat to face them. "Why didn't you go inside to get warm?"

Peter made a face. "We did, but sitting through one long mass is enough. We've been here for hours."

"You poor things." Jordan scoffed. "At least *you* didn't have to climb out of a river, and then hike miles in this cold."

Roland leaned forward. "What are you talking about?"

Jordan groaned. "Before we wow and amaze you guys, can someone tell me where we are going?"

"Salt Lake City," I said.

The three of them stared at me.

"David has a friend there who is holding a laptop and some cell phones for me. We can stop over there on our way to Albuquerque."

Jordan spoke first. "That has to be six hours away."

"Almost five. I looked it up."

"Sara, don't you think it would be better to stay in Boise tonight and leave in the morning?" Roland asked.

"Boise is going to be crawling with Mohiri in an hour... if it isn't already. I don't know about you guys, but I'd rather not be here when that happens."

"She's right." Jordan said. "They probably have a team here already, and the rest will come when they find out we're gone."

Roland rested his chin on the back of my seat. "He's gonna lose it, isn't he?"

I didn't have to ask who "he" was. "Probably."

His hand touched my shoulder. "It's not too late to turn back."

"No. I have to do this, but I understand if any of you have changed your mind."

"We go where you go," Roland stated with finality, and Jordan and Peter agreed.

"Salt Lake City, here we come." Jordan put the car in drive and pulled away from the church.

Roland settled back in his seat. "So how did you girls manage to sneak away?"

Jordan and I exchanged smiles. Then she glanced over her shoulder at Roland. "It wasn't easy. After you guys left, Sara acquired two personal bodyguards who wouldn't let her out of their sight. Not hard to guess *who* gave them that job."

"I'm surprised Nikolas was willing to let someone else watch you," Roland said.

I looked down at my hands. "We weren't exactly talking before I left."

"Since when has that ever stopped him?"

Peter snorted. "You girls are here, so your bodyguards couldn't have been *that* good."

"You don't know Seamus and Niall," I said.

"Once we realized they were going to follow Sara everywhere, we had to get a little creative. Actually, it was all Sara's idea." Jordan chuckled. "She set a little trap for them, and they fell right into it."

I took up the story. "Sahir takes care of the menagerie, but he was hurt during the attack and he has to stay in the medical ward for a few days. I went to the menagerie during dinner to feed Hugo, Woolf, and Minuet, and Jordan came along to help."

"Of course. I'm such a good friend."

I rolled my eyes at her. "Seamus and Niall waited by the door while I fed everyone, and Jordan went into Sahir's office where she could see us on the security monitors. I gave her a signal and she turned out the lights."

"But can't warriors see pretty well in the dark?" Roland asked.

"Yep. And the twins went right for Sara, which is what we wanted them to do." Jordan snickered. "Then she zapped their Irish asses."

Roland guffawed. "You didn't."

"It wasn't much. I just needed to freeze them long enough for us to take their radios and lock them in Alex's cage. They were already swearing up a storm by the time Jordan and I left the building. I figured no one would go to the menagerie looking for us for at least an hour. It's not like Seamus and Niall will have to spend the night there."

"Now comes the best part," Jordan said. "Bet you're thinking we snuck away through the woods, right? Not us. We jumped in the river."

"Sure you did." Peter scoffed. "Seriously, how did you get away?"

"We rode the river. I used my power to keep us warm and to get the water to take us where we wanted to go." I'd gotten the idea from the night of the attack when Jordan and I had ridden the river to the stronghold to escape vampires.

Peter's mouth fell open and Roland yelled, "Are you insane? You could have died!"

"I'm really good at controlling water. We were perfectly safe. Besides,

Feeorin and Fiannar were with us the whole time."

"What?" Jordan jerked the steering wheel and the car swerved a little before she corrected it. "What do you mean they were with us?"

"I think they like to watch over me. I saw them a few times along the way. I didn't tell you because I didn't want you to freak out. Kelpies don't have the best reputation."

"With good reason! You couldn't tell me after we left the river?"

"I was kind of preoccupied, trying not to freeze to death, and to get out of town. I guess it didn't seem important compared to everything else." I told Roland and Peter about meeting Derek and Wes and buying the car. "And here we are."

"And here we are." Roland looked excited and nervous at the same time.

"You have our stuff, right?" I asked, and he nodded. I'd known there was no way to sneak out with backpacks, so Jordan and I had given the boys our things to stuff inside their larger packs. Once we got to Salt Lake City, she and I could buy backpacks for ourselves.

"Jordan, you might want to step on it," Roland said. "I have no desire to run into a Mohiri warrior after hearing about the stunt you two pulled. Something tells me they aren't going to take it well."

"Way ahead of you, Wolf Boy."

I glanced at the speedometer and saw we were doing ninety. "Just don't get pulled over." She didn't have a driver's license or insurance. All we needed was some state trooper poking around and asking questions.

Once we hit the interstate, talk turned to Albuquerque and the chances of finding Madeline. Or more importantly, what I was going to do when I found her. Now that I was getting closer to confronting her, I didn't know what I was going to say. It wasn't going to be a sweet mother-daughter reunion. Madeline was a stranger to me, one with information I needed to keep the people I loved safe.

The conversation quieted after an hour or so, and I retreated into my thoughts. Now that we were safely away, guilt settled in. I hated to think of what Tristan and Nate would go through when they discovered what I'd done. Tristan was almost as protective as Nikolas. I promised myself I would call them as often as I could, though I knew that wasn't going to alleviate their fears. I thought about calling Nikolas and swallowed hard. Already his absence was a hollow pain in my chest.

"Sara, wake up!"

"Huh?" I opened my eyes and sat up straight. "Sorry, didn't mean to fall asleep."

Roland leaned away from me. "You can sleep all you want as long as you don't start glowing again."

"What?"

"You were lit up like a giant glow stick," Jordan said, not taking her eyes off the road. "It's kind of hard to remain inconspicuous when they can see you from the space station. Does that happen a lot?"

"I don't know. I mean, I don't think so." I held up my hands, but they looked normal. "A month ago I was having little episodes where my power acted up. I thought I was done with them once I learned to control my power. It must be starting again."

Roland whistled. "If that was a little episode, I don't want to see a big one."

"I didn't glow before, so this must be something new." My teeth worried my lower lip. I was pretty sure glowing wasn't normal even for an undine. Aine had said my power would grow, but not when it would stop, and I had no idea what to expect next.

Roland's hand squeezed my shoulder. "We'll figure it out. Don't worry."

It was well after midnight when we reached Salt Lake City. I wasn't the only one who let out a big sigh. It had been a long day for all of us, and a five-hour car ride would tire anyone.

"I don't know about you guys, but I'm beat." Roland yawned loudly. "What do you say we find a motel and catch some Zs?"

Peter stretched. "Sounds good to me."

"I have to go to David's friend's place first to get the stuff he's holding for me," I said, rubbing the back of my neck.

Jordan shot me a glance. "Now? It's awfully late to be making a house call."

"David said his friend, Kelvan, sleeps during the day. If we don't go now, we won't be able to see him until tomorrow night, and I don't want to spend two nights here."

"Fine, but I have to find a gas station first. My bladder is about to burst."

"Same here," Peter added.

I pulled a folded piece of paper from the back pocket of my jeans and studied the address I'd written on it. We were going to need a map, too. None of us knew our way around this city.

It didn't take long to locate a gas station. The four of us went in search of the restrooms, and then I found a little souvenir rack up front that had a map of the city. I bought it along with bottles of water and some premade sandwiches from the cooler. Not exactly an ideal meal, but it would tide us over until breakfast. By the time I walked outside, Jordan had finished refueling the car. We devoured the sandwiches, and I realized it wasn't going to be cheap to feed four large appetites. I decided to worry about that later and focus on finding David's friend right now.

Peter chuckled when I spread out the map. "Why are you wasting time with that when we can look it up on our phones?"

"We don't have any phones yet," I said, tracing a route with my finger. "You two ditched yours, right?"

"Uh..."

My head snapped up and I spun in my seat to stare at him. "Please tell me you tossed your phones at the airport."

Peter flushed. "We thought we should have phones on us in case we needed them."

I groaned and rubbed my temple where a headache had started to form. "Peter, the Mohiri are very good at tracking people. How long do you think it's going to take them to figure out we're all together? We have to get rid of them *now*."

"Are they really that good?" Roland asked.

"This is Nikolas we're talking about," Jordan told him. "What do you think?"

Roland pulled out his phone and held it up. "What do we do with them? Throw them in the trash?"

"No, they'd still track us." Jordan lowered the map and looked around. A smile spread across her face. "Hand them over. I have an idea."

Roland and Peter passed their phones to her, and she got out of the car. We watched her walk toward the gas pumps where an RV was parked. She disappeared behind it and returned a minute later without the phones. She wore a smug expression when she climbed into the car. Before I could ask what she'd done with the phones, she pointed at the RV pulling away from the pump.

A few seconds later I saw what she was grinning about. The rear of the RV was covered in stickers that said things like "Snow Birds" and "Beach Bound," and the license plate was from Alberta. "Brilliant!"

"I hope Nikolas likes Florida." Her smile grew. "See, I told you you'd need me on this trip."

It took us a few minutes to locate Kelvan's address on the map and for Jordan to figure out the best route to get there. Twenty minutes later, we pulled up outside a dingy four-story apartment building. Jordan cut off the engine, and I looked down the empty street that was dark in places because of missing streetlights. Garbage littered the street that was badly in need of repair, and graffiti covered some of the buildings.

"Not exactly welcoming, is it?" Roland muttered, and I silently agreed with him. "Are you sure this place is safe, Sara?"

"If David says we can trust his friend, I believe him."

"What if it's not his friend we have to worry about? For all we know there could be a dozen suckers hiding in that building."

I tapped my chest. "Trust me, if there was a vampire close by, I'd know it."

The four of us climbed out of the car, and Roland led the way into the poorly lit lobby on the main floor. A cluster of mailboxes lined one side of the hallway and two elevators took up the other side. I hit the elevator button and could hear the groan and creak of gears as the car slowly descended. From the sounds it was making, I wasn't sure we shouldn't take the stairs instead.

We got off on the fourth floor, which looked even more rundown than the lobby with stained carpet and peeling wallpaper that had probably been put up in the seventies. I led the way to apartment 410 and knocked briskly on the door.

I heard someone moving around inside the apartment and then the sounds of locks being undone on the door. One, two, three... four locks? This guy was seriously paranoid. The door cracked open and a male voice spoke. "Who are you?"

"I'm David's friend, Sara. Are you Kelvan?"

The door opened another inch, but instead of admitting us, the man held up a cell phone and snapped a picture of me. Then the door shut in my face.

"Hey!" I yelled, knocking again. *What the heck was that about?*

After a minute of knocking, the door opened again and the man said, "Come in."

I walked into the apartment, followed closely by the others, and the door shut behind us with a loud click. Immediately, my power flared up and static crackled through my hair. I whirled around and got my first look at our host, one word racing through my mind. *Demon!*

CHAPTER 2

THE DEMON STARED at me with wide eyes as I took in his appearance: my height with a rounded face and curly brown hair. If it weren't for his black eyes and the two small horns peeking through his curls, I might have mistaken him for human. That and the fact that my power was going a little berserk. What the hell was David thinking? Why hadn't he told me he was sending me to see a demon?

Kelvan put up a hand and fear flashed across his face. He stepped back until he was pressed against the door. "You're Mohiri... and Lycans! David, why did you send hunters into my home?" he asked shrilly, and I glimpsed tiny fangs where his canines should be.

A faint voice issued from the cell phone in his hand, and he hit the speaker button.

"Kelvan, this is my friend Sara I told you about," said David's familiar voice. "Sara, meet my good friend Kelvan. You've probably figured out that Kelvan is a vrell demon."

I looked at Jordan, who had studied demonology a lot longer than I had. She gave a slight nod, which I assumed meant vrell demons were not dangerous.

"Hi." I smiled at Kelvan but didn't extend my hand. I didn't think he would appreciate my power's reaction to him.

"Hello," he replied stiffly, without returning the smile.

David spoke again. "Kelvan is one of the best hackers in the business. He's actually the one who tracked Madeline to Albuquerque."

"Thank you," I said.

Kelvan shifted from one foot to the other. It struck me then that he was not being unpleasant on purpose. He was genuinely afraid of us, afraid of everything if all the locks on the door were any indication.

Someone moved behind me and Kelvan's eyes widened even further.

"David vouches for *you*, but what about the other hunter and the wolves?"

I glanced over my shoulder at Roland who looked ready to pounce if Kelvan made one false move. Turning back to Kelvan, I said, "Are you going to try to eat us or anything equally unpleasant?"

The look of horror on his face was almost comical. "Of course not!"

"Then we're good." I faced my friends. "Chill out, guys."

Roland's jaw dropped. "But he's a *demon*, Sara."

I arched an eyebrow, and he reddened. "I didn't mean it that way. You're different."

"David trusts him and so do I. Not all demons are evil, you know."

They all stared at me like I'd sprouted my own pair of horns, and I could feel Kelvan's eyes boring into the back of my head.

Jordan looked at Kelvan. "You see what I have to live with? Watch out or she'll be trying to feed you blueberry muffins next." She went to the coffee table, grabbed a National Geographic magazine, and settled down in the stuffed armchair as if she hung out in demon lairs every day.

Roland relaxed his stance, and he and Peter took the couch. He picked up the TV remote. "Hey, do you mind if we watch TV while we wait?"

"Um, sure, go ahead," Kelvan replied weakly as if he didn't know what to make of the strangers invading his living room.

"If you guys don't need me anymore, I have something to take care of," David said. He told me to contact him when I got to Albuquerque then said goodbye and hung up, leaving me standing with a nervous demon. I tried not to stare at Kelvan, but it's not every day you meet a demon. Sure I'd seen a few, but none that were humanoid.

"David said you have a laptop and some phones for me," I said to break the awkward silence.

Kelvan nodded and went to the far corner of the living room that served as his office. The large desk was almost impossible to see beneath the computers and multiple monitors that were mounted on stands to make room for them all. Soda bottles and Chinese takeout containers also littered the top, and he muttered an apology as he hurried to clean it up.

I took the opportunity to study the apartment. It was cluttered, but much cleaner than I'd expected based on what I'd seen of the building. Books, magazines, and newspapers lay around the living room, and the kitchen table was covered in what appeared to be model airplane pieces. There was a stereo with an actual turntable and a large stack of albums beside it. The top one was a Fleetwood Mac album, and my fingers itched to find out what others lay beneath it.

All in all, it looked like a pretty normal place, not what I'd expected a demon's home to look like. But then, I'd never really imagined demons living among humans this way. I'd pictured them living in sewers and abandoned buildings, not in a little apartment with throw pillows and a ficus tree.

I did take note of the thick bars on the windows, and I couldn't help but wonder who or what Kelvan was hiding from. Granted, it wasn't the nicest part of town, but his defenses seemed a bit extreme. Maybe he was afraid someone was going to steal all his computer equipment.

"I hope you like Macs. They're all I use, and David didn't give me much notice."

I turned to find Kelvan holding out a thin, silver laptop. "Wow, it's so light," I marveled when I took it from him. And small. This would easily fit in a backpack. "Nice!"

"It gets great battery life, and you can go a few days without charging if you don't use it much. I got you a padded case to protect it."

"This is great, Kelvan. Thanks."

Kelvan smiled for the first time, and his fangs flashed again. It was a little strange to be talking computers with a guy who had fangs, but I did my best to act like it was no big deal.

He held up a small rectangular gadget. "This is a mobile hotspot and it'll let you connect to the internet from almost anywhere. The account is not in your name, and there's no way to trace it back to you or us. I also installed some of my own apps on the Mac that will allow you to browse the internet and make secure calls that can't be traced to your IP. Come over to my desk and I'll show you how to use them."

Twenty minutes later, I closed the laptop after a crash course in how to use a Mac and Kelvan's special software. In addition to the laptop, he gave me a bag containing four prepaid cell phones and an envelope containing five hundred dollars in cash. I tried to refuse the money, but he said it was from David, not him. When I asked him if David could afford it, Kelvin chuckled and said their clients paid generously for their services. His statement made me wonder exactly what they did for their clients and why he chose to stay in this rundown building when he could afford to live in a better neighborhood. He seemed like a nice guy, a bit shy around strangers. But then it wasn't as if a guy with horns could go out and socialize a lot. From the look of his apartment, he didn't have many visitors either.

I was getting to my feet when a scrawny white cat entered the living room and headed straight for Kelvan. It was easy to tell from the cat's matted fur and staggering walk that it was unwell, and I automatically bent to pick it up. The poor creature weighed next to nothing, and it could barely manage a weak hiss in my direction.

Kelvan immediately reached for the cat. "Please, don't hurt her."

I was so shocked anyone would think I could harm an animal that I answered more sharply than I meant to. "Don't be ridiculous." I cradled the cat in my arms, my power already searching for the source of her illness. It didn't take long to discover the tumors riddling her frail body. The poor creature would be lucky if she lived another two weeks. "She's full of cancer. Didn't you take her to a vet?"

His eyes widened until they looked like large black buttons. "How do you...? I took her to one of our doctors, and he said there was nothing he could do for her." He held out his hands and I saw they were trembling. "Please, Lulu is all I have."

I gave him a reassuring smile and sat on the couch between Roland and Peter with the cat on my lap. I had healed very sick animals before, but never one so full of cancer. I didn't want to make any promises to Kelvan until I knew I could help Lulu. I laid both hands on her stomach and cringed as my power explored the extent of her tumors. They were so big that some of them had fused together. She should have been put to sleep weeks ago. The agony on Kelvan's face told me he knew that, but couldn't bring himself to part with her.

Kelvan came to stand before me, clenching his hands together. "What are you going to do to her?"

Roland stood beside him to watch me. "Dude, I think this is Lulu's lucky day."

"What do you mean?"

"Watch."

Hoping Roland was right, I stroked Lulu's head, letting my power soothe her. Soon her head drooped limply against my thigh, and my power went to work. I went after the smallest tumors first, gently consuming them with healing fire that repaired the organs they had damaged. The largest growth was attached to her lungs, and it took me a good five minutes to destroy that one. Then I had to fix her weakened heart and remove the remaining impurities from her blood. I smiled in satisfaction as the glow faded from my hands. *That should do it.*

"You killed her!"

I looked up at Kelvan's grief-stricken face and shook my head. "No, she's just sleeping. See? She'll be perfectly fine when she wakes up. The really sick ones always do this after they're healed."

"Healed?" His eyes darted from me to his cat. "How... how is that possible?"

"It's something I do, and I'd really appreciate it if you'd keep it to yourself." It had been careless of me to show my power to a stranger, especially a demon, but all logic had gone out the window when I'd picked up the sick cat. Standing, I placed the sleeping cat in his outstretched hands. One of my fingers grazed his hand, and he jumped as if he'd received a shock. "Sorry." My power was a bit amped because of the healing and the presence of a demon. I forced it back down. The lessons with Nikolas and Chris had really paid off.

Kelvan's next action shocked us. He sat on the coffee table, cradling

Lulu to his chest while fat tears rolled down his cheeks. "I'm sorry," he said hoarsely when he could talk again. "Lulu was my brother's cat, and she's all I have left of him."

"Your brother?" I prodded gently.

"Mallar, my older brother. He brought Lulu home five years ago when she was just a kitten."

Jordan came to stand beside me. "Where is he?"

Kelvan sniffled and wiped his face with his hand. "He was killed two years ago. He and his friend, Jaesop, went out one night and ran into some vampires."

"Vampires?" Peter asked. "Why would they kill another demon?"

Kelvan shrugged sadly. "Why do humans kill other humans? They are evil. Vampires think themselves superior to all other races, and they kill anyone who crosses them. There are few demons who would not rejoice if every vampire was wiped from the face of the earth."

"Is that why you're helping us?" I asked him. "Because of your brother?"

"David and I have been friends for years, so I would have helped him anyway. When he told me Madeline could lead the Mohiri to the Master, I made tracking her my first priority." He stroked his sleeping cat's head. "Hunters don't help my kind, and we don't help them. But if you need *anything*, you let David know and he'll contact me. I can never repay you for helping Lulu."

"You don't owe me for that. I would have done it anyway."

He gave me a watery smile. "You are not like other hunters, are you?"

Jordan snorted. "You have no idea."

"How did you know what we are anyway?" I asked him.

He shrugged. "Most demons can sense another demon when we get close enough. My people have a very good sense of smell, which is why I knew those two were werewolves."

Jordan covered a yawn with her hand and looked at me. "As fun as all of this is, I'm ready to crash for a few hours."

"Me too." I gathered up the laptop, cell phones, and cash and looked around for my backpack before I remembered I still had to buy one. I spotted a paper bag on the kitchen counter and stuffed everything into it. If we ran into anyone on the way to the car, I doubted they'd take much notice of a Chinese takeout bag.

"Thanks for everything," I said to Kelvan before I followed the others into the hallway. He held out his hand, and I shook my head. My control was a lot better now, but I didn't want to risk hurting him. "Better not."

"Oh, right." He withdrew his hand and ran it through his curls. "Listen, I know you're more than a hunter. It doesn't take a genius to see that. David said the Master is looking for you, and I'm sure it has something to do with whatever you did to Lulu. Be careful out there. Word is that this is the most dangerous vampire anyone's heard of in a long time. They say he's insane, and he really has it out for the Mohiri. All vampires do, but he's the worst."

"If you know that, you must know more about him."

"No one really knows anything about him, except what comes from other vampires, and they're not saying anything. There have been some demon disappearances that have been blamed on him, too. No one knows what he's doing with them, but everyone's afraid. Just watch your step."

"I will. Thanks."

The four of us were quiet as we walked back to the car. Jordan started the engine and looked over at me. "I'm going to stop at the first decent motel I see."

"Someplace cheap," I reminded her. "We have to make this money stretch until we can get more." David's five hundred dollars would help a lot, but between gas, food, and hotels, it wouldn't take us long to run through it. I had some diamonds that would fetch a good price if I could find a buyer. I put that on my mental list of things to do – after I got some sleep.

"As long as it's not a total roach motel." She reached into the back pocket of her jeans and pulled out a thin wad of bills, which she handed to me. "Here's four hundred. It's all I could get."

Roland leaned forward. "I have five hundred. I found a bank machine at the airport."

"I can't take that. It's your car money."

He laughed and sank back against his seat. "I don't think a car is very high on my list of priorities right now."

"I have two fifty," Peter chimed in.

I opened my mouth but Roland spoke first. "We're in this together."

Jordan pulled away from the building. "See, we're better off than we thought we were."

Ten minutes later, we parked outside a Motel 6. Jordan and I went inside to get two rooms, and the boys stayed with the car. I leaned wearily against the front desk as I waited for the clerk to finish whatever she was doing and check us in. It had been a long, stressful day, and all I could think about was how good it would feel to lie down and close my eyes.

The featherlike touch against my mind was so faint I thought I imagined it at first. It came again, and I jolted away from the counter. Nikolas was here. Not at the hotel but definitely close-by. And if I could sense him...

I grabbed Jordan's hand and pulled her toward the door. "We have to get out of here."

"What? Why?"

"Nikolas is here."

She scanned the parking lot as she ran after me to the car. "I don't see him."

"You know that bond thing? He's here, trust me."

"Shit!"

Roland and Peter were in the front seats so Jordan and I dove into the back. "Get us out of here, Roland," I cried, sinking low in the seat.

He turned in his seat to look at me. "What's wrong?"

"Nikolas," I gasped as the sensation grew stronger. Roland continued to stare at me, and I yelled, "Drive, damn it! Nikolas is here."

"Fuck." He started the car and eased out of the parking spot.

"Hurry," Jordan barked. "I'd rather face a couple of hungry vampires than Nikolas right now."

"If I drive too fast it'll draw attention." He pulled out onto the road and slowly picked up speed. "And I've seen what Nikolas is like when he's pissed."

"You've never seen him like this," Jordan muttered.

I didn't speak because I was too busy trying to sense Nikolas's presence. It disappeared and reappeared several times, and each time my breath caught in my throat. His nearness awakened a storm of emotions inside me, and my Mori moved restlessly. It hadn't even been a day, but I missed him so much. I hated the way things had been between us before I left, and part of me wanted to tell Roland to stop the car and let Nikolas find us. Shaking it off, I reminded myself why I was out here and what was at stake if I didn't do what I'd set out to do. There would be no future for any us until the threat of the Master no longer hung over our heads.

"We're clear," I said at last.

Roland merged onto the highway. "How do you know?"

I swallowed past the small lump in my throat. "I just do. I'll explain it later."

"How the hell did they find us so fast?" Peter asked.

Jordan harrumphed. "My guess is they tracked the cell phones you were supposed to ditch in Boise. There's no way they could have guessed we'd come to Salt Lake City."

"But how'd they know we were at that motel?" Peter wondered out loud.

"I don't think they did. They were probably driving around checking out motels." *And seeing if he could sense me nearby.* It had almost worked. Another twenty minutes and I would have been asleep in my hotel room, unaware he was anywhere close by until he showed up at the door. Something told me he wouldn't have knocked either.

It was just past four in the morning when Roland pulled into a roadside motel and declared that we weren't driving any farther tonight. I had no idea where we were, and I didn't care as long as there was a bed. I paid for a room with two beds at the front desk, and the four of us said good night. I didn't even bother to undress. I fell on top of the covers and was out within minutes.

*   *   *

I leaned against the car, sipping the hot coffee Roland had brought back for me along with breakfast. The morning air was cold, but I was enjoying my first real view of Utah too much to sit inside the hotel room with the others. We were in a town called Green River, which the motel clerk told me was popular with outdoor enthusiasts. Watching the sun slowly turn the peaks of the distant rock formations to gold, I understood why.

I stared at the laptop sitting on the hood of the car, which was my other reason for being out here alone. I dreaded making the call, dreaded the worry and anger I would hear in Nate's and Tristan's voices, but I had to call and let them know we were okay. I wasn't sure if Tristan would even be there or if he was out looking for me, but Nate would be there for sure. Kelvan had warned me not to use the cell phones to call home because they could be traced, but he'd assured me the software on the laptop would prevent the Mohiri from tracing my location.

I hope you're right, Kelvan. I opened the app and typed in the number to Tristan's office phone. There was a short delay before it began to ring. I held my breath until I heard someone pick up on the other end.

"Hello?"

"Tristan?"

"Sara! Is Jordan with you? Are you girls okay?" The relief in his voice brought tears of guilt to my eyes.

"Yes, she's –"

"Where is she? Is she alright?" Someone demanded in the background, and I knew it was Nate before Tristan put me on speaker. "Sara, what the hell were you thinking running off like that? Where are you?"

I took a deep breath. "I can't tell you that. I'm sorry I worried you, but I had to do this."

"Worried? I've been half out of my mind that one of those monsters will find you." I had never heard Nate so upset. "I know you're angry about the decision to take you away, but this is not the way to handle it."

"His decision, not mine." I squeezed my eyes shut. "I know you all want to protect me, but I can't live that way, to be constantly guarded and never allowed to have any control over my own life. You know me, Nate. That would kill me."

His tone softened. "Then we'll figure something out. Just come home."

The plea in his voice made my stomach knot, and I tried to think of something to say that wouldn't cause him more pain.

"Tell us where you are and someone will be there in hours," Tristan said, mistaking my silence for concession.

I stared at the ruggedly beautiful terrain and steeled myself to say what I had to say. "I can't do that. This is about more than controlling my life. I'm tired of hiding and watching people I love get hurt. I don't want us to spend our lives looking over our shoulders."

"What are you saying?" Tristan asked slowly.

"I'm saying that as long as the Master is alive, none of us are free."

Tristan sucked in a sharp breath. "Sara, you can't mean to go after him alone? That would be suicide."

"I know that. I'm just going to find the person who knows his identity."

"Madeline."

"Once I find out what she knows, I'll tell you and you can take care of the rest."

"What makes you think you can find your mother when Tristan's people can't?" Nate asked. "She could be anywhere in the world."

I heard clicking in the background and knew Tristan was on his computer, most likely asking his security guys to trace the call. I sent up a silent prayer that Kelvan's software blocked them from tracking me.

"I have my sources too, and according to them, Madeline is a few hundred miles from where I'm standing. If they're right, I'll be paying her a visit tonight."

The clicking stopped. "Sara, if you know where Madeline is, tell me and I will bring her in."

"She'll see you coming, but she won't expect me." I let out a short laugh. "Who knows, maybe she'll be curious enough to meet her daughter that she won't try to run."

A door opened behind me, and I turned to see Roland leave our room and start toward me. It was time to get on the road again.

"Listen, I have to go." Nate and Tristan began to protest, but I cut them off. "I only called to let you know we're okay. I'll call again in a day or so."

"You haven't asked to speak to Nikolas," Tristan said. I suspected he was trying to keep me on the line as long as he could, which meant he was having trouble tracing the call.

"That's because I know he isn't there."

"You should call him."

"I'm in no mood to be yelled at right now." I bit my lip. I did want to hear Nikolas's voice, even if he was yelling at me. I just didn't trust myself to speak to him yet.

I changed the topic. "By the way, how are Seamus and Niall?"

"Furious they were tricked so easily. It may take them a while to live it down." Tristan released a slow breath. "You can't go around using your power on the warriors, Sara."

"Nikolas taught me anything is fair in a fight. They use their strength and speed against me. My power is my strength, so why shouldn't I use it to level the field?"

"I don't think that is how he intended for you to use it." Tristan was stalling now, trying to keep me talking. Kelvan's software was obviously working as he'd promised, but I didn't want to take any chances.

"Tell Seamus and Niall I'm sorry." My hand hovered over the keyboard. "I have to hang up now. I love you both and I'll talk to you again soon."

"Sara, wait —" Tristan said, but I ended the call before he could finish. I swallowed hard and closed the laptop with a shaky hand.

Roland leaned against the car. "Rough call?"

"It was a lot harder than I thought it would be." I picked up my cup and drained the last of my coffee. "Do you want to use the laptop to call your mom? She must be worried."

"I called her from the Boise airport and told her we were staying a few more days with you. She wasn't happy, but she said she'd let the school know." He made a face. "She's going to flip when I tell her it's going to be more than a few days."

"Who knows? It *might* be only a couple of days if we find Madeline," I said hopefully. "And if not, you can always go back."

"Stop trying to get me to go home. We're in this together, and that's it."

I smiled and gave him a quick hug. "I'm really glad you're here."

Jordan walked up to us, jiggling the car keys. "We ready to get this show on the road?"

"Yes." A thrill went through me. Today we would reach Albuquerque, and I might finally get some of the answers I was looking for.

Peter joined us, carrying his and Roland's packs. "What if we find Madeline and she won't talk?" he asked, dampening my excitement.

"She'll talk." Madeline owed me that much, and she was going to help me whether she wanted to or not.

We were leaving town when I spotted a sign for a thrift store. It didn't take us long to find two small backpacks, coats, and a few needed toiletries. I moved my stuff from Roland's pack to my own, smiling when the laptop fit easily inside. Tucked in with my clothes was a silver necklace, and I fastened it around my neck, letting the plain silver cross settle on my chest. It had been my grandmother's and a gift from Nate on my sixteenth birthday. Wearing it made me feel like he and my dad were with me in a small way.

Eight hours and two pit stops later, we reached the Albuquerque city limits. I wasn't the only one who released a happy sigh. Jordan and Roland had switched places at the last stop, and he glanced over at me as we drove into the city. "Where to?"

"Let's get something to eat before we do anything else."

"Really? I mean, I thought you'd want to go after Madeline as soon as we got here."

"I need to check in with David first, and we're all hungry." We'd only been on the run for a day, but they all looked worn out and in need of a break. Spending so many hours in a car is tough for anyone, and it didn't help that we were all a bit on edge. "Just make sure it's someplace we can afford."

I wasn't the least bit surprised when Roland found a little mom-and-pop burger joint. When it came to burgers, he and Peter had built-in radar. We filled a booth and the waitress took our orders. While we waited for our food, I stepped outside to call David, using one of the prepaid phones.

"You made good time," he said when I told him where we were. "I didn't expect you to get there until tomorrow."

"We were motivated to move quickly." There were things David didn't know about me, so I was vague on the details of our near run-in with Nikolas.

"This is good actually. We've been keeping a close eye on Madeline's movements, and she's still in Albuquerque, but for how long I don't know. Since we've been tracking her, she hasn't stayed in a place longer than a week."

My pulse quickened. "So she's here now, for sure?"

"Yes. Do you have your laptop with you? I'm sending you something."

I tucked the phone between my ear and shoulder and opened the laptop. It powered up in seconds, and I opened the browser and logged into the new email account David had set up for me. Before I'd left home, I'd wiped the computer in my room as he'd instructed, but I had no idea what Tristan's security guys were capable of.

There was a message from David in my inbox, and I opened it to find a black and white security photo of a dark-haired woman leaving what looked like a hotel lobby. She had either dyed her hair or was wearing a wig, but there was no mistaking Madeline's beautiful features. I studied her for a long moment, expecting to experience anger, pain, *something* for the woman who had abandoned me, but all I felt was cool detachment.

"When was this taken?"

"This morning at Hotel Andaluz. She was checked in under the name Teresa King. It's the first actual picture of her we've been able to get. She's good at hiding from cameras. Is it her?"

"Yes." My breath caught, and I immediately began to Google the hotel name for directions.

"She's no longer there," David said. "She stays only one night at a hotel before she gets a new one. She hasn't checked into another one yet."

My heart sank. "Then she might have left town already."

"We have reason to believe she is still there. Kelvan has friends in the demon community in Albuquerque, and he found out through them that

Madeline has gone to see a local warlock named Orias for the last two nights. His friends tell him she is expected back tonight."

There's a demon community? "Why would demons help us?" I asked when I'd gotten over my shock.

"They wouldn't, but they'd help Kelvan. You must have made quite an impression on him."

I closed the laptop so I could hold the phone again. "What do you mean?"

"Kelvan is a nice guy, but he doesn't do well with strangers, especially hunters. That's why I didn't tell him what you are. After you left, he told me that if you ever needed anything, to let him know. He took it upon himself to reach out to his friends in Albuquerque."

"I think his cat really liked me."

David let out a laugh. "Lulu likes people even less than Kelvan does."

I grinned. "I have a way with animals. It's all part of my charm."

"Okay, I get it. You're going to be mysterious about it." I could tell by his voice that he was still smiling. "I hope your charm works on warlocks, too."

"I've never met a warlock. I've heard they can be into some heavy stuff." Like capturing baby griffins and using their blood to raise demons. I shuddered. I had no desire to meet someone who practiced that kind of magic. Everything I knew about warlocks had come from Remy. Warlocks were born with magic, but they needed demon essence to make them strong. They raised higher demons and kept them captive so they could draw from the demon's power. The stronger the demon, the stronger the warlock.

"Orias is a powerful warlock. He offers his services to anyone for the right price. He doesn't care if you are demon, human, or something else as long as you can pay and don't cause him any trouble. He doesn't have a problem with Mohiri, like many of his clientele do, but he never gives anything away for free either, and that includes information."

"Great," I muttered. If we were lucky, we'd find Madeline at the warlock's place and I wouldn't have to deal with him at all. I sighed. Since when had I ever been *that* lucky?

"I'm sending you directions to Orias's place now. It's a little tricky to find if you don't know exactly where you're going. I think that is by design."

Someone tapped on the window behind me, and I turned to see Roland waving for me to come in.

"Thanks, David. Listen, I have to go but I'll let you know how it goes. And tell Kelvan thanks for me."

"Will do. Stay safe."

I hung up and joined the others in the booth where a burger and fries waited for me. Looking over at Jordan's plate, I shook my head at the two monstrous cheeseburgers. "You aren't actually going to eat all of that, are you?"

"Duh." She smirked and took a huge bite from one.

I picked up my own and took a much smaller bite. It was homemade and so delicious after twenty-four hours of gas station food. I gave a contented sigh that drew smiles from my friends.

"What's the plan?" Jordan asked in a lowered voice after she finished off her first burger. "Do we know where Madeline is?"

"She's here in town, but she moves around a lot." I told them about the picture David had sent me, and they all started talking at once.

"So we wait for her to check into another hotel?" Peter asked.

I took a sip of my soda. "We don't know if she will get another hotel. But I have the name of a person she has been going to see, and there is a very good chance she'll be there tonight. David is sending me the address."

"Great." Roland grinned at me. "So who are we going to see?"

I smiled at their expectant faces. "We're off to see the wizard."

CHAPTER 3

"SARA, ARE YOU sure these directions are right?" Roland twisted the wheel to the left and the headlights bounced over the cactus growing along the edge of the twisting desert road. Not a road actually, more like a track that wound through the uneven terrain with occasional markers to let you know you were still on it. We had been following it for forty minutes, and so far there was no sign of buildings or any kind of life.

"David said it was a bit out of the way."

"Out of the way or out of the state?" he retorted. "If this road gets any worse, we're probably going to lose the exhaust... or worse."

"We should almost be there." The car crested a rise, and I pointed to a small cluster of lights less than a quarter of a mile away. "There it is."

Jordan leaned forward in her seat. "Where? I don't see anything."

"Right there, those lights."

She shook her head. "I don't see any lights."

"Me either," Roland said.

"Ha-ha, you guys. Very funny."

By now we were close enough to make out a large, two-story adobe structure with lights shining from some of the downstairs windows. Outside lights illuminated the front of the building where half a dozen cars were parked.

Roland maneuvered the car across a small wooden bridge. "I don't know what you're talking —" He hit the brakes. "Whoa! Where did that come from?"

"What the hell?" Jordan yelled close to my ear. "That was *not* there a minute ago."

One look at their shocked expressions told me they were not kidding me. "You really didn't see it before?"

Roland shook his head, still gawking at the building.

I studied the structure, which appeared pretty normal to me – well, as normal as any building in the middle of the desert. "It must be some kind of spell to hide the place until you get close to it. He's a warlock, so he could probably do something like that."

"But you saw through it," Peter said.

I chewed my lip, just as mystified as they were. "Maybe my power makes me immune to it. I don't know."

Roland parked the car in front of the building. He rested his hands on the steering wheel and looked at me. "Are you sure you want to go in there?"

"No, but I think I have to," I replied. "You guys can stay in the car if you want."

He reached for his door. "No way am I letting you go in there alone."

The four of us got out of the car and walked to the entrance. I stopped in front of the arched wooden door and read the sign affixed to it. NO WEAPONS. NO BLOODSHED. NO CREDIT. "Nice."

"No weapons?" Jordan blustered. "That's ridiculous."

I removed my dagger from the inner pocket of my coat and motioned for Roland to unlock the car. "It makes sense if you think about it. He does business with everyone, so he must get clients who hate each other. It would be bad for business if they killed each other at his place."

Jordan didn't remove the knives I knew she was carrying, and I waved a hand at the door. "I bet he has a ward in place to detect weapons."

She glared at me for a long moment then stalked to the car. "Fine, but I'm going on record as saying this is a bad idea."

"We're not completely unarmed. We still have Roland and Peter."

She made a sound that told me she'd rather have her knives.

Roland opened the door, and we filed inside. I was at the rear and had to move up between him and Peter to get a look at the room we were in. For some reason, I'd expected the inside of a warlock's house to be dark and creepy with candles and wands and spell books all over the place. This room resembled nothing from my imaginings. It was warm and inviting with pale stucco walls, red ceramic tile floor, and a high beamed ceiling. Several pieces of what looked like local art adorned the walls. Brown leather couches, small tables bearing pretty stained glass lamps, and several large potted plants completed the décor.

The occupants of the room were another story.

Seated on one couch was a diminutive man with a ruddy complexion and small pointed ears who looked suspiciously like a dwarf. Across from him, two old crones in identical gray dresses bickered quietly over something. A burly man with shaggy yellow hair held a magazine in his clawed hands. He appeared to be some kind of werecat on the verge of shifting. Next to him, a slightly balding man in a dark suit was playing with the silver-tipped cane that lay across his knees. Everyone looked up when we entered and watched us curiously for a moment before going back to whatever they were doing. There was no sign of Madeline.

To the left of the door, a pretty young Hispanic woman sat behind a desk. She smiled and beckoned us over. "Welcome to Casa Orias. Do you have an appointment?"

"I don't have an appointment, but I have an important matter to discuss with Orias," I told her.

She flashed her dimples. "Orias is a very busy man, and as you can see he is booked tonight. If you'll leave me your name and phone number, I'll add you to his schedule." She glanced at her computer. "How about tomorrow at 5:00 p.m.?"

Jordan tapped her fingernails impatiently on the desk. "This can't wait until tomorrow."

The receptionist's smile never faltered. "I understand, but everyone's business with Orias is important. It wouldn't be fair to the clients with appointments."

Something told me sweet talk wasn't going to work on this woman. I unzipped the small front pocket of my coat and pulled out a rolled-up tissue. Discreetly, I opened the tissue and let a perfect, fat diamond bounce across the polished wooden desk. The diamond had to be four or five carats, and it sparkled under the small desk lamp. Beside me, Jordan let out a small gasp while the receptionist's mouth made a perfect O.

The phone on the desk rang and the receptionist answered it. "Yes, sir. Canceled? I do have a walk-in I could schedule instead. I'll do that." She hung up and smiled again. "Wonderful news. One of our clients just canceled and we have an opening tonight. Mr. Orias will see you right now."

"What luck." I picked up the diamond. "Lead the way."

She walked around the desk and led us through a closed door, down a hallway, and up a flight of stairs. At the top, she knocked on a door and a male voice rumbled for us to come in. I took a deep breath and stepped inside.

"Welcome," said the man sitting behind a large mahogany desk. He looked to be in his thirties, with long black hair and sharp brown eyes. He wore a plain blue dress shirt and black pants, and he looked more like a businessman than a powerful warlock.

He looked at the four of us and his eyes widened almost imperceptibly. "Mohiri children and werewolf pups, what an intriguing group."

"We get that a lot." I walked farther into the room and my power stirred, sensing the presence of a demon nearby. Warlocks kept their demons with them at all times so it made sense that Orias had one in his office. The demon felt oddly muted, as if it was under glass, but even so I could tell it was somewhere to my left. It was strange and disconcerting to be in a room with a higher demon, and I forgot to introduce myself.

Orias steepled his fingers, and his shrewd gaze shifted to me. "And how may I be of service to you this evening?"

Trying to ignore the demon, I walked forward until I stood behind one of the three visitor chairs in front of his desk. I rested my hands on the back of the chair, thinking about how to broach the subject of the reason for our visit. "I'm looking for information."

"I know many things. What kind of information are you seeking?"

"I'm looking for someone, a Mohiri woman who has been to see you a couple of times this week. I need to find her."

"Indeed. And does this woman have a name?"

"She probably goes by a lot of different names, but I doubt you have many Mohiri clients."

He rested his forearms on his desk. "And what business do you have with this woman?"

"It's personal."

"Indeed." Orias smiled, showing off even, white teeth. "It's not often I have three beautiful Mohiri women visitors in as many days."

My breath caught. "So she was here?"

"I do have a client who matches that description, yes."

His short evasive answers were starting to annoy me. "Can you tell me where she is? It's really important that I find her. I can pay."

He leaned back in his chair and shook his head. "I can't give out sensitive information about another client." I started to speak, and he raised a hand. "My clients pay well for my discretion as well as my services. It would not be good for my business if they felt like they could not trust me."

His expression told me he wasn't going to be persuaded to give up Madeline. I wanted to scream. I couldn't believe we had driven all this way to the middle of nowhere for nothing.

"What kind of services do you offer, if you don't mind me asking?" Jordan said from behind me.

"I offer many services, spells mostly. Protection and locations spells. My specialty is glamours."

"Glamours?"

Orias smiled at her. "As you probably saw on your way in, many of my clients can't go out in public in their natural form. My glamour spells allow them to live among humans undetected. They look and sound human for as long as the spell lasts. Of course, the stronger the spell, the shorter it lasts. Mine are very strong so my clients have to come back for a new one every month. I have many repeat customers, and I've found it to be a very lucrative business."

Roland spoke up. "What if someone asked for a spell to kill someone else? Do you do those, too?"

"At one time, yes," the warlock replied without remorse. "But I found it to be too messy, so I don't deal in that type of magic anymore." He waved a hand at his richly furnished office. "As I said, my current business is very profitable. It also keeps a certain warrior organization that likes to raid my peers at bay."

I sighed inwardly. It was obvious we weren't going to get anything useful from Orias. Hopefully, Madeline was still in the city and Kelvan could locate her again before she moved on.

Orias tapped his long fingers on his desk. "Speaking of the Mohiri, I received some very interesting news this afternoon. It seems they are looking for two of their young people, and they are offering a generous reward for their safe return. It's not often that they reach out to their contacts in the community, so these two lost children must be very important to them."

"All their children are important to them." I swallowed and walked over to look at a painting to hide the panic flaring inside me.

"And imagine my surprise when two of their young people show up in my office on the same day. A coincidence, no?"

Jordan snorted. "Do we look lost to you?"

I could only muster a small laugh as I strolled toward a bookcase that held an odd assortment of books and ornaments. The demon's presence grew stronger until it was impossible to ignore. I turned away from the shelves to find Orias watching me with a calculating gleam in his eye. It was time to get out of there.

"Thanks for taking the time to meet with –" I gasped as Orias raised a hand and the office door slammed shut behind Roland and Peter.

Roland grabbed the knob and pulled, but the door refused to open. He spun to glare at the warlock. "Not funny, dude. Open the door."

Orias reached for his phone, looking very pleased with himself. "Why don't you children get comfortable while I make a call? Don't worry; you won't come to any harm here."

Roland, Peter, and Jordan started toward the warlock. Orias flicked a finger and the three of them suddenly found themselves sitting on the three chairs with their arms and legs bound by some invisible force. They yelled and were gagged until all they could do was struggle mutely in their bonds.

Orias glanced at me. "I only have three chairs, but you don't look like much trouble. Behave yourself while I make this call or I'll stick you in the closet until they get here."

Why did everyone always assume I was the helpless one? I spun back to the bookcase, looking for something to use as a weapon. I laid my hand on one of the shelves and blue sparks danced across my skin. The demon was very close, the same demon the warlock needed to feed his magic.

I scanned the items on the shelves and my eyes lit on a small brass replica of Aladdin's lamp. I couldn't help the laugh that slipped out. "How original."

As soon as my fingers touched the lamp, I felt something move inside it. I picked up the lamp in both hands and turned to face Orias, too desperate to ponder how a powerful demon could fit into such a small space. Orias was looking through the phone book on his computer and completely ignoring me.

I let a small amount of power infuse my palms. The lamp jumped in my hands, making the lid rattle.

Orias's head whipped in my direction and he paled slightly when he saw what I was holding. "That is very valuable. Put it down."

More of my power surrounded the lamp, and it began to quiver and issue a faint whining sound. I ran a hand along the side. "I wonder; if I rub this, will a genie appear?"

"That... that is not a toy, you meddlesome child." Orias's words were stern, but he had gone a shade whiter and small beads of moisture appeared on his brow. "You don't know what you are messing with. Set it down before you get hurt."

"I know exactly what this is." I gave the lamp a shake and the whining grew louder. "You have one pissed off demon in here. I'm afraid he doesn't like me at all. Tell me, how do you fit a demon in a lamp anyway?"

Orias stood and held out his hands, which I noticed weren't so steady anymore. "Give that to me."

I looked at my friends to see them all watching me with a mixture of curiosity and worry. I gave them a small smile and let my power brush against the brass sides of the lamp again. The demon rumbled and I thought I could actually feel its fear. *That's new.*

"Stop!" Orias cried, panting. He put a hand on the wall to steady himself, and fear filled his eyes. "Please."

I tilted my head toward my friends. "Release them."

Jordan sputtered and yelled the second her magical gag fell away. She jumped up from the chair and reached for her weapons... which were in the car. By the look on her face, she might not need anything but her bare hands.

"If this is how you treat clients, it's no wonder you have that 'no weapons' rule," she shouted at the warlock.

Orias ignored her. "They are free. Now please hand over the lamp."

"Do you honestly think I am that stupid? I give you this, and you'll have us all tied up before we know what hit us."

"What are you going to do with it? You can't take it."

Jordan made a face. "There is no way I'm getting in the car with that thing."

I touched the lamp's ornate lid and the demon actually growled.

"Oh, be quiet," I said to the lamp. I met Orias's worried gaze. "You can have your pet demon back *after* you promise to let us go and tell no one we were here."

"Done."

Jordan scoffed. "You actually expect him to keep his word?"

"No. That's why he's going to take the White Oath."

Orias inhaled sharply, and my friends shot me questioning looks. "What's that?" Peter asked.

"The White Oath is the only oath that can bind a warlock to their word." *Thank you, Remy, for everything you ever taught me.*

"How could you possibly know about that?" Orias demanded, not bothering to deny it. "That is something known only to my kind."

"Doesn't matter how I know. Are you going to take the oath?"

Anger replaced the fear in Orias's eyes. "Fine. I'll do it. I swear that –"

"Not so fast." I knew the oath had to be worded right so there was no way for him to wriggle out of it. I walked over and grabbed a pen and notepad from his desk. It took me a few minutes to write something, and then I handed the notepad to him. "Read this."

Orias pored over what I'd written, and when his mouth set in a straight angry line, I knew I'd gotten it right. "I swear under the White Oath to the following terms: I will allow Sara, Jordan, Roland, and Peter to leave this place unharmed. I will not try to harm them or bring them back once they leave here, nor will I have someone else harm them or bring them back for me. I will tell no one I have seen Sara, Jordan, Roland, or Peter, and if anyone asks about them, I will not reveal they were here. And..." He paused and scowled at me. "I will tell them how to find the woman they are looking for."

"Brilliant!" Jordan crowed.

I hadn't planned to add the bit about Madeline, but Orias had brought it on himself when he'd tried to turn us in. I watched him expectantly.

He gritted his teeth. "I don't know where the woman is now, but she is headed to LA. Go see Adele at the Blue Nyx club. She knows everything that goes on in the city, and she can find anyone. That's all I have." He held out his hands. "Now can I please have that?"

I handed the lamp to him, and he cradled it like it was a baby. His eyes met mine. "What are you?"

"I'm just a girl looking for answers." I reached into my pocket for the diamond and set it on his desk. "Payment for the information you gave me."

Roland huffed. "Are you nuts? The dude tied us up. He doesn't deserve payment."

I turned, ignoring his outburst. "Come on, guys. Let's get out of here." The last thing I wanted was a powerful warlock holding a grudge against me. Anyone who could raise a demon and imprison it in a lamp was not someone I wanted as an enemy. Hopefully, the diamond would soothe his wounded ego and make up for some of the reward money he'd lost out on.

The door opened this time when Roland tried it, and we filed out into the hallway. We hurried down the stairs and along the hallway to the waiting area, all of us eager to quit this place.

"How the hell did you know about that oath thing, Sara?" Roland asked from behind me. "That was genius by the way."

"Remy. He taught me a lot of stuff. I just never thought I'd have to use it."

The waiting room had a few more occupants, and I knew immediately that at least one of them was a demon. It was either the short man with yellow skin and pointed ears or the young gray-skinned woman with long white hair. She glanced at us then looked away. Tucked against her side was a tiny version of her that had to be her child. I smiled at the little one, and she returned it shyly before burying her face in her mother's sleeve.

I was halfway across the room when cold stabbed me in the chest. "Oh, no," I uttered, looking around frantically. But the vampire wasn't in the waiting room. He was outside and coming closer.

Jordan grabbed my arm. "What is it?"

"Trouble." I met her eyes and said, "Radar."

Her eyes widened and she cursed softly. "I told you it was a mistake to leave the weapons in the car. How many? Can you tell?"

"One, I think. I can't be sure."

Roland came to my side. "What's wrong?"

"Vampire," I whispered, and he let out a low growl. I'd never heard him do that in human form, and I had a suspicion he was very close to going furry.

"What should we do?" Peter asked in a low voice.

Before I could answer, the door opened and the vampire stepped into the room. He was medium height with black hair, and he wore a brown leather jacket. Fear stole my breath as his eyes passed over us on his way to the receptionist's desk. A second later, he stopped and I saw him sniff the air. I wondered if he was picking up the werewolf scent in the room.

When I'd almost lost Nate I made a vow to destroy every vampire that crossed my path. But we were weaponless, and I had no idea how old the vampire was. The smartest thing to do right now was get out of there.

Roland's fingers closed around my wrist. *Come on*, he mouthed.

Peter was the first one through the door with Jordan close at his heels, eager to retrieve her knives. I was about to follow them when there was a sudden breeze and the door slammed in my face. I found myself face-to-face with the vampire. My heart thrummed against my ribs and I let out a small scream. Someone pounded on the door, but the vampire held it shut with one hand.

The vampire let out a hiss. "A Mohiri child all alone without her protectors." He reached for my face, and Roland growled. The vampire's eyes flicked to him. "I am a lot older than you, pup. Stay out of this and I might not kill you."

I tried to step in front of Roland, but he put an arm across my chest to stop me.

"Don't touch her," he snarled in a voice that was several octaves deeper than his normal one.

I looked down and saw dark wiry hair sprout from his arm as claws grew from his fingers. I flexed my own fingers, feeling power hum through them. *Between us, we can handle this.*

"Heel, dog," the vampire spat, showing his fangs. He reached for me again.

Roland lunged at him. The vampire moved so fast he blurred, and Roland flew backward across the room to crash into a tall ceramic vase. Shards of pottery flew everywhere.

"Roland!" I turned to run to him but my arm was held in an iron grip.

"Now where were we?" The vampire stared at me with dark hungry eyes. "I had a young Mohiri once, but his blood smelled nothing like yours. It's so sweet."

Revulsion coiled in my stomach. I brought my free hand up between us, and it took the vampire several seconds to notice it was glowing.

"What –?"

My hand slammed into his chest and power exploded from me. His eyes widened in shock, and he let go of my arm. Before he could recover I laid my other hand on his chest and pushed another wave of power toward his heart. He didn't go down as I'd hoped, but he wavered stiffly as if he was momentarily frozen. I'd never taken down a mature vampire, and I had a feeling this one was strong. I hit him with another blast, and he made a strange keening sound but stayed on his feet. Jesus, what did it take to kill one of these bastards?

The door crashed open, knocking us both off balance and severing my contact with him. I fell backward and landed on the two old hags, who shrieked indignantly. Mumbling an apology, I scrambled up just as the vampire gained his own footing. He wasn't moving nearly as fast, and his confident sneer was gone as he crouched, facing Jordan, who was now armed with two long knives. Peter crowded the doorway in wolf form.

"You weren't going to keep him all to yourself, were you?" Jordan quipped. "Friends share, Sara."

"Help yourself." I darted a glance at Roland, relieved to see him sitting up. He looked dazed but otherwise okay.

The vampire glared at me. "First, I'm going to take care of this little piece, and then you and I are going to get to know each other a lot better."

"Ew! Dude, you look old enough to be her father." Jordan twirled one of her knives. "And don't call me a piece, you sexist pig."

The vampire shifted his stance.

"Jordan, watch out!" I shouted.

A shriek split the air, and the vampire grabbed at the knife that had just missed his heart. His hand smoked as he ripped the blade out of his chest. He had to be very strong if he could withstand touching pure silver. He raised his hand, his intent clear. There was no way Jordan would survive a blow at such a close range.

I dove at him.

I felt a sharp pain in my shoulder, but it faded as magic surged in me. Lightning bolts leapt from my hand before it even made contact with his chest. This time, instead of drawing back for another strike, I fed more power into him. I felt it surround the demon inside him as he sank to his knees, his face frozen in a silent scream.

Something shiny caught my eye, and I turned my head to see the knife protruding from my shoulder. Bracing myself for the pain, I grasped the handle and yanked it free. Fire lanced through my shoulder, but I ignored it. I wasn't giving the bastard time to recover. With gritted teeth I lifted my glowing hand from his chest and plunged the silver blade into his heart. He made a sound like air leaking from a balloon, and his eyes grew round in disbelief before he toppled over and was still.

"What have you done?" I turned to see Orias emerging from the hallway. He wore a look of horror mixed with shock. "Do you know who that is?"

"You mean *was*." Jordan reached down, pulled her knife free from the vampire's chest, and wiped it on his shirt. "And it's nice of you to show up and lend us a hand by the way."

Orias ignored her. "That was Stefan Price."

I lifted my uninjured shoulder. "Is that supposed to mean something to us?"

"He was the oldest vampire in these parts, over one hundred and fifty years old, and very strong." The warlock stepped into the room and stared at the dead vampire. "No one has ever fought him and lived."

Roland limped over to us and laid an arm across my shoulders. "That's because old Stefan never met a couple of real warriors before."

Orias took in the state of his waiting room. "You four are nothing but trouble. You tore up my place and killed one of my clients."

"That client tried to kill us first. Ask anyone here." I looked around the room and caught sight of the stunned faces of the other occupants. My gaze met the eyes of the man with the yellow skin, and he jumped up and bolted for the door. Peter moved aside and the man disappeared into the night. He was followed by the two crones, who moved a lot faster than I would have expected them to.

I heard a whimper behind me, and I turned to look at the gray-skinned woman. The woman's child clung to her neck, her little body trembling. Poor thing. I didn't blame her for being terrified of that monster.

I walked toward them, intending to reassure the little girl, but her mother shrank away from me, holding her daughter tightly. "Please... my child," she whispered, her black eyes glistening with tears.

"It's okay. He's dead."

The woman seemed not to have heard me. She raised a hand to ward me off. "Don't hurt us."

Her plea stopped me in my tracks. She was afraid of *me*? "I wouldn't..." I looked at my friends helplessly, but they were as surprised as I was. Facing the woman again, I took a tentative step. My fingers tingled with power. It took me a few seconds to put it all together. I stopped walking and locked my power away.

"You're demons," I said gently, remembering Kelvan's reaction when he realized what Jordan and I were. Apparently, the Mohiri were known and feared everywhere.

"We've never hurt anyone. I promise. Please, don't kill us."

"No one is going to hurt you." I knelt in front of her so she would feel less threatened. This was new territory for me. If they had been animals or some other kind of creature, I could use my power to calm their fear and earn their trust, but my power had the opposite effect on demons. "I give you my word that you and your little one are safe. What kind of demon are you?"

"She is a mox demon," Orias said when the woman did not reply. "A very passive race, I assure you. She buys my glamour spells for her daughter, so she can attend school."

I smiled at the woman. She didn't return it, and I wasn't surprised considering the situation. "I don't know what you've heard about the Mohiri, but you don't have to fear us." I stood and looked around the room, meeting the eyes of the remaining visitors. "My friends and I aren't here to hurt anyone." I pointed at the dead vampire. "He was different. We kill vampires, but we don't hurt innocent people, no matter what they are. That includes demons."

I looked at Roland. "Are you okay?"

"I'm fine. What about you? You're the one who is bleeding."

My shoulder chose that moment to twitch, and I sucked in a sharp breath at the pain I had forgotten until now. Adrenaline is a great pain buffer, apparently. I put up a hand to cover the wound made by the knife.

It didn't feel like anything major had been hit, and the blood was already beginning to slow. I suddenly felt tired and wanted nothing more than to lie down. It felt like forever since I'd last slept.

"Come on. Let's get out of here," Jordan said. "I have something in my bag that will fix you up."

I scrunched up my nose. "Please don't say it's gunna paste."

Jordan grinned. "What else? I snagged a can before we left. I figured if I didn't use it, you definitely would."

I cast one last glance at the demon woman. She was rocking her child gently, and I heard her say softly, *"Talael esledur."* Whatever it meant, it worked and the child stopped crying.

"I'm really sorry I frightened her," I told the woman before I walked out.

Jordan retrieved the dreaded can of gunna paste from her backpack and laughed at my expression as I dutifully swallowed some. The stuff was horrid, but it worked amazingly fast to numb pain and speed healing. She was smart for remembering to take some. It wasn't as if we could go to a hospital if we got sick or hurt. She got a towel from Orias to staunch the flow of blood until the gunna paste and my accelerated healing kicked in. The warlock happily provided one, and then he politely asked us to leave and never come back because we were bad for business.

"Sara, do you realize what you did back there?" Roland asked as he drove us back to the city. "That vampire was super old, and you killed him by yourself."

Jordan and I were sitting in the back, and she laid her hand on my arm. "I have to admit, that was *the* most badass thing I've ever seen. When you pulled that knife out of your shoulder and stabbed him with it, my jaw nearly hit the floor."

I grimaced and adjusted my hold on the towel pressed against my shoulder. "What is it with vampires stabbing me anyway?"

"At least you aren't picking pieces of pottery out of your skull," Roland complained. "You were amazing, Sara. Nikolas would be proud of you if he'd seen that."

"Are you kidding? Nikolas wouldn't let me get within ten miles of a vampire that old. And we might want to keep the whole stabbing thing between us."

Laying my head against the headrest, I stared out the window at the dark desert landscape. I couldn't help but wonder where Nikolas was now and what he was doing and thinking. I had no doubt Chris was with him, and they had probably scoured every square mile of Salt Lake City after he'd sensed me there. How long would it take him to figure out where we'd gone? I was sure he would eventually. If there was one thing I had learned, it was to never underestimate Nikolas.

I thought about the vampire I'd just killed and smiled sadly at the darkness. Maybe, when all of this was over, Nikolas would feel the same way about me.

CHAPTER 4

WE SPENT THE night in another cheap motel, and for the second night in a row, I quickly succumbed to exhaustion. I had planned to contact David when we got there, but the long day of driving, followed by battling a vampire and getting stabbed, did me in. Surprisingly, I felt no ill effects from using so much power on the vampire. Every time I thought about it, the whole thing seemed unreal. I had killed a mature vampire. Me. My power wasn't strong enough yet to do the job on its own, but I could feel it growing every time I used it.

I awoke the next morning, sweating under a pile of blankets. I sat up and pushed them off me. "What the hell? Are you guys trying to smother me?"

Jordan was sitting on the other bed watching TV. "You did that glowing thing again, and we couldn't get you to wake up. All we could think to do was cover you up so no one would notice it."

"Oh." I went to the window and pushed aside the heavy drapes to see it was around midmorning. I must have been more tired than I'd realized. "Where are the boys?"

"They went to get breakfast. We weren't sure when you would wake up, and it freaked them out a bit. Me too, actually."

"Sorry."

She waved a hand. "At least you'll be handy to have around if we ever have a blackout."

Shaking my head, I picked up my backpack and went to take a shower. I received my second surprise of the day when I pulled off the T-shirt I'd slept in and saw my shoulder was completely healed. Not healed as in the scars looked a few weeks old, but as in there wasn't a trace of a scar at all. It usually took my body two or three days to do that.

The boys were back by the time I stepped out of the bathroom, freshly showered and dressed in my only clean outfit. Travelling light meant not packing a lot of clothes, and killing vampires was dirty work. We were going to have to spend some of our money on extra clothes. Plus, the coat I'd bought at the thrift shop yesterday morning was torn and covered in blood. Between hotels, food, and gas, it wasn't going to take us long to burn through our cash. I sighed heavily. It was time to sell some of the diamonds.

We sat on the beds and discussed our plans as we devoured our fast food breakfast. It wasn't the best breakfast we'd ever had, but it was cheap so the boys were able to buy plenty to satisfy our appetites. I was ravenous, and I caught them staring at me as I reached for my fourth hash brown patty.

I scowled at them. "What? Using all that power made me hungry."

Jordan raised an eyebrow. "And cranky too, apparently."

I muttered an apology because she was right. I'd been in a funk since I woke up and I had no reason to be. Last night, I'd killed a powerful vampire and learned where Madeline was headed next. I should be feeling pretty good, but instead I was snapping at my friends.

After breakfast, I made a few calls. The first was to David to tell him what we had learned about Madeline. He said they couldn't find any signs she was still in Albuquerque, but that he and his friends would pick up her trail in Los Angeles.

My second call was to an old contact named Malloy, who was pretty shocked to hear from me. "Ain't you supposed to be dead?" he asked, referring to my rumored drowning.

"I just needed a change of scenery. You know how it is."

"It's a cutthroat business, kid." His loud exhale said it all. "So what can I do for you?"

"I'm headed to LA, and I need to sell a few rocks for my boss." Malloy had always assumed I worked for someone powerful, and I was happy to let him keep believing that. "Who do you trust out there?"

He barked a laugh. "I don't trust anyone. But you're in luck. My brother, Jeff, does business out that way. I'll give him a call."

We talked for a few minutes about the stones I was selling, and he said it would probably take a few days for his brother to set something up. I agreed to call him again when I got to Los Angeles. I didn't like the idea of dealing with strangers in unfamiliar territory, but we needed money. I'd worked with Malloy a number of times, and I trusted him as much as you could trust anyone in his business. He'd get a cut of the business he sent his brother's way, so he would make sure it was a solid deal.

According to Google, it was about a twelve-hour drive from Albuquerque to Los Angeles. None of us were thrilled about the prospect of another long day cooped up in a car. Roland, Peter, and Jordan drew for driving shifts, and I felt bad because I couldn't share the work, especially since they were out here for me. Roland said I'd done enough work last night and I deserved a rest, but I still felt like they were letting me off easy. I got him to stop at a convenience store where I stocked up on a ton of snacks and bottled drinks for the trip. I planned to treat us all to a nice steak dinner when we got to Los Angeles. If I got a fair price for the diamonds, we wouldn't have to worry about money anymore.

It was after midnight when we finally rolled into Los Angeles. We were too tired and irritable to be excited about where we were, and we immediately found a hotel room for the night. It had two queen beds so the girls could have one and the boys the other. Within thirty minutes, everyone but me was sound asleep.

I lay there listening to the sounds of the city and watching neon lights play across the ceiling. My mind refused to turn off, and my emotions were all over the map. Disappointment over missing Madeline in Albuquerque still gnawed at me. I wondered how we were going to find her in a city this big. The vampire attack at Orias's had made this all very real, and I worried about my friends' safety. I was also anxious about selling the diamonds and meeting this Adele person.

And then there was the growing emptiness inside me and the sadness emanating from my demon. I knew with all of my heart that I was doing the right thing, but being away from Nikolas was much harder than I'd thought it would be. I rubbed my chest. Was it normal to feel a physical ache from missing someone? If it hurt this much being separated from your bond mate, I couldn't imagine the pain of severing a bond.

I rolled out of bed with a groan and padded to the bathroom, grabbing my backpack on the way. Closing the door with a soft click, I took out the laptop and set it on the edge of the vanity. When it powered up, I opened the phone app and stared at it for several minutes. *I'll call Chris, just to let him know we're okay.* I was sure Chris was with Nikolas. Maybe talking to him would make me feel less lonely, knowing that Nikolas was nearby.

The number I dialed was not Chris's. The phone rang twice. I didn't have time to brace myself before his husky voice answered.

"Hello?"

My breath caught.

"Hello?" he said again.

I opened my mouth, but no words came out.

"Sara? Is that you?"

I closed my eyes against the frustration and hope in his voice. *This was a mistake.*

"Sara, talk to me."

I disconnected the call and sat on the toilet with my arms wrapped tightly around me, as if that would help. The only arms I wanted around me were his.

"Stop this." I paced the small bathroom. I was behaving like one of those lovesick girls back home who used to pine after Roland. I missed Nikolas, but getting all weepy over him wasn't going to solve anything. I was the one who had put this distance between us, and I was just going to have to deal with it.

I stuffed the laptop in the backpack and heard the soft rustle of plastic. My hand came out holding a clear plastic bag containing a folded navy blue T-shirt. I didn't hesitate. I pulled my T-shirt off and held up the shirt from the bag. The material was soft, and it was miles too big for me. When I slipped it over my head, it fell to mid-thigh. I lifted the material to my nose and breathed in deeply. If I closed my eyes, I could almost believe he was standing in front of me.

The room was quiet when I left the bathroom and crawled back into bed. I curled up on my side, facing the window, and closed my eyes. It was another hour before I relaxed enough to sleep, and I drifted off surrounded by his comforting scent.

*   *   *

"It's about time you two got back," Jordan blurted the second I opened the door to our hotel room. "You were gone forever."

"It's only been two hours." I waited for Roland to lock the door behind us before I pulled two bundles of one hundred dollar bills from inside my coat and tossed them on the bed beside her. "A very profitable two hours."

"Whoa!" Peter gaped at the money. "You got all that for four diamonds?"

Roland produced two more bundles of cash and tossed them next to mine. "Oh man, I wish you two had been there. That guy Garrett took one look at Sara and offered her five grand, like he was doing her a favor. You should have seen his face when Sara told him twenty or no deal. Then she told him the diamonds were at least twice what she was asking, and she knew he already had a buyer lined up. Next thing I knew, the two of them were chatting it up like old friends."

Jordan picked up one of the bundles, turning it over in her hands as if she couldn't believe it was real. "How did you know he had another buyer lined up?"

I shrugged off my coat and sat on the foot of the bed she and I had shared the last two nights. "Malloy told me. He also told me Garrett tries to lowball everyone at first."

Peter stared at the bundles of cash. "Wow, I've never seen that much money. Is it really twenty grand?"

I flopped back on the bed, happy not to have to worry about money anymore. "Yep."

"What are we going to do with it?" he asked. "You can't carry around that much cash."

"We're going to split it up between the four of us so no one has to carry it all," I informed him. "And we're going to eat something besides burgers and pizza."

"And get a better hotel?" Jordan added hopefully. "I'm not talking about the Ritz, but something that doesn't have a neon sign would be a step in the right direction. And I'd really like not to have to share a bathroom with two boys."

I looked around the cramped room and remembered listening to music from the bar down the street at 2:00 a.m. "Sounds like a plan. We also need to buy some clothes."

Jordan's eyes lit up. "Clothes?"

I laughed and sat up. "We're not going to Rodeo Drive. But you and I could use a few extra tops and jeans."

"Not to mention outfits for tonight." She waved at my clothes. "You can't wear that to a place like Blue Nyx."

"I guess you're right." The last thing I cared about was dressing up to go out, but we needed to blend in when we went to the nightclub.

Excitement curled in my stomach. Two days ago when we'd gotten to Los Angeles, we'd learned that Adele, the proprietor of Blue Nyx, was out of town and not due back until tonight. I was hoping she could tell me something about Madeline. We were close; I could feel it in my gut.

"Of course I'm right." She jumped off the bed with a gleam in her eyes that I had come to dread. "What are you lying around for? We have shopping to do."

I groaned and let her pull me to my feet. "Okay, but I'm telling you right now I draw the line at wearing a dress. I don't care how hot you think it looks."

Two hours later, I was threatening to strangle Jordan with the next scrap of cloth she claimed was "club wear." Those outfits might be what everyone was wearing, but they were definitely not me, and no amount of coaxing or bullying was going to get me into one of them.

I tossed one of the offending dresses over the dressing room door at her. "What the heck, Jordan? I wear more than this to bed."

She snickered loudly, enjoying herself way too much.

"I'm getting this." I opened the door and held up a pair of skinny black pants and a loose green sleeveless top. The top was pretty without looking like a second skin, and I'd just found a nice pair of black boots that would go great with the outfit.

Jordan looked it over with a critical eye. "It's still a bit overdressed, but I guess it'll have to do."

"Overdressed?" I gave her a hard look. "Are we done now?" We'd already purchased some jeans and tops for everyday wear along with a few other necessities. I had one more stop planned for today – if we ever finished trying on clothes.

"Almost. You need one more outfit, maybe two, before we go." She headed for the checkout with me close at her heels.

"More outfits? What for?"

She smiled over her shoulder. "Don't sound so worried. You'll like these."

"I doubt it."

Outside, she pulled me down the street to another shop. I stopped struggling when I saw the mannequins in the window were wearing jeans and tank tops, and there wasn't a skimpy dress in sight.

"People like Orias and that guy, Garret, don't take you seriously because you look like you just walked out of a high school. You need to start dressing like the badass chick you are." She pushed open the door. "I think you'll find something in here more to your taste."

Jordan was right on both counts. I did like the store, and I did need a wardrobe change. I was tired of people not taking me seriously. Hoodies weren't going to cut it anymore.

By the time we left the shop, I had splurged on several pairs of dark jeans, some tank tops, a pair of black combat boots, and a soft, black bomber-style leather jacket. I had to admit the clothes had looked pretty damn good on me when I'd modeled them for Jordan.

"You're actually smiling," Jordan said as we walked to the car. "I told you you'd like that last place."

"You were right. It was time for a change."

She gasped dramatically. "What? Did... did you just admit I was right? I feel faint."

We laughed as we dropped our bags in the trunk. It struck me that this was the most normal outing I'd had in months, and the first time I had ever gone shopping with another girl. And I was actually enjoying myself.

Jordan started the car. "Hotel?"

"Actually, we have one more stop." I pulled a slip of paper from my pocket and read off the address I'd written down last night.

"Where are we going?" Jordan asked.

"It's a surprise. You'll like it."

"Really?" Her face glowed with excitement. "Are we going to kill something nasty?"

I snorted. "Out of all the things we could do in LA, you come up with that one?"

She shrugged one shoulder. "You said I'd like it, and you always seem to find the bad guys. Or they find you."

"Well it's not that, but I'm pretty sure you'll like it even more."

It was her turn to snort. "More than killing things? Doubt it."

"Bloodthirsty much?"

We pulled up in front of a two-story pawnshop with bars on the windows and colorful graffiti across the brick front. Jordan leaned forward, peering at the building. "A pawnshop? Is this some kind of payback for the dresses?"

"Nope." I grinned because I couldn't wait to show her what waited for us inside. "Come on."

The shop was empty except for a middle-aged employee sitting behind the counter, playing solitaire with a deck of cards. The balding man gave us a dismissive glance and went back to his game. I walked up to him and tapped the counter to get his attention. The tag on his shirt had the name Rick on it.

"Hi, Mr. Garrett sent me."

Rick's bald head jerked up. "Mr. Garrett?"

I took a business card from my back pocket and slid it across the counter. The man's eyes followed it and as soon as he saw the name, he straightened up and gave me an ingratiating smile.

"Of course. Come with me." He ducked out from behind the counter, hurried over to lock the door, and put up the closed sign. Then he motioned for us to follow him to a set of stairs leading to the basement. "You don't look like Mr. Garrett's usual customers."

"Sara," Jordan hissed in my ear. "What is going on?"

I tossed her a grin over my shoulder before I started down the stairs. "You'll see."

At the bottom, Rick crossed the basement and entered a combination to unlock a heavy door at the other end. He flipped a switch just inside the door and waved us in.

"Wha –?" Jordan's mouth fell open and her eyes grew round. She whirled to face me. "Is... this for real?"

I couldn't contain my laughter. "Enjoy."

She flung herself at me, almost knocking me over. "You are the most amazing friend in the whole fucking world!"

"Uh, Jordan, you're crushing my ribs," I wheezed.

"Sorry." She stepped back, and I could have sworn I saw the glimmer of tears in her eyes before she turned away. The happiness on her face was worth the extra diamond I'd given Garrett for access to the contents of this room. Jordan had been such a great friend to me at Westhorne, and then coming with me on this journey to God only knew where. She'd earned this.

I let my gaze roam over the large array of weapons covering every bit of wall space in the room. One whole wall held nothing but guns, from handguns to semi-automatic weapons and even a grenade launcher.

Seriously? Who the heck needed a grenade launcher in Los Angeles?

I followed Jordan past the guns to the interesting stuff. Garrett had not been exaggerating when he'd told me about his supply of weapons. I saw swords of every shape and size, daggers, staffs, whips, axes, throwing knives and stars, and things I had no name for. There were half a dozen crossbows of different sizes, flamethrowers, and enough ammo to arm a platoon.

Rick followed us into the room, talking on his cell phone. He hung up and gave me a smile. "Mr. Garrett says you're all paid up and to take what you agreed on."

Jordan stared at us. "Seriously?"

I nodded. "Within reason. And no guns."

She let out a squeal and headed straight for the swords, just as I knew she would. Jordan was a purist when it came to weapons. In her mind, nothing but a finely-crafted sword was good enough for a warrior. I watched her lift a beautiful katana from the wall and heft it in both hands, getting a feel for it. Her movements were practiced and smooth as she sliced the blade through the air.

"Perfect!"

"Don't you think you should get something smaller? That thing will be kind of conspicuous if you carry it around."

"Can't I get two? Pretty please. I *have* to have this sword, Sara. It was made for me."

I laughed and shook my head. "Fine. Go crazy."

Leaving Jordan in a blissful haze, I went to pick out some weapons for myself. I avoided the swords because I'd be more likely to cut my own head off than someone else's. I already had my silver dagger, but it never hurt to have an extra. I chose two smaller ones that I could tuck inside a boot or under my clothes. My power was my real weapon, but it wasn't strong enough yet to kill a vampire. I could incapacitate them for a minute, but I still needed a blade to finish them off.

It had struck me as odd that I hadn't sensed a single vampire since we got to LA, but I knew they were here somewhere. A city this size was bound to have a lot of them, and with my track record, I'd be meeting some sooner or later.

A small black crossbow caught my eye and I picked it up. It was light and tiny compared to the other crossbows on the wall, and it felt good in my hands. "How do you use this thing?"

Jordan came over and showed me the basic workings of the weapon. She inserted a small arrow, cocked it, and fired at a target hanging on the far wall. The arrow hit the target a few inches off center. She cocked the crossbow again and gave it back to me. "Give it a try."

I lined up the small scope with the target and pulled the trigger. The arrow whistled through the air and embedded itself an inch from the bullseye.

"Not bad." Jordan loaded another arrow into the crossbow. "Take another shot."

My second arrow nicked the bullseye. My third one hit dead center. My fourth one bounced off the center one and skidded across the floor.

"Damn, you have crazy aim." She took the bow and hefted it in one hand. "It's small and light. If we had some silver-tipped arrows, this would be a great weapon for you."

"It's too big to conceal."

She pointed at the sword she had been admiring. "So is that, but I'm getting it."

Rick interrupted us. "I believe there are silver-tipped arrows in the ammo chest."

Jordan grinned and nudged my shoulder with hers. "Every girl needs a few accessories to go with her new outfits."

Forty minutes later, we pulled into the parking lot of our new hotel where we'd left the boys earlier. Between the two of us we managed to lug the shopping bags and a large black duffle bag full of weapons to our room. Jordan dropped her bags on the floor and flopped down on her bed while I knocked on the door of the adjoining room to let the boys know we were back. Roland raised an eyebrow when he saw all the shopping bags, but he soon forgot them when I showed him and Peter the contents of the duffle bag.

He held up a belt of small throwing knives. "What are you going to do with all of this?"

Jordan sighed heavily and closed her eyes. "A girl can never have enough weapons."

"I really hope we don't need to use any of this," said Peter as he poked around in the bag.

I picked up one of the small silver daggers I'd gotten for myself. "So do I." *But it doesn't hurt to be prepared.*

* * *

Blue Nyx wasn't like any of the other nightclubs we'd driven past on our way here. There was no flashy sign to attract clubbers and no lineup outside the door. It was a nondescript brick building with a plain steel door bearing no decoration. In fact, if it wasn't for the small blue letters painted above the door, we would not have known we were at the right place. We couldn't even hear music until we stood in front of the door, and even then it was very faint.

Jordan tried the handle and found it locked. She rapped on the steel door and took a hasty step back as the heavy door swung outward. I think we all gasped as the biggest man I'd ever seen towered over us. He must have been seven feet tall with a blond buzz cut and dressed in jeans and a black T-shirt that stretched across his massive chest and arms. With his flat nose, wide forehead, and small dark eyes, he reminded me of a picture of an ogre I'd seen in a book at Westhorne. Hell, I wouldn't be surprised if he did have ogre in his blood.

"Holy crap, you could bench press a bus," I blurted.

His thin lips twitched, and his gaze settled on me before sweeping over my friends. I wasn't sure what he was checking for, but he looked satisfied by whatever he did or didn't see. He stepped back, still holding the door open with one hand, and waved us in. We had to walk under his arm, and he was so tall none of us had to duck. That seemed to amuse the bouncer because he chuckled. I looked up and caught a flash of fang. *Definitely ogre.*

We walked down a short hallway where another bouncer, almost as big as the first one, stood in front of a second door. "Talk about security," I muttered to Jordan, who nodded.

At first glance, Blue Nyx was like the nightclubs I'd seen in movies. There was a crowded dance floor and a long bar where three bartenders rushed to fill orders. Waitresses in tiny black dresses maneuvered through the tables and couches that surrounded the dance floor, carrying trays of colorful drinks. In one corner a DJ sat on a raised platform surrounded by equipment while loud music pumped through the club's sound system in synch with the colored strobe lights. A staircase curved upward to the second floor where people milled near the railing, talking and watching the gyrating bodies below.

Even before my eyes had time to adjust to the lights, I knew this place was nothing like those other clubs. My senses were assailed by the different kinds of magic that permeated the air, filling my nose and raising gooseflesh on my arms. Magic pulsed with the music like a living thing and made me want to move with it. It was a heady sensation.

My power twitched, wanting to break free, and not just because of the other magic. There were demons here.

But not just demons. Scanning the dance floor, I could barely keep my jaw up at the sight of the diverse group of people. Tall, slender elven women with long blond hair and pointed ears rubbed against faerie males. A nymph in an almost transparent dress did a slow sensual dance, surrounded by five men who could only be dwarves. A werewolf couple was engaged in a heavy make-out session, oblivious to the people moving around them. At least, I suspected they were weres based on the hair I saw sprouting along their arms. Four gray-skinned mox demons danced in a small group at the edge of the dance floor, and a vrell demon who reminded me of Kelvan danced with a blue-haired girl who raised her hands in the air and shot blue sparks from her fingertips. There were other people who I suspected were demons and a number of humans too, and they all moved together in a mass of sweaty, undulating bodies.

My face grew warm just watching the dancers, and I didn't even want to imagine what was happening on the couches in the darker corners of the club. I looked at my friends to gauge their reactions and found Roland and Peter gawking at the nymph while Jordan looked the faerie males up and down. I shook my head. "Roland, if your tongue hangs any lower it'll be on the floor."

He gave me a goofy grin. "Why don't we have clubs like this back home?"

"Or men who look like that?" Jordan said with a gusty sigh, still staring at the faeries.

I followed her gaze, but when I looked directly at the faeries, their outlines blurred for several seconds. One second they were muscled with blond hair and handsome faces, and in the next they were slender and blue-skinned with long black hair and pointed ears. Once I focused all I saw were the blue bodies. It hit me what I was seeing and I let out a laugh. "Um, Jordan, you know that thing where I can see through glamours? Trust me, those guys aren't your type."

She slanted a look at me. "You're kidding."

"Not unless you like your men blue and pointy-eared."

"Pixies? Shit. That is so wrong."

"You can't trust a faerie." I smirked at her. "Trust me."

She punched my arm. "All right, smartass, let's go find this Adele chick."

I had to nudge Roland and Peter twice to drag their eyes away from the dance floor. "Men," I muttered, even though I was beginning to suspect the magic I sensed in the room might be partly responsible for the promiscuous behavior of the people there.

Roland showed off the dimples that had charmed many girls back home. "Come on, Sara. Live a little." He looked over his shoulder at the nymph. "Try something new."

"No, thanks." All I was interested in was talking to Adele and finding out if she knew where Madeline was. The club scene was not my thing, even if the people in this one were fascinating. I just wanted to get what I came for and leave.

We made our way to the bar, and I waved down one of the bartenders who, surprisingly, turned out to be human. I asked him if Adele was here, and he said she usually got in around eleven, which wasn't for another forty-five minutes. Jordan and I ordered sodas and the boys got beers to sip while we waited. A few people approached us for dances, but we decided to stick together. The place didn't look dangerous, but trouble had a way of finding us.

Before long I noticed a tall, well-built, blond faerie with dark blue eyes and finely chiseled features watching us. I squinted to see beneath his glamour, and I was surprised to find there wasn't one. Our eyes met, and he smiled and started toward us. I suppressed a groan. Aine was the only faerie I'd met and she was very good to me. But it was common knowledge that faeries in general were nothing but trouble. They were bored immortals always looking for amusement, and they had rather unbridled appetites for fun and pleasure.

"I did not expect to find such fresh young beauties at Adele's tonight," the faerie said when he reached us.

My eyebrow rose. "Does that line really work?"

Instead of being offended, he laughed huskily. "Most of the time."

I couldn't help it, I smiled back. Stupid faerie charm.

"I am Eldeorin." He extended a hand, and I took it automatically.

"Sara." I studied his face. His voice sounded vaguely familiar to me even though I was sure we had never met. "Excuse me; do I know you from somewhere?"

Eldeorin's grip was firm and he covered my hand with his other one. "We haven't formally met, but I'd know you anywhere, little Cousin. I tended you when you were in Faerie."

"*You* healed me?" Memories surfaced of soothing faceless voices I thought I had dreamed. "I remember hearing your voice..."

His smile widened. "I stayed with you until you were through the worst of it. I have never seen anyone fight to live as hard as you did. And here you are." His gaze moved past me to my friends, who were oddly quiet. "You keep unusual company, but I can see why. Your friends are quite fetching."

I resisted the urge to roll my eyes as I turned to introduce him to the others. Roland and Peter stared at him with a mix of fascination and wariness. Eldeorin turned his dazzling smile on them, and I saw a glazed look enter Roland's eyes.

"Hey!" I smacked Eldeorin on the arm. "None of that faerie mojo on my friends."

"I apologize. I got carried away." He leaned down to whisper in my ear. "Is he...?"

"No."

Eldeorin sighed. "Pity."

I made the introductions. Roland and Peter nodded, and I had a feeling that neither of them realized how close they had been to falling under a faerie's charm. I'd have to watch Eldeorin and make sure he didn't try it again. Cousin or not, faeries had their reputation for a reason.

Eldeorin turned his attention to Jordan, who took a step back. I stared at her pained expression in confusion for several seconds before it dawned on me that her Mori probably wasn't too happy to be close to a full-blooded faerie.

"My apologies, Mohiri," Eldeorin said to her. She merely nodded in reply.

Just then a group of faerie males paused behind Roland and Peter. Eldeorin gave them a small shake of his head. One of the faeries gave me a disappointed smile before they moved on.

"Hey!" Roland spun around to stare after the departing faeries. "Someone just grabbed my ass."

I bit back a smile. "Roland, no one here wants to grab your butt."

"I would. It is a very nice one," Eldeorin said.

"What?" Roland croaked. The look on his face was priceless.

"Well, you did say we should live a little," I said. "Maybe try something new."

Panic filled his eyes. "That's not what I meant!"

Laughter burst from me, and it took me a full minute to be able to speak. "We're just messing with you, Roland."

He did not look convinced.

Peter glanced around warily. "It's five after eleven. Shouldn't that woman be here by now?"

"What woman?" Eldeorin asked.

"Adele. We came here to talk to her." I looked for the bartender I'd spoken to earlier.

Eldeorin's eyes gleamed with curiosity. "Now why would you young people want to see Adele?"

"It's business," Jordan stated coolly, not bothering to hide her dislike for the faerie.

Eldeorin's rich laugh drew the attention of several human women nearby and they smiled appreciatively at him. "I know what kind of business Adele deals in, and I doubt the four of you would want any part of it."

I shrugged. "I need to talk to her; that's all."

"Then allow me." He waved toward the stairs. "Adele and I are old friends, and I'd be happy to take you to her."

I hesitated. "Why do you want to help us?"

His smile dimmed. "I am helping you, little Cousin, because you are too innocent for your own good. I could not permit you to face someone like Adele on your own. She has sweet little things like you for lunch."

A cold tingle ran up the back of my neck. "I really hope you are speaking figuratively and not literally."

"It is all a matter of perspective. You need not worry. She will behave herself if I accompany you." He pointed to the stairs again. "Shall we?"

CHAPTER 5

THE FOUR OF us followed him up the winding stairs to the second floor. At the top, he turned right and walked up to the door of a room with a large, darkened window that overlooked the entire club. Outside the door stood a huge man who resembled the two bouncers, and he scowled at us as we approached.

"Evening, Bruce," Eldeorin said, apparently unfazed by the brute's unwelcome stare. "Is she in? My cousin and I would like to see her."

Bruce's small dark eyes moved over me. He grunted and stepped aside, but held up a hand when all of us made to follow Eldeorin. "Only the faeries," he said in a deep rumbling voice.

A volley of protests came from my friends. "No way," Roland and Peter uttered.

Jordan moved to stand beside me. "We go where she goes."

Bruce crossed his huge arms. "Only her."

"It's okay, guys," I said, ignoring the knot in my stomach. "I'll be fine."

"No harm will come to her. I promise you," Eldeorin told them.

Jordan gave him a hard stare, and he met it with a smile. "Stop scowling, warrior. We faeries take care of our own."

"Let's go," I said to him. I just wanted to get this over with so we could get out of this place.

Eldeorin opened the door and ushered me inside ahead of him. My eyes went immediately to the blond woman lounging on a couch in front of the window. She looked to be in her early twenties with flawless porcelain skin, generous red lips, and eyes the most striking shade of violet. She wore a long silver dress that hugged her curves, and she held a wine glass in her hand.

Adele was exquisitely beautiful. She was also a demon. I couldn't tell what kind of demon she was, but the way my power pressed to get out, she was a strong one. It was no wonder Eldeorin had insisted on accompanying me. I couldn't help but wonder how a faerie had come to be friends with a demon.

"Eldeorin, what a pleasure." She seemed genuinely pleased to see the faerie.

He steered me toward a couch on the other side of the room, keeping his distance from her. "Adele, you are as lovely as ever."

Her gaze shifted to me, and I saw a spark of interest. "And who is this pretty thing you have on your arm tonight? She doesn't seem like your type."

"You should know by now that all beautiful people are my type," he replied with a soft laugh. "This is my little cousin, Sara. Sara, meet Adele."

"Hello," I said.

"Sara? That is a human name." A slow smile spread across her face. "Cousin indeed. Are you playing with me, Eldeorin? Did you bring a present for me?"

A present? Indignation rose in me. How dare she talk about humans like they were toys for her pleasure? Blue sparks played over the bare skin of my arms, making the hairs stand on end.

Eldeorin laid a hand on my arm. "Now, Cousin, Adele meant no insult."

"What kind of demon are you?" I asked her.

That earned a throaty laugh from her. She set down her glass and sat up. "Oh my, you are an innocent. I'm shocked Eldeorin even brought you to my club."

"Adele is a succubus," Eldeorin informed me.

I inhaled sharply. Succubi survived by feeding off sexual energy, sometimes killing their victims when they were done with them. Their power allowed them to enthrall and arouse people to the point where they were helpless to defend themselves. Not that any male caught in a succubus's hold would want to be freed. Women were not immune to their power either, although most Succubi preferred men.

A horrifying thought struck me. "All those people downstairs, you're feeding off them."

"Yes," she said, as if it was no big deal. "Don't look so shocked. I provide a place where they can let go and explore their sexuality. In return, I feed off all their excess energy. It does not harm them, and most of them are aware of what I do. It also keeps me sated so I don't have to look for someone to feed off. It is a good arrangement for everyone."

The thought of someone feeding off my energy made bile rise in my throat. I couldn't believe people willingly subjected themselves to that. Yes, it was better than Adele finding some unsuspecting victim, but it still felt wrong.

She picked up her glass again and took a sip of wine. "I'm surprised

Eldeorin didn't tell you about me before he brought you here."

"That is because I didn't know she was coming here tonight," he said in mock aggravation.

Adele gave me a knowing smile. "Spreading your little faerie wings, hmm?"

"I came to talk to you actually."

"Is that so?" A perfectly shaped eyebrow shot up. "You have my undivided attention."

"A warlock named Orias told me to come see you. I'm looking for someone, and he said you can find anyone in LA."

"Orias? I haven't seen him in ages. Is he still living at that ghastly place out in the desert?"

"Yes."

She shook her head. "Why anyone with his power would choose to live like that is beyond my comprehension. So tell me, who are you looking for?"

"Her name is Madeline Croix, but you might know her by another –"

"Madeline?" Adele's eyes narrowed. "Why would a faerie youngling be looking for a Mohiri?"

My heart began to thump against my ribs. "You know Madeline?"

"I know her well enough."

"Do you know where she is?"

"You have to answer my question first. Why are you looking for her?"

"I'm looking for her for her daughter."

Adele's eyebrows shot up again. "I did not know Madeline had a daughter."

Wow, what a shocker. "She does, and it's very important that her daughter finds her. Only I'm not sure Madeline will want to talk to her. She left when her daughter was only two and hasn't seen her since."

Adele tapped a finger against her lips. "That explains why I have never heard of the child. Madeline does not like to talk about her past."

"You sound like you've known her a while. Are you friends?"

The succubus paused before answering. "She saved my life a few years ago, and I guess you could say we are friends now, as much as anyone can be friends with her. She visits once or twice a year when she's in town."

"She saved your life?" It was hard to imagine Madeline doing a kindness for anyone.

"A vampire decided he liked my club and wanted it for himself. Madeline was in the right place at the right time." She smoothed the fabric of her dress over her thighs. "After that I hired new security. No one gets past my men, not even vampires."

I swallowed, trying to hide my excitement. If Adele was telling the truth, then Madeline would come to see her when she got to Los Angeles – if she wasn't here already."

"Orias told me Madeline was on her way to LA. Have you seen her?"

"I haven't seen her in over a year, and I don't know when she plans to visit again."

Something in her tone told me she wasn't being honest. If they really were friends, I couldn't fault her for trying to protect Madeline. But I hadn't come this far only to let Madeline slip through my fingers. "Would you tell me if she does come to see you? I promise I just want to talk to her."

Adele studied me for a long moment. "I'll consider your request. I make no promises, though."

"Thank you." I made a mental note to call David as soon as we got back to the hotel and ask him to find out everything he could on Adele. I should have done that before I came to see her. I didn't believe she would really let me know when Madeline arrived, so we were going to have to watch her.

"On that note, I think it is time to get you home, Cousin." Eldeorin stood and extended his hand to me. "Adele knows how to contact me if she needs to reach you." He inclined his head toward the succubus. "It's been a pleasure as always, Adele."

Adele didn't bother to rise from her couch to see us out. "It was wonderful to see you and to meet your young cousin. Are you calling it a night then?"

Eldeorin laughed as he gently tugged me to the door. "You should know me better than that. I'll be back after I see Sara home."

Roland, Peter, and Jordan were standing right where I'd left them, and their anxious expressions softened when they saw me. Roland reached my side first. "Are you okay?"

"Did you find out anything?" Jordan asked impatiently.

"Yes, I'm fine, and I'll tell you everything in the car," I said in a low voice. "I'm so ready to get out of here." I smiled at Roland. "Unless you want to stay?"

Roland shook his head vigorously. "I've seen enough, thanks."

"Come then, and I'll see you out." Eldeorin took my hand and laid it on his arm. It reminded me of Desmund, and I suddenly wished I was back in the library with him instead of in this hot, noisy club that reeked of magic and something dark and wanton that made my stomach churn.

Movement by the main door caught my eye as we made our way around the dance floor. Two tall young men walked through the door and slowly perused the room. They were both dark-haired and good looking, but that wasn't what drew my attention. There was something about the way they moved that was familiar, but I couldn't put my finger on it.

A third man appeared behind them, and the bottom fell out of my stomach. "Oh shit!" I grabbed Jordan's arm and pulled her down to sit on a couch.

Roland, Peter, and Eldeorin crowded around us. "What is it?" Peter asked.

"Trouble."

Jordan's eyes lit up. "Vampires?"

"Worse. It's Chris, and he's not alone."

Roland swore softly. "Nikolas and Chris are here? We're so screwed."

"I don't... I don't think Nikolas is here." At least I couldn't sense him nearby, but that didn't mean he wouldn't arrive any minute.

"They're spreading out," Roland said in a frantic tone. "Chris is still by the door, but the other two are definitely looking for someone."

"Who is Chris?" Concern colored Eldeorin's tone. "Are you in danger?"

I shook my head. "He's my Mohiri cousin, and he's looking for Jordan and me. If he catches us, he's going to drag us home, and I can't go yet. I have to find Madeline first."

"We kind of left home without permission," Jordan explained. She peered around Peter. "I don't know the two with him. They look foreign."

How the hell had they found us? There was no way Chris showing up here tonight was a coincidence. Not with my luck. "We have to get out of here before they see us. Is there a back door to this place, Eldeorin?"

"Um, guys." Peter nodded toward the back of the club. "I think they thought of that, too."

Jordan turned to look behind us. "Fuck! There're two more of them back there." Her eyes were resigned when they met mine.

I wasn't ready to throw in the towel yet. I reached up and tugged on Eldeorin's arm, and he sat beside me.

"Will you help us?" I'd only met him an hour ago, but it felt like I'd known him for a lot longer than that. I couldn't explain it, but I trusted him like I trusted Aine.

"I am not sure you are ready to be out in the world, little Cousin," he replied, taking one of my hands in his. "The Mohiri are strong warriors. Perhaps it would be best if they took you home where it is safe."

"No place is safe for me." I shook my head at his puzzled expression. "It's a long story, and I'll tell it to you later. But first, we need to get out of here. Please."

"If he's going to do something, he'd better do it soon," Roland whispered urgently. "They are closing fast."

My fingers tightened on Eldeorin's arm. "Please."

Eldeorin's blue eyes stared intently into mine. Behind me Jordan made a sound of dismay and my heart sank. I broke away from his gaze and looked up at the warrior who stood several feet away. His brown eyes passed over my friends and settled on me. I swallowed hard. And then he smiled.

It was not a "gotcha" smile, which was what I expected. It was sensual and inviting, the kind of smile a man gives a woman he wants, and it made heat invade my face. I looked down after a few seconds, waiting for him to call out to Chris. Disappointment burned in my throat like bile. I had been so close to finding Madeline, and now it was all over.

Jordan's gasp brought my head up again in time to see the warrior continuing his slow trek through the crowded club. "What the hell?" she whispered. She looked at me and her mouth fell open. "Oh, this is priceless."

"What?" I asked.

Eldeorin leaned toward me. "I pray I am not doing you a disservice, Cousin."

"What the...?" Roland sputtered. He looked down at himself and then at Peter.

Jordan let out a short laugh. "You two look good as elves. I think it might be an improvement."

"Speak for yourself, pixie," he retorted.

"What?" Jordan rounded on Eldeorin. "You made me look like a pixie?"

It took me a few seconds to realize what they were all going on about. Eldeorin had cast glamours over us. I could see through them, so everyone looked the same to me. "What am I?"

Roland grinned. "You are the hottest nymph I've ever seen."

"What?" I pictured the almost naked nymph I'd seen dancing earlier. "I'd better be wearing real clothes."

Jordan stood and pulled me to my feet. "It's probably best that you can't see it. As long as it gets us out of here, right?"

"Ugh! Let's go." I glowered at Roland and Peter who were staring at me, as was every other male around us. "Stop that."

"Sorry," my friends said sheepishly, and turned away.

"If it makes you feel any better, it doesn't look like you," Roland said without looking at me.

Eldeorin led us to the main entrance, right past Chris, who was scanning the room. I tried to look straight ahead, but I couldn't help myself. I glanced at Chris and found him watching me. *Oh, crap, he knows it's me.* But then he gave me a slow smile. *Okay, this is beyond awkward.* I wanted to run out of there, but I looked away and forced myself to walk at a normal pace.

The moment the heavy outside door shut behind us, I released the breath I was holding and smacked Eldeorin on the arm. "A freaking nymph? Really? I think my cousin was about to hit on me. Do you know how gross that is?"

His smile was pure mischief. "It got you out of there, didn't it? And we are all cousins in one way or another."

I didn't examine that statement too deeply. I had a feeling Eldeorin had no boundaries when it came to cousins, species, or gender. "Thank you for helping us," I said instead. "Can you take the glamours off us now?"

"There may be more warriors around. Once you are safely inside your vehicle, I will remove them."

"Good idea," Roland said with a smirk as we walked to our car. "In fact, maybe Sara should keep hers for a few days. It's the perfect disguise."

"Careful, Roland," I told him sweetly. "I don't know how to create glamours yet, but I might someday. How would you like to spend a day walking around in a bikini?"

He winced and raised his hands. "Point taken."

When we reached the car, Eldeorin hugged me before I could open the door. It was a good thing I had gotten used to hugging, because faeries were an affectionate bunch.

"Stay safe, Cousin. I will check on you soon."

"How will you find me? Do you have some kind of radar for finding other faeries?"

He laughed softly as he released me. "Something like that. Now get out of here. It won't take those warriors long to see that you aren't in the club."

Jordan started the car, and I climbed into the front passenger seat. By the time I closed the door and buckled my seat belt, Eldeorin had vanished. *I really wish I knew how to do that.* After meeting Eldeorin, I saw there were a lot more advantages to Fae magic than being able to kill vampires.

I rolled down my window a few inches for some air and sank back against my seat. What a night.

Roland let out a deep breath. "Damn, that was close."

"If we hadn't met the faerie, they would have had us for sure," Peter added.

I nodded. "And I'm not sure I would have gotten in to see Adele without him. After meeting her, I'm really glad he was with me."

Jordan glanced at me as she started driving us back to the hotel. "Why? What happened?"

I told them about meeting Adele and what I had learned about Madeline.

"A succubus?" Jordan made a face. "Madeline has strange taste in friends."

"If Madeline really is in LA, I think she'll visit her soon. We just have to watch Adele."

Roland laid his hand on my shoulder. "I hate to put a crimp in your plans, but the Mohiri were all over that place. We can't exactly do a stakeout with all those warriors nosing around."

"Not to mention we have no idea where Adele lives," Jordan said, stopping at a red light.

"That's why I'm going to ask David to —" I broke off and looked around the intersection. "Did you guys hear that?"

Jordan looked over at me. "Hear what?"

I rolled the window all the way dawn. "I thought I heard —"

A girl's terrified scream split the air.

I gasped, not because of the scream, but because of the cold spot forming in my chest. We'd been in Los Angeles for two days and I was surprised it had taken this long to come across one of them. "Vampire."

Roland slapped the back of Jordan's seat. "Drive, Jordan!"

"We have to do something," I told them.

"We have to get out of here," Roland argued. "We can't go looking for trouble."

"I'm not looking for trouble, but I can't stand by while one of those things murders someone." My statement was punctuated by another scream.

Jordan jerked the wheel to the right and sped down a less busy side street. The cold spot in my chest grew until I knew we were there. I motioned to her, and she parked in front of a closed drycleaner and jumped out. I followed her to the trunk where we began pulling weapons from the duffle bag we had stored there earlier. I armed myself with a long dagger and the mini crossbow, and Jordan grabbed her new sword.

I held a knife out to Roland, but he shook his head. He and Peter ran into the darkened loading dock between the drycleaner and a laundromat. Less than thirty seconds later, I heard the scratch of claws on pavement.

"No!" a girl cried. It came from the alley across the street. The terror in her voice spurred me forward, and I was halfway across the street before Roland let out a soft growl and started after me.

The alley was lit by the streetlight, and I came up short at the sight before me. The blue-haired girl from the club was backed against a dumpster with her hands held in front of her. Flames flew from her fingertips, holding off the blond vampire advancing on her. At her feet lay her vrell demon friend from the club. He was unconscious and blood ran down one side of his face.

A few feet away from them, two vampires were feeding on a female mox demon. Their noisy slurping and the sight of the ravaged body made my stomach revolt. All I could see was Olivia and Mark lying on the snow that was soaked with their blood.

Rage burned through me. Before I knew what I was doing, I had the crossbow cocked and aimed at one of the vampires kneeling over the mox demon. He jerked and screamed when the silver-coated arrow pierced his back. It wasn't close enough to hit his heart, but he screeched when he grabbed the arrow and tried to pull it out.

The other two vampires turned their attention to us. "What have we here?" the blond drawled, and then his eyes widened at something behind me. I didn't have to look to know Roland and Peter were flanking me.

Jordan came to stand beside me. "Vampires eating demons? That's like cannibalism, isn't it?"

"What do you care about a couple of dead demons?" asked the red-headed vampire still kneeling over the mox demon. He rose slowly to his feet, and I saw his eyes flit between Jordan and me, assessing who was the bigger threat.

Jordan raised her sword. "We don't care about dead demons. We do, however, have a problem with live blood suckers."

The redhead's attention shifted back to me and instead of fear I felt a flash of annoyance. Why did everyone assume I was the weak one? I looked at Jordan's sword and listened to the two growling werewolves behind me. Okay, maybe this time they were right.

"I think he likes you," Jordan said, laughter in her voice.

The blond vampire yelled at his friend who was still making a God-awful racket as he tried to remove my arrow. "Shut up, Trevor!"

"I can shut him up for you," Jordan said sweetly. "Wouldn't take more than a second."

"You can have her," snarled the redhead. "I want the little one. "

Roland let out a deep growl that made the hair stand up on the back of my neck. I put my hand back and touched his furry snout.

Jordan scoffed. "Sorry, guys, you aren't really our types."

The blond vampire sniffed the air. "Mohiri children out walking their pets. I wonder if your blood is as sweet as they say it is."

I loaded another arrow into the crossbow. At the same time, I opened my power, relishing the comforting heat spreading through me. The way they moved told me they weren't mature vampires, but they weren't new, either. My eyes went to the blue-haired girl who was crouched in a defensive stance between her demon friend and the vampires.

"You guys need some new material," Jordan quipped. "Sara, what was the name of the last sucker who thought you smelled good? You know the one you killed in Albuquerque?"

"Stefan Price."

Both vampires stared at me. "*You* killed Stefan Price? Impossible," declared the redhead.

Jordan brandished her sword. "Why don't you come over here and find out for yourself?"

Trevor, who had finally managed to extricate the arrow from his back, strutted over to stand beside his friends. He looked a lot cockier when he wasn't jumping around and screeching his head off. "What are we standing around for? Let's take care of these bitches and their pups." He pointed a clawed finger at me. "That one is mine."

"Sorry, I'm already taken." I swung the crossbow up and aimed it, earning a laugh from him.

He bared his fangs at me. "You took me by surprise the first time. Do you really think you can hit me in the heart with that thing before I get to – ?"

Trevor let out an earsplitting shriek and doubled over, clutching at the arrow protruding from his smoking crotch.

"I wasn't aiming for your heart."

Jordan whistled. "Damn, girl, you do have an evil streak after all."

"If he can't walk, he can't attack."

Roland growled impatiently. The other two vampires took a step back.

"Right, let's get this over with. Jordan and I will take the redhead, and you guys handle the other two." It seemed like a fair fight since Trevor was now trying to crawl away. The alley was a dead end, so I wasn't sure where he thought he was going.

I couldn't help but compare this to the first time I ended up in an alley with a vampire. I had been so terrified of Eli I could barely move. Back then, I could never imagine me willingly going after a vampire, let alone three of them. So much had changed since that night in Portland. The irony of it all was that vampires were responsible for a lot of it.

The vampires realized playtime was over when the four of us split into pairs. They crouched side-by-side and bared their fangs and claws at us. Tendrils of fear curled in my stomach and adrenaline spiked through me even though we had them outnumbered. I welcomed it. Fear keeps you alive.

Roland and Peter moved first. Snarling, they ran toward the blond vampire. I saw the vampire's face contort in fear a second before he spun and fled deeper into the alley with the werewolves on his heels. I heard growls and screams, but the dumpster was blocking my view.

The redhead's lips curled as Jordan and I advanced on him. "You shouldn't have let your guard dogs run off. Now it's just us."

I reloaded the crossbow and pulled out the dagger I had stuck in the waistband of my pants. "Can you take him?" I asked Jordan, knowing she was itching for a vampire kill. But he wasn't as young as most of the vampires she had killed.

"Probably," she replied without her usual cockiness.

"Go for it. I've got your back."

She smiled and started forward. "I know you do."

The vampire didn't wait for her to reach him. He rushed at her, claws outstretched. He was fast, but Jordan was faster. She leapt to one side and whirled in a lithe movement to slice the sword across his back. He screamed and spun, lashing out at her. I heard a soft grunt as his claws scored her bare arm, but she didn't falter. The sword came up again and this time it severed the hand that had injured her. Blood splattered across the front of the new top she'd bought for tonight. She was going to be pissed about that.

He let out a screech and ran at her again. One thing I'd learned over the last few months was that immortality did not equal intelligence. No person in their right mind would attack someone who looked as fierce as Jordan did in that moment, especially if that someone was holding a big ass sword. Her movements when she met his attack were easy and graceful like the steps in a deadly dance. She reminded me of Nikolas.

Jordan's sword opened a gaping gash in the vampire's stomach. He stumbled back in shock and grabbed his gut. Like a predator, she advanced. Metal glinted. The vampire's next scream was cut off as his head separated from his body.

We looked at each other over the vampire's body. Her chest rose and fell sharply, but I knew it was from excitement, not exertion. She lifted the bloody sword and smiled. "I told you this sword was made for me."

I started to reply but stopped when I realized I no longer heard any sounds of fighting from the end of the alley. My stomach twisted in fear. "Roland? Peter?"

Their big wolf forms appeared around the dumpster, bloody in places but otherwise looking okay. Roland looked at the dead vampire at Jordan's feet then nodded to let us know the other two were dead as well.

A whimper drew my attention to the blue-haired girl and her friend, and I rushed over to help them. I couldn't touch the vrell demon, so I laid a hand on the girl's bare arm to comfort her. I'm not sure which of us was more shocked when my power flared and lashed out at her. I'd gotten pretty good at keeping it under control, but I was a bit worked up and not expecting her to be a demon. I yanked my hand away. "Shit, you're a demon."

She leaned protectively over her friend, who moaned softly. "Please, don't hurt us."

No one had ever looked at me with that much fear in their eyes, and it felt like someone had socked me in the gut. I moved back to give her some space. "No one is going to hurt you or your friend."

She stared at my hands, and I rested them on my thighs. "I'm sorry about zapping you. It was an accident."

"This one's gone," Jordan called, and I looked over my shoulder to where she was checking the mox demon for signs of life.

The vrell demon opened his eyes. "Nell?" he rasped, looking up at the blue-haired demon.

"Aiden!" She kissed his forehead. He tried to move, and she helped him into a sitting position until they were both facing me. She clung to his hand as if it was a lifeline.

"Who are you?" Aiden asked warily, covering his bleeding head with a hand.

"My name is Sara and this is my friend, Jordan. The werewolves over there are my friends, Roland and Peter. We heard screams and came to help. I'm sorry. We were too late to save your friend."

"You killed them all?"

"My friends did."

He stared at the vampire's body. "You are Mohiri, aren't you? Why would you help us?"

I fought to hold back the scowl that threatened. The Mohiri were supposed to be the good guys, but every demon we encountered acted like we were the boogeymen. I didn't like having to defend myself over and over.

"The Mohiri kill vampires, but we don't hurt innocent people. You're safe with us."

Aiden's eyes grew round and he hugged Nell close, whispering to her in demon tongue.

I stood and walked a few feet away because it was obvious my closeness was distressing Nell. "We probably shouldn't stay here much longer. Can you walk, or do you need help?"

"I am well enough to walk." Aiden got to his feet with Nell's help. He looked at Jordan and me. "Thank you."

"Anytime," Jordan said. "Just stay away from alleys at night from now on."

Aiden gave her a pained smile. "Sound advice." He laid an arm over Nell's shoulders and looked sadly at the dead mox demon. "Let's go home. We have to call Moira's family so they can collect her body."

"I'm really sorry about your friend," I said as they limped past us.

"Well, our work here is done," Jordan declared, watching the two demons leave. She wiped her blade on the dead vampire's clothes. "We should get out of here, too. We're less than a block from Blue Nyx and this might attract some attention."

We ran across the road, thankful there was no traffic, and the boys went into the loading dock to change back and dress. Roland had a scratch on his chin and Peter was sporting a bruised eye. I was the only one among us who wasn't wounded or bloody. I chuckled at that as we got into the car, and Jordan asked what was funny.

"This is the first time I've encountered a vampire and didn't need a shower or medical attention after. I think my luck is improving."

She looked down at her ruined top and made a face. "I wish my clothes could say the same. Hanging with you is a blast, but it's murder on my wardrobe."

"Sorry. Next time, I'll kill the vampire."

She started the car. "Not on your life."

The three of them immediately started going over the fight and arguing over who had made the best kill. All I could do was shake my head and wonder when this crazy night would be over.

I still couldn't believe Chris had been at the club. There was no way it could have been a coincidence. And if Chris was in Los Angeles then Nikolas was here too. But why wasn't Nikolas with him tonight? If they'd had any reason to suspect I'd be at the club, I couldn't see Nikolas not being there. My heart fluttered at the thought of Nikolas being somewhere in this city right now, and a pang of longing twisted my stomach.

Roland let out a whoop. "All night diner. I could really go for a burger with the works."

"Me too!" Peter chimed in.

"You want to eat *now*?" Jordan asked, already putting on her signal to get into the other lane.

I chuckled. "Werewolves are always hungry. You should know that after almost a week with these two."

As soon as we pulled up in front of the diner, Roland and Peter started to get out and I stopped them. "You guys have blood on you. I'd better go in."

"Oh, yeah." Roland sat again, and he and Peter told me what they wanted. I looked at Jordan, who shrugged and said that since we were here, she might as well get something too.

It was after midnight so the diner was pretty quiet. It was one of those fifties-style diners with a checkered tile floor and red vinyl seats. The young waitress at the counter wore a pink poodle skirt and looked none too happy about it. I ordered three burgers with the works, and she disappeared into the kitchen after she rang them up.

I couldn't think about eating after what I'd seen in that alley. My stomach rolled every time I remembered those vampires ripping into that poor mox demon. If we'd gotten there just a few minutes earlier we could have saved her. I sighed wearily. We had saved two lives and there were three fewer vampires stalking the streets of Los Angeles. I should be happy with that.

The waitress brought me a large paper bag. I thanked her and headed back to the car. A man opened the door for me when I reached it, and I mumbled a thank-you to him, still lost in my thoughts.

"Sara?"

My breath caught. I knew that voice.

I spun and stared at the friend I hadn't seen in months. "Greg?"

CHAPTER 6

BEFORE I KNEW what was happening, Greg pulled me into his arms and swung me around as if I weighed nothing. The bag of food slipped from my hands and hit the ground as my arms went around his neck to hug him back.

"I can't believe it's you. What on earth are you doing in LA?" he asked when he finally set me back on my feet.

"I could ask the same of you." I stared at him, reeling from the fact that he was standing in front of me. Greg was the last person I'd expected to run into in California. I hadn't seen him since he'd graduated from school last spring, and he hadn't changed much in that time. His dark blond hair hung in long, careless waves to his shoulders, and his brown eyes still had that intensity that used to make the boys back home give him a wide berth. He wore jeans and his old leather jacket on his six-foot frame, and he looked like he'd been working out more since he moved to Philly last spring. I looked around and sure enough, his motorcycle was a few feet away.

A few days after I got to Westhorne, I'd called Greg to let him know I wasn't dead like the rest of the world believed I was. It had been a huge shock for him, especially after attending my memorial service two weeks before. We'd talked for an hour and I'd planned to tell him everything, but he'd been too shaken up to have all of that laid on him at once. So I told him I'd explain it all the next time we talked, and he'd sounded okay with that. I'd figured I could ease him into it over time. But he'd never called me back, and he'd stopped answering his phone and emails.

"What happened to you, Greg? We talked and then I didn't hear from you again." I fought to keep the hurt out of my voice.

He ran a hand through his hair and stared like he still couldn't believe it was me. "Ah shit, I'm sorry, Sara. Things have been kind of crazy. My uncle

Leo passed away last month, and I came out here to take care of things for my aunt and cousin."

"Oh, I'm sorry. Was he the musician?" I remembered Greg talking about him a few times.

"Yeah, that's him."

"Greg?" Roland said from behind me.

"I should have known you two would be with her. What the hell brings you all to LA?" Greg frowned at me. "You told me you had to hide and pretend to be dead because someone was after you. What is going on, Sara?"

"It's a long story." One I wasn't sure he was ready to hear.

"I have time if you do. In fact, why don't you come back to —?" He stared at something behind me, and I looked back at Jordan who had joined us, still wearing her bloodstained clothes.

"Um..." I fumbled for something to say.

Greg fixed me with a hard stare. "Let me guess, long story?"

"Yes." I waved at Jordan. "Greg, this is Jordan. Jordan, Greg is my friend from back home."

He bent and picked up the greasy paper bag, handing it to me. "My uncle's place is not far from here. Why don't you guys come over and we'll catch up there? Something tells me this is not the place for that talk."

I looked at the others. Roland and Peter nodded and Jordan lifted a shoulder. "All right. We'll follow you."

Greg's uncle's place turned out to be a remodeled firehouse. The lower floor was used for storage and parking, and the upper floor had been converted into a very spacious and comfortable apartment. There were two bedrooms, a bathroom, a small recording studio, and an open area that served as the kitchen, dining room, and living room. Large windows gave us a great view of the busy city lights.

Greg offered Jordan a clean T-shirt so she could change out of her bloody top. Then he and I sat facing each other on the couch while the others ate their burgers in the kitchen.

"Talk," he said in his gruff, no-nonsense tone.

"I don't know where to start."

"How about the beginning?"

I hesitated. This would have been so much easier over the phone.

He folded his arms. "Sara."

"Okay, but I have to warn you, this is going to sound crazy. You probably won't believe me."

A shadow passed over his face. "You'd be amazed at what I'd believe."

I took a deep breath. "It all started when my dad died." As soon as the words began to pour from me, I couldn't stop. I told him how my dad had really died, about my healing ability, and all the things I'd kept hidden from

Nate and my friends for so many years. Shock registered on his face more than once, but he didn't interrupt me. I was grateful for that because I was afraid if I stopped, I wouldn't know how to continue.

The others joined us in the living room when I started to talk about the last few months, beginning with that fateful night in Portland. I paused when I remembered I couldn't tell Greg the truth about Roland and Peter. It wasn't my place to reveal their secret to anyone, even to someone I trusted as much as I did Greg.

I looked at Roland and he nodded. So I told Greg the story of that night, including the boys' part in it. Roland and Peter joined in, helping me relate the rest of the events that had happened in Maine. I tried to gauge Greg's thoughts as he listened to our story, but he had always been hard to read. He nodded grimly at times and said little. He had never been one to speak much, even when we used to sit together at lunch. Neither had I. It was probably one of the reasons we'd gotten along so well.

My body tensed when I told him about the Mohiri and the demon inside me. I'd come to accept and care for my Mori, but I remembered the fear and revulsion I'd felt when Nikolas had told me what I was. I couldn't bear it if Greg looked at me that way.

He wore an expression of disbelief as he looked from me to Roland and Peter who smiled and nodded reassuringly. I waited for the truth to sink in and for him to recoil from me, not that I would blame him. I just hoped he would get used to the idea eventually and we could stay friends. That was why I'd wanted to ease him into this slowly. It was a lot for anyone to take in.

His face paled a bit when he realized I was not joking, but he showed none of the abhorrence I'd expected. Encouraged, I continued to tell my story with Roland and Peter's help. Greg listened quietly when we told him about the events leading up to me leaving New Hastings, and it wasn't until I got to the part where everyone had believed I was dead, that he finally spoke.

"That was one of the roughest days of my life."

The emotion in his voice caught me off guard. I swallowed past a lump in my throat, amazed I'd gotten this far without crying. "I'm sorry, Greg."

"Wasn't your fault."

I didn't reply. I wasn't responsible for the things the vampires had done, but a lot of the other happenings in Maine were consequences of things I'd done. I had a lot of regrets from that time, and my biggest one was hurting Nate and my friends with my lies. That was why I wanted to be completely honest with Greg, even if it meant risking our friendship.

He rubbed the back of his neck and let out a puff of air. "So you're a demon *and* a faerie?"

"I'm half faerie. And I'm not half demon; I have one demon inside me.

There's a big difference."

"Okay," he said slowly. He looked at Roland and Peter. "And you two are werewolves?"

"Yes," Roland answered.

"I see."

"Greg, you're taking this a lot better than I thought you would." Maybe he was in shock and he just wasn't showing it. Or maybe he thought we were all nuts.

His gaze swung back to me. "I admit, it's not every day you hear your friends aren't human, but..."

It was something in his eyes and his voice that made me understand his quiet acceptance. "You've seen things, haven't you?"

He hesitated before he nodded.

"What?"

His expression darkened. "Enough to know you're not messing with me."

"I wouldn't do that to you."

"I know." He reached over and took my hand, surprising me again. Greg wasn't an affectionate person. The last time I'd seen him touch someone was when he'd grabbed another boy by the shirt front for bullying Jeffrey Crumb at school. "If you're supposed to be hiding from vampires, what the hell are you doing in LA?"

"That's where the story gets more interesting." I told him about Westhorne, the vampire attacks, and our journey to LA. I didn't say a lot about Nikolas because it was hard to talk about him. Greg seemed to understand and didn't prod me about it, although I could tell he was curious.

"So let me see if I got this right. You have a demon inside you, but you can fry other demons by touching them?"

"I don't think 'fry' is the right word."

Jordan snorted. "She made a lamprey demon explode once. Totally awesome, but gross." She went on to describe it in detail. "And she can paralyze vampires long enough to stake them or chop their heads off."

I made a face. "Thanks for that colorful description, Jordan."

"Anytime."

"Does this power work on all demons?"

I nodded. "I started out with small demons and I've used it on a few vampires. I did kill one vampire with my power, but he was new. It's harder the older the vampire is, and I've never tried to use it on a large demon."

"That's amazing."

I smiled. "It comes in handy."

He studied me quietly for a long moment. "And now you are on a mission to find your mother and make her tell you about this Master who's after you? Did I miss anything?"

"I think that sums it up."

He leaned forward and waved at the others. "Can I ask why these three have blood on them and you don't?"

I made a face. "We ran into three vampires, and we had to take them out. They did all the dirty work."

"Jesus." He sank back against the cushions. "To think I used to worry about you walking home after school."

Roland chuckled. "Dude, you should have seen Foley after she kicked his ass."

Fighting with Scott was not something I was proud of, especially since I'd used my Mori strength against him. If his friend Ryan hadn't been there, God knows what I might have done to him. "That's not funny, Roland. I really could have hurt him."

"Scott is an asshole," Greg said scornfully.

After all I'd learned, I didn't think Scott was as bad as they made him out to be. But it would be futile to try to convince Greg otherwise. I was more concerned with how Greg was handling all we'd dumped on him in the last hour. I could only imagine the thoughts that must be going through his mind after everything he'd learned tonight.

I turned to him and found him giving me a pensive look. "What are you thinking about?"

His head tilted, and he gave me a roguish smile. "I'm trying to picture you in that faerie dress."

I grabbed a small pillow and hit him with it. He laughed as he easily deflected it.

"Greg, be serious. Are you okay with all of this? I know it's a lot to take in."

His grin faded. "I'm good, really, though it might take a few days for it all to sink in."

I sagged in relief. "Now it's your turn. What have you seen?"

"I'll tell you later. I want to hear more about those hellhounds. What were their names?"

"Greg!" He was evading my question and I wanted to know why.

Roland laughed. "Dude, when she gets that look on her face, it's easier to just give in."

Greg opened his mouth at the same time his cell phone rang. He pulled it out and looked at the number. "Excuse me, guys. I have to get this." He disappeared into one of the bedrooms, talking softly. I couldn't hear the words, but it was easy to detect the strain in his voice. Whatever the call was about, it wasn't good.

Ten minutes later, he came back. "Sorry about that. My cousin Danny is only ten and he's having a real hard time with his father's death. He and his mom live in Dallas."

"You don't have to apologize for that." I realized for the first time how tired he looked. And it was obvious he had a lot of family stuff on his mind. "We should get going anyway. Can I have your number so I can call you tomorrow?"

"Why don't you guys stay here?"

I really wanted to say yes to have more time catching up with him, especially since we had no idea where we'd be off to next. "Don't you think this place might get a bit cramped with five of us staying here?"

Greg waved it off. "I've got two bedrooms, a couch out here, and another one in the studio. Plus, a fridge full of food and a big screen TV. This has to be a lot nicer than your hotel."

Roland gave the TV a longing look. "I don't mind sleeping on the couch."

"Jordan?" She didn't know Greg, and she probably didn't want to be stuck sharing a bathroom with four other people. If she wasn't comfortable with the idea of staying here, we had to respect that.

She pursed her lips and her eyes lingered on the bathroom door. "I suppose it wouldn't hurt to stay for a few days."

I turned to Greg. "I guess we're staying. But we have to go get our stuff and check out first. It's pretty late so we'll stay there tonight and come back tomorrow."

"I'll see you in the morning then." He walked us to our car and gave me another hug. It was so out of character for him that it worried me. He looked emotionally worn down and in need of a good night's sleep.

Tomorrow I was going to find out what he was hiding from me. Something was weighing on him and it bothered me to see him this way.

"Greg seems different," Roland said on the way back to the hotel.

I watched the streets go by. "He definitely has something on his mind. I'll talk to him tomorrow."

Jordan jumped in the shower as soon as we got back to our room, and I called David to tell him what I'd learned about Madeline. He said Kelvan and another friend would handle the surveillance. When I asked him if his friends minded doing all this work for us, he laughed and said, "Are you kidding? This is the most fun we've had in ages."

Jordan walked out of the bathroom, toweling her hair. "All right, what's the deal?"

"Huh?" I said, distracted.

She snapped her towel at me. "Hello, earth to Sara. How the hell did your virginity make it through high school intact with a guy like that around?"

"It's not like that with Greg and me. We're friends." I decided not to mention the short-lived crush I'd had on him a few years ago.

She climbed into her bed. "Uh-huh. Well, I can't wait to see Nikolas's face when he gets a load of your high school friend."

After Jordan settled down, I took a shower and got into my own bed. But my mind and body were too wound up to go to sleep. I rolled over and puffed up my pillows for the fifth time, telling myself that all the excitement tonight was the cause for my sleeplessness. But the truth was I hadn't slept well since I'd left Westhorne.

There was one thing I knew would help me sleep. I pressed my face into the pillow. *No way.* I'd given in to that weakness the past two nights. I would not do it again.

That's what I kept telling myself as I buried my face in the T-shirt that still carried his scent. And when I grabbed my laptop and went into the bathroom. And when I opened the phone app and dialed the number.

"Hello?"

I closed my eyes. How could one word wreak so much havoc on my emotions, and yet fill me with a sense of peace at the same time?

"Sara? Will you talk to me tonight?"

I listened to him breathe, wanting more than anything to talk to him. The longer we were apart, the harder it was to be away from him. But I was afraid once we started talking, he'd convince me to tell him where I was.

"Okay." He exhaled slowly. "Tristan said you sounded tired when you called him today. I know you're not sleeping. You know you can call me anytime, even if you're not ready to talk yet."

A tear leaked out from beneath my closed lid. *I miss you.*

"It's late. You should try to get some sleep. Call me again tomorrow so I know you're all right. And Sara... I need to hear your voice, too."

Hearing him say that nearly broke me. "I'm okay," I said hoarsely before my finger hit the button to end the call.

I sat on the edge of the bathtub, trying not to give in to my tears. All I needed was to have red puffy eyes tomorrow. It took me a few minutes to compose myself, and then I left the bathroom and slipped into bed as quietly as I could.

Jordan's sleepy voice startled me as I pulled the covers over me. "I give you five days tops before you cave and tell him where you are."

"What do you mean?"

"You have it so bad for that guy you call him every night just to hear his voice. You're like an addict sneaking away for a fix. You even stole his T-shirt." She rolled over, and her voice was slightly muffled by her pillow. "Forget what I said. I give you three days max."

"Just because I miss him doesn't mean I'm going to give up looking for Madeline. This is too important."

"Maybe you can have both. Nikolas can be a little – okay, *a lot* – overbearing, but that's because he just wants you to be safe. I admit he can go overboard with the whole alpha male bit, and I can definitely see how that would bug you. But you've both had time to cool down. I bet if you talked to him, he'd be more willing to compromise."

I stared at the ceiling, blinking away tears. "I wish it was that simple."

Jordan raised herself up on one elbow. "I know you're hurting. We all do. You don't hide it as well as you think you do."

"I knew this wasn't going to be easy." I let out a shaky laugh. "Some warrior I turned out to be, huh?"

"You're still a bit rough around the edges, but you have potential. Plus, you have excellent taste in friends."

I wiped my eyes with the sheet. "I'm glad you're here with me, Jordan."

She fell back onto her pillow and yawned. "You couldn't have stopped me if you'd tried."

* * *

"Do you guys want to order in or go out?" Greg waved some takeout menus. "There's a great Chinese place a block away and they deliver."

I looked up from the email I'd just gotten from David. He and Kelvan had already located Adele's home, and they were watching that and the club while they looked for any sign that Madeline was in the city. I was so lucky to have David on my side. There was no way I could have done this without his help.

"Chinese sounds great."

"Works for me," Jordan said, and the boys echoed her.

We decided what to order and Greg called it in. His cell phone rang a few minutes later, and he took it into the studio and shut the door. I watched him go, wishing I knew what was going on with him. We'd gotten here around noon, and I'd spent most of the afternoon catching up with him while the others enjoyed the big TV and stocked fridge. He still hadn't confided in me about what was bothering him, but I saw worry cross his face a few times when he thought I wasn't looking. He hadn't slept well either, judging by the shadows under his eyes. Twice, when I thought he was close to opening up, his cell phone rang and he left the room to talk. Both times he came back looking like he carried the weight of the world on his shoulders. Greg had always been so strong and nothing had ever seemed to get to him. It was hard seeing him like this.

After dinner, Greg grabbed two beers from the fridge and handed me a warm sweater. "Come on. I want to show you something."

I followed him to a set of stairs I thought led to an attic. But they actually took us to the roof where his uncle had created a pretty little patio area lit by strings of lights. I walked to the edge of the roof and looked up at the Hollywood sign in the distance. "Wow, this is amazing."

He stood beside me and set his beer on the ledge. "It's nothing like home, is it?"

"You're not kidding. Have you seen what women wear to clubs here? They'd get pneumonia if they dressed like that back home."

He laughed, and it was the first real one I'd heard from him all day. "Sara, don't ever change."

"I'll always be me, but some change is good."

"True." He took a long drink from his beer and leaned against the ledge, looking out at the city. "I'll never forget the day you started at St. Patrick's. You looked so shy when you walked in with Roland, and then at lunch you ran off two guys who were messing with Jeffrey."

I thought back to my first day of high school. "I don't remember seeing you that day."

He laughed deeply. "No, you didn't, but I saw you. Everyone saw you."

"What do you mean?"

"I don't know. You were just different. All the other girls were trying to get the guys' attention, but you were doing everything *not* to be noticed. And you talked only to Roland and Peter, ignoring the rest of us."

I made a face. "Was I really that stuck up?"

Greg laughed again. "No, no, that's not what I meant. You just seemed content to do your own thing. What you didn't know is that a pretty girl ignoring a bunch of high school boys is like waving a red flag at them."

I was glad the darkness hid my blush. "I think you might be exaggerating a bit."

"Have you ever known me to exaggerate? I couldn't figure out what it was about you, but I wanted to get to know you." He gave me a sideways look. "I didn't give a shit for anyone in that school, so it shocked the hell out of me. I can still remember your face when me and Mike sat at your table. You were reading some old book and you looked like you wanted to tell us to get lost."

I smiled at the memory. "Well, Mike *was* kind of loud."

"I thought you were going to take off, but you just went back to your book." He stared at the city. "I wasn't exactly a nice person back then. Anyone besides you would have run away."

"I knew there were things out there a lot scarier than you." I sipped my beer. "And I actually liked you guys."

"I don't know why you liked us. We were on the fast track to nowhere back then." He turned his face toward me. "I know your uncle didn't think much of me, and he was right. I was bad news, and I don't blame him for not wanting me around you."

"Nate and I didn't agree on a lot of things. And you weren't that bad. You were always good to me."

He frowned. "Before I met you I was a total asshole. I had a juvie record, and I was headed down a pretty bad road. Mike and me were all ready to drop out and join up with a bike gang out of Boston. They were hard core. You had to pull an armed robbery in order to get into the gang."

His revelation stunned me. I knew he'd had a bad rep, but I'd never thought of him as a criminal. "What stopped you?"

"You did."

"Me?"

"There was something about you that made me want to be a better person." He blew out his breath. "I know that sounds cheesy, but it's true. After I met you, I didn't want to do that crazy stuff anymore."

It took me a minute to recover from my shock. "Remember what I told you last night about me being half undine? It can affect humans, especially guys, and they start acting different around me."

"Maybe that's true, and it might be what made me sit at your table, but you're a good person, Sara. You were too good for me and the rest of the guys back home."

"Is that why you threatened violence on any boy at school who hurt me?" I smiled at his look of surprise. "Roland told me."

He grinned, not the least bit embarrassed. "I meant it, too."

"Greg, I –" I started to asked him again about whatever had been worrying him, but I was interrupted by his cell phone.

"Sorry, have to take this." He walked to the other side of the roof and I watched him as he spoke to the caller. His voice rose a few times and I picked up snatches of the conversation. I heard him say the name Draegan several times, as well as his uncle's and cousin's names. He looked haggard when he hung up and joined me again.

I crossed my arms and confronted him before he even reached me. "Greg, who was that? What is going on?"

"It's nothing."

"It's not nothing. You look like hell every time you get one of those calls."

He drank down the last of his beer. "It's just family stuff. I told you my cousin is having a rough time."

I wasn't going to let him off the hook this time. I'd seen real fear on his face a minute ago. "Who is Draegan, and what does he have to do with your cousin?"

Panic flashed in his eyes before he schooled his expression. "He's no one," he answered in a hard voice. "Leave it alone, Sara."

"Don't do that," I pleaded. "I know you're in trouble, and I'm betting it has to do with your uncle. Tell me. Maybe I can help you."

He sighed roughly. "You can't help me with this. No one can."

The defeat in his voice shook me. Greg had never sounded so helpless. I laid my hand on his arm. "How do you know that if you don't tell me what it is?"

He pulled away and put a few feet between us. "I'm not getting you involved in this. It's too dangerous."

"Greg, in the last few months, I have been attacked by vampires, demons, witches, mutant hyenas, you name it. I've seen things that would give anyone nightmares for the rest of their lives. I can take care of myself, and I'm not alone. I have two werewolves and a Mohiri warrior downstairs. You know Roland and Peter will want to help you, too. Trust me when I tell you we are exactly the people you want to get involved in this."

He reached for his beer and saw it was empty. I handed him my bottle which was still half full. He took a long swig before he looked at me again. "I can't do that."

"Yes, you can." I took his hand, something I'd never done before, and his callused fingers closed around mine. "Just tell me, and we'll figure it out together."

He made an angry noise and pulled me over to the patio area. Once we were seated on the couch, he raked his hands through his hair. I waited quietly for him to speak.

"In June, my cousin Danny got sick and they found out it was leukemia. He went through a round of treatments, and the doctors told Uncle Leo and Aunt Mary that it didn't look good. In October, he just went into remission. The doctors didn't know what to make of it.

"Then Uncle Leo was killed in a car crash on his way to visit them. It was a big blow, especially with everything Danny was going through. Aunt Mary couldn't leave him so she asked me to come out here and take care of everything for her. It was only supposed to take a week or so. But a few days after I got here, a guy showed up at the door, saying he worked for someone named Draegan, and he was here to collect on a debt Uncle Leo owed him. I told him I needed to see proof of how much money Uncle Leo owed, and we would pay him when we sold off this place."

"How much did he owe this Draegan guy?"

Greg laughed harshly. "More than you can imagine. I was worried about paying off a stupid money debt. I had no idea."

"Tell me."

He looked away for a long moment and his eyes were haunted when they met mine again. "Have you ever heard of a blood debt?"

I shook my head as dread coiled in my stomach.

"When the doctors told Uncle Leo they couldn't do anything for Danny, he went to a demon named Draegan and asked him for help. Don't ask me how he even knew anything about demons, because I don't know. Draegan gave him some kind of medicine to give to Danny to drink. Whatever it was, it worked. But the price was steep. Uncle Leo signed a contract saying he would give his life to Draegan if Danny got better."

"No."

He nodded grimly. "Uncle Leo had a month to pay his debt. But he was killed in a car accident before he could."

"But doesn't that cancel the contract?"

"No. What Draegan didn't tell Uncle Leo was that if he couldn't or wouldn't pay the debt, it could be collected from a male family member who shares the same blood. Draegan's flunky told me Danny was the closest male relative so he has to pay the debt."

I inhaled sharply. "No."

"I've been trying to get them to take money instead. I even offered them this place, but Draegan won't take it. I tried to go talk to him, but he won't see me. All his people will tell me is that blood is the only thing that will cover the debt, unless Draegan decides not to collect. And he's not going to do that."

"Oh, Greg." I couldn't imagine what he'd been going through the last few weeks, dealing with something like this by himself and worrying about his cousin. "I promise we'll fix this."

He stared off into the distance. "I found out yesterday that there is another way to pay off the debt. I'm Danny's first cousin, and we share the same blood."

"No!" I jumped up and stood over him so he was forced to look at me. "No. That's not going to happen, ever! Don't even think about it."

"Sara, if you just listen —"

"Stop. I don't want to hear it. I'm not letting you die over some stupid debt, Greg." My voice rose as I became hysterical.

He stood and put his hands on my shoulders. "It's okay. Please, don't get upset."

"Don't get upset? You're talking about letting some demon take your life." I gasped for air. "I'll kill him before I let him hurt you."

"No, you won't. The only way to see Draegan is if he wants to see you. I asked around and word is he is strong, and he's surrounded by these other demons who work for him. You can't get near him." His shoulders sagged. "Trust me. This is the only way."

"I refuse to believe that."

He pushed me away, physically and emotionally. "Sara, this is my choice. I know it's hard, but you have to accept it. If you can't do that, then... maybe you should go."

"You don't mean that."

"Yes, I do. I knew it was a mistake to invite you to stay here, but I just wanted to spend time with someone I actually care about before I..." He cleared his throat. "I never should have told you about this. I just wanted to tell someone. It means a lot that you want to help me, but you can't."

I spun away from him and ran to the stairs. He didn't try to stop me, not that he could have. Did he really think I would stand back while some demon murdered him?

"What's wrong?" Roland asked when I ran into the apartment and went straight for my phone.

"Nothing. I just remembered something I have to talk to David about."

"Are you sure? You look upset."

"I'm fine."

He looked at me for a long moment before he turned back to his movie. "Okay."

I carried the phone into the bedroom I was sharing with Jordan and shut the door. David answered on the second ring.

"I didn't expect to hear from you today. Is everything alright?"

I sucked in a trembling breath. "I'm not sure. What can you tell me about a demon in LA named Draegan?"

CHAPTER 7

"WHOA!" ROLAND STARED up at the high-rise building with his mouth hanging open. He wasn't the only one staring. The thirty-story glass and steel structure was pretty impressive, even if I thought it was totally impractical in a state with an active fault line running beneath it.

Jordan craned her neck. "Nice."

The building's glass doors slid open and the four of us entered the pink marble lobby together, then stopped and stared again. In each corner stood a tall, abstract sculpture and there were more security cameras than you'd find at a bank. Directly in front of us was a pair of elevators and to our left was a desk, behind which sat a burly security guard. He watched us suspiciously then asked us what our business was there. I told him we were there to see Draegan, and he didn't even blink an eye.

"Damn, who lives like this?" Peter said when the elevator doors closed.

"Rich demons, I guess." I hit the button for the top floor then faced the three of them. "You guys ready for this?"

Jordan smiled and opened her long coat to reveal the knives strapped to her thighs. Then she turned around and pulled up the back of the coat to show us the short sword in the harness on her back. "I was born ready for this."

Roland rolled his eyes and gave me a reassuring smile. "We're good. You look ready to kick a little demon ass yourself."

I glanced down at my outfit. I was wearing my new dark jeans and a black tank top with combat boots and my leather bomber jacket. Around my neck I wore my grandmother's silver cross on a long chain, and I kept it tucked inside the tank top. Demons didn't like silver, but wearing the cross gave me a little extra courage. The silver dagger inside my jacket didn't hurt either.

The elevator stopped on the thirtieth floor, and the door slid open to reveal a richly carpeted hallway. We walked to the door at the end of the hall, and I rang the doorbell. Almost immediately, it was opened by a large demon with red-tinged skin. He was bald with tiny nubs where his ears should be, a huge bulbous nose, and his eyes were black with red rings around the pupils. He didn't have horns, but two fangs protruded from beneath his upper lip.

"What do you want?" he asked in a gravelly voice that grated on my eardrums.

"We're here to see Draegan," I said.

He scowled. "Everyone wants to see Draegan. He's busy."

I put my hand on the door when he moved to close it. "I'm here about a debt."

"A debt, huh?" He looked us over then sniffed the air. "No shifters allowed."

Roland looked incensed. "What?"

"Draegan has a demon-only policy. Keeps all the undesirables out."

Jordan pushed forward until she stood beside me. "I'm not a shifter."

The demon leaned down and sniffed her hair. "Hmm, Mori demon. We don't get your kind here."

"You can tell what kind of demon someone is just by smelling them?" I could see why this guy would make a perfect bouncer for someone like Draegan.

"Yes." He sniffed at me and wrinkled his nose. "Mori demon, but you don't smell right. What is wrong with you?"

"She's been sick," Jordan said.

The demon narrowed his eyes at me. "I didn't think Mohiri got sick."

I gave a short laugh. "Of course we get sick. Where do people come up with this stuff?"

He peered down at me a moment longer before he nodded and waved us inside.

I looked at Roland. "We won't be long."

"I don't think you two should go in there alone." His eyes were dark with worry. "Maybe we should leave."

"We can't leave. Greg needs us." Not that Greg knew where we were. He thought we were meeting a man about Madeline. Things had been strained between Greg and me since last night, but when I'd offered to go to a hotel, he'd gotten upset. It tore me apart to see him hurting, and I was determined to keep him safe. He'd watched out for me when we were younger, and it was my turn to do the same for him now.

Roland nodded reluctantly. "Just be careful."

I squeezed his hand then moved past the demon into the foyer. My heart pounded as I followed Jordan into the spacious, opulently furnished penthouse. Except for the art on the walls, almost everything in the room was white. White leather couches, white tile floor, white tables and shelves. Even the pieces of art around the room were made of white marble. It looked like someone had doused the place in bleach to remove all the color. I couldn't imagine why anyone would want to live in a place so sterile looking.

The apartment had floor-to-ceiling windows that boasted an incredible view of the city. But I was too busy staring at the twenty or so demons mingling in the room and keeping a strong grip on my power to care about the view. I had never seen this many demons together in one place and my Fae side was not happy about it. Jordan and I stood off to one side to survey the room, and to let me have time to get used to the large demon presence. She recognized most of the demon races, and she identified each one for me.

The short, thin ones with dark skin, catlike eyes, and small curved horns were ranc demons and they liked to drink blood. Unlike vampires, they preferred animal blood. Sheroc demons were green-skinned with long black hair to their waist and drooping purple eyes. They looked harmless enough until Jordan explained that they fed off pain and grief, sometimes driving their victims insane. The rotund, pasty white demons with red eyes and white hair were femal demons. Physically, they were harmless, but they were known to traffic a highly addictive demon drug called *heffion* to humans.

My eyes fell on a tall, tanned blond man whom I mistook for a human until he looked my way and I saw the silver eyes that appeared to glow softly. Jordan didn't have to tell me that this one was an incubus, a demon who preyed on women the same way a succubus preyed on men.

"Lovely company Draegan keeps," I muttered.

Two female mox demons in short white dresses and jeweled collars walked among the guests, carrying trays of food and drinks. Every now and then one of the guests would run a lecherous hand up females' arms or grope their backsides as they passed. There was no mistaking the fear and revulsion on the females' faces, and I wondered why they worked in a place like this.

A burst of raucous laughter led my gaze to the gulak demon I had come here to see. Broad shouldered with scaly skin, bat-like wings, reptilian eyes, and a single horn in the center of his forehead, Draegan was easily the scariest looking demon here. He sat at a table with two ranc demons and a sheroc demon, pouring a luminescent, milky substance from a crystal decanter into shot glasses. He set one glass in front of each of them and barked out something I couldn't understand. One by one, the demons at the table tossed money on top of a stack in the center of the table. Then they put their glasses to their lips and downed the contents. None but Draegan looked happy about it, which told me this was no ordinary drinking game. One of the ranc demons wobbled and caught himself on the table while the other fell over sideways and hit the floor with a thud. The sheroc's eyes rolled back in his head a second before it hit the table.

Draegan let out a deep rumbling laugh and tipped back his own glass. He slammed it back on the table and said something to the ranc demon that hadn't passed out yet. The ranc demon held up his hands in defeat and stumbled away from the table to collapse on one of the couches. Draegan laughed again and pulled the large pile of money toward him. He stacked it and handed it off to one of two smaller gulak demons standing behind him.

This was the demon that held Greg's life in his hands. He had to be seven feet tall and weigh over four hundred pounds. According to David, gulaks were known for their brute strength, and they were the closest the demon community had to organized crime. There wasn't much they weren't into and most demons feared them.

Draegan had set up his own little crime syndicate in Los Angeles, running drugs and weapons and intimidating the crap out of other demons. He threw parties to show off his power and wealth, but he also surrounded himself with security, which told me he wasn't as strong as he liked to portray. Looking at him now in the flesh, I saw nothing more than a loud-mouthed bully who could afford to hire others to do his dirty work. I really hated bullies.

"What is that game they're playing?" I wondered if it might be the way I could get close to Draegan.

"It is called *Glaen*," answered a silky voice on my left, startling me.

I looked at the incubus who had approached while Jordan and I were distracted by the other demons. He smiled, showing off even white teeth. Knowing what he was made my skin crawl, but I forced myself to remain cool. All the demons here filled me with disgust, but I had to put my emotions aside and keep in mind why I was here.

"Glaen?" I asked.

"The game is named after the drink. You ante up before each shot, and the last one conscious wins the pot. Draegan never loses, but these idiots keep trying."

"It's that strong?"

The incubus laughed as if I'd made a joke. "It's poison."

"Poison?" Jordan repeated.

"To us it is. It'll kill you if you drink enough of it. I guess the Mohiri don't teach you about things like that." His silvery gaze appraised Jordan and me. "And what brings two beautiful young Mohiri to Draegan's of all places? I'm surprised Wilhem let you in. You aren't exactly like Draegan's usual guests."

I ignored his flirting. "We're here on business."

"Draegan doesn't like to do business at his parties." One of the mox demons came over to us and handed the incubus a glass of liquor. He took a sip and smiled. "He does serve good brandy, though. Would either of you care for a drink?"

"No, thanks," Jordan and I said together. Even if I could handle liquor, there was no way I'd accept a drink from an incubus. I couldn't believe I was still standing here talking to one. Just being near him made my skin itch and my gut twist. My power strained against my control, and I clamped down on it even more. Losing control now would be disastrous.

The mox demon turned to leave, and I noticed an unusual black tattoo that resembled a hieroglyphic on the right side of her jaw.

"What does that tattoo mean?" I asked the incubus, my curiosity overriding my aversion to him.

"That is her owner's mark."

My spine stiffened. "Owner's mark?"

"Draegan owns her, and that is his brand to show she is his property," the incubus explained casually, unaware of the anger igniting inside me. Slaves? Blood debts? My nostrils flared, and I gripped the edge of the small marble table beside me.

Jordan shot me a "keep it together" look then turned to the incubus. "Do you know Draegan well?"

"As well as anyone here. I live in the building so I come to his parties when I have nothing more exciting planned." His eyes glowed, and I fought the urge to shudder. "I'm Lucien, by the way. I can introduce you to Draegan, but I assure you he won't do business tonight. The only money that exchanges hands at his parties is during Glaen."

Jordan and I exchanged looks and my heart sank. We both knew my lack of tolerance for liquor meant I couldn't play the game if I wanted to. And I wouldn't ask her to endanger herself to save someone she barely knew. My throat tightened painfully.

"You said it's poisonous to demons, but Mohiri have human bodies. Does it have the same effect on us?" Jordan asked Lucien.

"Glaen is toxic to all demons. I've seen a mature vampire pass out after four glasses. He lasted a bit longer than most demons do."

"If it's so strong, how can Draegan drink it?" I already suspected it was sheer strength that kept the huge demon from passing out. His body mass allowed him to consume more than everyone else.

Lucien laughed. "Look at him. Gulaks have a high tolerance for pain."

"But what is Glaen and where does it come from?" Jordan asked him.

He shook his head. "Ah, the ignorance of youth. Glaen is a Fae drink."

I gawked at him, my heart racing. "A Fae drink? At a demon party?"

"You can buy anything if you have enough money and know where to find it. Some demons like to amuse themselves by taking risks. Drinking Glaen is a status symbol to them. They like to tell others they played Glaen and to talk about how long they lasted in the game."

Jordan wrinkled her nose. "That's sick."

The incubus raised his glass to her. "I agree. I prefer to get my thrills in other ways."

This time I could not repress a shudder. "I'd prefer not to hear about how you get your thrills."

Instead of being insulted, Lucien was amused. "I wondered how long you'd hold back."

I gave him a questioning look, and he chuckled. "I can sense how females react to me, and your aversion is quite strong, even though you don't know it. It's actually refreshing to be around females who don't want me."

Jordan narrowed her eyes at him. "Poor fellow. I'm sure it must be a hardship for you."

I didn't hear his reply because my attention was fixed on the decanter sitting on Draegan's table. What were the odds of finding a Fae drink at a demon party, especially this one? I'd never tried Glaen, but Aine had assured me that Fae food and drink would have no effect on me. Did that include this drink? I wasn't eager to repeat my last experience with drinking, but I would take any kind of hangover for Greg.

"I'm going to play," I announced.

"That would not be wise," Lucien warned. "Look at you. There is no way you could last against Draegan."

Jordan pulled me aside. "I don't think that's a good idea," she whispered. "You don't know if that stuff won't hurt your Mori."

"I had food and drink in Faerie and it didn't hurt my Mori," I whispered to her. "This is the best shot we have, and I just have to outlast him. He's tough, but I have an advantage here."

Her eyes swung between me and the big demon still sitting at the table. "I still don't like it."

"Just stand close to me and catch me if I look like I'm going to pass out."

"That's not funny."

"If you have a better plan, I'm all ears."

She gave me an unhappy look and shook her head.

I walked back to the incubus who was watching us with open curiosity. "Will you introduce us?"

He sighed. "If you wish, but I agree with your friend. This is a bad idea."

Draegan bellowed a greeting when we approached his table. "Lucien, glad you could make it tonight!"

"How could I miss one of your parties?" He waved a hand at me. "My young Mohiri friend here wanted to meet you. She would like to play Glaen with you."

Draegan's cold reptilian eyes slid over me, and his mouth opened in surprise. Then he threw back his head and roared with laughter. The two demons standing behind him joined in.

"Play indeed," he rumbled. "Go away, little Mohiri. Who let you out after dark?"

I pulled out the chair across from him and sat down. "But all the fun stuff happens after dark."

Draegan waved a scaly hand at me. "You're too puny, and I'll not have your papa coming after me because you got sick at my place."

"Or maybe you're afraid I might win."

The laughter around us died.

"No one beats Draegan," said one of his companions.

"Then he shouldn't have anything to worry about."

Draegan's thin lips pulled tight and he glared at me. "The ante is five hundred dollars per shot. You don't look like someone who carries that kind of cash."

I unzipped a pocket of my jacket and pulled out one of the diamonds I'd brought with me to pay off Greg's debt. "Will this do?"

Draegan's eyes widened when he saw the sparkling gem. He swallowed greedily. "That will do nicely, and it'll look great in the new ring I'm going to have made."

I laid the diamond on the table in front of me, amazed at how steady my hands were. "Let's play then."

He barked at one of the mox demons who ran to get clean glasses from the bar. One of the other gulak demons handed him a wad of cash, and he began counting out five hundred dollars.

I waved away his money. "I don't want money. I want to play for something else."

He looked up from his money. "Like what?"

I rolled the diamond around the table, watching how Draegan's eyes followed it. "You're holding a debt against a friend of mine. I want it."

He chuckled, but his eyes were shrewd. "I hold a lot of debts. You'll have to be more specific."

"His name is Greg McCoy."

"McCoy? Ah, the blood debt." He shrugged as if my friend's life meant nothing. "What does a Mohiri care for a human's debt?"

"I just said he was my friend."

"So you did." He scratched his scaly chin with a clawed hand. "One little diamond hardly covers a blood debt. I already have a buyer lined up for him, and she's willing to pay handsomely for a fit young human male."

Over my dead body. My breathing increased and my control slipped a little in my anger. I struggled to compose myself before I lost it and leapt across the table at the gulak.

"That's a five carat diamond." I patted my pocket. "I have two more in here just like it, and I'm sure they will more than cover the debt."

Draegan's hungry eyes hovered on my pocket. "Show them, then."

I shook my head. "I'll show them *if* you win."

The gulak was barely able to take his eyes off the glittering diamond I rolled between my fingers. David had done his homework well. He'd said the one thing Draegan loved more than money was precious stones.

"Crak, bring the box," Draegan barked, and one of his henchmen disappeared down a hallway. He returned a minute later carrying a dark wooden box, which he laid in front of his boss. Draegan lifted the cover and shuffled some papers before he pulled out a folded one. He opened the paper to reveal a long one-page contract with Greg's uncle's name signed in blood at the bottom.

I nodded, and he laid the contract in the center of the table then handed the box to Crak.

"Your turn," he said.

The room had grown quiet around us, and it was as if everyone held their breath when I laid the diamond on top of the contract. Demons moved in closer, forming a wide circle around us. Jordan stood at my left, and Lucien stood at my right as if he and I were suddenly friends. When this was over, I hoped I never laid eyes on him or anyone else in this room again.

Draegan could not hold back his satisfied smirk as he filled two shot glasses and pushed one toward me. "Ladies first."

I picked up the glass and sniffed the pearly substance. It smelled sweet and made me think of flowers and honey. I put it to my lips and tilted my head back. *Here goes everything.*

Flavors burst across my tongue: cream, honey, lavender, and too many others to identify. It was the most amazing thing I'd ever tasted. I swallowed and delicious warmth spread through my body, making me want to laugh and run barefoot through a sunny meadow. I licked every last drop from my lips before I set the glass down and looked at Draegan, who wore a puzzled expression. Around us, demons were staring at me like I'd just sprouted angel wings.

"What?" I asked.

Jordan tapped my shoulder. "How do you feel?"

I gave her a grin. "Wonderful."

Draegan made a noise, and I faced him again to find him watching me with narrowed eyes.

"Your turn."

He snatched up his glass and downed the contents in one gulp. I watched him enviously. Next time I saw Aine, I was going to ask her why she'd never told me about this stuff.

Draegan grimaced slightly as he put his glass back on the table. It was the only sign he gave that the drink affected him at all, and not in a pleasant way. He picked up the decanter and filled our glasses again.

I reached for mine before he had a chance to push it across the table. My mouth was already watering in anticipation by the time I put the glass to my lips and drank. *Mmmm.* I sighed happily as I laid my empty glass on the table.

I smiled at Draegan as he took his turn. I couldn't understand why he was scowling when he should be happy. This stuff was incredible. I could drink it all night.

Two shots later, Draegan started swaying in his chair, and whispers broke out around us.

After the fifth shot, I burped loudly and slapped a hand over my mouth. "Excuse me."

By the sixth shot, his eyes were crossing, and he had to hold onto the table to stay upright.

I pressed my legs together tightly, suddenly feeling the effects of all the drinks. "Listen, how much longer do you think this will take?"

"Are you ready to give up?" he asked in a slurred voice. His eyes couldn't focus on my face.

"No, I really need to pee."

Someone snickered. One corner of Draegan's jaw sagged and drool ran down his chin. Behind him, his two henchmen watched me with expressions of anger and disbelief.

Draegan tried to scowl, but his lips wouldn't cooperate. "It's over when I say it's —"

His face hit the table so hard I was sure there would be cracks in the wood.

"That's gonna hurt." I looked up at Lucien, who was watching me with an indecipherable expression. "Did I win?" He nodded, and I couldn't hold back my grin. "Awesome! Now could you point me to the bathroom? I really do have to go."

He pointed down the hallway. "Second door on the left."

Draegan's bathroom was as white as the rest of his apartment. "What does this guy have against color?" I muttered as I washed my hands and dried them with a plush white towel.

I grinned at my reflection in the mirror. *I did it!* Greg and his cousin would never have to worry about Draegan or blood debts again. "Not bad for a night's work."

My power surged and I clamped down on it. "What the hell?"

A small tug on my coat caught my attention, and I looked down at the tiny pale creature clinging to my front pocket that held the diamonds.

"Hey, get out of there." I grabbed the back of the imp's loincloth and set him down on the vanity. He chattered angrily and snapped his sharp little teeth at my hand.

I flicked a spark at him, making him squeak and scurry backward. "Don't bite off more than you can chew, buddy. Now go steal from someone else."

When I came out of the bathroom, Jordan was standing in the hallway waiting for me. In her hands were the diamond and the contract. She handed them to me and watched as I stuffed them in my pockets. "Do you feel okay?"

"Never felt better."

She peered into my eyes. "You're acting weird. I'd say you were drunk, but Lucian said Glaen isn't alcohol."

"I'm great!" I gave her a quick hug.

She stepped back. "What was that for?"

"I'm just glad we're friends."

"Whoa, too much of the happy juice." She took my arm and led me back to the main room. "I hope this faerie shit wears off soon because it's kind of freaking me out."

We were met by Draegan's two henchmen as soon as we entered the living room. They moved to block our path to the door. The rest of the demons moved back, giving the four of us a wide berth.

"You aren't going anywhere," Crak said. "You cheated and Draegan will deal with you when he wakes up."

Jordan stepped in front of me. "She drank the same stuff he drank. Everyone here saw it, including you. How is that cheating?"

"She is not a demon. No demon can drink that much Glaen," argued the other gulak demon.

"Lorne, she is Mohiri, you idiot," Lucien said.

"Wilhem!" Lorne bellowed. The demon who had admitted us came into the room. "You let a human in here."

Wilhem walked up to me and sniffed. "These two have Mori demons." He touched his nose when Lorne started to shake his head. "This never fails."

Crak crossed his arms. "I don't care. Draegan will be pissed if he wakes up and finds out we let them leave, and I don't want him mad at me."

Jordan reached behind her and pulled her short sword free from its sheath. The two gulak demons took a step back. She pulled me around them. "We're leaving. Deal with it."

I shook my head to clear it. "You better listen to her, boys. She's scary with that thing."

We got halfway across the room before Crak let out a small roar and lunged at us. Jordan shoved me aside and turned to meet his attack. The gulak demon was not agile, but he came at us like a charging bull. Jordan dodged his advance and swung her sword, but the blade hit his shoulder and bounced off.

He grinned, showing off sharp teeth as he lashed at her with one of his clawed hands. "It's not that easy to kill a gulak, little Mohiri."

I let out a small scream when someone grabbed the back of my jacket and swung me around. I came face-to-face with the other gulak. The magic I'd been holding back erupted, and my whole body tingled as electric currents raced through it. Instead of trying to pull away from the demon, I reached for him, my hands glowing when they slammed into his chest. His eyes flew wide, and he let out a strangled scream before he flew backward and crashed into a white marble podium holding a sculpture that resembled a deformed swan. The heavy piece of art toppled over and bonked him squarely on the forehead, and he fell back on the floor moaning.

I turned to Jordan who was fending off Crak and two of the ranc demons that had joined the fight.

"Hey, no fair!" I yelled, jumping the closest ranc demon. He twisted and tried to gore me with one of his horns, but only managed to scrape my palm before I grabbed him by both horns. Power burst from my hands and the demon's horns shattered. "Oops," I said as he stepped back and felt the stumps that used to be his horns. "Sorry."

He made a keening sound and ran at me. I met him halfway and grabbed him around his thin neck with both glowing hands. His cry dissolved into a croak a few seconds before he sank to his knees. I gave him another blast of power for good measure then let him collapse to the floor.

Jordan had taken out the other ranc demon, and she and Crak were circling each other. "You got this?" I called, and she gave me a thumbs-up with her free hand.

Noise behind me alerted me to the fact that Lorne had gained his feet again. He shook his head to clear it and looked around until he found me. Instead of speaking, he roared and lumbered toward me. I sidestepped him easily because he was still disoriented, and before he could stop his headlong rush, I jumped on his back. My hands wrapped around his face, and I pushed power into him.

The gulak gasped and collapsed beneath me. I climbed off his unconscious – or maybe dead – body and looked around for Jordan. I smirked when I saw Crak facedown on the floor with Jordan straddling his back and wrenching his arms behind him. "I can do this all night, you overgrown lizard," she ground out, twisting his arm until he moaned in pain.

Chuckling, I brushed off my clothes. It hit me then how quiet the room was, and I looked up to see the rest of Draegan's guests watching me with expressions ranging from astonishment to fear. It wasn't until I moved to brush down my hair and felt it crackling with static that I understood their reactions.

"Anyone else here have a problem with us leaving?" I asked the room, and almost every head moved from side to side.

Lucien was the only one who spoke. "What are you?"

"Didn't you hear Wilhem? I'm a Mohiri."

"No Mohiri can do what you did."

I shrugged. "Apparently, at least one can."

Lucien studied the demons at my feet. "Something tells me people underestimate you a lot, little Mohiri."

I plucked a gulak scale from my hair. "They usually do. I'm working on that, though."

I heard swearing and a crack behind me, and I looked back to see Crak sprawled out with his head at an odd angle, and Jordan getting to her feet. "Bastard tried to bite me. What kind of fighting is that?"

I picked up her sword and handed it to her. She glared at the other demons then glanced at me. "Let's get out of here."

"You don't have to tell me twice." I felt for the crumpled contract in my pocket. I couldn't wait to get back to Greg and tell him his nightmare was over.

I took one last look at Draegan before I left, and behind him I saw the two mox demons huddled in a corner. "Hold up, Jordan," I said as I veered toward the two females.

"Do you two want to come with us?" I asked them. They stared at me with wide, frightened eyes. "Once we leave here, you can go wherever you want. You're free."

One of them darted a look at Draegan who was snoring loudly now. "Don't worry about him," I told her. "He can't hurt you anymore."

The two demons shared a look then nodded timidly at me. I waved toward the door, and they moved around Draegan and the other demons, giving them a wide berth. As soon as they were in the clear, they ran for the door. By the time Jordan and I reached the door, the mox demons had already disappeared down the stairs.

Roland and Peter were standing right where we'd left them, and they practically sagged in relief when we came through the door.

"What the hell happened in there?" Roland asked.

I hiccupped as I headed for the elevator. "We'll tell you in the car."

"Did you take care of Greg's debt?"

Jordan let out a burst of laughter. "Oh, she took care of it all right."

The elevator stopped on the first floor, and I pulled out my phone as I walked across the lobby. David answered before we'd reached the main exit.

"Everything go okay?" he asked.

"Perfectly." I stepped outside and stared up at the glass building. "I need one more favor tonight."

CHAPTER 8

I THREW THE covers off me and shivered in my T-shirt and shorts. Rolling out of bed, I quickly changed into jeans and a long sleeve top. I pulled a warm hoodie over the top and hunted around for a pair of socks. It almost felt like I was back in Idaho. "Damn, I thought LA was supposed to be warm," I grumbled as I opened the bedroom door.

"Morning, sleepy head," Roland called from the kitchen. "We thought you were going to sleep all day."

I looked at the clock on the TV, surprised to see it was almost 11:00 a.m. "Why didn't you guys wake me?"

Peter stirred something in a pan on the stove. "We figured you earned a good sleep after last night."

The door opened and Greg came in carrying a bag of groceries. He handed the bag to Roland and came over to me. He still looked tired, but less haggard than yesterday. It was probably going to take a little while for last night's shock to wear off. Suddenly finding out you're safe after weeks of living in fear was a lot for anyone to process.

"Hey," I said before he pulled me into a tight hug. "What's that for?" I asked when he released me.

"I think I was too stunned last night to thank you for what you did," he said hoarsely. "I still can't believe it's over."

"You were too busy yelling at me for going to Draegan's, remember? And then you drank half a bottle of rum."

He winced. "Oh, yeah."

Roland snickered. "And then you threatened to take her over your knee if she ever did anything like that again."

"I'd kill to see that." Jordan laughed as she set glasses on the table.

I started to retort, but the set table caught my attention. "Are we celebrating?"

Roland raised an eyebrow at me. "You forget what today is?"

I gave him a blank look.

"Happy birthday!" He sang and the others chimed in.

My birthday? How could I have forgotten that?

Greg nudged me, and we went to join the others at the table. "I didn't have time to get you a present yet," he said.

"Spending my birthday with you and knowing you're safe is the best present you could give me."

"Oooh, better not let Mr. Tall, Dark, and Moody hear you say that," Jordan teased when I took the chair next to her.

Roland and Peter piled my plate high with French toast, sausages, and every other breakfast food I could imagine. I tried a bit of everything, but I didn't have much of an appetite. Roland and Peter were more than happy to finish off the food that was left.

After breakfast, Jordan figured out how to work the espresso machine and treated me to a birthday latte. The coffee was heavenly, and I cradled it to ward off the chill in the apartment.

Greg sat beside me, drinking his coffee. "Sara, you don't seem worried that Draegan might come after you for killing his other demons."

I smiled over the top of my cup. "I'm not. And I have a strong feeling Draegan won't be collecting any more blood debts."

"What makes you say that?"

"Last night when we left Draegan's, I asked my friend David to contact the Mohiri and let them know about the dangerous demon living in that building. I'm betting the world has one less gulak demon in it today."

"Three less, actually, if you count the two we took out." Jordan looked very pleased with herself.

Greg crossed his arms and frowned at me. "I feel like I should be mad at you for going to see Draegan after I told you to stay out of it."

"But you see now that I was right and we *were* the best people to handle this."

"That's beside the point."

Roland chuckled. "Dude, it's easier if you just nod and move on. Trust me."

Greg opened his mouth, but he was interrupted by his phone. He smiled when he saw the number. "Hey, buddy." He looked at me and mouthed the word *Danny* before he went to sit in the living room. Hearing Greg sound like his old self again made my heart swell.

We stayed close to the apartment that afternoon. After lunch I made a quick call to Nate and Tristan because I knew they'd be upset if we didn't talk on my birthday. They spent half the time trying to get me to tell them where I was. I reassured them we were doing well, and I asked Nate to pass that on to Roland's mom, Judith. The boys couldn't call their families because they were afraid Maxwell would order them home. They couldn't refuse a direct command from their Alpha, even over the phone.

I talked to David twice that afternoon, and both times he told me there was still no sign of Madeline. Her trail had gone cold after she left Albuquerque. That news left me dejected and wondering how long it would take to locate her again. My whole reason for being here was to find out what Madeline knew about the Master.

David had other news the second time we spoke. "Kelvan heard that vampires attacked Orias's place last night. His receptionist and a couple of his clients were killed. Orias got away, but he took out two of the vampires first."

My stomach dropped. "Why would vampires attack a powerful warlock like him?"

"Word is that a well-known vampire was killed there five days ago... on the same night you went to see Orias, in fact." He made a disapproving sound. "You told me it went well. You didn't say anything about a vampire."

I scuffed my toe on the rug in front of the couch. "We might have run into a little trouble, but we handled it. I didn't want to worry you."

David sighed heavily. "Sara, we're supposed to be in this together, remember? That's the agreement we made before we started this. How am I supposed to help you if you keep things like this from me?"

I had no argument because he was right. "I'm sorry."

"Just don't do it again." I heard him typing and waited for him to speak again. "According to Kelvan's friends in Albuquerque, the vampires wanted to know about a girl who supposedly killed Stefan Price. When no one could tell them who she was, they started tearing the place apart. They torched it when they left."

I remembered how proud Orias was of his establishment, and I was sorry it had been destroyed. I felt worse about his poor receptionist and the others who had been killed.

"Did you really kill that vampire by yourself?" David asked.

"I had some help."

"Kelvan said there is a rumor among the demons about a girl warrior who slays only vampires. The other night a vrell demon and his friends were attacked by vampires in LA, and the girl came out of nowhere to save them." He cleared his throat. "I don't suppose you know anything about that?"

I almost laughed at the way people blew things out of proportion. "We were there, but it was my friends who killed the vampires."

He was quiet for a moment. "Listen, I get that you want to help people, but you need to be even more careful now. You don't want to draw attention to yourself."

"I know." As far as we knew, the Master still believed I was at Westhorne. If he even had the tiniest suspicion we were in LA, this city would be swarming with vampires. Not only would it put my friends' lives in grave danger, it would scare Madeline away. "We'll lay low until you pick up Madeline's trail again."

We spent the day hanging out at the apartment, watching movies, eating until we couldn't move, and laying low as I'd promised David we would do. By midafternoon, I tired of movies and went to look for a book from Leo's bookcase. His copy of *White Fang* kept me engrossed for an hour before I lost interest in that, too. I paced around the apartment feeling out of sorts and bursting with nervous energy as if I'd drunk five lattes instead of one. By the time dinner rolled around, I was nursing a small headache – something I rarely had – and I'd discovered that sitting around waiting for news was not fun.

Greg went out and picked up steaks for dinner and we grilled them on the roof. It was a beautiful night, even if it was a little chilly. I still didn't have much of an appetite, and I caught Jordan frowning at the half-eaten steak I slid onto Roland's plate. She gave me a questioning look and I shrugged it off.

After dinner, Greg brought out a cake, and I laughed when they sang "Happy Birthday" to me. *I wish you were here*, I said silently as I blew out the candles. It was a silly wish since I was the one keeping us apart, but I could think of nothing I wanted more in that moment.

"You're thinking about him, aren't you?" Jordan said a little while later when we carried our dishes to the kitchen.

I didn't try to deny it. "Yes."

"Call him," she urged. "Talk to him."

"I... can't."

She fixed me with a hard stare. "You know you want to. You're just being stubborn. If I had a man like Nikolas, you wouldn't have to tell me twice."

Greg opened the fridge and pulled out a beer. "Who is this Nikolas you guys keep mentioning?"

"He's my..." How did I describe Nikolas? Friend, protector, trainer: he was all of those and more. Boyfriend was too weak a word for someone like him, but soulmate felt like something out of a romance novel.

"He's her mate," Jordan answered, not having as much trouble as I was in summing up my relationship with Nikolas.

Greg choked on his beer. "Mate? You're married?"

"No, of course not." I couldn't stop the blush that crept up my face. "We're... dating." Interesting choice of words considering Nikolas and I had never been on anything remotely resembling a date. "It's different for the Mohiri. I don't know how to explain it." I gave Jordan a helpless look.

She smiled at Greg. "Sometimes, a Mohiri male and female have a special bond between their two demons. The male starts behaving like a Neanderthal and growling at anyone else who looks at his woman. The female tells him to get over himself even though she is secretly crazy about him. Eventually, the two of them do the deed and live happily ever after."

The look on Greg's face made me groan silently. I should have known better than to trust Jordan with something so delicate.

"Nikolas and I care about each other, and he's very protective of me." I explained the Mori bond without going into too much detail, particularly about the mating.

Greg relaxed when he realized I hadn't become a child bride since we last saw each other. I think, in his eyes, I was still the girl he'd sat with at lunch in high school.

Roland grabbed two beers from the fridge for Peter and him. He took a long drink from his before he said, "So if two Mohiri get drunk and have sex, are they mated for life? That would totally suck. What if you wake up the next day and realize you don't even like the other person?"

"It doesn't work that way, thank God," Jordan said. "The bond has to be there already for the couple to be mated. No bond, no mating."

Peter leaned against the counter. "So what happens if you meet your mate when you're five? Does the male beat up the other kids for playing with you?"

Jordan laughed. "Bonds don't form until we're mature." She nodded toward me. "Or close to it in some cases."

I sat on one of the bar stools at the kitchen counter. "It's kind of like werewolf imprinting except both people feel the bond instead of one."

Jordan sat beside me. "Only one werewolf bonds to the other? I didn't know that."

Roland picked at the label on his bottle, looking uncomfortable with the direction of the conversation. "A male werewolf imprints on the female their wolf claims as their mate. The female doesn't have to accept him, but she usually does."

"What happens if the female werewolf doesn't want the guy?" she asked. "Can he imprint on someone else?"

"Only if his wolf does," Peter said. "And if they haven't… you know."

Jordan looked between them. "And what if the guy doesn't like who his wolf chooses?"

Peter shook his head. "Same deal, but the wolf almost always imprints on someone they both like."

"Wow, that totally sucks," Jordan declared, and I couldn't help but agree. Being bound, for the rest of your life, to someone who didn't want you sounded like a miserable existence.

Greg whistled. "That's rough."

Roland nodded unhappily. "You're telling me."

"For a guy who hates the idea of being in a relationship, you date an awful lot," I teased Roland. "Aren't you afraid you'll imprint on one of those girls?"

"Werewolves don't imprint on humans." He smiled. "That's why I only date human girls."

Peter snickered. "And he stays the hell away from the Knolls when they have pack gatherings there."

"Why?" I asked.

Roland shuddered. "Because every eligible female between sixteen and thirty is there looking for a mate. Thank God, Uncle Max doesn't force us to go to gatherings. He's a tough Alpha, but he says it's up to you if you want to mate or not."

"So all those times you slept on my couch to give up your room for company, you were hiding from female werewolves?"

He blushed. "Um, yeah."

Jordan and I laughed, and his brows drew together. "You wouldn't think it was funny if it was you."

I raised an eyebrow. "Hello?"

Jordan snorted indelicately. "You poor, poor girl. I can see how being bound to a smoking hot warrior would be such a hardship."

"Says the girl who vows she doesn't need a man."

"I might be willing to make an exception if he came in a package like that." She let out a gusty sigh. "But I think Nikolas is one of a kind."

My chest squeezed. *He is.*

Roland finished his beer and got another one. "Enough of this mushy crap. Let's watch movies and get drunk since we can't go out."

"Sounds like a plan," Peter said.

"You guys don't have to stay in, you know. Jordan and I are the ones who have to hide."

Roland, Peter, and Greg laughed at the same time.

"You two were out of our sight for less than an hour last night, and you started a fight in a room full of demons." Roland shook his head. "We're staying together."

Jordan followed us into the living room, wearing a cocky smile. "We didn't start the fight, but we sure as hell finished it."

I made it two thirds of the way through the first *Fast and Furious* movie before restless energy sent me prowling around the apartment again. I read the titles of the books in Leo's bookcase so many times I could have recited them by heart. I checked my email half a dozen times. At one point, I wandered up to the roof for some fresh air, but the cold soon drove me back down again. The others kept shooting me questioning looks, which I ignored. I couldn't have explained my state of mind to them if I wanted to.

Jordan gave me a knowing look two hours later when I grabbed the laptop and headed to our bedroom. I sat on the bed and laid the laptop beside me. My hand hovered over the keyboard for a long moment before I hit the button.

"Hello?" said a warm male voice I'd missed more than I thought I would.

"Hey," I replied.

"Sara? Jesus!" Chris whispered hoarsely, alerting me to the fact that he wasn't alone. "Are you alright? Where are you?"

I pulled the blanket from the foot of the bed and wrapped it around my shoulders. "I'm fine, and you know I'm not going to tell you where I am."

"You don't sound fine."

The concern in his voice made tears prick my eyes. "I'm okay, really. I just wanted to check in and say hi."

He released a slow breath. "I'm surprised you have time. You've been pretty busy the last week."

"Busy?"

"Orias, Stephan Price, the gulak demons last night."

I chewed on my lower lip. "How do you know I had anything to do with those?"

Chris laughed softly. "Let's just say your handiwork is hard to miss, Cousin. And we got your friend's call last night."

That brought a smile to my lips. "Did the Mohiri take care of Draegan?"

"Oh, he's been taken care of. When we got there he was yelling about the girl who cheated him and killed his men. Then he started describing what he was going to do to this girl when he found her."

I grimaced. "That bad, huh?"

"Yes. Nikolas thought so, too."

"Oh..."

"Nikolas has been as surly as that wyvern of yours since you left, and it doesn't take much to set him off. Do you know what it's like being around him when he's like this?"

"Sorry."

Chris groaned. "No, you're not. If you were truly sorry you would tell me where you are right now and save me from this torture."

"Chris, I –"

"At least talk to the man," he pleaded. "Give him something."

I took a deep breath. "Is he there with you now?"

"He's nearby."

My pulse quickened. "Okay."

I heard Chris walking and a door opening and closing. There was a muffled sound as he handed his phone to someone. Then a deep impatient voice said, "Hello?"

"Hi," I replied hesitantly.

"Sara." He said my name so softly it was like a caress. Warmth curled in my stomach. "What's wrong? Are you hurt? Did he hurt you?"

"Chris?"

"The gulak demon."

"He didn't touch me."

I could hear his exhale. "You didn't call last night. I didn't know what to think."

I closed my eyes, wanting to kick myself. Last night had been crazy, and we were all so excited about getting the contract for Greg that I hadn't thought Nikolas might be expecting me to call him like I'd been doing every night. *God, I'm an awful person.*

"I'm sorry."

"I'm just glad you're okay and that you're talking to me."

The ache that had lingered in my chest for days began to ease. I tugged the blanket closer around me and curled up on my side, facing the laptop. "Me too."

He sighed and I imagined him running his hand through his black hair, his gray eyes dark and intense. "I know you're angry with me, but this isn't solving anything. Tell me where you are, and we'll talk this through."

"I'm not angry about that anymore."

"Then tell me where you are."

"If I do, will you try to stop me from looking for Madeline?"

He didn't reply.

"This is important to me, Nikolas. I've gotten closer than anyone else to finding her, and I can't stop now."

"We'll look for her together," he said, and I closed my eyes, wishing I could believe that.

"Does that mean you won't have any problem with me going to see warlocks and demons and anyone else who might lead us to Madeline?" Working together meant he'd have to stop trying to protect me from anyone who looked at me funny. It meant us being equals. I didn't have his fighting abilities, but I'd proven that I had my own strengths.

"We'll work something out."

I heard clicking in the background, and it took me a few seconds to realize he was using a computer. It didn't take a genius to figure out what he was doing. I should have been angry he was trying to trace the call, but I would have expected nothing less from him.

"You can't trace me. I made sure of it."

The clicking stopped. "So I see. You picked up a few tricks."

"Yes, and some new friends." It was strange thinking of a demon as a friend, but that was what Kelvan was becoming to me. "Listen, I have to go." I wanted nothing more than to lie there all night talking to him, but I didn't know how good Mohiri technology was or how long it would take them to trace my call. It was foolish to risk them finding me just because it made me feel better to hear Nikolas's voice.

Nikolas surprised me when he didn't try to keep me on the phone. "Call me tomorrow."

"I will," I promised. My heart felt lighter now that we'd actually talked. "Good night."

"Good night," he said huskily. "And, Sara, happy birthday."

*　　*　　*

"Are you going to stay in bed all day?"

"Mmm."

"Sara, wake up." Jordan pulled the covers off me, and I shivered as cold air touched my arms and legs. I opened my eyes to glare at her, and my head began to pound with a fierce headache.

I reached for the blankets and pulled them back up to my chin, burrowing beneath them until only my eyes were visible. "Go away," I moaned. "I don't feel well."

"What's wrong?"

"I have a splitting headache, and I feel achy and tired."

Her brows drew together. "You didn't drink last night. Why are you sick?"

"I don't know," I retorted miserably. "Can I go back to sleep now?"

Roland entered the room. "What's wrong with you?"

"She's sick." Jordan rooted around in her backpack and carried the can of gunna paste over to me. "Here, this will make you feel better." She stood over me as I dutifully took some of the bitter paste. Anything to get rid of this headache.

"Sick?" Roland repeated. "Sara never gets sick."

"Maybe it's the flu," Peter suggested from the doorway.

I didn't remember ever having the flu so I couldn't say if he was right or not. I closed my eyes and hoped the gunna paste would kick in soon.

"Go back to sleep," Jordan said, shooing Roland and Peter out of the room. "I bet you'll feel one hundred percent better when you wake up again."

When I opened my eyes again, it was three in the afternoon. My headache had eased a bit, but the rest of me felt like I'd just done a few rounds with my old trainer, Callum. My body was stiff and sore, and getting dressed made me so tired I wanted to lie down again. I was also freezing. I dressed in layers and wrapped the comforter around me before I left the bedroom.

"Hey, look who's up," Roland said when I joined him on the couch. "Feeling better?"

I tucked my legs underneath me and leaned my head against the cushioned armrest. "A little better," I said when I saw his look of concern. "It's freezing here."

Greg came over to stand beside the couch. "You *must* have the flu because it's not cold here. It's seventy degrees outside today."

"Oh."

He left the room and came back carrying the thick comforter from his bed. "Here. Maybe this will help."

"Thanks," I said as he laid it over me.

"Are you hungry?" Jordan asked. "You haven't eaten all day."

I wasn't hungry, but I said I could eat a little. She went into the kitchen, and I heard the microwave. A few minutes later she came back with a mug of hearty chicken soup. I sat up and took the mug between my cold hands, blowing on the soup to cool it.

"We went to that diner to get some of their soup," she explained. "It's homemade, and these guys said that when someone is sick, you're supposed to feed them soup."

I took a sip of the rich broth. "It's delicious, thanks."

I drank the whole cup of soup to make her happy, and then I lay back and took a nap, buried beneath a mountain of comforters. It was dark out when I woke again, and the others were sitting around quietly watching TV. Jordan got me more soup and added in some crackers. When I finished, she tried to tempt me with my favorite Ben & Jerry's ice cream, but my stomach couldn't handle anything else. I watched part of a movie before I dozed off for another hour.

"This makes no sense," Jordan said the next time I woke. "You're Mohiri... and Fae. You shouldn't get sick. And the gunna paste should have made you better by now."

"Maybe she picked up something from one of the demons at that party," Roland suggested. "Is that possible?"

Jordan chewed her lip. "I don't know." She looked at me. "Did you get bitten by one of those demons you fought?"

"No. The ranc demon's horn scratched my palm, but it didn't draw blood." I held up my hand. "There isn't even a mark."

"Still, we should look them up to make sure their horns don't have poisonous tips or something," she said.

"Can you bring me the cell phone I've been using to call David?" She went to get it for me. I called him and asked him to ask Kelvan about ranc demons. It didn't take long for him to come back and tell me ranc demons were not poisonous. So much for that theory.

It was hard to hide my illness from Nikolas when I called him that night. He asked me twice if I was okay and I lied and said I was only tired. He tried again to get me to tell him where I was, and for a moment I was tempted. I was miserable and I wanted nothing more than for him to come and take me home. I said goodbye soon after that because I knew I'd regret my moment of weakness once I felt better.

I slept fitfully and woke the next morning feeling worse than the day before. The headache was back and my stomach hurt now, too. And I couldn't get warm no matter how many blankets my friends piled on top of me. I didn't say anything, but my illness was starting to scare me. I found my vial of troll bile and took a small drop. If anything could make me better it was troll bile. It was even nastier than gunna paste, but I knew from experience how potent it was. After that, I took a nap on the couch, hoping the bile would work its magic.

By the time evening rolled around, I knew the bile wasn't helping. If anything, I was worse. I felt like someone had syphoned all the energy and heat from my body, and I could barely stomach the smell of food. The only thing my stomach could handle was water and a few dry crackers. I could barely keep my eyes open for five minutes at a time, and when I slept it was fitful and full of strange dreams I couldn't remember.

My Mori was upset, too. I could sense its distress and I tried to assure it that we were going to be fine, but it's not easy to be convincing when you aren't sure if what you're saying is true.

When I began to shiver uncontrollably despite all the blankets covering me, Greg stood up and said he was taking me to a hospital. Jordan told him he couldn't do that, but I could hear the uncertainty in her voice. If I could have spoken, I would have told them that human medicine would not cure whatever was wrong with me.

I passed out a few minutes later. The last thing I remembered thinking was that I'd broken my promise to call Nikolas and he was going to worry again.

CHAPTER 9

VOICES THREATENED TO drag me away from the wonderful dream I was having, and I fought consciousness to stay in the dream world. I knew I wasn't really back in my old living room in New Hastings, sitting by the fire with Nikolas and listening to the storm rage outside. I had no idea why my mind brought me back to that time and place, but I was warm and content and reluctant to leave.

The voices tugged at me again, and I felt the coldness of the real world pressing down on me. My eyes opened and Greg's uncle's living room slowly swam into focus. I saw Roland and Greg talking in low voices across the room and Peter dozing in a chair. The clock on the TV said it was 4:00 a.m., and I wondered groggily why everyone was still up. Jordan's voice came from the direction of the kitchen, and it took me a few seconds to realize she was talking to someone. Who was she on the phone with at this hour?

When I heard a low male voice answer Jordan, alarm filled my muddled brain. I tried to move beneath the pile of blankets, but my tired body refused to cooperate. Panic filled me, and I let out a small cry.

"Shhh," someone murmured in my ear.

I stilled as several realizations hit me at once. The first was that I was warm for the first time in days. The second was the absence of the hollow ache in my chest. The third was that I was lying on my side with my back pressed against a warm hard body.

"Nikolas?" I whispered.

"I'm here."

My breath hitched and a lump formed in my throat. I had no idea if I was crying because I was upset that he'd finally caught me, or because I was so happy he was here. My illness had made me weak and emotional, and I shook as the tears came.

"Don't cry." His arms tightened around me, pulling me closer. It took me a few minutes to get my emotions under control.

"How do you feel?"

"Rotten," I rasped. "What's wrong with me?"

"I don't know, but we'll figure it out." Beneath his reassuring tone, there was an edge of worry that frightened me.

I shifted in his arms, needing to see him. He lifted me easily, turning me toward him.

Eyes the color of dark smoke met mine, and I fell into their depths. I had missed him so much, and the need to touch him, to make sure he was real, overwhelmed me. I reached up to caress his jaw, which was covered in a day's growth of beard. My fingers grazed his full lips, and they parted slightly, sending warm breath across my skin. I touched his brow, smoothing out the furrows, hating that I had put them there.

"I'm sorry I didn't call."

His eyes softened, and he leaned down to press a tender kiss to my forehead. My stomach fluttered and warmth coursed through me. I closed my eyes and rested my head against his chest as his arms circled me protectively.

"It's okay," he said against my hair. "Go back to sleep."

When I woke again, his warmth was gone, and fear that it had all been a dream twisted my gut. A hand stroked my hair, and I realized I lay with my head on Nikolas's lap. He spoke and his voice was a balm for my fear.

"Tristan is sending two healers with the jet. I don't want to wait until we get her home."

"Good idea," Chris replied, his voice devoid of his usual good humor. "Do they have any ideas what it could be?"

"There are several species of demon with venom that can cause some of these symptoms, but according to Jordan, they didn't come into contact with any of them."

"Tell us again what happened at the party," Chris said, and I listened as Jordan related the events of that night exactly as they had happened.

"She didn't eat or drink anything except the Glaen, and the only demons I remember her touching were the ranc and the gulak. The only other demon that got close to us was an incubus."

Nikolas tensed. "An incubus?"

Jordan snorted. "Sara would have fried his man parts if he'd touched one of us, trust me. My girl doesn't mess around."

"How was she after she drank the Glaen?" Chris asked. "It's a powerful drink from what I hear."

"She was kind of silly like she was drunk, but not staggering. She even hugged me."

"Sara hugged you?" Roland said. "That must have been some good stuff."

"Could her Mori be sick from the Fae drink?" Chris suggested. "She's only half Fae after all."

I felt for my Mori, and I could sense no pain from it. It seemed to be content now that Nikolas was here.

"My Mori is fine," I rasped.

Nikolas's hand stilled. "How are you feeling?"

I took stock of my symptoms. I was freezing again, and every joint in my body ached. My stomach rolled, my head hurt, and my skin felt dry and itchy and stretched across my muscles. I shifted and everything hurt. "Same. Thirsty."

Jordan appeared at my side, holding a glass of water with a straw in it. "Here." She put the straw to my lips and I drank slowly, afraid to disturb my already unsettled stomach.

"Better?" she asked, and I noticed how pale and tired she looked.

"Yes."

She stayed by my side. "Are you mad at me?"

"No, why?" It took a moment for me to understand. "You called him?"

She nodded. "You were so sick. I didn't know what else to do."

"You did the right thing," I said, and she smiled wanly. I poked my hand out from under the blankets to touch hers. "Thanks, Jordan."

Her smile fell away, and she set the glass down to take my hand in both of hers. "Sara, your hand is like ice!"

A fit of shivering overtook me and my teeth began to chatter. "C-can't get w-warm."

She jumped to her feet. "Nikolas, look at her. I think she's turning blue from cold."

Seconds later, I was sitting on his lap with his arms around me. Jordan arranged the blankets over us and I curled into him. But no matter how close I got to him, I couldn't get warm. It felt like I was cold from the inside out, and my body shivered so violently it hurt.

Nikolas said something to Jordan, and she ran out of the room. I clung to him desperately, afraid that I was dying. I'd never feared death, but that was before I found him. I'd spent so much time running from him, but I didn't want to run anymore. I couldn't bear the thought of leaving him now.

He stood and let the blankets fall to the couch. I cried against the cold as he strode into the bathroom where Jordan had filled the large claw-foot tub with hot water. Carefully, he set me down in the tub. I tried to stay upright, but my body was so weak I slid down into the water.

Nikolas grabbed my shoulders and lifted me forward so he could sit behind me, positioning me between his legs so I was chest deep in the water with my back against his chest. Water sloshed out onto the floor, but

I was too cold to care, and I was only vaguely aware of Jordan throwing down towels to soak up the mess.

Steam rose up around us as Nikolas tried to rub warmth back into my arms, which were quickly growing numb. I could feel the heat of the water, but it did nothing to warm me. I sobbed from pain and frustration and the fear that this really was the end.

"Stay with me, Sara," Nikolas said hoarsely, and the helplessness in his voice broke my heart. I wanted to turn and hold him, but I was too weak to move.

"I'm scared."

He spoke gruffly in my ear. "I did not chase you halfway across the country to let you leave me again. You are one of the strongest, most stubborn people I've ever met, and you are going to beat this. Do you hear me?" I didn't reply and he asked more forcefully, "Do you hear me, Sara?"

"Yes," I said through chattering teeth. I summoned the last of my strength, determined to never leave him again.

"Look!" Jordan cried.

The others crowded into the bathroom behind her. "What is that?" Roland asked.

I opened my eyes and stared down at the glittering particles appearing around us in the water. The specks of light multiplied and moved toward me, clinging to every part of me that was under water. I watched in weary fascination while it covered me in a warm golden glow. A sigh escaped my lips as the familiar heat sank into my skin, my muscles, my bones, and every frozen part of me.

"It's her magic – or the water magic," Jordan said. "I'm not sure which."

"Whatever it is, it's helping." Chris moved closer. "Her color is improving."

I let my head fall back against Nikolas's chest as exhaustion weighed down my body. He wrapped his arms around me. "That's it. Hold on, Sara. The healers will be here soon."

I must have passed out because the next time I opened my eyes, I was warm and dry and wrapped up in blankets on the couch again. A face swam before my eyes, and it took a few seconds to focus on the woman who looked vaguely familiar.

"How do you feel?" she asked as she touched my forehead and peered into my eyes.

"How do you think?" I mumbled, earning a smile. I remembered her from Westhorne. "You're Margot."

"That's right. Now tell me where it hurts. Are you still cold?"

"I'm warm now, but my head is killing me. And I feel like I want to throw up, but I can't."

She nodded. "According to the others you haven't eaten much in days.

You need nourishment and liquids to help keep your strength up." She reached behind her for a red duffle bag. "I'm going to hook you up to an IV, and then we are going to transport you to the jet. We'll have you home in no time and we'll get you all fixed up."

"Okay." I started to ask where everyone was when I heard the low rumble of male voices from the kitchen.

"Hey, you're awake." Roland appeared at the foot of the couch. His blue eyes were dark with worry and dark shadows lay under them. "You scared the shit out of us. Please don't do that again."

I summoned a weak smile. "I'll see what I can do."

Blinding pain shot through my skull, robbing me of my breath and my voice. I pressed my hands to my head as explosions of light went off behind my eyes and waves of agonizing pain rippled through me. A whimper escaped my lips, and I doubled over as hammers pounded my skull mercilessly. I prayed for unconsciousness because if I had to endure this much longer, I would go insane.

Nikolas called my name, but he sounded far away. People spoke in urgent voices that were hard to hear above the roaring in my head. In the back of my mind, the walls around my Mori fell and it cried out in pain. I tried to put the protective walls back up, but my power would not respond.

A new voice broke through the haze of pain around me. It was warm and rich, yet commanding. "Let me help her, warrior, if you want her to live."

I tensed when a cool hand touched my forehead and then gasped as the stabbing pain rapidly drained away. A sob escaped me, and it was a minute before I opened my eyes to see Eldeorin smiling down at me.

"Hello, little Cousin. I told you I'd see you again soon."

"H-how did you find me?"

His smile dimmed. "Your pain is like a beacon to any Fae within fifty miles of here. I was away from the city or I would have come sooner." His hand stroked my cheek and each touch sent a wave of soothing energy through me. "I'm going to take care of you now."

"You healed her?" Roland asked.

"No, I merely eased her pain. I will take her to Faerie where we will tend her."

Nikolas stepped forward, towering over us. "She stays with me."

Eldeorin did not cower or flinch from Nikolas's anger. He continued to stroke my face as if nothing had happened. "Sara needs to be around my kind. She is going through *liannan*."

"*Liannan?*"

"Think of it as the Fae equivalent of puberty. Her powers are experiencing a growth spurt, and her body cannot handle the sudden changes. If she was full Fae and had grown up among our kind, this would have happened slowly, over months or years, and she would have been better able to deal with it. We were not sure she could even enter *liannan* since she is half Mohiri and lives outside of Faerie. Only exposure to our kind or a prolonged visit to Faerie should trigger *liannan*. I did not sense it in her when we met, and our brief encounter was not sufficient to cause it."

"What about Glaen?" Jordan asked him.

"What do you know of Glaen?"

"Sara drank a bunch of it at a demon party a few nights ago. She started getting sick a day later."

Roland came to stand beside Jordan. "Don't forget the times she glowed when she was asleep before she drank the Glaen. No way was that normal."

Eldeorin nodded thoughtfully. "It sounds like she was already approaching *liannan*. Consuming that much of our drink at one time could be a catalyst to someone like her."

"Will she be okay?" Roland asked, his voice strained.

Eldeorin gave me a reassuring smile. "Yes, but she needs proper care."

Nikolas looked at me with a closed expression. "What kind of care?"

"She will need to be near our kind, at least until she passes through the most difficult stage. The best place for her is Faerie."

"For how long?" Nikolas asked.

"I cannot say," Eldeorin replied. "It may take weeks or months."

Something unreadable flashed in Nikolas's eyes. "Do whatever it takes to help her."

"No," I rasped. "I don't want to go to Faerie." As much as I'd love to see that beautiful place, I did not want to leave Nikolas again.

Nikolas sat on his haunches so his face was close to mine. "You'll get better faster there."

"I can get better here. Eldeorin will stay here with me. Won't you?" I asked the faerie, silently pleading with him to say yes.

"I will stay if that will put you at ease, Cousin."

"Thank you." I tried to sit up, but my body was too weak to obey me. Nikolas stood and lifted me into a sitting position. His jaw hardened when Eldeorin sat beside me holding my hand, and I remembered what Desmund had told me about Mohiri males not liking another male touching their bond mate. I reached my free hand toward him, and he entwined his fingers with mine. Tugging gently, I made him sit on my other side so I could rest my head against his shoulder.

The tension in Nikolas's body eased, and he looked at Eldeorin. "It's not safe to stay in this apartment. Can you come to our stronghold?"

"That would be unwise. I and others of my kind will have to be near Sara for weeks. I don't think a prolonged Fae presence at a Mohiri compound would be received well. And we don't know yet how Sara's *liannan* might affect your people."

"None of our safe houses are big enough to hold all of us," Chris said. "We could take a large house for a few months and bring in some people to help with security."

Eldeorin shook his head. "That is not necessary. I have a place we can use, and it is big enough to accommodate all of us without Fae and Mohiri affecting each other."

"Is it safe?" Nikolas asked skeptically.

"It is glamoured and well-fortified with faerie protections. No vampire would dare attack it."

Nikolas's thumb rubbed soothing circles on the back of my hand. "Where is this place?"

"It is near Santa Cruz."

"We can be there in an hour on the jet," Chris observed.

Nikolas stood, releasing my hand. "Chris, call the pilot and tell him to be ready to leave within the hour. Jordan, pack your things and Sara's."

Roland came forward. "We're coming too."

"Be ready to leave here in five minutes."

I looked around the living room. "Where is Greg?"

Greg came out of the kitchen and approached me. His hair needed a brush and he looked like he hadn't slept in days.

He knelt beside me. "You need help that I can't give you, Sara. I wish I could after what you did for me. But just say the word and I'm there."

A selfish part of me didn't want to let him go because I didn't know when I'd see him again. But he'd been through hell the last month, and he needed to try to get back to some kind of normal life.

"You need to be with your family. I'll talk to you again soon." I grabbed his hand before he could stand. "And you better call me. Don't make me come looking for you."

His eyes warmed. "I'm putting you in my speed dial, I promise."

Eldeorin stood over me. "Now, Cousin, let's get you ready to travel. I could have the two of us there in seconds, but I have a feeling neither you nor your warrior would be happy with that." He laid his hands on either side of my face and they glowed like mine did when I did healings. Heat suffused my face, quickly spreading throughout my body. "This will keep you comfortable for the journey. I won't need to be in physical contact with you the entire time, but I will stay close."

"All packed," Jordan called.

Nikolas scooped me off the couch, and I protested that I could walk even though my limbs felt like warm jelly from Eldeorin's blast of power. He ignored my objection and carried me outside to the waiting SUVs that were guarded by two more warriors. They turned around when we drew near, and I was surprised to see Seamus and Niall. I expected harsh words from the twins after the way I'd left them, but they wore their usual boyish smiles. I gave Nikolas a questioning look and he smiled.

"They volunteered to come. I think they found Westhorne too tame after you left."

"Never a dull moment, lass," Niall quipped, walking toward us.

Seamus grinned. "What's this I hear about you giving a beatdown to some gulak demons?"

Cold exploded in my chest, and I stiffened in Nikolas's arms. "Vampires," I choked out. I had no idea how I knew it, but there were eight vampires coming at us fast. "Eight."

Nikolas tensed and Seamus and Niall drew their swords. Behind us I heard our weapons bag hit the ground and the soft whine of metal as more swords were drawn. I found myself suddenly passed from Nikolas's arms to Eldeorin's. "Get her out of here," Nikolas ordered before he spun away to take the sword offered to him by Jordan.

"No!" My cry was lost on the wind as the city disappeared into a black void I had experienced once before. Seconds later, Eldeorin stood in front of a large white mansion with a fountain in the middle of the well-lit driveway. I struggled in his arms, but I was as weak as a kitten. "Take me back. We can't leave them there alone."

"Calm yourself, Cousin," he soothed as he walked toward the mansion. "You cannot help your friends in your condition. It would only endanger them if you were there because they would try to protect you."

"Then leave me here and go back and help them, please."

He stopped at a set of double doors. "Your safety is my only concern. Do not fret. Your friends can handle a few vampires."

The doors opened and a short person in a white uniform ushered us inside. Eldeorin strode across the marble foyer and up a wide flight of stairs. At the end of the hallway, he opened the door to a large bedroom and set me down on the high four-poster bed.

Terrified for Nikolas and my friends, I slid off the bed, but my legs crumpled underneath me. Eldeorin caught me and lifted me back into the bed. The cold in my chest had been replaced with squeezing pain that made me gasp for breath. "I have to go back. Please take me back."

Eldeorin laid a hand on my forehead and muttered something in a language I did not understand. My mind filled with a warm fog that beckoned me and made me want to close my eyes. "No," I sobbed, fighting as the fog closed in around me.

"Sleep, little Cousin," Eldeorin said softly before blackness descended and I heard no more.

*   *   *

I awoke slowly to the cries of gulls and the roar of waves against the shore. A light breeze tickled my face and carried a slight ocean tang along with the sweet scent of roses. My eyes opened to a sunny room decorated in delicate shades of blue and white, and I looked around in confusion. *Where am I?*

A curtain fluttered and I stared at the open balcony doors past the foot of the queen-sized bed I lay in. I had no memory of how I'd gotten to this place. The last time I'd woken up in a strange room, I'd discovered I was in Seelie, but I didn't think they had oceans in Faerie. I rubbed my temples, trying to focus and remember what had brought me here and, more importantly, where I had come from. My mind refused to penetrate my foggy memories, and I sank back against the soft pillow. *Why can't I remember?* My eyes travelled around the unfamiliar room. *I must be dreaming. That's it. Time to wake up now.*

I pushed the covers off me and stared at the long white nightgown I wore. Now I knew I must be dreaming because I'd never wear something like this. I slid out of bed and had to grab the mattress to steady myself when a wave of dizziness hit me.

"Sara, you're awake!" Someone caught me from behind and turned me to envelope me in a warm hug.

"Nate? What are you doing here?" I pulled back to look around the room again. "Where are we?"

His brow furrowed. "What do you remember?"

"I. . ." I tried to focus on my memories, but it was like a thick curtain hid them from me. "I don't remember anything."

The bedroom door opened and a beautiful girl with long red curls entered carrying a tray. A smile lit her face when she saw me. "Welcome back, Sister!"

"Aine?" I looked from the sylph to Nate. "What's going on? Why can't I remember anything?"

She carried the tray to the balcony and set it on a table there. Then she came over and picked up a soft blue robe lying across the foot of the bed. "You have been very ill, and I came to help tend to you," she explained as she helped me into the robe. "I brought you some food. You have not eaten for some time, and it will help you get your strength back."

The mention of food made me aware of my growling stomach. I let Aine lead me out to a small table on the balcony that had a breathtaking view of the ocean. The house we were in sat atop a small cliff, and I could hear waves crashing against the rocks below. Aine sat me in a comfortable chair in the sun and settled a blanket over my lap before she moved the tray of food toward me. I knew it was faerie food as soon as I tasted the cold frothy milk. Nothing in this world tasted as good as faerie food.

Nate and Aine joined me at the table. "How do you feel?" Aine asked as I devoured a pastry.

I washed the pastry down with some milk. "Better. I still don't remember how I came to be here – wherever this is – or how I got sick."

"Is that normal?" Nate asked Aine.

She smiled. "It will all come back to her very soon. It is normal to be confused when you first awake from the healing sleep, especially when it is a long one."

I stared at my uncle and faerie friend talking as if it was an everyday occurrence, and I started to understand how Alice had felt down the rabbit hole. "How long was I asleep?"

"Almost a week. Eldeorin said you were very ill and distressed, and he had no choice but to put you in a sleep."

I blinked at her. I'd been asleep for a whole week? "Eldeorin?"

"You don't remember Eldeorin?" Her brows drew together delicately. "It must have been a very powerful healing he did on you. Eldeorin is one of our most gifted healers. You are fortunate he found you when he did."

A hazy image of a blond man emerged from the fog around my mind. It slowly came into focus, and I recognized the mischievous blue eyes and smiling mouth. He was standing at the edge of a bar in a night club, watching me. There was something not right about the club and it made my skin crawl. Why would I go to a nightclub of all places?

The veil blocking my memories fell away, and I gasped as everything came back to me at once. LA, Greg, Draegan, my illness, Nikolas. *Oh God!* We'd left them surrounded by all those vampires.

Fear threatened to suffocate me and my hands gripped the arms of my chair until my knuckles turned white. "Where is Nikolas? Where are Roland and the others?"

Aine laid a warm hand on mine. "Calm yourself, Sister. Your friends are all safe."

I looked at Nate and he nodded. I searched their faces, afraid they were only trying to placate me.

Aine touched my face. "I would not deceive you."

"Why aren't they here?"

"They are here, but we've had to keep them away from you, and we put protections on this room to contain your power. Your *liannan* made your magic uncontrollable, and it would not tolerate anyone but Fae being near you. After two days, your werewolf friends and uncle were able to sit with you."

"And Nikolas?"

"No demon could enter this room without your magic lashing out at them."

My chest tightened. "What does that mean? I can't go near him?"

"Once you are in control of your magic again, it should be safe."

"Should be? You don't know for sure?" I didn't want to think about what it would mean if I couldn't be with Nikolas. Or the other people I'd come to care so much for.

Aine shook her head. "Sara, there has never been another like you, and we did not know you could even go through *liannan*. It is progressing very quickly, and you have moved through the most difficult stage in a week. It normally takes months."

I remembered how sick I'd been before Eldeorin had arrived to help me. "I can't imagine going through *that* for months."

"Your symptoms were more severe than is normal for *liannan*. Eldeorin thinks it is because of the Mori. Your magic grew, but it had nowhere to go because half of you is inhabited by a demon."

"So where did it go?"

She pushed my plate toward me, and I picked up a piece of fruit that looked like one I'd eaten in Seelie. "The healing sleep allowed your body to adjust and make room for the magic. Do you not feel it inside you?"

I stopped eating and focused on the well of power at my core. It felt the same, but stronger, and it pushed against the walls holding it back. Tendrils of magic escaped, and I grabbed them and sent them back. I checked on my Mori and found it huddled fearfully, but safely, at the back of my mind. *It's okay*, I sent it soothing thoughts. *I won't let it hurt you.*

"Sara?" Nate said, and I realized I'd been quiet for several minutes.

"I'm fine." I summoned a smile for him.

"You appear to be in control of your power again," Aine said. "How do you feel?"

"I feel like me, but different. It's hard to explain." I sighed and found myself on the verge of tears again. "I can't stop crying. What's wrong with me?"

She smiled. "*Liannan* does that to you. I cried for weeks when I had mine."

"Weeks?" It was hard to imagine sweet, smiling Aine crying.

"It will pass. How is your control?"

I tested my power again. "I think it's good."

"There is only one way to know for sure. Please, do not move from this spot." Aine stood and went into the bedroom. I heard the door open, and I started to rise when I felt the soft caress of butterfly wings against my mind. *Nikolas!*

I was halfway out of my chair when static began to crackle across my skin. *No!* I fell back into the chair and grabbed for the power fighting to break away from me. Suddenly, Nikolas's presence was gone and my power receded. Tears burned my eyes, and I found it hard to breathe as the reality of what had just happened hit me.

Nate scooted his chair over and put an arm across my shoulders to draw me close. "It's going to be okay. You just woke up. In a day or two, you'll be back to your old self again."

My heart ached at the thought of having Nikolas so close and not being able to see him. But Nate was right; I was still very tired and weak. I just had to get through the next few days and everything would be okay. I refused to think about any other outcome.

A phone rang in the bedroom, and Nate went to answer it. He came out onto the balcony, handed it to me, and said he'd come back later.

I knew who was on the other end without hearing his voice. "Nikolas?" My voice cracked.

"I'm here," he said. "Don't cry."

My tears spilled over. "I'm sorry."

"You have nothing to apologize for. The faeries explained what is happening with your power."

"I could have killed you." Saying the words made them real, and my body began to shake.

"But you didn't."

I sniffled and wiped my eyes with the back of my hand. "I don't know how long it'll be before I can see you again."

"I know." He exhaled slowly. "I'm not going anywhere, and we can talk like this whenever you want to. You just focus on getting better."

"I will."

"Good. Now tell me, how do you feel?"

"A bit weak."

"But you aren't in any pain?"

"No pain," I assured him. "Aine said I'm over the worst of it."

His voice softened. "She told me that, too."

A yawn hit me. I couldn't believe I was still tired after sleeping for a week. I covered my mouth to hide it.

"You need to rest."

"I'm fine," I blurted, not wanting him to go.

He chuckled. "Liar. Get some sleep. We can talk again when you wake up."

"Okay," I conceded unhappily.

We hung up and I rested my head against the tall back of my chair. Nikolas was safe and I could talk to him even if I couldn't see him. That would have to be enough for now.

"Well, it's about time you got your lazy butt out of bed."

I jerked awake from my nap as Roland strolled out onto the balcony with Peter trailing behind him. The sight of them instantly raised my spirits. "Hey, guys."

The boys sat across from me, and their eyes immediately locked on the plate of uneaten pastries and fruit. I pulled the plate out of their reach and shook my head. "Faerie food."

Aine appeared in the doorway and laughed at their crestfallen expressions. "Heb says he has never seen anything like a werewolf's appetite. I will have him prepare a meal for you boys."

Roland watched Aine leave. "Why didn't you ever tell us your faerie friend was so hot?"

I rolled my eyes. "She's a sylph. What did you expect?"

Peter stretched out his legs. "You look pretty good for someone who's been asleep for a week. Feeling better?"

"Hundred percent better than the last time I saw you. I'm still a bit tired, but Aine said that's normal. I can't believe I slept for a whole week."

Roland's smile faded. "Eldeorin said you were in pretty bad shape and he had to put you to sleep to calm you down."

"I was upset because we left you guys there with all those vampires."

Peter snorted. "We totally kicked their asses. I don't think those suckers expected to find a bunch of warriors and two werewolves waiting for them. It didn't even last five minutes." He and Roland took turns telling me about the fight I'd missed.

"Those Mohiri don't mess around, especially Nikolas," Roland said. "That man is downright scary in a fight."

"How's he been?"

Roland made a face. "Imagine a polar bear with a sore tooth. Now imagine sharing a house with one."

"Please, get better soon so he'll stop growling at everyone," Peter begged, making me laugh.

I steered the conversation away from Nikolas because I was tired of being weepy. "What about Greg? Did he go home?"

"He's staying with his cousin and aunt in Dallas for a week before he heads back to Philly," Roland said. "He calls every day to check on you."

Peter leaned forward in his chair. "Before we left LA, Greg told Nikolas that he'd better take care of you, or else."

I could easily picture Greg going toe-to-toe with Nikolas. "What did Nikolas say?"

"He said Greg didn't have to worry about you anymore, and then Greg said you would always be his concern. Nikolas wasn't too happy about that."

Uh-oh. "What did he do?"

"Nothing. Chris got between them and said the plane was ready to go." Peter smirked at me. "And Roland told Nikolas you'd never forgive him if he hurt Greg."

Roland let out a snort. "I said you'd kick his ass."

I would have done it too, but Nikolas would not have hurt Greg no matter how annoyed he got. He protected humans; he didn't harm them.

"So what has everyone been doing for the last week?"

Roland grinned. "Hanging out in style. This place is crazy. Do you know they have a movie theater and a game room downstairs?"

"I must have missed that part of the tour," I replied dryly. "When did Nate get here? Is Tristan here, too?"

"They came the day after we did," Roland told me. "Tristan couldn't come in to see you, but Nate's been in here every day. Tristan had to go back to Westhorne, but he said he'd be back when you woke up."

There was a knock on the bedroom door and a diminutive person with curly red hair and a goatee arrived bearing a tray laden with food. At least I thought he was a man until I saw the pointed ears and realized he was actually a dwarf. He set the tray on the table and smiled when Roland and Peter dug into the thick burgers. Bowing to me, the dwarf left without saying a word.

"You gotta try this, Sara," Roland moaned through a mouthful of food. "Heb makes the best burgers you've ever tasted."

"Heb?"

"The dwarf. He does all the cooking here."

Peter nodded in agreement. "That faerie food's not gonna fill you up. Have one of these."

I picked at one of the pastries on my plate. I didn't really have much of an appetite, even for the delicious faerie food. "I'm good."

Roland took one of the burgers and laid it on my plate. "Eat," he ordered.

"I'm not hungry."

"Yes, you are. You're just moping because you can't see Nikolas." He shook his head. "You spent a week running from him, and now you're upset because you can't see him for a few days. You really are a normal chick after all."

I took a French fry from the tray and lobbed it at him. "Shut up."

He ducked and the fry flew over the railing. "Look on the bright side. You get to spend the next few days with Pete and me in this big ass mansion, eating anything you want. Before you know it, you'll be all better and leading Nikolas on another merry chase across the country."

I shook my head. "No more chases." I was done running.

CHAPTER 10

I RESTED MY head against the cushioned back of the chaise lounge chair and turned my face toward the sun, letting its warmth soak into my skin. The sounds of the birds and the ocean reminded me of home and when I closed my eyes, I could almost pretend I was back in Maine.

I missed home. But not as much as I missed Nikolas. He and the others had left the estate three days ago so I could move around freely without hurting one of them. They had rented the property next door, but they might as well have been on the other end of the state. Would they have to stay away until my training was complete? Aine said my control was a lot better now, and I didn't know if I could bear being separated from them that long.

"You look much improved today, Cousin."

I opened an eye to peer at Eldeorin who had the annoying habit of appearing in front of me instead of walking up like everyone else.

"I wish you wouldn't do that."

He chuckled and bent down to kiss my forehead. Faeries were an affectionate bunch, and I was still trying to get used to their ways. Over the last three days, I'd spent a lot of time with Eldeorin and Aine, regaining my strength and learning to control my power again. They were patient and kind teachers, and very good at cheering me up whenever I got emotional. That happened a lot after I found out they had sent all the Mohiri away so their demons would not disturb me. I'd been pretty upset until Eldeorin had explained that this was the best way to speed my recovery. After that, I spent hours every day practicing with my power and getting back the control I'd built up over the years.

"I came to tell you I am leaving for a few days now that you are recovered. I will be back in a week or two to begin your training."

"Training?"

Eldeorin gave me a look of fond exasperation. "If you are determined to live in the human world you must learn to use your power to protect yourself. Aine and I will teach you what you need to know."

"Does that mean I have to stay here? For how long?"

"How long depends on you." He winked mischievously. "Until then, Cousin."

Just like that, he was gone. I grumbled under my breath and closed my eyes again. What kind of training did he have planned for me? I was eager to learn more about my power, but I hated being kept in the dark.

A yawn escaped me, and I let the ocean lull me into a light sleep. I hadn't slept well the last three nights, and I found myself napping throughout the day when I wasn't working with Aine and Eldeorin. What I wouldn't give for just one good night's sleep.

"Sara."

"Hmm?" I turned my face toward the voice that sounded so achingly familiar. "Nikolas?" My eyes opened and for a second I thought I was dreaming when I saw him crouched beside my chair. Before he could speak again, I threw myself at him, wrapping my arms tightly around his neck and knocking him backward. He ended up on the grass with me lying on top of him. I raised myself on my elbows and drank in the sight of him. His surprise over my attack passed, and he gave me a lazy smile that made my stomach do flips.

"Miss me?" he asked in a low, rough voice.

There were no words to describe what I'd been through the last three days. Emotion choked me until I couldn't speak, and I did the only thing I could.

His lips were warm and firm and they parted under mine, our breath mingling as I explored his mouth. The taste, the smell, that could only be Nikolas, invaded my senses, and I trembled as my Mori reacted to him. After a minute, his hands came up to frame my face, and he took possession of my lips with a hunger that made my head spin. Fire raced through my veins as the kiss consumed me.

He whispered my name and brushed his lips against the corner of my mouth, my nose, my eyelids. I melted under the tender assault. Then he pulled me down so my cheek lay over his heart, and wrapped his arms around me. I tried to get my heart rate and breathing back to normal, and I smiled when I felt his heart racing as well.

"I'll take that as a yes," he said huskily. "I should go away for another week."

I lifted my head and scowled at his satisfied expression. Before I could make a retort, someone cleared their throat a few feet away.

"Maybe I should come back later," Chris said in a voice laced with laughter.

Nikolas's gaze didn't leave mine. "Good idea."

"Where is she?" Jordan called. A few seconds later, she said, "Oh. Well I guess she's feeling better."

"Come along, Jordan. Let's give these two some time together."

"But —"

"We'll see you two later," Chris said and then I heard him lead Jordan away.

Nikolas's hand came up to brush away the hair falling around my face. "You look tired."

"I haven't been sleeping well." I rested my cheek against his chest. "Are you really here?"

He kissed the top of my head and held me close. "Yes."

I closed my eyes, content to lie there wrapped in his arms and breathe in his scent. I didn't care that we were lying in the middle of the lawn or who saw us. Three days ago, I'd feared I would never be able to touch him again. I wanted to hold onto him as long as I could.

"Aine said you've been working hard to get your control back. Looks like she was right."

"She and Eldeorin are so good to me." I sighed deeply. "Eldeorin said I have to start training next week."

"Yes, he told me that."

"He didn't say how long it would take." I bit my lip. I couldn't expect Nikolas and the others to hang around here indefinitely, and the thought of being here without them put a damper on my happiness.

"What's wrong?"

"Nothing."

He rolled us until we were lying side by side in the grass. Then he put a finger under my chin and forced me to look at him. "You are a terrible liar. Tell me what's bothering you."

It was hard to think straight when he was so close and looking at me with such tenderness. "I was just wondering how long I'll have to be here. I know you have responsibilities and I don't expect..."

His smile made me forget whatever I was going to say. "I'm not going anywhere. I may have to leave for a day or two sometimes, but I'll come back."

"Oh."

"You thought I'd leave you after the chase you led me on?"

I took a deep breath. "I'm sorry I took off the way I did. I was upset, but I should have talked to you instead of running away."

His hand toyed with my hair, sending delicious shivers down my back. "I'm sorry too. I handled the whole thing badly. I saw how upset you were, and I should have known you would run."

A smile played around my lips. "You did know. That's why you had the twins follow me everywhere."

"A lot of good it did." His smile matched mine. "At least Seamus and Niall won't be making any more wisecracks about how you never would have given them the slip in Maine."

"How long did it take you to find them and realize we were gone?"

"About thirty minutes. Then we spent the next thirty scouring the woods." He frowned. "How did you two get past all our sentries?"

"Jordan didn't tell you?"

"She said she was going to let you tell that story." He arched an eyebrow. "Well?"

I plucked at a blade of grass. "You promise you won't get angry?"

"I think we're beyond that after everything else that's happened, don't you?"

I told him how Jordan and I had left Westhorne, and he stared at me in disbelief. All traces of humor left his face when he heard how we'd changed in the mill and hiked to Derek's to buy the car. To his credit, he didn't comment on it, but I could tell he wanted to.

"Then you drove to Boise to pick up Roland and Peter." His brow creased. "What was in Salt Lake City? Jordan and the others wouldn't tell us much about it."

"A friend who set me up with a laptop. You traced Roland's and Peter's cell phones there?"

"Yes."

"You almost caught us at our hotel and we had to take off."

"I know, and I spent the better part of a day searching for you there. Why did you go to Albuquerque?"

"How did you know we were in Albuquerque?"

He gave me a smug look. "You aren't the only one with resources. Although, I have to say yours are impressive to help you get as far as you did with us on your trail."

"Aren't you full of yourself?"

He laughed softly. "I do have some experience in this area."

"What? Chasing runaways... orphans?" I almost said "girlfriends" but I stopped myself.

"Among other things." He gave me an impatient look. "Are you going to tell me why you went to New Mexico?"

I sighed. "Madeline was there. We were so close, and we just missed her. But we got a good lead that she was headed for LA." I met his gaze. "Now it's your turn. How did you know we went there?"

"Let's just say that when a vampire as old as Stefan Price is killed, news travels fast. We've been hunting him for years, but he's always managed to evade us." His eyes darkened. "When we heard a rumor that he was killed by a girl warrior who looked suspiciously like you, we went to Orias's place to check it out for ourselves."

"You know Orias?"

"Everyone knows Orias. He's a powerful warlock, but he usually stays under the radar." Nikolas fixed me with a hard stare. "For some reason he couldn't mention the names of the warrior and her friends or where they'd gone."

I lifted my hand. "Warlocks are a strange breed."

He caught my hand. "Tell me the truth. Did you kill Stefan Price by yourself?"

"Roland and Jordan helped, but I did kill him."

"With your power?"

"That and one of Jordan's knives."

He exhaled deeply. "And then you went to LA, and you met the faerie at Adele's club."

"You know Adele, too?" My jaw clenched at the thought of him anywhere near the gorgeous succubus.

"Jealous?"

"No."

He lifted my hand to his lips and kissed my fingertips, sending a thrill through me. "Adele is well-known in the Los Angeles underworld, and she has given us helpful information in the past."

"I bet she didn't tell you that she and Madeline are pals, or that Madeline goes to visit her once or twice a year."

His eyes widened. "She told you that?"

It was my turn to be smug. "I told you I was close to finding Madeline."

Footsteps alerted us that we were no longer alone. "Um, what are you guys doing down there?"

I looked up at Roland, who wore a knowing smirk. "What does it look like?"

His grin grew. "Looks like you got started without the mistletoe."

"Mistletoe?" I glanced from him to Nikolas. "It's Christmas?"

"Christmas Eve," Roland said. "And we're getting ready to decorate the tree. You two coming?"

"We'll be there in a few minutes," Nikolas answered.

"Right." Roland walked away.

Nikolas rubbed my arm. "You're quiet all of a sudden."

"I can't believe I forgot Christmas." Our *first* Christmas together.

His gaze softened. "You had more important things on your mind."

"But I don't have gifts for anyone." Knowing Jordan, she had already been on a shopping spree. I knew Nate and Tristan would have presents for me as well. And Roland and Peter. "I need to –"

Nikolas moved suddenly, and I found myself pinned on my back beneath him. The intensity of his gaze made my stomach flutter wildly.

"Are you going to run away from me again?"

I swallowed hard. "No."

"Then that's all I want."

"Oh," I said breathlessly, unable to stop staring at his mouth inches away.

"There is one other thing." He closed the distance between us and his lips found mine again.

*   *   *

Jordan tossed me a sly look as she hung an ornament on the tree. She'd been wearing a Cheshire grin ever since Nikolas and I had joined everyone in the living room twenty minutes ago.

"What?" I demanded.

She leaned around the tree toward me. "You look thoroughly kissed. I don't know whether to hate you or high-five you."

Heat filled my cheeks. "You can tell that?"

Her laugh made the others look our way, and she lowered her voice. "You obviously haven't looked in a mirror. You're practically glowing." She reached over and plucked a blade of grass from my hair. "You and I are having a chat later, and you are not leaving out a single detail. That is, if he lets you out of his sight."

I peered through the branches at Nikolas, who stood by the window talking to Chris and Tristan. As if he felt my eyes on him, Nikolas looked my way, and his gaze warmed me from across the room. This was a side of him I'd never seen, and I was finding it hard to focus on anything else with him nearby. My thoughts flew back to his kisses, and I put a hand to my mouth absently. His mouth quirked as if he knew exactly what I was thinking, and I pulled my gaze from his before my face burst into flames.

Jordan threw a rope of garland at me. "Am I going to have to take a water hose to you two again?"

I made a face at her and hung my last ornament on the tree. "He's different, less intense."

"He hasn't taken his eyes off you since you came in. If that's less intense, I'd hate to see him worked up."

"I mean he's not as fierce as he usually is. He's hasn't yelled at me once for taking off."

She moved closer. "Almost losing your mate-to-be would affect anyone, even Nikolas. I'm sure he'll be back to his old charming self soon enough."

"You're probably right." I glanced surreptitiously at Nikolas again then turned toward the couches where Nate sat talking to Roland and Peter. Roland had called his mom a few days ago, and she hadn't been pleased with either of them. He'd had to promise her that he and Peter would go home after Christmas. I was happy to get to spend Christmas with them, and I tried not to think of them leaving.

"The tree looks nice," Nate said when I sat beside him.

I admired the tall Christmas tree. "It's a lot bigger than ours." The holidays had always been quiet at our place with just the two of us, and it was strange to be spending Christmas Eve with so many people. I looked around the room and my heart swelled. Most of the people I cared about were in this room, everyone except Remy, Desmund, and Greg. At least Remy and Greg were with family. It saddened me to think of Desmund spending Christmas alone, but he had volunteered to stay behind in case there was another attack on Westhorne.

"I wonder what they're all doing back home," Roland said. Christmas was big in the Knolls, and many of the families there celebrated together.

"Probably eating Nan's cookies," Peter replied longingly.

I couldn't help but feel a little homesick, too. "California is nothing like Maine; that's for sure."

Nikolas came over and sat on my other side. He reached over and took one of my hands in his as if it was something we did every day. "We'll go back there someday when this is all over."

I tried to ignore the warm tingle his touch sent up my arm. "If this is *ever* over. I guess we can assume the Master knows I'm no longer at Westhorne."

Tristan took a seat across from us. "Judging by the reports out of Los Angeles I'd say that is a safe assumption."

"How bad is it?" This was the first I'd heard any news about LA since I'd awakened from my week-long sleep.

"Over twenty attacks on humans in the last week that we know of," Tristan said grimly. "The council has dispatched three teams to the area to deal with it."

"Twenty attacks?" My stomach knotted thinking about all those poor people.

"If the vampires weren't killing in Los Angeles, they'd be killing elsewhere," Tristan said. "This is not your fault."

"I wonder how they knew we were in LA." Roland pondered. "The vampires we ran into didn't live to tell anyone about it."

"What vampires?" Nikolas asked in a deceptively calm voice as his fingers flexed slightly around mine.

Jordan, Roland, and Peter suddenly became mute, leaving me to explain. "We, um, might have run into a couple after we left Blue Nyx."

Chris had been leaning against the fireplace mantle, and he straightened to stare at me. "*You* killed the vampires in the alley? So you *were* at the club that night?"

"We saw you come in with those other warriors. Eldeorin glamoured us so we could get away." I looked at Nikolas, who was not happy. "Why weren't you with Chris that night?"

"I was there, just a little too late by the sound of it. We got word that two girls were attacked at a hotel, and I went to check it out." His brows lowered into a scowl. "What happened with the vampires?"

"We were driving back to the hotel when we came across three vampires attacking some people." I waved at Roland, Peter, and Jordan. "They killed them. I didn't even fight."

Chris rubbed his chin. "We found the vampires, but no human bodies, just a dead mox demon."

"That's because they were attacking demons, not humans."

Tristan frowned. "You rescued demons?"

"A vrell demon and his friend. They were harmless."

Nikolas exhaled slowly. "You don't endanger yourself for demons, no matter what kind they are."

"Not all demons are bad, you know," I argued. "The guy who gave me the laptop and helped me track Madeline is a vrell demon. He's actually a very nice guy."

Jordan spoke up. "We've learned that it's easier if you don't argue with her about this." I glowered at her and she added, "And I guess Kelvan is cool... for a demon."

"And the vampires?" Nikolas prodded.

Jordan dared a look at him. "They weren't that old, no match for all of us."

Nate spoke up. "I thought Sara didn't fight them."

"I didn't go near them. I shot one with a crossbow and the boys took him out."

Chris gave me a dubious look. "A crossbow?"

Roland barked a laugh. "Yeah. He started mouthing off to her and she shot him right between the legs."

"Sara has wicked aim with that thing," Jordan told Chris, who was the best archer at Westhorne. "She definitely should start training with one."

"What happened to our weapons anyway? Did we leave them at Greg's uncle's place?" I asked her.

"You honestly think I'd leave that sword behind? It would take more than a few vamps to separate us."

"What I would like to know is how vampires knew you were at that apartment in the first place," Nikolas said. "How well do you know that human who was with you?"

"Dude, don't even go there," Roland warned him.

"Greg is one of my closest friends from high school, and he would *never* do anything to hurt me." I tried to pull my hand away, but Nikolas refused to let it go.

"Greg's a solid guy," Roland said. "He used to watch over Sara like she was his sister. I can't see him betraying her."

"Especially after she saved his life," Peter added.

Nate nodded. "I always thought Greg McCoy was trouble, but he did seem to care for Sara."

Jordan pursed her lips thoughtfully. "It could have been one of those demons at Draegan's. They all knew Sara was playing Draegan for the blood contract, and one of them could have known who Greg was and where he was staying. I wouldn't put anything past that bunch."

Nate's voice wavered a little when he spoke. "It's a good thing you called Nikolas when you did. I don't want to think about what would have happened to you all if he hadn't been there."

"Promise us you won't take off like that again," Tristan said. He had hugged me so tightly when I had come in and then told me he was saving the scolding for later.

"I promise," I replied sincerely.

We were interrupted by the arrival of Heb bearing a tray of finger foods to tide us over until dinner. The dwarf set the tray on the wide glass coffee table, and Roland and Peter immediately dug in. My stomach rumbled, reminding me I hadn't eaten since that morning.

Nikolas released my hand and leaned over to pile some food on a napkin, which he placed on my lap.

"Thanks," I whispered self-consciously, feeling the others' eyes on us. I picked up a canapé and nibbled on it. It was smoked salmon on a little round of toast, and it was delicious. My stomach growled again, wanting me to eat faster, and I plopped the whole canapé in my mouth.

"So what happens now?" Roland asked between bites of food. "Are you all going home?"

Tristan shook his head. "Sara has to stay here to train with the faeries. Jordan and I will return to Westhorne after Christmas. Nate too, unless he wants to stay here."

Jordan didn't try to hide her dismay. "I thought I could stay here with Sara."

"Sara will be busy training, and Nikolas is staying with her. You need to continue your own training."

"But I can train here with Sara," Jordan insisted.

I looked from Tristan to Nikolas. "I have to do faerie training *and* Mohiri training?"

"We'll pick it up where we left off," Nikolas said with a gleam in his eyes.

Chris chuckled and winked at me. "I smell payback."

"You want me to stay, right?" Jordan asked me. "We can train together."

"Yes." I couldn't imagine her not being here after all we'd been through together.

Tristan leaned forward to pick up a canapé. "We'll see. I'm not sure of the wisdom in keeping you two girls together. You seem to have a remarkable talent for attracting trouble."

"At least no one could ever accuse us of being dull," Jordan quipped. "Besides, Nikolas will be here. How much trouble could we get into?"

Everyone but Jordan and I burst out laughing. Chris smirked at Tristan. "You might want to think about sending a unit here for backup."

Tristan nodded. "You may be right."

I folded my arms. "Everyone's a comedian."

* * *

It was almost midnight when Nikolas walked me to my room. We stopped at my door and I was loath to say good night to him, but too shy to ask him not to go. The thought of being alone with him made my stomach flutter, especially after the way he'd kissed me on the lawn, but I didn't think I was ready to take it beyond that. Sometimes it felt like I'd known him forever, and other times I felt like I didn't know that much about him. I knew Nikolas the warrior, but how much did I know about Nikolas the man? From the very beginning, there had been nothing normal about our relationship, and part of me wished we could do something normal like go on a real date and get to know each other like regular people did.

I turned to face him, but before I could speak, he tugged me to him and enveloped me in his warm embrace. I rested my forehead against his chest, savoring his closeness. As tired as I was, I could have stood there like that all night.

"It's late. You should get some sleep," he murmured against my hair.

"Stay." The plea came out before I could stop it and heat flooded my face. "I don't mean..."

He lifted my chin and dropped a light kiss on my lips. "I know." Opening the door, he ushered me into my room. The soft click of the door behind him did funny things to my stomach, and I faced him uncertainly.

His soft chuckle took me by surprise. "Get ready for bed. I'll just stay until you fall asleep."

I released the breath I was holding, and went to pull a T-shirt and a pair of shorts from the dresser. Excusing myself, I closed myself in the bathroom to change. When I came out, I didn't see Nikolas at first and I thought he'd left. A sound made me turn, and I found him standing by the balcony door.

His eyes moved over me and he raised an eyebrow. "I wondered what happened to that T-shirt."

I fingered the hem of the shirt I'd stolen from him and shrugged to hide my blush. "It's really comfortable."

He walked toward me, and I retreated until the backs of my thighs hit the bed. Reaching around me, he lifted the covers. "In you go."

I climbed into bed, and he pulled the covers over me. Then he kicked off his shoes and stretched out on top of the comforter. His arm lifted, and I scooted over to lay my head on his shoulder. He wrapped his arm around me and I sighed, happier than I'd been in weeks.

"Nikolas?" I said after a few minutes of comfortable silence.

"Hmm?"

"Why haven't you yelled at me for leaving Westhorne?"

The hand that was toying with my hair stopped. "Do you want me to yell at you?"

"No, but you're taking this too well." Jordan's words came back to me. "Are you being nice because I was sick?"

His chest rumbled. "Yes, but don't worry. I'm sure you'll give me more reasons to yell soon enough."

I smiled because he was probably right.

After another minute of silence I felt him sigh. "I was furious when I found out you'd left, and all I could think about was what could happen to you out there. I always want to keep you safe, but after the attack I couldn't think of anything but getting you away from there. I'm sorry I made you feel like you had no other choice but to leave. I want you to be able to come to me about anything."

"I'm sorry I left the way I did. I was upset about the attack, and all I wanted to do was fight back." I breathed deeply. "It hurt when you and Tristan said you were taking me away to hide, especially after people were hurt and killed because of me."

"You're not responsible for what happened that night."

"I know, but it's impossible not to feel guilty when some of my friends were killed by vampires who were after me. And I knew it wasn't going to stop and they'd keep coming. Sooner or later, someone I love will die and I can't live with that. I had to do something to try to end this. I should have told you what I knew about Madeline instead of going after her without you. I kept telling myself I could find her and that she'd run if she saw the Mohiri. But the truth is I needed to be the one to find her. I needed to feel like I was in control of my life again."

He was quiet for a moment. "You've spent most of your life taking care of yourself, and I've spent mine protecting others. It's not easy for either of us to go against our nature. I didn't realize how much I was pushing you to change yours until you left."

"And now?"

Another sigh. "I won't lie to you. I'm not going to try to take you away, but I can't stand to see you in danger either. You're a fighter, but I'm an experienced warrior, and I'm going to do what I have to do to keep you safe."

"I understand why you feel so protective, but you have to see that I'm not helpless."

"I never thought you were helpless. I just don't think you're ready to face what's out there."

My chest squeezed as I realized the futility of our conversation. I didn't want to argue with him on our first day together since my illness, so I didn't say anything.

I didn't realize I was pulling away from him until his arm tightened around me. "Let's not fight," he implored softly.

My body relaxed against him again, and he kissed the top of my head. "You should go to sleep. I don't want Nate and Tristan shooting me dirty looks tomorrow when you can't stay awake at Christmas dinner."

A yawn came upon me. "You'll stay until I fall asleep?"

"I'll stay until I hear snoring."

"I don't snore."

"Like a motorboat."

I poked him in the ribs with my finger. "I do *not* snore!"

He laughed and captured my hand, holding it against him. "Okay it's more like a kitten purring. Did I ever tell you how much I like kittens?"

I had no reply for that. I fell asleep with a smile on my face.

CHAPTER 11

"ARE YOU SURE you don't want to fly home? It'll take you four or five days to drive all the way across the country."

Roland laughed and twirled the car keys in his hand. "Yeah, and that's an extra four or five days before we have to face Uncle Max."

Peter paled at the mention of his dad. "Maybe we should take our time. We could tell him the car broke down."

"Hey, there's nothing wrong with my car." Jordan walked over and patted the hood of the Ford Escort she had bought in Butler Falls. She smirked at Roland. "But you should probably put some blankets on the seats to protect them from dog hair."

He made a face at her but didn't offer a retort, most likely because he was still feeling a heap of goodwill toward her. Yesterday, she had shocked him when she'd signed the car over to him, saying it had served its purpose and he might as well take it off her hands. I had a feeling that he'd be trading it for that Mustang he wanted as soon as he got home.

I smiled at their exchange, but my heart constricted painfully. Roland and Peter had been with me through so much, and I didn't know how to do this without them. But they'd already lost weeks of school, and they had to get home if they had any hope of catching up and graduating this year. Plus, Roland had promised his mom they would head home the day after New Year's, which was today.

Roland looked at me. "I guess we should get on the road."

I pressed my lips together and nodded. I managed to hold back the tears until he walked over and pulled me into a tight hug.

"Don't do that or we'll never leave," he ordered hoarsely. "And then you'll have to explain to my mom and Uncle Max why we're not coming home."

"Sorry." I let go of him and wiped my eyes. "You'll call me every day until you get home, right? Do you have the new phone we got you?"

He rolled his eyes. "Yes, Mom."

I pulled a thick bundle of cash from my pocket and placed it in his hand. His blue eyes widened. "Whoa, what's this?"

"You need money for the trip home."

He tried to hand it back to me. "This is your money from the diamonds."

"I don't need it." He continued to shake his head, and I gave him a watery smile. "It'll make me feel better if I know you're staying in decent hotels instead of sleeping in the car. You and Peter can split the rest when you get home."

Peter came over and snatched the money from Roland. "I need a car too, buddy." He grinned as he stuffed the money in his coat pocket and turned to hug me. "You gonna stay out of trouble?"

"Yes," Nikolas answered for me as he and Chris came out of the house. He walked over to stand beside me. "Watch yourselves out there and have a good trip home."

"Thanks, we will." Roland held out his hand and Nikolas shook it. He gave me another quick hug before he and Peter headed to the car. A lump formed in my throat as they climbed in and Roland started the car. He rolled down his window and they yelled, "See ya." Then with a wave they pulled away.

I watched until the white car disappeared around a bend in the long driveway. When I turned toward the house, Nikolas put a hand on my arm. "You okay?"

"Yes," I lied. "Are you going out?"

"Chris and I are headed next door for a few hours to help them set up. I'll be back before dinner." The increased vampire activity in California had prompted the Mohiri to set up a temporary command center in the large house they had rented next door. Two units were arriving today with a truckload of equipment and supplies.

The thought of how quiet this place would be without Roland and Peter almost made me ask Nikolas if I could help him. I kept quiet because I didn't want to be in his way.

After Nikolas and Chris left, Jordan and I went into the huge house that suddenly felt very empty. I turned to the stairs, intending to mope in my room for the rest of the afternoon.

Jordan caught my arm and swung me around. "Oh no, you don't. You and I finally have this place to ourselves, and you are not hiding out in your room. Heb is making us some yummy snacks, and we are going to watch movies and stuff our faces."

I let her drag me to the home theater room. "I think I'm getting sick of movies."

"You're not sick of these. I picked them out just for you." She started the first movie and I turned my head to stare at her.

"*Jane Eyre?*"

She shrugged and settled back in her seat. "You love that book and I wanted to know what the big deal was. I also got *Pride and Prejudice* and *Emma* since you seem to like that stuff." She watched the opening credits. "I don't suppose there is any action in this?"

I didn't respond at first until she gave me a questioning look. "Thanks, Jordan."

She scrunched her nose. "Ah shit, don't get all weepy on me. I thought you were past that faerie puberty thing."

Her expression pulled a laugh from me. "Not quite. Aine says the worst of it is over, but I might have mood swings for a few more weeks."

"Great," she muttered.

We watched the first movie and were halfway through the second before Jordan began to fidget. I had to give her credit for making it that far since romantic period movies weren't her thing. We ended up stopping the movie and talking about where Roland and Peter were now and wondering how the new command center was coming along. Eventually the conversation came around to Nikolas and me.

"So," she began with a determined gleam in her eyes. "You never told me what happened Christmas Eve night. We're alone now and I need details."

"That's because there is nothing to tell. We talked and fell asleep."

She nodded slowly. "In your bed. *Right.* That's why Nate and Tristan looked ready to skewer him with the turkey fork at dinner."

I blushed, thinking about waking up sprawled across Nikolas on Christmas morning. He had planned to leave after I'd fallen asleep, but he'd dozed off, too, and I'd spent the entire night in his arms. Best Christmas present *ever.*

It would have been perfect if Nate hadn't come looking for me when neither of us showed up for breakfast. I'd thought it was awkward the morning Tristan had found me in Nikolas's apartment, but that was nothing compared to Nate catching us lying in bed together. The fact that we were both clothed and Nikolas was on top of the covers did nothing to placate Nate, and it had taken a whole day for him to stop glaring at Nikolas.

Jordan propped her feet up on the back of the seat in front of her. "You know, you must be the only female on the planet who would share a room – correction, a *bed* – with Nikolas Danshov and just sleep. Nuns would forget their vows if that male looked at them the way he looks at you."

"We're taking it slow," was all I could say. Since Christmas Eve Nikolas hadn't come into my room. He would walk me to my door and say good night with a tender kiss. In a way it felt like he was courting me. I would be lying if I said I didn't wish he would ask to stay again. The more time I spent with him, the more I wanted.

She let out a pained groan. "How the hell can I live vicariously through you if you're not getting any action?"

"You want action? I start my Fae training tomorrow. That should be a blast."

She grinned. "No thanks. While you're playing in the water, I'll be sparring with your warrior."

Coming from anyone else, that statement might have stirred some jealousy in me. I fixed her with a mock scowl. "Just as long as you remember he's *my* warrior."

*   *   *

A wall of cold water dropped down onto my head, and my arms flailed as the weight of the water knocked me off balance. I disappeared beneath the surface of the lake and came up sputtering and shivering.

"Why can't I do this?" I wailed, pushing my dripping hair out of my face.

"You are not concentrating," Aine called, warm and dry, from the shore.

I crossed my arms over my chest. "No matter what I do it gets away from me. It doesn't feel the same anymore."

Aine smiled patiently. "It is still your power, just more potent. You will soon get accustomed to it. "

"Tell that to the gazebo." The two of us looked at the ruins of the pretty little structure that had stood at the edge of the small lake at the back of the estate, until two days ago when a thirty-foot waterspout had turned it to kindling. Thankfully, no one had been close enough to get hurt.

Before the lake, we'd practiced in the pool. Chris had been sitting on one end, watching us, when I'd attempted to change the temperature of the water by a few degrees. He'd managed to get his legs out of the water right before it turned to solid ice. I wasn't so lucky and it took me ten very cold minutes to melt enough ice around me so I could escape. I was still trying to live that one down.

Then there was yesterday's debacle. Standing outside in the rain, I'd tried to use the magic in the water to form a shield over me. It might have been a nifty trick if I hadn't created a mini lightning storm on the back lawn. It took Aine and me working together for a full thirty minutes to make it dissipate. Aine had attempted to cheer me up by informing me that most water elementals couldn't even create a storm until they were fully matured, which for me would be in another five years or so.

"Perhaps we should start with something easier," Aine suggested softly. She walked to the water's edge. "Do you remember the first time you used your magic to call to the fishes in the valley lake?"

Despite my cold, wet state, I smiled at the memory of the trout nibbling at my feet that day. That whole afternoon held nothing but happy memories for me.

"Good. Now release a small amount of your magic to call to the fish in this lake."

I opened my power and immediately a golden cloud began to form around me in the waist-deep water. Something tickled my toes and I peered down at the small school of carp swimming around my legs. On the surface of the water, a pair of turtles moved slowly toward me. Watching my magic finally behave the way it was supposed to gave me a much needed boost of confidence. Aine was right; I'd just needed to start small and get a feel for it again.

"Wonderful!" Aine called. "Now pull the magic back to you."

I summoned my power to pull it back inside me. But instead of moving toward me, the cloud continued to grow and spread out into the lake. "Just great," I muttered as I struggled to rein it in.

"Don't fight it. Call to it."

"What do you think I'm doing?" I said through clenched teeth. "It doesn't seem to want to listen."

"Your magic is a part of you, Sara, and you control it as you would your arm or leg. You do not fight to raise your hand; you simply do it."

I took a deep breath and made myself relax and stop fighting the magic. What was the worst that could happen anyway? As long as I didn't try to use the magic, it didn't matter if it filled the lake. Eventually, the water would absorb the magic and all would be normal again.

Right. Because that was always how things worked for me.

I don't know who was more shocked when a long brownish green... thing erupted from the center of the lake. A garbling roar rent the air before the creature dove beneath the surface again. Seconds later, it reappeared, skimming across the lake toward me. My mouth fell open at the sight of the ten-foot creature that had a dragon's head, legs, and wings and the long thick body of a snake.

I scrambled for the shore, struggling to run through the waist-deep water. Behind me the dragon snake thing roared again, but I didn't stop to look back. Whatever it was, it looked and sounded pretty pissed off, and I wasn't about to stay in the water with it.

Three feet from the shore, I slipped on a rock and landed on my back in the water. Frantically, I scuttled backward as the creature closed in on me.

"Sara!" Nikolas pulled me from the water. He threw me behind him and faced the creature with his sword raised.

The creature leapt at us and Nikolas's blade scored its underside as it sailed over our heads. It roared in pain and tried to fly away from us. It had been agile over the water, but it didn't fly as well over land, and it wobbled as its small wings fought to keep it airborne.

"Don't hurt it, please," Aine cried as Nikolas started toward the struggling creature. "It is a *drakon,* a water dragon, and they are almost extinct. It means no harm."

"I know what it is." Nikolas looked angrier than the drakon. "It could have killed Sara if I hadn't gotten to her first."

"It is merely distressed because it was awakened from its hibernation. Sara is undine. She never has to fear any creature that lives in the water."

"It attacked her," Nikolas countered stiffly.

Aine's red curls bobbed when she shook her head. "No. It attacked *you* because it thought you were hurting her."

I looked at the drakon that was flying dangerously close to the ground now. It certainly didn't look like much of a threat to anyone. If anything, it looked ready to collapse. I saw dark red blood dripping from the cut in its long belly.

"We need to get it back to the water," I told them. I made a move toward the *drakon,* but Nikolas caught my hand.

"Nikolas, come with me if you're worried, but we can't let the poor thing die."

"Poor thing?" He sighed and released my hand. "I can't wait to see what Tristan thinks about your newest pet."

"I didn't say I was keeping it," I muttered as the three of us approached the tiring drakon. Really, what the heck would I do with a water dragon, of all things? Although, the lake at Westhorne was much nicer than this puny one, so maybe he would be happier there. I wondered if water dragons and kelpies got along well together.

Nikolas laughed. "You're already trying to figure out how to get that thing back to Idaho, aren't you?"

"No," I retorted halfheartedly.

Aine raised a hand and a breeze came up, lifting the drakon three feet off the ground. It was barely moving through the air now and we had no trouble catching it. Nikolas reached out to turn its body toward the lake, and the drakon twisted and snapped its fanged jaws at him.

"Stop that," I scolded, and it swung its head in my direction, looking so much like a normal dragon that I expected flames to sprout from its mouth. Instead, it made a loud mewling sound and stared at me with large unblinking eyes.

I patted its scaly side and it didn't try to eat me, so I figured I was safe. I moved in front of it and began walking backward toward the lake. "Come on, fellow. We'll get you back home."

The drakon switched direction and followed me, assisted by Aine's breeze. Nikolas walked several feet out to my right, ready to come to my rescue in case Aine was wrong about the drakon not attacking me.

When I reached the water's edge I took one step into the water, and the drakon followed me in. Aine released it and it immediately dove into the lake, rolling on the muddy bottom and making the water too murky to see it. A minute later, it reappeared, floating on the top of the water, half submerged like an alligator.

I crouched in the water. "I'm sorry I woke you up, and that the mean warrior cut you." Behind me Nikolas snorted, and I smiled.

The drakon blinked at me but did not move.

"You can go back to sleep now. I'll try not to bother you again," I told him.

He answered by rolling over in the water and showing me his pale belly that sported a two-foot long gash created by Nikolas's sword. Blood still seeped from the wound that looked painful and deep.

I felt my power stirring at the sight of the injury, but I was afraid to attempt to heal the drakon. What if I used too much and hurt him instead?

"What's wrong, Sister?" Aine asked softly and I told her my fears. She came over to lay a hand on my shoulder. "You will not harm him."

"How can you be sure?"

"It is not in you to harm an innocent creature."

I looked at the drakon again. "Not intentionally, but I could hurt him by accident."

"Aine is right," Nikolas said, prompting me to face him. His gray eyes held mine. "Remember the day I made you use your power on me?"

How could I forget? For a long agonizing moment, I thought I'd killed him. I shivered at the memory of my power throwing him across the arena.

"Your power could have hurt me that day, but you wouldn't let it. Your instincts kicked in because you didn't want to hurt me, just like you don't want to hurt this creature."

My chest warmed at the unwavering faith I saw in his eyes, and I managed a small smile before I turned back to the drakon. It had drifted closer to me, and I reached for it tentatively. The scales covering its underside were softer than the ones on its back, and I was surprised to feel how warm it was. I ran my hand along its belly, and it wriggled closer to me until it was pressed against my side. I moved my hand closer to the wound, and my power pushed against the walls holding it back, trying to go to the injured creature. Nikolas and Aine had faith in me, but did I trust myself enough to release the power?

A shudder went through the *drakon* before a wave of pain assailed me. I couldn't let it suffer. *Please, don't let me hurt it.*

"Nikolas, I need you to leave," I said without looking at him. "I know you think I can do this, but I can't... not with you here. I won't risk it after what happened when I woke up."

"Okay. I'll see you back at the house."

It surprised me when he didn't argue. A month ago, he would have refused to leave me.

I waited until I could no longer sense him before I opened my power to let a trickle escape. As soon as I called on it, it tried to surge forward, and I pushed it back again. Before the *liannan*, my power had flowed through me like a warm, gentle current. Now it was hot and forceful like a river of lava. It didn't really burn me, but sometimes it felt like it wanted to consume me – or the part of me that was not Fae.

There was a time when I would have been happy to get rid of the "beast" in my head, but I would do anything to protect my Mori now. When I'd first awakened from my long sleep, my Mori had been huddled, terrified, in the back of my mind. Even unconscious, my body had instinctively erected a wall around the demon to keep it safe from my out-of-control power. Still, it had taken me days to soothe my Mori and convince it I would never let it be harmed.

I fortified the protections around my Mori, and then I reached for my power again. This time I anticipated my power's behavior, and I grasped it firmly as soon as I opened the gate. Instead of letting the power flow freely as I used to, I guided it through my body, down my arms, and into my hands. It tried to leap from me to the wound beneath my hands, but I maintained my hold on it. It took me a minute of deep breathing to gather my courage before I let my power trickle into the drakon.

As soon as I entered the creature's body, it was like the last few weeks had never happened. No longer fighting my control, my power immediately went to work knitting together the severed tissue. The drakon shuddered beneath my hands as the healing fire closed up its wound and eased its pain. I closed my eyes as relief swept through me. *I did it!*

I ran my hand along the drakon's belly where the cut had been. "I think you and I are both going to be okay," I crooned softly as I pulled the power back into me. It didn't come as easily as it should have, but I was too happy about my success to care. I finally had a feel for this new power and a better understanding of how to handle it. I remembered being six years old and having to learn how to use my strange new power. It was like that all over again, only this time I wasn't doing it alone.

"Okay, buddy, you are as good as new."

I stepped back and the drakon rolled until he was right side up. He stared at me for a few seconds, and then he leaned in and licked my face with a long forked tongue. Before I could react, he spun around with amazing speed and headed toward the center of the lake. He leapt into the air and dove into the water without making a splash.

I wiped my face with a wet sleeve. "Ugh, dragon spit."

"You did it, Sister. You healed him."

My face split in a wide smile as I trudged out of the lake. Aine rushed over to hug me despite my wet clothes, and we laughed together.

I pulled away. "I can't believe it. After all the times I lost control of my power this week, I think I finally get it."

She nodded happily. "I don't know why I did not see this sooner. Healing is second nature for you because you have been doing it since you were a young child. Water magic is still quite new to you, which explains why you have been struggling with it. We should have started with what you knew best."

"How can we do that? We don't exactly have any injured animals around here."

"No, but we can go find some that need your help."

Go out and help sick creatures? "Can we go now?"

Aine laughed and shook her head. "I think you've done enough for today. Plus, you are starting your other training this afternoon."

I grimaced at the reminder that I was resuming my Mohiri training today. It wasn't that I didn't want to work with Nikolas. Who was I kidding? He was going to push me until I collapsed or begged for mercy – maybe both. Jordan had trained with him yesterday, and she'd nodded off during dinner last night. That did not bode well for me.

"Tomorrow when I return, we will go find something you can heal," Aine promised. Even though the estate was surrounded by faerie protections, Aine did not like to stay here long. After our training she always returned to Faerie until our next session. Eldeorin, on the other hand, loved the human world. Now that I no longer needed his constant presence, he liked to go off on his "pleasure excursions" as he put them. I didn't ask and I hoped he never felt the need to share them with me.

"Okay," I conceded. "I'll see you tomorrow."

She hugged me goodbye and did her disappearing thing. I'd asked her yesterday if I would ever be able to do that and she'd said only time would tell.

Nikolas was waiting for me when I walked out of the woods. "I told you that you could do it."

"You were supposed to leave," I accused mildly.

He smiled as he fell into step beside me. "I did leave. I know it worked because you have that look."

"What look?"

"The one I like seeing on your face. You look happy."

"I'll be even happier if you tell me I don't have to train this afternoon," I suggested hopefully as we neared the house.

He chuckled and opened the door for me. "Nice try. Get cleaned up, and I'll see you after lunch. Oh, and you might want to eat light."

I groaned and tried to ignore the laughter that followed me as I climbed the stairs to my room. I should probably skip lunch altogether and take a nap instead. Something told me I was going to need it.

After a very light lunch, I joined Nikolas in the gym they had set up on the first floor of the huge house. When I walked in, I saw it was laid out like the training rooms at Westhorne. I bit back a groan when I saw the bag in the corner, and I think my muscles actually ached at the memory of the workouts Nikolas had put me through back then.

Nikolas was waiting for me, and he smiled as if he was remembering, too. He immediately got down to business and gave me some stretching exercises to do. Once I had warmed up, he waved me over to the center of the room.

"The first thing we're going to do is see what you remember from our training." He held up his hands. "Show me a straight punch."

I positioned my body like he'd taught me and struck his palm with my right fist. Then I shifted slightly and did a strike with my left one.

"Palm heel strike," he ordered and I executed it as I'd been taught. I was surprised at how easily it came back to me after all these weeks. The endless drills he'd put me through had worked.

"Good," he said after I'd done a number of strikes. "Now go to the bag and show me the kicks I taught you."

I demonstrated the front kick, back kick, and round kick several times. Then he began calling out strikes and kicks, forcing me to change positions quickly to perform each one. A fine sheen of sweat covered my body by the time we stopped twenty minutes later.

"Very good. You remembered everything."

"I had a good teacher," I said, absurdly happy that he was pleased.

His trainer expression slipped and a small smile appeared. "All right, I think you are ready to learn a new strike. This one is called an elbow strike." He proceeded to demonstrate it for me then had me try it. We worked on it for ten minutes before he switched to a vertical front kick. Once I had that technique down, he made me alternate between the two. I was panting by the time he was satisfied I had them down.

Dread filled me when he said we were done with the bag, because I knew what came next. This was when he would work me with the weights and skipping rope until I could barely stand. He called it conditioning. I called it torture.

He surprised me by heading for the door instead of the weights.

"We're done?"

"No, we're going to add something new to your training." He opened the door and waved me through it.

I couldn't imagine what it could be, but if it got me out of weight training, I was all for it.

We went outdoors and around the side of the house where three wooden targets had been set up. On the grass near them was an assortment of knives, crossbows, and swords. I chewed my lip nervously at the sight of the swords, hoping he wasn't going to ask me to use one. The deadliest weapon I'd held was a knife, and I didn't think I was ready for anything bigger than that.

"What would you like to start with?" Nikolas asked, surprising me again.

I didn't need to think about it; I immediately went for one of the crossbows. It was a lot bigger and heavier than the one I'd used in Los Angeles, and it felt awkward in my hands. "How do you use this thing?"

Nikolas took it and explained all the parts to me. "This is a recurve bow," he said as he put it to the ground and cocked it. "It's a little harder to load, but it has more power than a compound bow. It's a great weapon once you get a feel for it."

"I've never seen you use a bow," I said as he brought the bow up and faced the first target.

"I prefer a sword." He released the bolt and it whistled through the air to sink into the center of the target. "But I'm proficient with most weapons."

"Of course you are," I said dryly, earning a smile from him.

"Want to give it a go?"

"Sure, as soon as I grow enough muscles to cock it."

He chuckled and showed me how to put my foot in the stirrup and where to place my hands on the string. I pulled the string back and settled it in the locking mechanism.

"Okay, what now?"

"Now, you aim." Stepping behind me, he turned me to face the target. Then he showed me how to position the bow and aim. His warm breath on the back of my neck was more than a little distracting, and I had trouble paying attention to his instructions. That was probably why my bolt missed the target by a good three feet.

He picked up another bolt and handed it to me. "It'll take a while to get used to."

"They make it look so easy in the movies." I grunted as I cocked the bow again. Then I lifted it and aimed at the target. It was a lot easier to concentrate without Nikolas standing so close, and I let out a slow breath as I peered through the scope and lined up the target. I knew my aim was good as soon as the bolt left the bow, and I whooped when it embedded itself in the target next to Nikolas's.

Someone whistled, and I looked around as Chris approached us. He went to the target and examined the two bolts in the center. "Very nice, Sara. Now let's see you do that again."

I loaded another bolt and took aim. Chris put a good distance between himself and the target, but it wasn't necessary. My bolt hit so close to the center that it left a long gouge in the one Nikolas had put there. I shot two more and they lined up beside the others.

"I've never seen anything like it," Chris exclaimed when Nikolas and I walked over to examine the target. The three of us stared at the five bolts embedded in the center. They were so close it was difficult to pull them out.

"I told you she was a natural." Jordan jogged over to join us. "Freaky, isn't it? It must be some faerie thing."

I frowned. "Hey, maybe I'm just good at something."

Chris let out a laugh. "Sara, I'm not that good, and I've been doing this for a long time."

"Right." I rolled my eyes at him. "I saw you practicing at Westhorne, and no one is as good as you with a bow."

Nikolas studied the target. "There is another way to test your aim. Let's try you on the knives."

"Knives?" That didn't sound as safe as the crossbow.

"Throwing knives." He went to the pile of weapons and picked up a leather harness containing six silver knives like the ones I'd seen him use before. "These are different from the dagger I gave you. They are a little smaller and heavier, and balanced in the center." He laid one of the knives across his forefinger to show me. Then his hand blurred as he grasped the knife and sent it flying into the center of the second target.

Chris took one of the knives and copied Nikolas, nailing the third target. I hadn't even seen him aim. Not to be outdone, Jordan held out her hand and Nikolas laid a knife in it. Her knife hit just inside the center ring of the second target.

"Show-offs." I felt inadequate next to the three of them. Sure I was a good shot with the bow, but knives were a whole different matter.

Nikolas handed me a knife and I took it reluctantly. I must have made a face because he smiled. "It's actually fun when you get the hang of it."

I hefted the knife, trying to get a feel for it. Unlike my dagger, this knife was entirely silver to make it difficult for a vampire to pull it out. I couldn't help but remember the first time I'd seen knives like this. Nikolas had thrown them at Eli to stop him from taking me from the alley in Portland.

Chris came to stand beside me. "Here, watch me." He took a knife and slowly demonstrated how to position my body and where to hold the knife. He drew his arm back then swung it forward, more slowly this time, sending the knife into the target with a soft *thunk*. "Now you give it a go."

I mimicked his movements, but the knife felt awkward in my hand, and I was sure I was going to slice my fingers off. Chris repositioned my hand on the knife, then stepped back and told me to throw. I did and the knife spun through the air and hit the ground a good five feet from the target.

"Not bad for your first throw," Chris said as he went to collect my knife and those in the targets.

I snorted a laugh. "Not bad? I totally sucked."

"You still have all your fingers and none of us are bleeding, so I'd call it a good start." He walked back to me and held out one of the knives. "Want to go again?"

"If I say no, will you let me stop?"

He flashed his dimples. "We could always try the swords."

"No thanks." I took the knife and got into position again.

"Here, like this." Jordan moved to stand beside me. Chris handed her a knife and she showed me how to hold it, explaining how it should feel in my grip. Then she slowly drew her arm back and swung it forward without releasing the knife so I could see the angle of her arm and the point at which she would release the weapon. She did that several times until I thought I understood the basic principles of knife throwing. Then she released the knife and it hit a few inches from the center.

"Do you need me to show you again?"

"No, I think I got it." I lined up the target and threw my knife. It nicked the bottom of the target before it stuck into the ground.

"Much better." Chris passed me another knife. This one actually stuck into the bottom of the target. So did the next four.

"How many do I have to throw?" I asked when Jordan went to collect the knives.

"We'll stop when you can hit the second ring from the center," Nikolas said.

Chris laughed. "We might be here a while."

I punched Chris's arm. "You're family. Aren't you supposed to be encouraging me or something?"

He snickered and jumped back out of my reach.

He was right, it did take a while. I threw dozens of times, and my arm was aching and my fingers hurt by the time I finally landed a knife in the elusive second ring. It wasn't by chance either. It might have taken me a while to get a feel for the knives, but once I did, my aim improved. My next three knives hit the same ring. The fourth one nailed the center one. After that, every knife I threw hit home.

"Damn, you are lethal with those things," Jordan exclaimed. "If you weren't my BFF, I'd be totally jealous right now." She cocked her head to one side and studied my target. "Who am I kidding? I am *so* jealous."

Chris smiled broadly. "Cousin, if you are half as good with a sword, you are going to make one hell of a warrior."

I flushed from their praise. "Let's not get carried away."

Nikolas hadn't said anything, and I was nervous to look at him and see his expression. It surprised me how much I suddenly wanted his approval.

"Great work, Sara."

The sincerity in his voice sent warmth through me. I turned to face him and the admiration in his eyes made my stomach do a little flip. If someone had told me a month ago that I'd react this way to a man's approval, I would have laughed at them. But Nikolas wasn't just any man. He was a fierce warrior and a strict trainer, and he did not throw his praise around lightly.

"Thanks."

"We'll add weapons to your daily training routine."

I dared to hope. "Does that mean I don't have to use the skipping rope anymore?"

"Nice try. We'll start working out after this."

The three of them laughed. I thought Jordan, at least, should've had compassion for me after her workout with Nikolas yesterday.

I barely made it through dinner that night without falling out of my chair. Nikolas had made up for the lost weeks and had put me through a grueling workout. I was pretty sure Chris had been right and a little payback was involved. After dinner, Jordan wanted to watch a movie, but I declined and dragged my aching body to bed. What I wouldn't have given for thirty minutes in one of the healing baths they had at Westhorne. I was out as soon as my head touched the pillow.

CHAPTER 12

OVER THE NEXT two weeks, my life became an endless cycle of training and more training. In the mornings, I worked with Aine, who made good on her promise to find some sick or injured creatures that needed my help. I healed a lame mustang in Wyoming, a blind terrier in Florida, and a sickly werecougar cub in Oregon. It amazed me how we could pop away from the estate and arrive in some place a thousand miles away. I loved being able to heal things again, especially since it no longer drained my power.

As well as the healings went, I still could not control my power when I used it for anything else. I could feel it pushing against my walls like flood water against a dam, and the pressure inside me built a little more every time I failed to release it. Aine was a patient teacher, working endlessly with me, but my frustration grew with each day that passed.

I trained with Nikolas in the afternoons, and I was pretty sure he was trying to keep me so exhausted I wouldn't think about running away again. Each day he taught me a new move and made me work on it until he was satisfied it was perfect. Then we'd spend an hour on weapons training. Jordan suggested I try a sword, but after ten minutes with one, Nikolas declared I was not ready for that weapon. He focused on teaching me how to fight with a dagger instead.

After weapons came the dreaded conditioning. I thought it would get easier as the days passed, but as soon as I got used to something, Nikolas increased the intensity of the exercise or added a new one. In trainer mode, he was absolutely relentless. Every time I lagged, he pushed me to work harder, always reminding me that my enemies would not give me a break. Some days I wasn't sure if he was trying to make me into a warrior or trying to show me that I wasn't cut out to be one.

When he wasn't training me or Jordan, Nikolas spent most of his time at the new command center they'd set up next door, which I hadn't seen yet. Chris was gone so much he started sleeping over there. Left to our own devices, Jordan and I soon discovered living on an estate wasn't all it was cracked up to be. There were only so many movies you could watch, and even books lost their appeal after a while. Jordan amused herself with video games and online shopping, but those held no interest for me. I talked to Roland and Greg every other day and caught up with David, who had been worried when I stayed out of touch for so long. Madeline had completely disappeared from sight, but David and Kelvan were still looking for her.

Boredom and weariness drove me to bed early on the nights Nikolas worked. I'd toss and turn for hours before I could finally fall asleep, and then I'd wake up bleary-eyed and tired.

By the end of the second week, I was so irritable and frustrated I did the unthinkable and snapped at Aine in our training. She looked shocked and a little hurt, and I felt like the most horrible person alive for yelling at someone so sweet and patient. Eldeorin chose that moment to show up and ask how things were going. My response was to burst into tears, which mortified me and made the two of them start fussing over me. Their kindness made me feel even worse. I blurted an apology to Aine and ran off.

If Nikolas noticed how quiet I was during our training that afternoon, he didn't mention it. I put everything into the workout, just wanting to be done so I could hide away in my room and not talk to anyone for the rest of the day.

At six o'clock that evening, a knock at my door pulled me from my cocoon of blankets. Not caring about my bed hair, I answered the door and found Nikolas with his leather jacket in his hand, wearing a fitted V-neck sweater and a pair of low rise jeans that drew my eyes to his hard stomach. I swallowed, forgetting why I was hiding from him and everyone else.

He made a sound and I blushed as I lifted my gaze to meet his amused one. The twitch of his lips told me he knew exactly where my eyes had been.

"Grab a warm coat. We're going out."

I didn't hide my surprise. "We are?"

"If you'd rather stay —"

"No!" A husky chuckle followed me as I grabbed some clothes and closed myself in the bathroom. He could laugh at me all he wanted if it meant I could spend a few hours with him outside of this estate. I ran a brush through my tangled hair and quickly brushed my teeth. In minutes, I was back at the door, tugging on my coat.

"Where are we going?" I asked as we descended the stairs.

"I thought you might like to go out to dinner for a change." He opened the door, and my eyes lit on the shiny black Ducati sitting in the driveway.

I'd expected Jordan to join us, but three of us weren't going to fit on the motorcycle. It hit me that it was just going to be the two of us. It wasn't like I'd never been alone with Nikolas, but this would be our first date. I suddenly felt shy, which was ridiculous when you considered that he'd already slept in my bed.

"That sounds nice," I managed to say.

He lifted a black helmet from the seat and fitted it over my head. My breath caught when his warm fingers brushed against my throat, and I found myself staring at his full lips. It wasn't until he tapped on the visor and lifted it that I realized he was talking to me. My ears burned when he had to explain again how to use the built-in mic. *Gah! Get it together, Sara.*

Smiling, he slipped on his own helmet and got on the motorcycle, patting the seat behind him. I climbed on and wrapped my arms around his waist, my pulse leaping as I pressed my body against his and wrapped my arms around his waist.

He started the bike, and before I knew it, we were passing through the gates. I almost let out a whoop as we rode away from the estate.

It didn't take long to see why Nikolas had told me to wear a warm coat. California might be warmer than Maine or Idaho, but that didn't matter when you were on a motorcycle. I was grateful that he shielded me from the brunt of the wind, but that didn't help my hands. I flexed my fingers, trying to warm them.

His voice filled my helmet. "You okay?"

"Yes, but I should have brought gloves with me."

Nikolas took his left hand from the handlebar and laid it over mine. He wasn't wearing gloves either and his skin felt scorching hot against my cold hand. How was he not cold?

I almost objected when he removed his hand, but a few seconds later he took my hand and placed it in the pocket of his jacket. My right hand quickly sought out his other pocket, and I sighed audibly when warmth enveloped both hands.

"Better?"

"Much better."

We rode in silence for a few minutes before I asked, "Where are we going anyway?"

"Santa Cruz. What kind of food are you in the mood for?"

"I love Italian, but I'm not picky if you want something else."

Ten minutes later, Nikolas pulled into the parking lot of a small Italian restaurant. Judging by the number of cars in the lot, the place was popular, and I wasn't sure we were going to get a table. I shook my head when he smiled at the hostess, who immediately led us to a table by one of the windows. A candle in the center cast an intimate glow over the white tablecloth, making me remember this was an actual date. I fiddled with my napkin as a waiter appeared to fill our water glasses and lay a basket of rolls between us.

Why am I so nervous? It's just Nikolas. What do I say? What if we have nothing to say to each other?

We looked over the menu and gave the waiter our orders. Then he left us alone. I cast about for something to say. "This seems like a nice place."

He smiled and reached for a roll. "It is. I've been here before."

"Oh." I felt a pang of jealousy as I imagined him here with some other woman, a beautiful one like Celine. *Don't even go there.* I knew Nikolas had been with women before me; I wasn't that naïve. I was *not* going to be one of those ridiculous girls who dwelled on things that happened before the man even knew she existed.

"I came here with Chris last week." He pulled his roll apart. "You should grab one of these before I eat them all."

Laughing, I took one of the savory rolls and spread some butter on it. I took a bite, and it practically melted on my tongue. "Mmm, this is amazing."

I looked up and found Nikolas watching me with an expression that made it hard to swallow the food in my mouth.

He picked up his water glass, breaking the spell between us. "I talked to Tristan today. He said Sahir is hoping to use Hugo and Woolf to patrol the grounds."

"I heard that too. They've been great with him ever since the night of the attack. I'm glad they don't have to be caged all the time now." I smiled at the thought of the two huge hellhounds running free through the miles of woods around Westhorne.

"You miss them, don't you?"

"Yes, but I know Sahir is taking good care of them. He doesn't have a lot to do without Minuet and Alex there."

Nikolas smiled. "The wyvern didn't go as far as you think. They've spotted him twice in the mountains near Westhorne. Sahir thinks he's found a cave to live in, and there is plenty of game for him to hunt. They've been too busy with everything else that's been going on to try to catch him. So far he's kept out of sight of the humans, and Tristan said he's going to leave him alone for now, unless he poses a threat to people."

I imagined some poor hunter out in the woods, looking up and seeing what looked like a small dragon flying overhead. They'd probably spend the next five years in therapy and never hunt again.

"The night of the attack he could have hurt a lot of people, but he only went after the crocotta and vampires. I hope that means he's no longer a danger to humans."

"We'll see," Nikolas said as the waiter arrived with our food.

I'm pretty sure my linguine was delicious, but it was hard to think of food with Nikolas sitting across from me. His eyes smoldered in the candle light, and I kept catching myself staring at his mouth. For his part, he seemed completely unaware of his effect on my appetite as he dug into his huge plate of lasagna.

Trying to focus on something besides him, I looked around the dining room. It reminded me of a little family restaurant Nate and I used to eat at sometimes. That life and Maine seemed so far away now, and I wondered, if I went back to New Hastings, would it still feel like home? Some things, I knew, would never be the same.

"Heavy thoughts?"

"Sorry." I realized I had been quiet for several minutes. "I was just thinking about New Hastings. It seems like forever since I was there."

"Do you still miss it?"

"Yes, but not as much as I used to. I miss Remy more than anything, but even if I was there, I couldn't see him." Remy's elders had forbidden him from seeing me after what happened to his little cousins. It still hurt that I hadn't gotten to say goodbye to him. I knew he would always be my friend even if we couldn't see each other.

"We can go back again when it's safe. And trolls live a very long time. I'm sure you'll see him again."

The way he said "we" made me warm inside and out. No matter what happened in my life, I knew he would be there, and that filled me with an emotion I couldn't put into words.

"Other than Maine, where would you like to go?"

"Everywhere," I said without hesitation.

He raised an eyebrow at me.

"Okay not *everywhere*, but there are so many places I'd like to see. Europe, South America, Africa. Sahir told me so much about Africa that I won't be happy until I see one of those sunsets he described."

"I think you'll like Africa. It has more wild animals than even you can tame." He wiped his mouth with his napkin. "And I think we can find you plenty of pretty sunsets."

There was that "we" again. My heart fluttered in response. I took a few sips from my water glass as I thought of something to say. "You've been all over the world. Do you have a favorite place?"

"I was usually too focused on my missions to enjoy a lot of the places I visited."

I toyed with my fork. "Maybe we can go back and visit some of them. You can show me Russia."

"I'd like that."

Nikolas's smile made my stomach dip. How was it that I hadn't fallen head over heels for this man back in Maine? I had the crazy urge to lean across the small table and kiss him. What had gotten into me tonight? At this rate, I was going to jump him before we got to the dessert. *It has to be the liannan. It's making me hormonal or something.*

We talked about some of the other places we'd like to see, and he told me about a few of the ones he'd been to and some of the strange things he'd seen and foods he'd tried. That turned the conversation to our favorite foods followed by a discussion about music. We argued for at least ten minutes over whether the sixties or seventies was the best decade for music, and I was surprised to learn that we liked a lot of the same stuff.

The waiter came to clear our plates and asked if we wanted dessert. There was no way I could leave without having tiramisu so we ordered a piece to share. I took my time, trying to draw out the meal as long as possible.

Walking to his motorcycle after our meal, it hit me that we'd just had our first normal conversation that didn't involve training or vampires or anything that a regular couple wouldn't discuss. And I'd liked it a lot.

Nikolas stopped at the motorcycle and looked at me. "So what would you like to do now?"

"We aren't going home?" I asked hopefully.

"Not unless you want to."

I didn't want our date to be over. "Can we ride around and see the city?"

"Are you sure won't be too cold?"

"Not if I can use your pockets again." I slipped my helmet on. "How is it that you're so hot...? I mean your skin is hot when mine is cold." Heat scorched my cheeks, and I was so glad for the helmet that hid my face.

Nikolas grinned. "My Mori controls my body temperature," he explained as he donned his own helmet. "You'll be able to do that too, eventually."

"That'll come in handy."

He straddled the seat, and I climbed up behind him, tucking my hands into his pockets again. The motorcycle purred to life and Nikolas pulled out of the parking lot, taking us on a slow tour of the city. Santa Cruz was very pretty at night, from what I saw. I spent most of the ride with my eyes closed, my arms around Nikolas, savoring the experience of the two of us alone out here.

"You're not cold, are you?" he asked after a few minutes.

"No, this is great. It's not as cold at this speed."

"We'll go slower on the way back. I should have taken one of the SUVs instead."

"I'd rather ride a motorcycle than in a car," I replied as we slowed for a red light. "Greg used to give me rides on his bike, and I loved it. I asked him to teach me to ride, but he didn't want to upset Nate."

He turned us down a different street, and I saw a lot of lights against the skyline. "I can teach you, if you still want to learn."

A disbelieving laugh slipped out. "You'll let me ride your motorcycle?"

His deep chuckle made warmth flood my belly.

"No, I'll get you something smaller and less powerful than the Ducati to start on."

A thrill went through me at the idea of the two of us riding our motorcycles side by side down a highway. "When can we start?"

Nikolas laughed again, but his reaction told me he was pleased by my eagerness. "Let's focus on your training right now. Besides, I need to find the right bike for you first."

We approached a brightly lit amusement park. "What is that?" I asked.

"That's the Boardwalk. The rides are closed, but I thought you might like to walk through it."

We parked the bike and began strolling through the colorful park. Nikolas asked if I wanted to check out some of the attractions, but I was happy just to walk with him. I did have to stop when I saw a vendor selling funnel cakes. I'd never had one and they smelled amazing. Nikolas smiled when I asked for one with powdered sugar and chocolate drizzled over it.

"Thank God for a high metabolism." I bit into my cake. "This is so good. You sure you don't want some?"

Humor flashed in his eyes. "No, thanks."

I took another bite and licked chocolate off my lips. "You don't know what you're missing."

I stopped chewing when he reached over and swiped his thumb across my chin. When he put his thumb to his mouth and licked off the chocolate he'd picked up, my stomach went to visit my feet.

"You're right, it's delicious." He tore off a piece of the cake and bit into it as if he hadn't just sent my insides into a tailspin.

We continued to the end of the Boardwalk, and then he suggested we walk back along the beach. Away from the people, we could talk without being overheard, and our conversation turned to less normal things, in particular my training with Aine.

"I don't understand why I can heal things, but I can't do anything else," I vented. "Sometimes it feels like I'm going to explode if I don't use my power. It's so frustrating."

"Is that why you were upset when you came to training today?"

I told him about snapping at Aine and then running away. "I feel awful about it. She's been so good to me and I yelled at her."

He stopped walking and tugged on my arm until I faced him. "Aine understands what you're going through. I only wish there was something I could do to help you through this."

"You are doing something," I said quietly. "I needed this."

We turned to continue our walk.

"What else is troubling you?" he asked.

"Nothing."

"Liar."

"It's just that there's not much to do at Eldeorin's. I have my training during the day, but it's kind of boring at night. I'm not used to being idle." I fell silent, hating how silly my complaint sounded with everything that was going on. "Never mind. It's nothing."

"It's not nothing if it's bothering you. I know I've been spending a lot of time next door, and I'm sorry for leaving you alone so much."

"It's not that. You have an important job to do, and I don't want to be coddled or entertained. I just need *something* to do. I need to feel useful."

We reached a wharf and we wordlessly decided to take a stroll along it. A light wind tossed my hair around my face until I held it to the side with one hand.

"You and Jordan don't have to stay at the house all the time. You can go next door whenever you want."

"Oh."

"The work we're doing concerns you, too. I'm sorry you thought I didn't want you there."

His words warmed me despite the wind. "I should have asked instead of assuming it was off limits."

At the end of the wharf, I walked to the rail and peered down at the foaming waves rushing between the pilings. It was too dark to see much, but I could feel the power of the waves. I'd always been drawn to the ocean, but since my *liannan* the pull was much stronger. The ocean teemed with so much life and magic it filled me with awe.

"You're not planning on jumping, are you?"

The teasing question transported me back to the wharf in New Hastings when he'd asked me the same thing. All I'd wanted that day was for him to go away and let my life go back to normal. I'd been so angry and afraid of what he'd stood for, the changes he'd brought with him. Now, I couldn't imagine him and the others not being in my life.

We stood quietly at the rail for a few minutes before he tapped my arm. "We should be heading back."

"Okay." I didn't want this night to be over yet, but I knew he had work to do.

We made our way back to where he'd parked the motorcycle, and soon we were on the road back to the estate. Neither of us said much on the return trip. I hugged his waist and closed my eyes, wishing we could drive past the estate and keep going until we hit Canada. Just the two of us.

I held back a sigh of disappointment when we pulled up in front of the main entrance. Dismounting, I pulled off my helmet. "I had a great time tonight. Next time I'll remember to bring gloves."

His eyes were dark and unfathomable as he smoothed down some of my hair that had been mussed by the helmet. "I don't mind if you forget them."

My breath caught. It amazed me how the smallest touch or look from him could affect me so much. "I guess I should go in. Jordan's probably waiting to grill me about every detail."

A knowing smile curved his lips, and he put a hand under my chin to tilt my face toward his.

My stomach fluttered in anticipation. Any kiss from Nikolas was enough to turn my legs to jelly, but this would be my first date kiss.

"Good, you're back at last."

Eldeorin's voice startled me so much that I took a step back from Nikolas to stare at the faerie. He hadn't been around much in the last two weeks, and he never visited at at night. "What are you doing here?" I asked, unable to keep my irritation from my tone. I liked Eldeorin, but his timing really sucked. Didn't he see we were in the middle of something important here?

He smiled indulgently. "I've been thinking about the problems you've been having with your magic, and I have an idea that will help you."

"That's great, but shouldn't we talk about it tomorrow when Aine is here?"

"This is not part of Aine's training." He took my hand in his, ignoring the dark look Nikolas shot him. "It's time for you to start your training with me."

I realized Eldeorin's intention a second too late. The last thing I saw was Nikolas's surprised face as the familiar black void settled around me.

CHAPTER 13

WE REAPPEARED IN the middle of what looked like a village. Around the small square were several brightly colored shops and some low buildings in need of repairs. Behind the buildings, I could see small mountains rising up in the darkness.

I yanked my hand from Eldeorin's and turned on him. "What the hell? You can't just grab people and disappear like that. Take me back."

He shook his head calmly. "I apologize for interrupting your romantic moment, but this could not wait."

I folded my arms across my chest and scowled at him. "The least you could have done is let me say goodbye. Nikolas is probably freaking out right now."

"I am sure he is not."

"You obviously don't know him very well."

Eldeorin smiled. "He may not like it, but he knows you are safe with me."

"*I'm* not even sure I'm safe with you," I muttered angrily, earning a laugh from him. I scanned the square, struck by how empty and quiet it was. A few lights lit up the square, but all the buildings were dark. A sign on one of the buildings was in another language that looked like Spanish. "Where the hell are we, and where are the people?"

Eldeorin leaned against a small fountain at the center of the square. "We are in Mexico. This village has been terrorized by a pair of vampires for a week, and the people hide in their homes after dark. Three people have been killed, and last night, the vampires took a young boy."

"A boy?" Tears pricked my eyes at the thought of a child in the clutches of those monsters. "Are we here to find him?" *Please, say yes.*

"No, it is too late for him," he said regretfully.

My eyes welled. "If you knew about this, why didn't you help them?"

He sighed softly. "Cousin, the Fae are powerful, but we are not all-knowing. I learned about this village's troubles a few hours ago, which is why I came for you. We cannot return their loved ones, but we can avenge them and free these people from the threat to their village."

"You don't need me for that. Surely you can take out a couple of vampires?"

He huffed as if he couldn't believe I would question his ability. "I can, but I'm not the one who needs an outlet for all the magic she has built up inside her."

Nervous excitement flared in my chest. My body literally ached with the need to release some of this pent-up energy, but the idea of facing two vampires was terrifying, even if Eldeorin was with me. "Are we talking about baby vamps or mature vamps?"

Eldeorin shrugged. "Does it matter?"

I threw up my hands. "Of course it matters. Mature vamps are super-fast and strong, and I can't take one down with just my power. In case you haven't noticed, I'm not packing a weapon."

"You are thinking like a Mohiri, like your power is finite."

"Isn't it? Healings don't drain me anymore, but I still get tired if I used too much of my power. Westhorne was attacked before I left and I was barely standing by the end of it."

"Your body was tired from channeling your magic, but you never could have depleted it. And now that you have been through *liannan*, your magic is purer and stronger, which is why you struggle with it."

I stared at him. "If that's true then why did I have to use a knife to finish off an old vampire I killed in New Mexico? I gave him what I had and it wasn't enough."

He shook his head slowly. "You gave him what you *thought* you had."

"So I –" I broke off and spun around as cold blossomed in my chest. "They're coming!"

"Good. It is time for you to 'let off a little steam', as they say."

The cold spread until the vampires appeared between two of the buildings. The male was tall and blond and the female a few inches shorter with dark hair. Both wore jeans and knit tops, and if I hadn't known better, I might have mistaken them for a couple of twenty-something American tourists. They spotted us and started walking leisurely in our direction.

My pulse raced, and my knees felt weak, but I held my ground. "Which one do you want?"

Silence.

"Eldeorin?" I looked behind me to discover I was alone. "Shit!" My heart hammered against my ribs. *Okay, calm down. You've got this.*

Who was I kidding? I was going to die in the middle of God only knows where, and I hadn't even gotten my first date kiss.

I'm going to come back and haunt that goddamn faerie for the rest of his immortal life.

"You're not one of the locals," the male said when they were within speaking distance.

"Are you lost, sweetie?" his companion asked in a falsely sweet voice. Both of them had what sounded like Texas accents, and I sent up a prayer that they were newly turned.

I swallowed and tried to control the tremble in my voice. "I think I am."

They stopped about ten feet away, as if they were a kind human couple not wanting to frighten the poor lost girl. I resisted the urge to rub my chest where an icy lump was lodged.

The male looked around. "How did you get here? Are you alone?"

I scrambled for a believable story. "I'm on a road trip with my cousin. Our Jeep broke down a few miles away, and I walked here for help. But I can't find anyone to help me."

A look passed between them. "So it's the two of you?" he asked. "Your cousin stayed with the car and you walked here alone?"

"Yes. He's a lazy jerk who expects me to do all the work," I said loudly, real annoyance clashing with my fear. "Last trip I take with him."

The female smiled sympathetically. "We have a car. If you'd like, we can take you to your cousin. Douglas is great with cars, and I'm sure he can help you with yours."

"That's very kind of you, but I should stay here in case my cousin gets it running and comes looking for me." I wondered why they were bothering to keep up the charade when they could have grabbed me and forced me to show them where my supposed cousin was.

They exchanged another look and Douglas said, "I tell you what. I'll go and see if I can help your cousin, and Carla will stay here with you. We'd hate to leave a fellow American all alone here at night."

They were going to split up? I might actually get out of this alive. "That would be great. Thanks."

Douglas nodded in satisfaction. "Now, where is your car? You said it was a few miles from town."

"I-I can't remember." I gave them what I hoped was a helpless look. "It was dark and I got all turned around. I really am lost."

"No worries. There are only two roads in and out of town. I'll find him." He gave Carla a kiss and whispered something to her. Then he headed back the way they had come.

Carla smiled and took several steps toward me, and I backed up until my calves hit the fountain. She stopped a few feet away, and I gritted my teeth because it felt like ice was going to burst from my chest.

"Don't worry. Douglas will take care of your cousin." She gave me a small smile, and I knew she was thinking about exactly how her companion would "take care" of my cousin. She sniffed the air and leaned slightly toward me. "Do you smell that?"

I swallowed hard. "What?"

"I don't know, but it smells amazing." She took another step in my direction and sniffed again like a dog picking up a scent. Bile threatened to rise in my throat when she licked her lips. "I've never smelled anything like it. It's –" She stopped and stared hungrily at me. "It's you."

She was on me before I could reach for my knife, and her speed and strength told me she had been a vampire for years. Her hands grabbed my shoulders in an iron grip, and she pressed her nose to my throat and inhaled deeply. A shudder passed through her as she breathed in the intoxicating scent of faerie that had probably grown stronger since my *liannan*. "What are you?" she moaned, her fangs distending to brush against my skin.

I resisted the urge to whimper as she pressed me back against the fountain. My mind threatened to blank out, and I battled with the memory of Eli holding me captive just like this.

"Douglas will be so angry if I don't wait for him, but I have to taste you." She pushed my head to the side. "Sorry, sweetheart, nothing personal."

Her words brought me back to my senses. What was I doing? I was a vampire killer, not some defenseless girl ready to be their next meal.

Power roared through me. Carla's hands were ripped from my shoulders, and she flew backward to land in the dirt a dozen feet away. *That's more like it,* I thought as I watched the vampire sit up wearing a dazed expression.

"What-what did you do?"

"I decided I didn't want to be tasted. I like my blood right where it is." My hands began to glow as power filled them. It felt so good to be able to release my power without fear of hurting someone. Someone other than the vampire, that was.

Carla's eyes narrowed in fear. "What the hell are you?"

Static rolled across my skin, and I resisted the urge to turn up the power. If I scared her too much she might run after Douglas and I'd have to face both of them at once. I needed to take care of her before her boyfriend discovered there was no cousin and came back for me.

"You have no idea how many times I get asked that. The way I heard it, one of my great grandmothers was a faerie. Can you believe that? I guess this" – I held up my hands – "is some kind of faerie thing. Beats the hell out of me, but it does come in handy."

Hunger replaced the fear in Carla's eyes. It looked like she had heard how yummy faerie blood was. She stood slowly, never taking her eyes from me. "So you are only half Fae?"

"Something like that." I could see her mind working, calculating how strong a half faerie was compared to a vampire her age. *Come and get me.*

Carla leapt at me. I raised my hands, but the force of her attack knocked me off balance, and I put out a hand to keep from falling backward into the fountain. My fingers touched the water, and it felt like I'd grasped a live power line as the water's magic fed mine. The hand crushed between our bodies found Carla's chest and my power pushed forward. She screamed, and I gagged as the stench of burnt flesh filled my nostrils.

Regaining my balance, I shoved her away from me and she toppled to the ground. A hole had been burnt through her top and my handprint was seared into her chest. She twitched and gasped for breath, her eyes full of pain and terror as I stood over her.

I crouched beside her, and all I could think about was the family hidden in one of those dark buildings, grieving for their little boy.

"Please..."

I laid my hands on her smoking chest and summoned my power. "Sorry, sweetheart, nothing personal."

I was washing my hands in the fountain when I sensed Douglas's return. He let out a howl of outrage when he spied the body of his girlfriend, and then he spun, searching the square for whoever had killed her.

"It's just you and me," I said with a calmness I'd never felt before when facing a vampire.

"How?" he demanded, hatred burning in his eyes.

I held up a hand and watched his eyes follow the blue sparks dancing across it. "Half Fae versus vampire. Fae wins."

"Half Fae?" A familiar hunger filled his eyes.

I sighed at the single-mindedness of these vampires. They were so mesmerized by the chance to taste Fae blood they didn't stop to consider the danger. Douglas's girlfriend was dead at my hands, but instead of running, he was planning his attack on me.

This time I would be ready. My hand slipped behind me and touched the water again in preparation for the assault.

I was not, however, expecting the water to turn to ice, and I managed to yank my hand away just in time. *Stupid power!* What a time for it to act up.

Douglas grinned and sped toward me. I whirled to the side in a burst of speed and called on my power. I wasn't fast enough to evade him, and he grabbed my right arm painfully. Lurching toward the fountain, I ducked to avoid the large icicles hanging from the second tier. Several broke and shattered on the icy surface. Instinct drove me and I grabbed for a long shard of ice, as Douglas jerked me toward him. I let momentum carry me to him and power the strike to his chest.

He shrieked and released me to grab at the icicle protruding from his chest. It took him several seconds to realize it was ice and not silver buried in his heart. His eyes gleamed with triumph when he looked at me. "Nice try, but ice can't hurt me."

"Maybe not, but this can." I grabbed the end of the icicle and sent my power into it. The ice was a perfect conductor, amplifying my power and carrying it straight to the vamhir demon. Douglas didn't even have time to scream before his heart and demon exploded in his chest. I jumped back as he fell across his dead girlfriend.

"Death by icicle. Very creative."

I whirled on Eldeorin who stood a few feet away. "You left me! You... you asshole! I could have been killed."

"Language, Cousin," he reproached mildly. "I did not leave you. I was merely observing your training."

"Training? You made me face off against two vampires without any warning. What kind of training is that?"

He raised an eyebrow and waved at the bodies. "The effective kind."

I crossed my arms. "I got lucky."

"Nonsense. You performed admirably. I am very proud of you."

The retort that was on the tip of my tongue died. "You are?"

"Yes. You did well, Cousin." He gave me a bright smile. "You separated them and took them both out very quickly, and you did it without your Mohiri weapons. The ice was ingenious."

I decided not to mention that the ice had been an accident.

Eldeorin inclined his head toward the dead vampires. "That was an impressive display of power. How do you feel now?"

I took a moment to do a self-check, and I was pleasantly surprised to find the pressure that had been building inside me for weeks was gone. Also gone were the anxiety and the fear that I would slip and lose control of my power. For the first time since I'd awakened from the healing sleep, my power felt normal, manageable. I told Eldeorin how it felt and he nodded.

"You needed to release your magic without holding back out of fear of hurting your friends. I think you will find your next training with Aine will be better." He looked quite pleased with himself. "Now, shall we go home? I'm sure your warrior is waiting for your return."

I pointed to the dead vampires. "Shouldn't we get rid of them?"

"No. We'll leave them so the people can see the vampires are dead and their village is safe." He walked over to me. "If I take you home looking like that, your warrior is not going to be happy."

"Like what?" I looked down at my clothes and found then splattered with vampire blood. "Exploding vampires is a messy business."

"So it would seem." Eldeorin waved a hand and the blood vanished. "Next time we'll work on your technique."

"Next time?" My question went unanswered as he took my hand and the village disappeared. A few seconds later, we arrived in my bedroom at the mansion.

"Home sweet home." Eldeorin wrapped me in a loose hug and kissed my cheek. "Sleep well, Cousin. I will see you soon."

"I really wish he'd stop doing that," I grumbled when he disappeared again.

A glance at the clock beside my bed told me I'd been gone no more than forty minutes. It didn't seem real that I had travelled to Mexico, killed two vampires, and freed a village in less than an hour.

I threw my coat on a chair and went to look for Nikolas. I could only imagine the mood he was in right now. Not that I blamed him. I'd be angry too if some faerie took him away right in front of my eyes.

Voices carried to me from the living room when I reached the top of the stairs.

"They could be anywhere," Nikolas bit out, leaving no doubt that he was royally pissed.

"He won't let anything happen to her," Chris replied calmly.

Nikolas appeared at the bottom of the stairs before I started down them. "Are you okay?" he asked harshly as I descended the stairs.

I gave him a reassuring smile. "Better than okay."

When I reached him he took my face in his hands. His eyes searched mine and what he saw must have satisfied him. "Where did he take you?" he asked in a softer tone.

I hesitated, unsure what to tell him. I didn't want to keep secrets from him, but he would freak if he knew what had happened. Based on Eldeorin's comments, there were going to be more training sessions like this one, and I didn't want Nikolas worrying every time Eldeorin took me away.

"We went to a place where there were no people around, and he helped me release my power. He said I needed to let it out without worrying about hurting you guys."

Nikolas dropped his hands. "Did it help?"

"Yes. I almost feel like my old self again." I laid a hand on his chest. "I'm sorry if you were worried."

The anger drained from his expression. "You don't have to apologize." His hand grazed my cheek and his gaze held mine. It was as if the last forty minutes hadn't happened, and we were out in the driveway again, returning from our date.

His phone rang.

He smiled apologetically and stepped back to answer it. "Here." He listened for a minute. "What did they find? No, I want to talk to them. We'll be there shortly."

I hid my disappointment behind a smile. It looked like another movie night with Jordan.

Nikolas looked at me. "It's still early. Do you want to come see the command center?"

Jordan was beside us before I could open my mouth. "Hell yes, we do."

I grinned. "What she said."

"Grab your coats and we'll head over," Nikolas said, returning his phone to his pocket.

The house they had rented was impressive, though not as big or as opulent as Eldeorin's. Warriors patrolled the iron fence, and at least half a dozen black SUVs and motorcycles were parked in the driveway. As soon as we entered the house, I heard men's voices coming from the living room. I followed Nikolas into the room that had been transformed into a temporary command center. Folding tables had been set up around the large room, and each of them was covered in computers and other electronic equipment. I looked at the closest one that held three large monitors displaying maps of Los Angeles, San Diego, and San Francisco. On each map were small clusters of blinking red, blue, green, and yellow dots.

"What are the dots?" I asked the blond warrior sitting at the table. He was someone I hadn't seen before.

"The colored dots are our people. Each unit's signature is coded for a different color, which makes it easier for us to track them." He moved his cursor over one of the dots and a small box appeared on the screen, showing the person's name, status, and last check-in time.

"How big is a unit?" I asked, impressed.

"A unit has six members."

My eyes found Nikolas and Chris, who were talking to another warrior on the other side of the room. "When I met Nikolas and Chris it was just the two of them. They don't have a unit?"

The blond warrior smiled as if I'd said something funny. "Nikolas and Chris normally work alone. If you saw them in action, you'd know why."

Jordan elbowed me. "She's seen Nikolas in action alright."

I smiled at the warrior's questioning look. "Nikolas found me in Maine last fall."

"Oh, you're *that* girl." His blue eyes sparkled with laughter. "We've heard all about you."

"See, Sara, you're famous."

We walked to another table where an Indian warrior named Raj was tinkering with tiny electronic devices the size of a dime. When we expressed an interest in his work, he was more than happy to explain it to us.

"These are transmitters we use for surveillance." He held up one of the devices. "They work well most of the time, but some of our targets have started using warlock magic to detect and disable them. I'm working on a transmitter that is undetectable and impervious to magic."

I took the device and turned it over in my fingers. "Are you close?"

"I believe so. I've been working with a warlock in Jaipur for two years, and I think we are close to perfecting it."

"That's pretty cool." I gave the device back to him. "Thanks for the show-and-tell."

He smiled widely. "Anytime."

Jordan tugged on my arm. "Let's check out the rest of this place."

"Nice talking to you," I said to the warrior as she dragged me away.

We circled the room, stopping at each of the work stations, which were manned by warriors. A couple of them showed security feeds from cameras in Los Angeles, and I recognized Blue Nyx on one of the monitors. One station was dedicated to police bands and news feeds, and another showed a map of Los Angeles with a dot for every confirmed vampire victim. There had to be almost fifty. My stomach churned as I turned away.

We wandered around the first floor and made a detour to the huge kitchen for snacks and sodas. When we returned to the living room, Nikolas and Chris were nowhere to be seen, though I could feel Nikolas's presence close-by. Jordan and I claimed a sofa that had been pushed against the cold fireplace to make room for the equipment. Our location gave us a view of the entire room, and the equipment and voices in the room made it easy for us to talk privately.

"Okay, spill it," Jordan ordered. "What did you and the faerie really do?"

I started to shake my head and stopped. I hadn't told Nikolas the truth because I knew how upset he'd be, but there was no reason not to tell Jordan. She'd keep it to herself if I asked her to, and I really wanted to talk to someone about what had happened.

"This stays between us," I said in a low voice.

She moved closer. "That good? So what did you do, go hunt down a vampire to practice on?"

Her guess was so close to the truth that I was at a loss for words for several seconds. My silence made her eyes go round and she grabbed my arm. "Shut up! You did not!"

I nodded slowly as I watched the door in case Nikolas returned. "I had no idea what Eldeorin was planning and it happened so fast."

"Well, don't leave me in suspense."

I related the entire story to her, leaving nothing out, as I kept an eye out for Nikolas. Some of the warriors glanced our way and smiled at us like we were two school girls whispering about boys. If they only knew what really passed between us.

"You killed two vamps without a weapon?" Jordan croaked, staring at me with something akin to awe. "Sara, that is..."

"Crazy, I know, but it's not like I had a choice. Eldeorin has very different ideas about training."

"I'll say."

I chewed my lip. "Now that you know everything, what do you think I should do?"

"About Eldeorin? Doesn't sound like there is much you can do."

"No, about Nikolas. If I tell him, he'll be so upset and he'll worry every time Eldeorin shows up."

"That's putting it mildly." She rubbed her chin. "I don't know. It's a tough call."

"What would you do?"

"I'd keep quiet and go kill some vampires." She shrugged. "But I don't have a Nikolas to consider. I honestly don't know what I'd do in your shoes."

I sighed heavily. "You're no help."

She pursed her lips. "Okay, let's look at it another way. You took out two vampires who killed a kid and were probably going to kill that whole village. You saved a lot of lives, and you burned off some of that power that's been making you miserable."

I nodded.

"If there's nothing Nikolas can do to stop Eldeorin from training you, then it's probably best not to say anything right now."

"I guess." I looked at the doorway as Nikolas walked through it. His eyes found me, and a small smile touched his lips. One of the warriors called to him, and it was easy to see the way the others looked to him to lead them.

My eyes were drawn back to the doorway as two more warriors came in. They were both tall, but one towered over everyone in the room. His features and coloring were Middle Eastern, and he wore his black hair tied back in a short ponytail. He was by far the biggest warrior I'd ever seen, and maybe the surliest if his scowl was any indication. I watched him absently hold the hilt of the sword sheathed at his hip, and I wondered if he was one of the foreign warriors sent here by the Council to help hunt the Master.

"That guy must be six-seven at least. What do you think?"

Jordan didn't reply and I gave her a sideways look, only to find her staring at the large warrior.

"Hello? Earth to Jordan."

"Mmm."

A smirk spread across my face. "Is it love at first sight?"

That got her attention and she fanned herself. "I think you mean lust at first sight. That has to be the hottest male I've ever seen."

I raised an eyebrow. "Hotter than Nikolas?" Not possible.

She tilted her head and studied the man as if she hadn't heard me. "There is something about him, something..."

"Dangerous?" I offered, thinking he was one man I wouldn't want to face in a dark alley.

"Yeah. He looks like he could take out a nest of vampires by himself."

"You don't think he's kinda scary looking?"

She exhaled slowly, her eyes never leaving the warrior. "He's perfect."

I nudged her with my shoulder. "Are you sure it's not love?"

Her rich laugh drew the attention of some of the warriors, including the new one. He aimed his scowl in our direction and stared at her for several seconds before looking away again.

"I don't think he likes us," I said.

"Not yet." She winked at me. "Did you see the size of that sword?"

I felt my eyes widen before the two of us dissolved into laughter. Every eye in the room turned our way. Nikolas gave me a questioning look, but all I could do was shake my head and laugh.

CHAPTER 14

"VERY GOOD, SISTER." Aine clapped as I sent small controlled waves across the lake. I passed my hand through the water and a five-foot waterspout formed a few feet from me. I held it for a minute then let it collapse. It was hard to believe that a week ago I couldn't use my power without causing a near disaster.

Aine's eyes shone. "You have improved so much these last few days."

"That's because you are a great teacher." I couldn't imagine someone sweeter or more patient than my sylph friend.

"Am I not a great teacher as well?" asked Eldeorin, appearing at Aine's side.

"The jury's still out on that," I retorted as a mixture of excitement and trepidation stirred in my stomach at the sight of him. It had been a little over a week since our trip to the Mexican village, and Eldeorin had made good on his promise to continue my "education" as he put it. Every second day, he appeared to whisk me away on one of his training sessions, which always ended with me killing something.

First, it had been the drex demon in New Orleans, a nasty scaly thing that resembled an upright crocodile and disabled its victims by injecting them with venom that created severe hallucinations. I'd had to follow that thing as it dragged a young man into the bayou, not one of my more pleasant experiences. After the demon was dead, Eldeorin had helped me get the man back home again, and he'd assured me the guy wouldn't remember the experience because of the aftereffects of the venom.

Next, we'd gone to Miami to hunt some vampires that had been preying on the residents of a retirement community. What Eldeorin hadn't told me was that there were five vampires living in a newly formed nest in a nearby industrial park. Luckily for me, the vampires were all less than a few months old, and I had relatively little difficulty taking them out. Still, it would have been nice to have had a heads-up. When I'd said that to Eldeorin, he'd replied that I needed to learn to think on my feet because I never knew what I'd be facing out there.

Two days ago, we'd travelled to Seattle where I'd killed a vampire who was responsible for at least three missing teenagers. He'd been older than the vampires in Miami and he'd put up a little more of a fight, so the kill had been pretty messy. Eldeorin had to clean me up and heal a few scratches before he'd taken me home. But it had been worth it because I'd found two of the missing teenagers in the old house the vampire had holed up in. They'd been traumatized, but they were alive. Eldeorin used his magic to heal them and wipe their memories of their horrible ordeals before we'd dropped them off at the nearest hospital.

Every time Eldeorin arrived I had no idea what he had in store for me, and it scared me. At the same time, I couldn't deny that I liked how it felt to kill those monsters and to save people from them. I felt like I had a purpose, like I was doing what I was born to do. Not to mention that unleashing all that power helped me focus during my training with Aine.

The only downside – and it was a big one – was keeping my adventures a secret from Nikolas. Whenever he asked me about my trips with Eldeorin I said we went to the desert to work on my power. Not telling him the truth gnawed at me, but Jordan reminded me I didn't have another option, unless I wanted him to lose it. As much as I hated it, I decided to wait until I could prove I was capable of taking care of myself before I told him.

"So, Cousin, are you ready for our next little excursion?"

I waded out of the water and waited for Aine to do her little drying trick. "I don't suppose we're going somewhere fun for a change. They have vampires in Hawaii, don't they?"

Eldeorin laughed and hugged me because he knew it bugged me when he did that. "Oh, I have something very fun for you today. You like snow, don't you?"

"Snow?"

The word was barely out of my mouth when the world went black. I found myself standing in a foot of snow in the parking lot of what looked like a storage facility. I wrapped my arms around myself and shivered in the bitter cold as fat snowflakes swirled around me. "Are you trying to freeze me to death?"

"Oops." Eldeorin waved a hand and I was suddenly wearing soft-soled boots that came to my knees, a warm jacket, and a knit cap that I pulled down over my ears.

I waved a hand over my form-fitting outfit. "What's with all the black? I feel like a cat burglar."

He gave me a lopsided smile. "I figured we might as well have some fun."

"You always have fun," I reminded him, sticking my hands in my pockets to warm them. "I do all the work, remember?" I looked around the empty parking lot. "Where are we, and what are we doing here?"

"We are in Minneapolis to see a gulak demon that has decided to enter the slave business."

Anger burned away the tiny knot of fear in my stomach. "Human or demon slaves?"

"Both, most likely."

"This place looks deserted. Where are they?"

He took my arm and led me around to the front of the building. Then he pointed to a two-story warehouse across the road. "They are in that building."

I studied the warehouse. There were two loading doors and four upper windows on the side facing us, but I could see no sign of activity. Several inches of untouched snow lay on the ramps in front of the doors, indicating that no one had gone in or out that way in the last few hours.

The sound of an approaching truck broke the silence. A few seconds later, I spotted a white moving truck at the end of the street. "Um, shouldn't we hide before they see us?"

"They can't see us."

"Oh, right, glamour." I exhaled in relief. "When will I be able to do that?"

"Baby steps, Cousin."

"You know, for a teacher you're not that big on sharing." I thought about our other excursions. "I'm not going to go in there and find a dozen gulaks, am I? It's just one, right?"

Eldeorin shrugged. "A gulak usually has a second and third but they won't be as strong as he is, and none of them is as strong as you."

"Why doesn't that make me feel better?" I recalled the fight at Draegan's party. I'd only had to take out one of the gulaks because Jordan had killed the other one. And neither of us had faced Draegan because he'd been unconscious. Something told me he would not have been an easy kill.

The truck reached the warehouse and the driver put it in reverse to back up to one of the loading doors. The doors opened and a gulak and a ranc demon got out.

"How are they able to drive around in broad daylight without someone seeing what they are?"

"Glamours," Eldeorin replied. "Warlock made, if I'm not mistaken."

Silently cursing warlocks everywhere, I watched as one of the gulak demons typed in a code on the panel next to the door and the door began to rise. The ranc demon moved to the back of the truck, and I heard the truck door slide up followed by the unmistakable sound of crying.

"You're up, Cousin. Get in there and go all Fae on their demon asses."

In less than a minute, I was across the street and crouched in front of the truck as the two demons led seven bound and shackled humans into the warehouse. The four women and three men all looked to be in their late teens or early twenties, and judging by their various states of undress, they had been taken from their beds. I watched a pale red-haired woman stumble only to be yanked up violently by the gulak demon. She cried out, and my nostrils flared in outrage. The bastard didn't know it yet, but he'd just hurt his last human.

The warehouse door began to close, and I jumped from my hiding place to slip inside before I was locked out. Knowing Eldeorin, the glamour hiding me would only last until I entered the building. That was his way of keeping things interesting. But, hopefully, that would be all the time I needed.

Just inside the loading door I ducked behind a stack of wooden pallets to size up the situation and get my bearings. The open area of the interior was lined with rows of floor-to-ceiling shelves that were empty except for a few crates on the upper shelves. That made it easier to follow the progress of the demons and their prisoners as they moved toward a door on the far side of the open space.

The ranc demon shoved the humans into the room, and I waited several minutes for them to reappear. They spoke in a language I couldn't understand before the ranc demon headed for a room a few doors away from where the humans were being held. The gulak demon climbed a set of stairs to the second floor. I had a feeling he was going to report in to this boss. I'd deal with that later. First, I needed to take care of his friend and get those people out of here.

Remembering what Eldeorin had said about a gulak never working alone, I scanned the room to make sure it was empty before I slipped out from my hiding place. I stayed close to the wall as I silently made my way to the room where the humans were, and I let out a relieved sigh when I tried the door and found it unlocked.

I wasn't prepared for the sight that greeted me when I opened the door, and my hand flew to my mouth when I saw the large dog cages lining the walls of the room. They were stacked three high, and from each one a pair of terrified eyes stared at me. All but two of the cages held humans; the last two were occupied by mox demons.

"Please, help us," sobbed a girl who couldn't have been much older than I was. Her fingers curled around the bars of the cage and tears streaked her dirty face.

I put my finger to my lips and went to her cage. "Shhh. I'm going to get you all out of here, but you have to be quiet. Okay?"

She clutched at my fingers. "I w-want to go h-home."

The girl's broken plea shook me, and I was torn between the urge to comfort her and the need to free them all. My pragmatic side won. I squeezed her fingers before I pulled my hand away and whispered, "I'll take you home. I promise. First, I need to get these cages unlocked. Do any of you know where the key is?"

"You mean this key?" asked a deep rumbling voice from behind me. There were cries from the cages as I whirled to face the gulak demon who dangled a set of keys from his clawed hand. He leered at me as he filled the doorway. "Hello there. Where did you come from?"

If I hadn't seen and fought a gulak before that moment I might have been scared by the sight of the scaly demon. Instead, I was worried about how I was going to kill him without hurting anyone else. My power strained to be free, but I had to get this guy out of the room before I unleashed it. And I had to hurry before all his buddies showed up.

"I was just passing by and thought I'd check this place out."

His reptilian eyes swept me from head to toe. "Is that so? I think I should take you to see the boss."

"Okay, but can my friends come too?" I glanced over his shoulder.

He spun to look behind him. It was all the opening I needed. I tackled him and knocked him to the floor outside the room. "I can't believe you actually fell for that." My glowing hands covered his mouth before he had a chance to shout for help. Power flowed into him, and he gagged as it encased his head and filled his mouth and nose, suffocating him. I tried to make it fast, to get it over with before someone heard us and came to see what was going on. The gulak decided not to go easily, and it took him a good minute to die.

I climbed off his body and dragged it back into the room, ignoring the two dozen pairs of eyes watching me. The demon had dropped the keys and I grabbed them off the floor.

"Okay, let's get you guys out of here."

A minute later, I swore when I realized that none of the keys on the ring fit the cage locks. The bastard had been playing me.

"The o-other one has the key," stammered a blond man.

"The one who brought you here?" The man nodded, and I moved toward the door. "Hold tight. I'll be back."

I chewed my lip as I studied the door to the room the ranc demon had entered. I couldn't just barge in because, for all I knew, there might be a dozen demons in there. But I couldn't stand here waiting for him to come out either.

Before I could change my mind, I rapped on the door. There were sounds from within before the door opened to reveal a shocked ranc demon who was also very much alone. Using the element of surprise against him, I pushed him into the room and kicked the door shut behind me. Away from the humans, I didn't have to restrain my power and I let him have it in the chest.

"Shit!" I backed away as his skin turned dry and brittle and began to fall away in chunks. His mouth opened in a silent scream before his whole head crumbled, followed by the rest of his body.

I stared at the pile of what used to be the demon then looked at my hands. "Maybe a little *too* much."

I let out a groan when I realized the keys I was looking for were probably in that pile of demon bits. It would be just my luck to have melted the damn things.

It took a few minutes to locate the keys, and I let out a relieved sigh when I saw they were intact. On a table was another set of keys that looked like they belonged to the truck outside. I grabbed them and shoved them into my pocket. Wiping my hands on my jeans, I hurried back to the first room and fitted a key into the lock on the first cage. *Thank you, God*, I said silently when the padlock clicked open. I moved to the next cage, making a mental note to learn how to pick locks in the very near future. Either that or figure out how to blast them open with my power. Now that would be a handy trick to know.

The blond man whose cage I'd unlocked first climbed out and stood beside me, rubbing his arms. It was cold in here, and the poor guy was wearing a T-shirt and boxers.

"How are we going to get out of here?" he asked, following me. "There are more of those things out there."

I focused on the lock I was working on. "How many?"

"I don't know. At least one more of the scaly ones and it's huge."

The lock opened, and I removed the padlock before going to the next cage, which held the girl I'd spoken to.

"We're going home now," I told her in a soothing voice as I freed her. When the door opened she flung her arms around me, her body shaking in terror. I gently set her away from me. "I know you're scared. I need to get everyone else out, and then we'll leave."

"Where are the others?" asked a dark-haired man as I unlocked his cage.

"Others?" Dear God, there were more prisoners here?

"The people with you who came to help us," the man said as I helped him out of the cramped cage.

"It's just me."

"Are you serious?" he asked incredulously.

"Yes." I tried to move past him, but he was blocking my way. "This will go a lot faster if you let me open the rest of these cages."

The blond man pulled the dumbfounded brunette aside, and I continued to unlock the cages. When I got to the two mox demons, a hand grabbed my arm roughly.

"What are you doing? You can't let those things out!" the dark-haired man hissed.

I shook off his grip and faced him. "These two are victims here just like the rest of you."

"They're monsters," he spat. "I'm not going to die in this hellhole because you took pity on those things."

I turned back to the cages again. "You don't have to wait for me. I'm not leaving anyone behind."

He gripped my arm again. "But they're not human. Look at them."

I swung around again, letting power flow to my hands until they glowed softly. The man took a step back and stared at them.

"What makes you think *I'm* human?" I looked at the people huddled together and staring at me with a mixture of fear and astonishment. "Listen, I know you've all been through a lot and you're scared, but I've met creatures like these before and they are very gentle. I promise they won't hurt you."

The man who had confronted me nodded slowly and stepped back. I gave him a reassuring smile and crouched in front of the bottom cage where the female mox demon watched me warily. I couldn't blame her after she'd witnessed what I'd done to the gulak demon.

"Can you understand me?" I asked gently and she nodded. "Don't be afraid. I'm going to get you out of here." I unlocked the door and swung it open, but she didn't move. Figuring she was scared, I unlocked the last cage and stepped back so the two demons felt safe to climb out. The female did, but the male in the top cage stayed where he was.

"What's wrong with him?" I asked her.

"The gulak hurt his legs. I think they are broken."

It didn't take long to size up the situation. The male couldn't walk and the female was too weak to carry him. I couldn't touch him without hurting him. That left one solution. I looked at the humans who watched us warily. "They broke his legs and I can't help him." I held up my hands for emphasis. "Will one of you men carry him?"

The men exchanged looks, but no one volunteered.

"Please."

A man who looked like he played college football stepped forward. "I'll do it."

I gave him a grateful smile and stepped aside so he could lift the mox demon from the cage. I opened the door and peered out to make sure the way was clear. Then I pulled the truck keys from my pocket. "Can one of you drive that truck?"

"Briig?" roared a deep gravelly voice that could only belong to the dead demons' boss. "Where the hell is that slave I asked for?"

One of the girls whimpered. "Oh God, it's coming!"

"Quiet," I ordered softly, trying to keep my voice from shaking. I couldn't help but remember how big and powerful Draegan had been. If this gulak was as big as Draegan, was I strong enough to take him? And how many more demons were out there with him?

Eldeorin thinks you can do this or he wouldn't have brought you here.

I set my shoulders and put on my brave face. "You stay here and keep this door closed."

"You're leaving us?" someone cried fearfully.

"Just for a little while. I have to deal with the rest of them so we can leave."

The guy holding the mox demon frowned. "You're doing it alone?"

I smiled with a confidence I wished I felt. "Piece of cake," I lied as I slipped out of the room and closed the door behind me.

"Briig, you worthless dung heap!" The gulak bellowed again. "Do I have to do everything myself?"

Heavy footsteps thumped down the stairs, matching the rhythm of my pounding heart. I cast a furtive glance around, dismayed to see there weren't any places to hide on this side of the warehouse. I wanted to get a look at what I was facing before I confronted it.

There was only one place to go. I grabbed the metal shelving, very glad for all the years I'd spent climbing trees back home, and scaled it quickly. The third shelf was about fifteen feet off the floor and I had time to reach it and lie flat before the huge scaled demon came into view.

I smothered a gasp. "Huge" was not the right word to describe this demon. At least eight feet tall, the gulak was massive. The fact that he was alone did not offer any comfort because he looked like he could crush a car with those arms. Not to mention the inch-long claws on each hand and the sharp teeth protruding from the corners of his mouth.

If I survive this, I'm going to kill that faerie.

The gulak stopped at the bottom of the stairs and swung his large horned head from side to side before his eyes narrowed on the closed door of the room where the people were hiding. A growl came from him as he started toward the room. "Briig, you better not be playing with my slaves again if you know what's good for you."

My heart leapt into my throat. If he opened that door and saw everyone out of their cages, there was no telling what he would do. I had to stop him.

"Briig quit... permanently."

The gulak stopped in his tracks. "Who said that?"

I stood and ran quietly to the other end of the long row of shelves to draw him as far away as I could from the room. "I did," I called boldly from my new hiding place.

He spun and followed my voice. "Where are you? Show yourself!" he roared.

Taking a deep breath, I moved to the edge of the wide shelf.

A sneer twisted his thin lips when he stopped and glared up at me. "How did you get out of your cage?"

"Do I look like I was in a cage?" I swallowed dryly. Holy crap, he was even bigger and scarier up close.

He tilted his head. "Maybe not, but you'll be in one soon enough. I have an incubus client who'll pay a hefty price for a pretty little thing like you."

"I think I'll pass." My stomach churned. How many girls had he sent to his incubus friend or to other horrible fates?

"You should have thought of that before you came into my place." He grabbed the lower shelf supports to shake them, but they were cemented to the floor. "Don't make me come up there after you, little mouse."

"Or what?" I taunted with false bravado, knowing that sooner or later I was going to have to get very close to the gulak. The only way those people were getting out of there was if he was dead. Even if I could get them out somehow, I still had to kill him. I couldn't leave him alive to kidnap and sell more innocent people.

"Can you climb, you overgrown iguana?"

A deep laugh rumbled from him. "No, but I can do this." Leathery wings spread out from his back, spanning twenty feet across. I barely had time to think there wasn't enough room for him to fly when he lifted straight off the floor toward me.

I stumbled back and caught a support bar before I fell off the other side of the shelf. There was no time to run, and I gasped as a clawed hand wrapped around my arm.

"Gotcha," he gloated.

My pulse skyrocketed, and I didn't know if it was fear or adrenaline. I grabbed his arm with both hands. He bellowed as the first jolt of power slammed into him, and he dropped out of the air, pulling me with him.

His back hit the cement floor, and I landed on top of him. My teeth shook from the impact, and I was temporarily winded, giving him enough time to recover. An arm snaked around my waist as he moved to get up.

"I think I'll get double my usual price for you. My clients like some fire in their slaves."

"I'm. Not. For. Sale." I gritted my teeth and slammed a hand into his chest.

The gulak's roar shook the building as he threw me away from him. I sailed through the air and hit the floor hard, and a small scream tore from me when I felt a bone in my wrist snap. Gasping in pain, I rolled over and struggled to get to my feet before he attacked again. That was when I realized I'd twisted an ankle too, and I was in no shape to fight him.

Then I'd better end this quickly. I limped to where he was sprawled paralyzed on his back with a large black mark covering his chest. My eyes widened when I saw the leather had been burnt from his wings and all that was left were the spines.

"What are you?" he rasped, hatred burning in his eyes instead of fear.

"I'm one of the good guys."

He tried to laugh and it came out as a croak. "Good guys never win."

"I guess I'll have to change that." I knelt beside him, holding my injured arm to my stomach, and laid my free hand on his charred chest. He didn't blink or utter a sound when I finished the job. His mouth gaped open and his tongue hung out as he stared unseeing at the ceiling.

"Is-is it dead?"

I looked up and nodded at the dark-haired man who was standing a dozen feet away. "Do you think you could help me up?"

He hesitated for several seconds then rushed over to help me to my feet. I tried not to moan when he jolted my broken wrist.

"Come on; let's get you guys out of here." I limped to the people crowding the doorway of the room. "You're safe now, but you should go to the hospital to get checked out. Can one of you drive the truck?"

"I can," said the man beside me.

We were a sorry-looking bunch when we filed outside. Everyone but me was barefoot and shivering, but they were too happy to be free to care about the cold. The dark-haired man climbed up into the cab to start the truck and the rest of them hurried to pile into the back. The mox demon held back, as well as the blond man holding her friend.

"What about these two?" the man asked.

"Set him down here. I'll take care of them."

"You're not coming with us? You need a doctor more than we do."

"Don't worry about me. My ride will be here soon."

"Here." One of the women held out a blanket that had been in the back of the truck. "Wrap him in this."

The kindness of these people after their terrifying ordeal warmed me. I took the blanket and wrapped it around the mox demon before the man laid him on the ground. There were a lot of tears and cries of thank you before the truck finally pulled away, leaving me alone with the two mox demons.

"Perfection." Eldeorin appeared before us, startling the already frightened demons. "You were amazing, Cousin."

"Not exactly perfect." I grimaced. "I should kick your ass for this one."

"As if you could." He laughed and touched my hand, making the pain in my wrist and ankle disappear. "Admit it, you enjoyed that."

"Yeah, I always like getting tackled by demons ten times my size." I shook out my newly healed wrist. "Do you have the phone?"

He waved and a cell phone appeared in his hand.

"Show-off." I took it and called David, who let Kelvan know about the mox demons so he could send someone for them. I refused to leave them until help arrived, for fear some more of the gulak's henchmen were nearby. Ten minutes later, I saw three mox demons walking up the street toward us, and I let out a sigh of relief.

"Will you be okay?" I asked the female demon and she nodded timidly.

"Good." I turned to Eldeorin. "Can we go home now?"

Mischief sparkled in his dark blue eyes. "Already? The day is still young."

I waved a finger in his face. "No way, Eldeorin. That was enough training for one day."

He took my hand and laid it in the crook of his arm. "This one will be fun; trust me."

"That's what you always say," I complained before Minneapolis faded around us.

CHAPTER 15

"DO WE HAVE any intel on who might be doing this?"

Nikolas's voice drew my attention away from my laptop where I was chatting with David and Kelvan. Almost two months had passed since I'd gotten sick and we'd lost Madeline's trail. Now I was determined to pick it up again with the help of my two talented hacker friends, and for the last three days we'd been working together to try to figure out where Madeline was. The difference this time was that I was sharing anything we learned with Nikolas. The Mohiri had wanted to work directly with my friends, but David and Kelvan didn't trust anyone but me. Nikolas wasn't happy about the arrangement until I reminded him that David, Kelvan, and I had gotten closer to finding Madeline than the Mohiri ever had.

Nikolas walked into the command center with Chris and another warrior named Raoul whom I'd seen here a lot. Nikolas's eyes scanned the room until they met mine, and we exchanged smiles. I liked being able to spend my evenings here working alongside him, and the looks he gave me told me he felt the same way.

Raoul shook his head. "Whoever they are, they are deadly and fast. I hate to admit it, but their kill rate is better than ours right now with zero human casualties. They move around a lot too, which makes it impossible to get a lead on them. We have reports coming in from all over the country."

Instead of sitting at one of the tables, the three of them walked toward me. Chris and Raoul each took a chair and Nikolas sat on the couch with me. I pulled my legs up to make room for him, and he rested a warm hand on my foot. He was so caught up in his conversation I didn't think he was even aware he'd done it. When his thumb began to absently stroke my bare ankle, a tingle spread up my leg and I found it hard to concentrate on my computer or their conversation.

"Are you sure it's the same people?" Chris asked.

"No, but my gut tells me it is. All the strikes have the same feel to them, and the hostiles were killed by some kind of weapon we haven't seen before. The warehouse in Minneapolis, the vampire in Seattle, the nest at the old amusement park in New Jersey."

My head jerked up at the mention of New Jersey. Two days ago, I'd wiped out a nest of seven vampires and rescued a family of four from an abandoned amusement park in that state. It had been my most difficult kill yet, and at one point I'd thought I was done for. I was glad I saved that family, but I'd been in over my head on that one. It was only my vampire radar that had kept me alive, and I'd sworn to Eldeorin that if he ever pulled another stunt like that I was never speaking to him again.

"...and each time the victims recovered had no clear memory of their rescuer or what happened to them. It's like someone messed with their memories. Twenty-two people were rescued from the gulak in Minneapolis, and every one of them gave a different description of the person who helped them."

"One person?" Nikolas's thumb stopped moving. "Didn't you say we found a dead gulak master in the warehouse? It would take an experienced warrior to kill a demon that powerful."

Raj, the transmitter guy, chuckled. "Maybe we have a rogue warrior taking it on the road."

"Or it could be a human hunter with a new kind of weapon," someone else suggested. "Whoever he is, he has a pair to go into that nest on his own."

Chris laughed. "Maybe we should try to recruit him."

Jordan snorted and looked up from the workstation she was monitoring. "You guys automatically assume it's a male."

Raoul gave her an indulgent smile. "No offense, Jordan, but the odds are small that this is a female."

I couldn't resist speaking up. "Why?"

"Most females don't have the stomach for that kind of killing," Raoul said, earning a scowl from Jordan. "Mohiri females do," he amended, "but I doubt one of them is behind this. I think we are dealing with someone new."

"Why does it matter who they are as long as they are helping people and killing the bad guys?" I asked.

Nikolas's hand gently squeezed my foot. "It doesn't as long as they keep a low profile and don't endanger humans. We monitor the police bands in most cities, so we heard about the warehouse in Minneapolis and were able to get it contained before the local authorities arrived."

A warrior named Brock chimed in. "It looks like we aren't the only ones with a vigilante at work. A month ago, we also picked up a story about a village in Mexico that claims an 'angel' appeared out of nowhere to destroy the demons terrorizing their village. One of our teams down there checked it out and found two dead vampires."

My eyes met Jordan's across the room, and she didn't have to speak for me to know what she was thinking. She knew about every one of my adventures, and she would have traded places with me in a heartbeat.

A message flashing on my screen pulled my attention back to my chat. I smiled when a picture of a fluffy white cat appeared with the caption "Lulu says hello."

Me: Give her a hug for me.
Kelvan: Already did.
Me: Any luck with that lead in Canada?
David: No, but we might be onto something else. K is on it.
Pause.
Me: Guys, don't keep me in suspense here!
Kelvan: Hold on. Running a new algorithm.
Me: English please.
David: He wrote a new routine with new search parameters.
Me: Oh.
Kelvan: Give me a few minutes.
Long pause.
Kelvan: Think I have something.

A black and white photo appeared in the chat window, and I clicked on it to make it larger. The woman in the picture had a strong resemblance to Madeline, but it was hard to be sure.

"Nikolas." I turned the laptop to face him, and his eyes narrowed on the screen. He leaned over for a closer look and Chris crowded in behind him.

"It's Madeline," Chris breathed. "How the hell did they find her?"

I lifted a shoulder. "I told you they're the best."

Nikolas looked at me. "Where was this taken?"

"One second." I pulled the laptop around and asked David, who replied immediately. "Yesterday in Vancouver," I told Nikolas. More words appeared on the screen and my pulse sped up. "David sent an address where they think she's staying."

Nikolas stood and began issuing orders for a team to be ready to depart within the hour. One of the warriors brought up Vancouver on his monitors, preparing to track the team once they got there.

I set the laptop on the couch and followed Nikolas. He finished talking to one of the warriors then turned to smile at me. "Great work, Sara."

"Thanks, but David did most of the work."

He laid a hand on my arm. "Why don't you grab your stuff, and I'll walk you and Jordan home before I leave?"

My smile faltered. "What do you mean? I'm coming with you."

"It's too dangerous," he replied firmly.

"I can take care of myself, Nikolas. Besides, it's only Madeline."

He shook his head. "You're not ready. We'll handle this."

I refused to back down. "She's my mother, so if anyone should be there, it's me. I didn't work this hard to find her just so you could leave me behind." My voice had gotten louder and people were staring at us, but I didn't care. This was too important to me.

His jaw hardened. "You can talk to her when we bring her back here."

"So that's it. We're back to you making all the decisions and me having no say at all?" Angry hurt made my chest ache. "I thought we were in this together."

"We are."

I waved an arm at the room. "You mean as long as I'm doing something you don't think is dangerous. Why have I been working my butt off in training if you're not going to take me seriously?"

"I do take you seriously." He rubbed the back of his neck. "Listen, this is not the time or place for this discussion. We'll talk about it when I get back."

"Fine." I grabbed my laptop and backpack from the couch and marched to the door. "Chris, will you walk me back?"

Nikolas followed me. "I said I'd take you home."

I couldn't look at him and let him see how much his dismissal had hurt. "You have a mission to organize. One of the others can make sure I get home."

"Chris can get things ready here." He picked up my coat where it lay over the back of a chair and held it up for me. I had no choice but to let him help me into it.

Silence hung over us during the short walk back to the house. At the door he took my hand and laced his fingers with mine. "I hate to leave you upset, but I have to go. We'll talk when I get back, okay?"

I nodded, still not able to look at him.

He let go of my hand and pulled me against him, wrapping his arms around me. "I'll see you in a day or two," he said against my hair.

As upset as I was with him, I couldn't let him leave without saying anything. My arms went around his waist, and I pressed my cheek to his chest. "Be careful."

"Always." He pulled away and pressed a tender kiss to my lips before he opened the door and ushered me inside. I waited until I could no longer sense him before I let the tears come.

* * *

"Have you heard anything yet?" Jordan ran up to me as I walked to the house after my training with Aine. It was noon and Nikolas and Chris had been gone about sixteen hours.

"Just that the first place they checked didn't pan out. David sent me a new address and I passed it on to Raoul to give to the team."

Jordan studied my face then fell into step beside me. "You're still mad at Nikolas, aren't you?"

"Wouldn't you be?"

She lifted a shoulder. "Probably. But it's *Nikolas*."

I scowled at her. "If you say I should forgive him just because he's hot, I may have to rethink our friendship."

"Wow, you really are pissed." She opened the door and entered the house ahead of me. "I'm just saying that you should be used to him being this way by now. A bonded male is overbearing enough without him being Nikolas Danshov. Add to that the fact that you ran off, almost died, and spent a week in a faerie coma, and you've got one very overprotective warrior on your hands."

"I thought he was starting to see me as an equal. Maybe if he knew about the things I've done he'd change his mind." I'd been trying for weeks to find the nerve to tell Nikolas the truth about my training with Eldeorin, but I'd chickened out every time I came close. He was even more protective now than he'd been before I'd left Westhorne.

Jordan barked a laugh. "He'd lose it, and in a big way."

I rubbed my temple. "I don't know what to do, Jordan. I can't live this way."

A gleam entered her eyes. "Well, there is one way to get him to ease up."

"You know I'm not ready for that." The idea of Nikolas and me being intimate made my stomach do funny things. It wasn't that I hadn't thought about it, because I had – more than once. But it was a huge step to take. "Come on. I'm starving. Let's see what Heb is making for lunch."

She shook her head as she always did when I brushed off the topic. "Since you don't have training this afternoon, we'll call the wolf boys and get them to play *World of Warcraft* with us. I totally kicked their asses last time."

I groaned. "Jordan, you know I don't like computer games."

"Perhaps you'd prefer a game of draughts instead?"

I whirled around to stare at the tall and impossibly handsome warrior sauntering out of the living room. His dark wavy hair touched his shoulders and his eyes mirrored the smirk on his lips. A choked sound escaped me, and I launched myself at him. He laughed and enfolded me in his strong embrace.

"Hello, little one. It's good to see you again."

"Desmund, what are you doing here?" I stepped back and stared at him in wonder. "I mean, I'm so happy you're here, but I didn't think you wanted to leave Westhorne."

He led me into the living room. "Westhorne has become quite dull of late, and I find I don't enjoy my solitude as much as I used to. I was planning to take a trip to England until Nikolas called last night to ask if I'd like to visit for a few days."

"Nikolas called you?"

He chuckled as he sat and patted the couch beside him. "I was as surprised as you are. What have you done to that warrior?"

"She's mad at him, and he's trying to soften her up." Jordan took a seat across from us, and I was surprised to see her grin at Desmund. Up until a few months ago, Desmund had been a reclusive and sometimes dangerous warrior all the trainees had avoided. Even Jordan had been more than a little intimidated by his legend.

"Is that so? And what has he done that requires bribery to gain your forgiveness?"

"He thinks I'm useless."

Desmund arched an eyebrow, and I flushed.

"I mean as a fighter. No matter what I do or how much I train, he refuses to think I might be able to take care of myself." I told him about all the progress I'd made with my combat and Fae training, omitting my trips with Eldeorin. "If anyone deserves to be there when Madeline is caught, it's me."

"You are right about Madeline, but Nikolas was also right not to take you into what could be a very dangerous situation. It sounds like you have come a long way in your training. However, Nikolas is an experienced warrior, and he knows it takes more than a few months of training to prepare you for what is out there."

"But I *have* seen what's out there. If he only knew what I've −" My outburst died on my lips when I realized what I'd almost said.

"What does Nikolas not know?" Desmund's eyes bored into mine. "Sara?"

"I..." I looked to Jordan for help, and she gave me a "you're on your own for this one" look. I bit my lip and met Desmund's unyielding gaze. "If I tell you this, will you promise to keep it between us for now?"

"I won't make any promises until I know what is going on."

Great. I took a fortifying breath. "There is this faerie named Eldeorin who took care of me when I was sick, and he has been training me for the last month."

Desmund nodded. "Tristan has mentioned him."

"After my illness, my Fae power got a lot stronger, and I couldn't use it without destroying something. Eldeorin's been training me to use my new power."

"And what is wrong with that if it is helping you? Moreover, why would it upset Nikolas? Is he jealous of the faerie?"

"He doesn't like Eldeorin, but he knows he's just my friend." I swallowed. "He wouldn't be happy if he knew what my training with Eldeorin was really like."

Jordan snorted. "There's the understatement of the year. Do the words 'DEFCON 1 mean anything to you?"

Desmund's brows drew together. "Sara?"

"I've been using my power to kill vampires," I blurted.

Jordan stretched a leg over the arm of her chair. "Among other things."

"Explain." Desmund's tone did not change so it was impossible to know what he was thinking. I started by telling him about my *liannan*. I explained how out of control my power had been and how terrified I'd been of losing control around Nikolas and the others. And then Eldeorin had shown me how to release all that pent-up energy.

Once I got started, the whole story poured out of me, and I spent the next hour filling him in on all my training sessions with Eldeorin. A mixture of shock, concern, and even pride showed on his face, until I got to the part about the vampire nest in New Jersey. I wasn't surprised that one angered him. I didn't want to think about how Nikolas was going to react when I finally told him – if Desmund didn't tell him first.

"I know how bad it sounds, but Eldeorin is always there with me, and I don't think he'd let me get seriously hurt. And I'm getting really good at using my power. I still need to work on my fighting, but I'm getting better every day."

Desmund leaned back and stared at me for a long moment until I couldn't take the silence anymore.

"Say something."

He shook his head. "Your friend, Jordan, is right. Nikolas is going to explode when he hears of this."

I sagged against the couch. "Are you going to tell him?"

He responded by laughing. "I consider myself a brave male, but even I am not brave enough to be the one to tell your mate what you have been up to."

I hugged him. "Thank you."

"That does not mean I agree with you keeping this from him. Nikolas and I have had our differences, but he is a good man and he cares for you."

I pulled back. "I'm going to tell him; I want to tell him. I just don't know how. He'll want me to stop, but I don't want to. I like helping people, and I'm really good at this."

I stared at Desmund as my words sank in. I had complained and yelled at Eldeorin every time I finished one of his training sessions. But the truth was, I felt completely alive and free every time I saved a life and rid the world of one more evil. And I wanted to do it again.

He let out a slow breath. "So you are the vigilante everyone has been talking about these last few weeks?"

"Yes."

He stood and held his hand out to me. I took it automatically, and he pulled me to my feet.

"Where are we going?" I asked when he started for the door, taking me with him.

"If you are intent on saving the world, we need to get you in fighting shape." A smirk curved his lips. "If nothing else, it will help you restrain your mate when he goes into a rage over this."

"*You're* going to train me?"

He laughed arrogantly. "It's been a while, but I do remember how to train someone. I'm sure I can show you some tricks that even Nikolas does not know."

We went to the gym with Jordan trailing behind us, probably hoping to learn some of those tricks Desmund had mentioned. She leaned against the wall as Desmund and I faced each other in the center of the room.

"Before we begin, I need to see what you've learned so far. Proceed."

"You want me to attack you?"

Amusement lit his eyes. "I want you to try."

I went through every kick and strike Nikolas had taught me, and Desmund deflected each one so fast he barely appeared to move. I knew my form was perfect, but there was no way to get past the defenses of someone as fast as him.

"Your technique is good, but where are your strength and your speed?"

I paused to catch my breath. "I still have trouble with that part."

His brow furrowed. "Then that is what we need to work on. It is no wonder Nikolas refused to let you accompany him."

It was my turn to scowl. "I have other strengths."

"Yes, you do, but they are not enough. You were fortunate when you entered that nest that you did not encounter all those vampires together. Your power may be strong, but can you kill that many vampires at once?"

"No, but neither can a warrior." Except maybe Nikolas. And Desmund.

"A warrior would not have attempted that on his own unless he had a death wish." He thought for a moment. "Can you not use your Mori strength at all?"

"A little, but not for long. It feels... strange to me."

"Strange?"

"I don't connect with my Mori the way you guys do, and it's uncomfortable sharing my mind with someone else. Whenever we join, it's a bit overwhelming and I can't keep it up for long."

"But how is it possible for you to be separated at all?"

I stared at the floor, unsure of how to explain my situation to someone who had never spent a day in his four hundred years disconnected from his Mori. No Mohiri, not even Nikolas, could understand what it was like to live with two opposite forces inside of you. Demons and Fae were enemies, and I should not even be possible. But here I was.

"When I was little, I didn't know what I was, just that I had something bad in my head. Then my Fae power developed, and I learned to use it to keep my demon locked away so it didn't make me do bad things." I met his astonished gaze. "That's how I grew up, and it was the only thing I knew until I met Nikolas. My Mori and I are like two minds in one body. I can feel it and talk to it, but I can't use its power unless we join."

Jordan leaned away from the wall. "Wait, you talk to it? Isn't that like talking to yourself?"

"No."

"And your Fae power does not harm your Mori?" Desmund asked, his shock turning to fascination.

"It hurts it a lot if I'm not careful. I keep my power locked away whenever I let it out."

Understanding lit Jordan's eyes. "That's how you were able to stay sane all those years? You just kept your Mori locked away?"

"Pretty much."

"Damn, Sara." Jordan shook her head. "Is there anything you *can't* do?"

I frowned. "Fight, apparently."

Desmund stroked his jaw. "You can fight, just not well enough to face a real adversary without using your power. To do that, you need to join with your demon. So that is what we must work on."

"How?" If he knew a way to help me join easier with my Mori I was all ears.

"The only way is for you to release the demon and join with it as often and as long as you can. It will be unpleasant at first, but eventually you will become accustomed to it."

I swallowed dryly. "And how are you going to help me with that?"

His smile was back. "I will offer moral support and teach you to use your new demon strength on your enemies."

"What about me?" Jordan asked almost reverently. "Can I train with you, too?"

He gave her an appraising look. "What would you like to work on?"

"Sword," Jordan and I said together and laughed.

Desmund glanced from Jordan to me. "Very well." He studied the layout of the room then looked at me. "First, we will spend some time working with your Mori, and then we'll have some weapons training. How does that sound?"

"Awesome," I said dryly, earning laughter from the two of them.

Something told me I was the only one who wasn't going to enjoy training, but at least it would help me keep my mind off other things, like Nikolas and what he was doing right now.

I took a deep breath. "Where do we begin?"

*   *   *

I knew something was wrong the moment I walked into the command center that evening. If the flurry of activity around several of the workstations wasn't enough evidence, the fact that a hush fell over the room when I entered spoke volumes.

"What is it?" I asked Raoul, and alarm shot through me when he couldn't quite meet my eyes. "Tell me."

He hesitated before answering. "The teams had a confirmed lock on the target, and they moved into retrieval position an hour ago. We just got word that they are under heavy attack by hostiles."

"How many?" Desmund asked calmly from behind me.

"Unsure, but they are surrounded. We've dispatched backup from Seattle, but they are still an hour away."

Fear clawed at my chest. Nikolas was in danger, fighting for his life. I'd been so angry at him when he left yesterday. What if he...? *No, don't think that! He's going to be okay.*

"Where are you going?" Jordan called as I spun toward the door.

"I need to find Eldeorin."

She ran after me. "He could be anywhere. How will you find him?"

I stopped and stared at her, flinching at the sympathy in her eyes. "I don't..." My mind raced desperately and the answer hit me. "Heb. He can find him." I took off running again, followed closely by Jordan and Desmund. Eldeorin had said if I ever needed him, to send the dwarf and he would come.

Heb was polishing the silver when I burst into the kitchen, and I almost sobbed in relief. "I need Eldeorin, Heb. Please!"

He disappeared without a word, leaving me clinging to the granite countertop for support. *Please, don't let us be too late.*

Desmund placed his strong hands on my shoulders and turned me to face him. Worry darkened his eyes. "What are you going to do when the faerie gets here, little one?"

"I'm going after Nikolas and Chris."

"Nikolas would not want you to endanger yourself that way."

"Don't!" I pulled away and he let me go. "Don't talk about him like he's gone."

He held up a hand. "I'm sorry. I didn't intend that the way it sounded. I only meant that if he was here, he would not be happy with what you are planning."

"I know, but I won't stand back and do nothing." I clenched my hands anxiously. "Where the hell are they?"

"Cousin, what is wrong? Are you ill?"

I almost hurled myself at Eldeorin when he appeared beside me. "Nikolas is in trouble. He needs me."

Eldeorin pulled me to him and his hand stroked the back of my head, sending his calming influence over me. "Hush. We will help your warrior. Where is he?"

"Vancouver," Desmund answered for me. "She is too upset and inexperienced for this. Take me instead."

Eldeorin patted my back and tucked me against his side, smiling as if nothing was wrong. His blue eyes gave Desmund an appraising look. "As much as I'd *love* to take you instead, that is not possible. My magic would harm you, maybe even kill you. Something tells me that my little cousin would be very upset by that." His arm gave me a squeeze. "Don't worry about her. She is much stronger than you know."

I clutched the hand that rested on my shoulder. "Can we please go?"

"Of course. Let's go find your warrior."

CHAPTER 16

COLD FILLED MY chest the moment we arrived on the quiet street lined with large older homes. Though not a vampire was in sight, I knew immediately that there were at least three dozen of them nearby, and my improved radar told me exactly where they were. So many vampires working together was almost unheard of, and no Mohiri team could expect to defeat that many at once.

"Do you feel them?" I asked Eldeorin.

"I sense demons, but I have trouble telling the Mohiri and the vampires apart."

I looked up and down the street. I couldn't sense Nikolas, but I told myself that was just because he wasn't close enough. *He's okay. If anyone is okay, it's him.*

"I can't do this alone. There are too many."

"We'll do it together." He waved a hand, and I found myself dressed in black again, this time with two silver blades strapped to my thighs.

Seconds later, a male vampire ran from between two houses. I knew Eldeorin had made us – or at least me – visible when the vampire stopped and stared at me across the well-lit street. Indecision showed clearly on his face, and he looked up the street before his gaze came back to me.

I saw it the moment he made up his mind, and I was ready when he attacked. He was fast and his fangs were already extended when he reached me. He grabbed my shoulders in an iron grip and pulled me against him.

My hand came up between us, and he let out a small scream and staggered back when the first blast of power ripped through him. I don't think he knew what was happening until I pressed my glowing hand to his chest a second time. Shock and fear filled his face as he crumpled to the pavement.

I stepped around the body in the direction he had been looking. "This way."

Two houses down we encountered two vampires feeding on an older man. I leapt on one of them and took him out quickly, leaving Eldeorin to handle the other one. There was nothing we could do for the man, so we moved on.

The need to find Nikolas burned through me, dampening my fear and lending speed to my movements. Methodically, I located vampires, and Eldeorin helped me kill them as we made our way up the street to a large white house where I sensed the largest concentration of vampires.

But no Nikolas. "Why can't I feel him?" The possible answer to that was something I refused to consider. If I did, I'd fall to pieces.

"My glamour prevents your demons from sensing each other," Eldeorin said. "It is the only way to shield you from detection."

"Oh thank God."

I didn't need to feel Nikolas to know he was in the white house that was crawling with vampires. "There are way too many vampires in there. We have to draw them out and give Nikolas and the others a chance."

Eldeorin studied the large house. "How would you like to do that?"

It occurred to me then that he was letting me make all the tactical decisions. I didn't care if he was turning this into another training session as long as we helped Nikolas and Chris.

"Nikolas won't recognize me, right?"

"Not unless you want him to."

The urge to laugh eased some of the tension coiled in my body. "Let's save that drama for another day." Putting my fingers to my lips, I let out a piercing whistle. "Hey, suckers, fresh meat."

Eldeorin shook his head as the front door crashed open. "I see we are going with the direct approach."

I should have been terrified to see six vampires spill from the house, but I felt strangely calm. Maybe it was the powerful faerie standing beside me or the result of our training sessions. Or maybe it was the knowledge that every vampire I drew out of the house gave Nikolas a better chance at survival.

"You are awfully young to be a hunter," drawled one of the vampires as they advanced slowly on us.

One of his companions laughed. "But not too young to die."

"I heard young Mohiri blood is very sweet," the first one said. "I get first drink."

Another vampire spoke up. "Hey, why do you get first drink? We all saw her at the same time."

"Because I'm the oldest and I say so, that's why."

"Are you guys for real?" Were they actually arguing over my blood in front of me?

They stopped bickering to stare at me.

"Before you draw straws to see who gets the first taste, you might want to ask yourselves one question."

The six of them formed a semicircle in front of us. The fact that they never looked at Eldeorin told me he was invisible again. These guys had no clue what was in store for them.

"What question?" asked the vampire who acted like their leader.

"You gotta ask why a defenseless girl would walk up to a house full of blood suckers." I watched their eyes go round as blue sparks rolled over my skin and lifted my hair from my shoulders. A thrill shot through me, and I knew how a hunter felt when they sighted their prey.

Six pairs of eyes suddenly shifted to my right as Eldeorin made his entrance. I used their surprise to my advantage, and I attacked before they knew what was happening. A few months ago, my power would have given a baby vampire a very painful but otherwise harmless shock. Not so anymore.

I hit the leader with a palm heel strike that sent him flying backward with flames sprouting from his chest. My leg swept another vampire off his feet. I grabbed his arm and shot power into him as a third vampire jumped on my back. The one on my back screamed and tried to get away from me as soon as he got a taste of my power. I flipped him over my shoulder and grabbed his throat before he hit the ground. After spending the last month killing older vampires, fighting a bunch of baby vamps was almost too easy. In less than two minutes, I killed four of them, while Eldeorin took care of the last two.

"That worked well."

I barely heard Eldeorin because I was listening to the sounds of fighting coming from inside the house. By my count we had killed about fifteen vampires so far. That still left twenty or so, and I knew they weren't all young or Nikolas and his team would have taken care of them already.

"There are still too many of them." I ran toward the house, but instead of going to the front door, I went around to the back. The door was wide open and I could see movement inside. I took a deep breath and prepared to call out again, hoping to trick a few more vampires into leaving the house.

Before I could open my mouth, my eyes were drawn to a movement above. A figure dove through a window and rolled across the roof of the back porch. Nimbly she came to her feet and jumped off the porch, landing silently in the grass. Shock immobilized me when I saw her hair gleaming like white gold in the moonlight.

"Madeline!"

She glanced at me in surprise, then she began to sprint away.

"Mother!"

Madeline stopped running, and her head swung in my direction again. At first she looked confused, and then I saw recognition in her eyes. I knew Eldeorin had lifted my glamour so she could see the real me. Shock and something I could not define passed over her face as we stared at each other for several seconds. I waited for her to say something to the daughter she hadn't seen in sixteen years.

She ran instead.

I didn't try to chase her, as much as I wanted to, because I could never catch her on foot. I watched as she raced toward the tall fence at the back of the yard and vaulted over it without once looking back.

Vampire screams drew my attention back to the house. There was no time to dwell on the fact that I'd finally caught up to Madeline and let her slip away. Or to question what kind of mother leaves her daughter – even an estranged one – behind with a vampire horde. Right now, my only concern was the vampire that had run outside at the sound of my voice. He wasn't young like the ones out front, and I barely had time to recover from my shock about Madeline before he was on me.

Eldeorin materialized and ripped the vampire away from me. I don't think I ever fully grasped the extent of my mentor's power until I saw a mature vampire almost disintegrate in his hands. Would I ever be that powerful? The prospect excited and frightened me at the same time.

A male shouted inside the house, and he was answered by another. *Nikolas!*

I was almost to the open door when three figures flew through it. The two vampires snarled and rounded on the blond warrior as he raised his long thin sword. I knew Chris could handle them. I wasn't so sure about the two more vampires sneaking up behind him.

I pulled out one of the knives I hadn't needed until now. It wasn't a throwing knife in my hand, but I knew from practice how to hold it and make it behave like one. I didn't hesitate as I drew back my arm and let the knife fly straight into the chest of one of the advancing vampires.

The vampire's strangled cry alerted Chris to the threat behind him and drew everyone's attention to me. Chris frowned, and his expression told me he was surprised to see someone else there. His lack of recognition told me Eldeorin had glamoured me again.

One of the vampires split away to come after me, and the others attacked Chris. I had my other knife out and my power ready before the vampire reached me. He lunged at me, but his eyes were on the blade in my right hand instead of my glowing left hand. I let him grab me before I brought my hand up between us. Shock registered on his face, and he shuddered violently as my power found its mark. I threw him away from me, and he twitched on the ground in his death throes.

My attention turned back to Chris, who had killed one vampire and was quickly dispatching the other. His opponent fell and he immediately scanned the yard for other dangers. His eyes fell on me, and he gave a slight nod before he raced back into the house again. I heard more shouts and screams and the sound of metal sliding through flesh. When two more vampires fled from the house with fear written plainly on their faces, I knew the battle had turned in our favor. I let Eldeorin have the pleasure of killing the vampires before they could escape.

A vampire crashed through a lower window and another ran out the back door. I was moving to intercept them when a warrior sped through the doorway and cut one down with one of his swords. He spun away from the dying vampire to impale the one that had gone through the window before it had a chance to stand.

My knees grew weak and relief washed over me as I watched Nikolas fight. He was magnificent. And he was safe. All I wanted to do was run to him, but I remembered in time that he couldn't know I was here.

His eyes swept the yard and settled on me. It was hard to read his expression, and I wondered what I looked like to him, or if he connected me with the vigilante whose movements they had been following.

"Who are you?"

My voice refused to work for several seconds. "A friend," I managed to say.

"That doesn't answer my question." He waved a hand at the bodies littering the yard. "No human could do this. What are you and how did you find us?"

"That is because I am not human. As for how I found you, I have my ways."

His furrowed brow told me he wasn't satisfied with my response – not that I'd expected anything else. He took a step toward me, and I suddenly realized the situation I was in. I couldn't outrun him, and I couldn't just disappear in front of his eyes either. That was a Fae ability, and he was too smart not to put the pieces together.

"Nikolas," someone called from inside the house.

He didn't take his eyes off me. "What is it, Devon?"

"We found a tablet and some other things, but she's not here. Looks like she got away."

Of course, she had. Madeline had done what she was best at and saved her own ass. Why would she care about the lives of people she knew, including her own daughter, when she'd never cared before?

Glass shattered loudly followed by screams, and Nikolas forgot about me to speed around to the front of the house. As soon as he was out of sight, Eldeorin appeared and laid his hand on my shoulder. "Time to go, Cousin."

We reappeared in the kitchen, surprising the hell out of Heb who was taking a large sheet of cookies from the oven. The metal sheet clattered across the tile floor, and the noise brought Jordan running into the room.

"You're back!" She skidded to a halt and her eyes swept over me. "You look amazing. Well, except for the blood and... is that a vampire fang in your hair?"

I thought she was kidding until I reached up and felt the sharp tooth tangled in my hair. My stomach churned and I threw the thing away from me, watching as it bounced across the kitchen floor. Wordlessly, Heb used a paper towel to pick it up and throw it in the trash.

"Say something. What happened up there? Is the team okay?"

Now that it was over and I knew Nikolas was safe, the weight of the night's events came crashing down on me. Killing vampires didn't bother me, but the sheer number of them that had attacked Nikolas's team scared the hell out of me. And then there was Madeline. After all the months of searching for her, I finally find her and she gets away. After this, I wouldn't be surprised if she fled the continent and disappeared for good.

Eldeorin waved his hand to clean me up, and then sat me at the small breakfast table. Jordan sat across from me with an expectant look on her face.

Desmund appeared in the doorway and started yelling at Eldeorin. "She looks terrible. I told you she was not up for this."

"Desmund, I'm fine, just a bit wiped." I smiled at Jordan. "Nikolas and the others are safe. At least I think everyone is safe. We didn't stick around long once it was over."

Jordan raised her hand in a high five. "I want to hear every detail."

I told her and Desmund everything that had happened from the moment we left here to the moment we returned. Jordan was wide-eyed as I recounted each fight, especially when Eldeorin added his own embellishments.

She muttered a few obscenities when she heard about Madeline. "I thought my mother was bad. Are you sure she knew who you were?"

I remembered the recognition in Madeline's eyes. "She knew."

"And Nikolas had no idea who you were?"

"None."

"What about the bond thing? Can't he sense you like you do him?"

"Not through a faerie glamour. I couldn't sense him either."

A phone rang and Heb went to answer it. He reappeared a minute later with a cordless phone, which he handed to Desmund.

Desmund spoke briefly to whoever it was, then hung up and smiled at us. "Nikolas called Raoul to let him know the team is safe. The Seattle team has just arrived on site, and they are taking over the cleanup operation."

Even though I'd been there and talked to Nikolas, it was still a huge relief to hear that the whole team had made it out. "Did he say when he's coming back?"

"They should be here sometime tomorrow morning."

I sagged in my chair, and Desmund laid a hand on my shoulder. "I don't like you going into such dangerous situations, but I understand why you had to do it." He looked at Eldeorin over my head. "Thank you for keeping her safe."

"You do not have to thank me, warrior. Sara is stronger than you could possibly imagine. One day, she will realize that as well."

Eldeorin spoke with such conviction it was impossible not to believe him. Training with him had shown me I was capable of more than I'd ever dreamed, but tonight had taken it to a whole new level. The whole time I was out there, my fear had been for Nikolas, not for me. When had I stopped being terrified of vampires? I still feared them, yes, but I was no longer the defenseless, frightened girl Eli had pulled into that alley.

I stood, covering a yawn with my hand. "If you guys don't mind, I think I'll go to bed."

Jordan nodded. "I think you've earned a good night's sleep. Too bad no one but us will know what you did tonight."

"For now. I'm going to tell Nikolas everything when I think he can handle it."

Laughter filled the kitchen. "Just let us know when you plan to do it so we can be far away," Jordan quipped.

I gave them a tired smile. "Good night, guys."

It felt strange entering my quiet bedroom after everything that had gone down tonight. I was so overwhelmed by it all that I barely knew what I was doing as I showered and got ready for bed. I burrowed under the comforter and snuggled my pillow, exhausted but happy. Nikolas was safe, and he would be home tomorrow.

My sleep was deep and restful, unmarred by a single bad dream. Sometime around dawn I awoke to a hand touching my face and an achingly familiar caress against my mind. "Nikolas," I said thickly, trying to come fully awake.

"Shhh. Go back to sleep." His lips brushed my forehead. "I'll see you in a few hours."

I felt his heat pulling away and I made a sound of protest. Reaching for him, my fingers slid through his soft hair as I tugged him back to me. My lips found his warm, full mouth and I kissed him urgently, driven by the joy of having him home and the fear of almost losing him. The intoxicating smell of him and the brush of his day-old beard against my face sent shivers racing through me. I wanted nothing else in that moment but to lose myself in him.

The bed dipped as he stretched out, half beside me, half over me. My stomach careened wildly when he whispered my name against my lips and took possession of them. His mouth was firm and demanding, yet gentle. I felt drunk from the taste of him, and my hands clung desperately to his hard arms.

My breath hitched as his hand left my shoulder to slide in a feather light caress down my ribs and rest against my bare stomach where my T-shirt had ridden up. The heat of his hand was like a brand against my skin, and a small noise escaped me.

Nikolas made a sound deep in his chest and broke the kiss, moving his head until it lay beside mine. I could feel his short warm breaths against my ear and his heart beating as hard as mine. After a minute, he lifted his head and his dark eyes peered down into mine. "I should go."

Confusion and hurt flared in my chest. "Okay," I whispered hoarsely.

He groaned and rested his forehead lightly against mine. "Jesus, Sara, don't look at me like that or I'll never be able to leave."

"I don't want you to leave."

"I know, but you're also not ready for where this is headed."

"I..." I wanted to deny it, but he was right. Getting caught up in a few heated kisses didn't make me ready to go farther. It wasn't that I believed you had to wait for marriage or anything. I just didn't feel like I was ready for that level of intimacy.

He rolled away until he lay on his back beside me. I heard a deep sigh and then his hand reached for mine. "I'm sorry about what happened before I left. I didn't handle it well and I hated leaving you upset. I know how important it is to you to find Madeline, and I should have known you'd expect to be there when we brought her in. But I'm also glad I listened to my gut and didn't take you with us. This was a rough one."

I know. "I was scared for you."

I felt his face turning toward me, and I turned mine so our eyes met.

"That's how I felt the whole time I was looking for you," he said gruffly. "I was afraid something would hurt you before I found you."

"I'm sorry."

He exhaled deeply. "I wish I could explain how it feels, this need to protect you, and how crazy it makes me when you're in danger. The bond is a part of me – us – and it's not something I can just turn off. Do you understand what I'm saying?"

I gave him a sad smile. "I'm trying to, but it's hard. Put yourself in my shoes. How would you feel if you suddenly lost your freedom and had people telling you what to do? I don't want to be pampered and taken care of. I'm not fragile, and I don't break that easily."

"I know you're not." He lifted our joined hands and held them to his chest. "Your spirit and independence make you who you are, Sara, and I never want to take them from you."

I didn't reply. How could I tell him his restrictions were slowly doing that?

"All I've known for a long time is how to be a warrior and how to command others. That's worked with everything else in my life. It's taken me a while to learn that won't work with us."

"You figured that out, huh?" I teased, and his answering smile lightened the mood in the room. "Do you think you'll ever get past it, this overprotectiveness?"

He sighed again. "I'll never stop worrying about your safety, but I think it will get easier."

"When I prove I can defend myself, will you treat me like the other warriors?"

He laughed softly. "I can safely say I will never see you as one of the other warriors. But I will try to be less of a tyrant. And when you demonstrate you are ready for a mission, I won't stop you from going on one. I guarantee I won't like it, but I won't hold you back."

"Thank you." It was a baby step, but one in the right direction. I wished I could tell him my secret, but I didn't want to ruin this moment. *Soon.*

He unclasped our hands and held his arm above my head. I didn't need more invitation than that, and I moved over to snuggle against his side with one arm across his chest. He stroked my hair as he often did, and I sighed blissfully.

"Do you want to talk about Vancouver?" I asked after we had been quiet for several minutes.

"Later. Right now I just want to hold you."

My chest swelled. How could I say no to that?

CHAPTER 17

"I THINK I'M starting to like California." Jordan leaned against the railing of the patio at the back of the house. "I could get used to this."

I inhaled deeply as I watched the waves crashing against the shore below us. "I missed the ocean when I was at Westhorne. It's pretty there, but nothing compares to the ocean."

"Is that an undine thing?"

A laugh escaped me. "Nope, I think it's just a Sara thing."

She was quiet for a minute. "So when are you going to tell me what happened when Nikolas got back from Vancouver?"

"Nothing happened, really."

She gave me a sly smile. "Nothing, huh? Is that why I saw him leaving your room that morning before breakfast?"

"He came to see me when he got here that morning because he knew I was worried about him."

"I take it you didn't tell him your secret since we still have a roof on the house."

I exhaled noisily. "I wanted to, but then he started talking about the bond, and how crazy it makes him when he thinks I'm in danger. He's not ready to know everything yet. I wish he was because I hate keeping this from him."

"Bonds are pretty complicated from everything I've seen and heard, and hell on the males. He'll come around eventually, maybe in a decade or two."

"Maybe."

She nudged me with her shoulder. "What's wrong? You have a smoking hot warrior visiting you in the wee hours of the morning. Why are you not grinning from ear to ear?"

I bit my lip, thinking about my talk with Nikolas two days ago. "Sometimes I wonder how much of what he feels for me comes from the bond. I know it makes males overprotective, and Tristan said it can give them some pretty intense emotions. What if there's no *us* outside of the bond?"

Jordan scoffed. "Are you blind? That man is crazy about you. And it's obvious you're head over heels for him."

"I know he cares about me. But he never talks about his feelings, except for how much he worries about my safety."

"Guys hate to talk about their feelings." She smiled again. "Nikolas seems more like a man of actions than words anyway."

I shook my head. "Not with me. He's taking it really slow."

"He headed straight for your bedroom when he got back that day. That doesn't sound slow to me."

Heat rose in my cheeks. "We've never done anything except kiss. He likes to hold me."

Her hand went to her heart. "Nikolas Danshov likes to kiss and hold you. You poor, poor thing." She sighed dramatically. "Where did I go wrong with you?"

I pushed her away. "Forget I said anything." I loved every second I spent with Nikolas, no matter what we were doing. But I'd give anything for him to tell me his feelings went deeper than caring and protective instincts. I loved him so much. What if he never felt the same way for me? I wished I was brave enough to tell him how I felt and hoped he loved me back. But I wasn't that brave, and my heart couldn't handle it if he didn't return my feelings.

"We are a sorry pair, aren't we? We're surrounded by hot male warriors every day and neither of us is getting any action."

Happy to move the conversation away from Nikolas and me, I said, "Whatever happened to that Egyptian warrior you liked – the one with the *big* sword? What was his name?"

"Hamid." Her eyes turned dreamy for a second before she huffed. "He left for LA before we could get better acquainted."

"Oh, that's too bad."

She grinned. "Don't worry. I'll see him again if I have anything to say about it."

Laughing, I turned to look at the water again. Poor Hamid. That man had no idea what he was in for.

"I've been meaning to ask you," Jordan said after a few minutes. "You haven't really said much about seeing Madeline in Vancouver. What was it like to finally see her face-to-face?"

"Strange. She looks our age."

"So does everyone else we know."

I shrugged. "I know, but it's different when it's your mother."

"Too bad you didn't get a chance to talk to her before she ran."

I nodded. "I shouldn't be surprised, but I can't believe she ran away like that."

"After everything I've heard about her, I can believe it." She grew quiet and I looked at her.

"What?"

She shifted weight from one foot to the other. "I was thinking. What happens if we find Madeline and she won't tell us anything? Or what if she really doesn't know anything about the Master?"

"Why would she be running all this time if she didn't know something?"

"I don't know. Why wouldn't she tell her father and let him take the Master down? She wouldn't have to run anymore if he was dead."

I couldn't answer that. I had asked myself the same question many times over the last few months. The possibility that Madeline might not know the Master's identity was one I wouldn't consider. I couldn't.

"There you are."

I turned around to see Desmund striding across the lawn toward us, wearing jeans and a thin gray sweater that clung to his muscular body. In the months since he'd recovered from his illness, he had returned to his former warrior physique and his skin had taken on a healthy glow again. Today his hair was tied back in a ponytail, showing off his handsome aristocratic features.

Jordan let out a low whistle. "Damn! He makes me wish I was male. And gay."

"Did you forget our training?" Desmund asked me as he stepped onto the patio.

"I was hoping you'd forget." After three days of training with Desmund, I longed for our quiet times together in the library at Westhorne. He was on an unrelenting mission to teach me to bond permanently with my Mori or to go insane in the process. It was like a freaking boot camp. If I thought hiding would get me out of working with him, I'd be under my bed right now.

His dark eyes gleamed wickedly. "Oh no. I have something new planned for us today."

I think I actually gulped. My eyes went to Jordan who gave me her "oh shit" look. "What is it?" I was almost afraid to hear the answer.

"Nothing you can't handle." He beckoned me with a wave of his hand.

"Later," Jordan called, and I thought I heard her mutter "maybe" under her breath.

We walked to the house, and he opened the door for me. "Wouldn't you rather play checkers?" I asked him when he steered me toward the training room.

He laughed richly. "I'd love a game later, if you're still talking to me."

That doesn't sound good.

I sensed Nikolas before we reached the gym. At the door to the room I stopped at the sight of him stacking weights on one of the mats. Desmund gently nudged me into the room. "Nikolas has agreed to join us today to help with a new training technique I've devised for you. We'll start with our normal routine and take it from there."

Our normal routine consisted of me joining with my Mori for as long as I could stand, which was usually less than thirty minutes. It wasn't that I didn't want to merge with the demon; I just couldn't handle the constant onslaught of emotions and the alien power flowing through me. I had no idea how the other Mohiri lived with it every second of their lives, and I wasn't surprised that orphans went insane if they were not taught to control their Mori.

Nikolas nodded to me but didn't speak as I walked to the center of the room where he had laid the weights. I closed my eyes and lowered the wall holding back my Mori. Its emotions, which had been muted, brushed against my mind – mainly its joy at being close to its mate. A few months ago, it would have rushed forward, but ever since the onset of my *liannan*, it moved slowly and warily. I assured it every day that I'd never hurt it, and I thought it was finally beginning to believe me.

It stopped and I knew it was feeling for my Fae power. *Glow?* it asked fearfully.

No glow, just us. I opened my mind to the black shapeless blob.

Solmi! A bonded Mori had a one track mind; all it cared about was its mate. The demon forgot its fear and pressed against my mind eagerly.

No matter how many times I merged with my Mori, I reeled from the sensations and myriad of emotions bombarding me. I gritted my teeth and let the initial wave wash over me. After a minute, my Mori reined in some of its emotions until I could think clearly again. It had taken us weeks, but we were both slowly learning how to join without overwhelming each other. I took a deep breath as it slowly released its dark power into my body until my muscles quivered from the increased strength.

"Are you good?" Desmund asked.

I opened my eyes. "Yes."

"Okay, we'll start with the smaller weights and work up to the larger ones. You know the drill."

I moved to the first set of kettlebells that were forty pounds each. After ten reps I moved on to the sixty-pound weights and did ten more reps. The heavier the weights, the more I had to tap into my demon's strength, allowing me to gradually widen our connection. By the time I got to the eighty-pound weights, I had so much power coursing through me I felt like I could lift one of my trainers.

Nikolas and Desmund stood off to one side as I went through my workout routine, and I heard enough to know they were talking about

Vancouver. I almost lost my concentration a few times, trying to listen to their conversation.

"I've never seen them behave that way," Nikolas said. "There were enough of them to wipe out several teams."

Desmund nodded thoughtfully. "It is unusual to hear of that many vampires working together." His voice lowered, but not enough that I couldn't hear him. "I am amazed you did not suffer casualties."

"I am too. If I didn't know better, I'd think they were trying to capture us, not kill us."

A tremor went through me and my Mori, and I lifted the kettlebells with more force than was necessary, sending one of them flying away from me. The thought of Nikolas in the hands of vampires made me want to retch and hit something at the same time.

Nikolas retrieved the weight and brought it back to me. "Are you okay?"

"Great," I lied. "Sometimes I don't know my own strength."

He smiled and laid the weight at my feet. Then he went back to stand near Desmund again. I tried to tune them out, but it was no use. Nikolas hadn't said much about what had happened that night in Vancouver, and I was dying to hear more.

"You are fortunate then that help arrived," Desmund said.

"Yes," Nikolas replied grimly. "We found almost twenty vampires dead in the street and near the house. I don't know how he knew where we were, but he's the reason we didn't lose anyone. The Seattle team wouldn't have made it in time."

Desmund's gaze flicked to me then back to Nikolas. "It sounds like you have a powerful ally out there."

"We need one. We are already getting reports of more vampire attacks on our people. The team in Houston nearly lost two warriors last night."

I lost track of what they were saying when I started to feel the strain of being joined with my Mori. Sweat beaded my upper lip and my legs began to tremble. The clock on the wall told me only twenty-five minutes had passed since I'd started, and I knew I wouldn't make it to thirty. Carefully, I set the heavy weights I was holding on the mat so I didn't hurt myself when the demon strength left me.

Desmund walked toward me. "You have thirty-five minutes left in this exercise."

I gaped at him. "I can't last an hour. I can barely do half an hour."

"Nonsense. You are stronger than that. Continue."

My hands curled into fists at my sides as I held the connection with my Mori. The hands on the clock seemed to be glued in place, and I was shaking by the time ten minutes had gone by. My Mori's presence began to buzz like a hornet's nest inside my skull, growing louder with each passing minute. "I can't," I gasped. I looked at Nikolas, who watched me with eyes full of concern but made no move to intercede.

"Am I late?"

I turned in confusion to the door as Eldeorin walked into the room. He smiled at me then looked at Desmund. "Sorry, I was detained."

"Your timing is perfect," Desmund said as the faerie joined him and Nikolas.

I spoke through clenched teeth as my Mori shifted again. "What are you doing here, Eldeorin?"

"Desmund and I talked last night about your training, and he mentioned the difficulties you are having with your demon. We came up with something that will help motivate you."

Desmund and Eldeorin had discussed me? What would a faerie know about joining with a demon? My eyes moved from Eldeorin to Desmund and then to Nikolas, whose expression gave nothing away. The smile on Eldeorin's face set off warning bells inside my head, and Desmund looked entirely too pleased with himself. What the hell were they up to?

Desmund approached. "We are going to try something new, and Nikolas has agreed to take part in our little experiment. You must stay joined with your Mori until the hour is up. If you don't we will start over, but I don't think that will happen."

"Why?"

Eldeorin moved before I could blink. He reappeared behind Nikolas with his hands on Nikolas's shoulders. A second later, Nikolas grunted and his jaw clenched as if he was very uncomfortable, but not in pain.

Solmi! my Mori cried. I forgot about my pain and ran toward Nikolas. "Stop!"

Desmund grabbed me from behind in an iron grip. "Your life could one day depend on you joining with your Mori. What if it was one of your friends' lives in danger? Or his? Could you do it then?"

I twisted, unable to break his hold. My eyes narrowed on Eldeorin, who met my furious glare without blinking. "Let him go, or so help me…" Eldeorin was very powerful. What if he accidently used too much of his magic? He could kill Nikolas or seriously harm him. I knew better than anyone what Fae magic could do to a demon, and I didn't want that anywhere near Nikolas.

"Imagine that is a vampire instead of the faerie," Desmund said mercilessly in my ear. "What will you do?"

He held me immobile and all I could do was watch Nikolas helplessly as minutes ticked by. My whole body trembled as fear and a violent urge to hurt someone boiled inside me. I was a pressure cooker that was about to explode.

Nikolas grimaced, and I saw pain flash briefly in his eyes.

Desmund slammed into the wall behind me. I moved so fast that

Eldeorin barely had time to show his surprise before I ripped him away from Nikolas. The faerie righted himself quickly as I went after him, shaking with rage.

A pair of arms wrapped around me from behind. "It's okay, Sara. Calm down," Nikolas said, pulling me back against him. My Mori and I immediately quieted at the sound of his voice and the touch of his skin on mine. I kept my eyes narrowed on Eldeorin, who watched us with blatant curiosity. Friend or no, I was going to kick his ass if he took a single step toward us.

"Fascinating." Eldeorin leaned against a wall nonchalantly, as if I hadn't just thrown him across a room. "Sara, are you still joined with your demon?"

"Yes," I bit out.

Desmund straightened his clothes as he walked over to stand a few feet from Eldeorin. "Interesting."

I scowled at them. "I'm glad I could entertain you guys."

Eldeorin ignored my angry retort. "You are not strong enough to throw off a warrior or me with your demon strength. You used your Fae magic."

"So?"

"You used it while joined with your demon."

"What?" Fear shot through me, and I turned my attention to my Mori. The demon was calm and unharmed, and happy now that Nikolas was holding us. The realization of what I'd done shook me to the center of my being. Somehow I had used my Fae power while connected to my Mori, without erecting a wall to protect the demon. How was that possible?

Nikolas pulled me closer to him. "What does that mean?"

"I am not sure," Eldeorin replied, his gaze never leaving me. "Sara has told me that her magic hurts her demon. Perhaps she and her demon have adapted. Or perhaps her Mori is safe from her power when they are joined."

"Whatever the reason, I was correct in my assumption." Desmund looked at me. "You think too much about merging with your Mori, instead of just letting it happen naturally. I thought that giving you something else to focus on would make you forget about the joining."

My anger rose again. "You couldn't have explained it to me instead?"

"We thought this would be more effective."

I pulled away from Nikolas, and he released me. "I can't believe you went along with this." I fought to keep my voice steady, but hurt crept into it.

Nikolas shook his head. "I didn't agree at first, but Desmund made me see that you needed incentive."

I rubbed my arms. "Hurting you is not incentive. It's cruel."

"You know Eldeorin would not really harm me." Nikolas took a step toward me, and I backed up.

Desmund sighed. "I'm sorry you are upset, little one, but I think you will see this was all for the best. We've made significant progress in your training today."

"It is no wonder she cannot join properly with her demon, the way you coddle her." Eldeorin's blue gaze locked with mine as he walked toward me. "Everything we do is to help keep you alive, Cousin. I won't apologize for that, just as I did not apologize for our training."

Nikolas looked from Eldeorin to me. "Apologize for what?"

"Nothing." I shot the faerie a warning look.

Eldeorin looked at Nikolas. "Sara did not care for my training techniques either at first."

I almost snorted. Eldeorin had very different ideas about training, and it wasn't like I'd had a choice in the matter. It was bad enough training with him and Nikolas separately. I didn't think I could handle the two of them and Desmund working together.

I breathed deeply, battling the emotions welling inside me. I felt manipulated and angry, and my Mori was still upset about seeing Nikolas in pain. And since we were still joined, I felt every one of its emotions as if they were my own. Looking at my three trainers only intensified my negative feelings.

"I think that's enough for today." Nikolas's tone left no room for argument. "We'll continue this tomorrow."

I couldn't get out of there fast enough. Once I was away from them, I gently nudged my Mori and it separated from my mind. I heaved a giant sigh as all the noise faded from my head.

I left the house and walked around the small lake twice before I stopped being hurt and angry. I understood their reasons for what they'd done, but it was hard not to be upset they had tricked me, even if their intentions had been honorable.

After the anger passed, I was left with the shock of what I had done. I'd used my power while joined with my Mori, something that before today had been inconceivable to me. But then, I'd never tried to use my power while joined because I didn't think I could.

I sat in the new gazebo that had been built near the lake. Closing my eyes, I lowered the wall around my Mori.

Are you okay? Did I hurt you?

Solmi hurt, it replied, still a little upset.

I almost rolled my eyes. One-track mind. *Solmi is okay*, I assured it. *Did the glow burn you?*

No burn. The demon moved forward a little. *Again?* It asked eagerly.

Not yet. Soon.

I opened my eyes and stared at the pretty little lake as I tried to make sense of it all. For the first time, I left the wall down, and my Mori and I sat quietly together, not joined, but as companions. I sighed in contentment. *This is nice, demon. I could get used to this.*

It curled up like a happy cat. *Me too.*

CHAPTER 18

"YOU'RE GOING TO Europe?"

"Tristan suggested it, and with everything that's going on, I think it's a good idea."

I leaned against my balcony railing. "But you don't like to travel."

Nate laughed on the other end of the line. "I used to love travelling when I was younger. I guess I lost interest in it for a while, but I'm looking forward to this trip."

"Are you going alone? Is it safe?"

"Safer than here." He sobered. "I wish I could convince you to come with me."

"I wish I could go too, but I can't right now." It was hard to think of him being so far away, but at the same time I was relieved he was leaving. It wasn't safe here anymore, if it ever had been. In the three weeks since the Vancouver mission, Mohiri across the country had come under increasing attacks by vampires. It was as if the entire US vampire population had rallied together to declare war against us. Strongholds were strengthening their security, and some compounds were sending their children overseas.

Whenever I got word that one of our teams was in trouble, Eldeorin and I went to help them. Sadly, we didn't learn about some of the attacks until they were over. So far, three warriors had been killed and two had been taken. Every day I was terrified that someone I cared about would be next.

Some days, Nikolas and Chris had to leave on Mohiri business, and I haunted the command center until they returned. I tried to be cool about it, but someone must have said something to Nikolas because he started calling me if he was gone more than a few hours. It helped to hear his voice, but I couldn't stop worrying.

Nate sighed. "I know, but I had to ask. Tell me again that you're safe there."

"I'm surrounded by warriors and faeries and this place is under Fae protections. And I've learned a lot in the last few months."

"Desmund told us you've come a long way."

"I have." My lips curved, and I wasn't sure if it was a grimace or a smile. Desmund had stayed for almost three weeks to help with my training. After the day I'd thrown him across the gym he hadn't tried to trick me again. He said he had newfound respect for my Fae powers, but I could tell he felt bad he'd upset me that day. That didn't mean he had gone easy on me. He'd spent every minute of our training pushing me to work with my Mori and to join with it for longer periods of time. It worked. I could stay connected with my demon for over two hours at a stretch now. And when I wasn't using my Fae power I often left the wall down between us, something that made us both happier. I no longer felt my demon's loneliness. It wanted nothing more than to join with me permanently, but it seemed content for now to be free from its cage and to be with me.

Nate chuckled. "To think I used to scold you about fighting, and here you are now, training with warriors."

"God. those days seem like so long ago, don't they?"

"A lifetime."

"Do you miss home?"

He was quiet for a moment. "Some days I do. I know I can't go back with things the way they are, but someday I'd like to visit again."

"Me too. I never knew how much I loved it until I had to leave." I closed my eyes and tried to imagine that the ocean I heard was the Atlantic instead of the Pacific and that instead of standing on a balcony, I was on the roof of our building back home.

"Actually, I wanted to talk to you about the apartment," he said, interrupting my daydream.

"What about it? You're not planning to sell it, are you?"

"I don't know. It's not like I need the money, but it seems like such a waste letting it sit there empty."

"But..." The thought of strangers living in our home made my chest squeeze a little, but it was unfair to ask Nate to hold onto it, especially after what had happened to him there. "You're right."

"I'm not going to make any decisions right now," he replied as if he knew exactly what I was thinking. "Judith is going to look after it until I decide what to do with it. I asked her to pack up the last of my books and have them shipped to me here since it'll probably be a while until I can go back."

Judith had been so good to Nate and me, watching over our place and taking in our dog, Daisy. According to Roland, Daisy was living on his Uncle Brendan's farm now and the Beagle loved it there. I had planned to bring Daisy to Westhorne, but I knew she'd be happier at the farm. Brendan had a soft spot for dogs and he'd take good care of her.

Judith had tried to catch my cat, Oscar, too, but he refused to be rescued, and had gone back to his life as a stray on the waterfront. She left food outside our door for him, and she said she caught a glimpse of him every now and then.

Nate spoke to someone in the background then came back to me. "Listen, I have to go. I promised Desmund I'd play a game of chess with him."

"Chess with Desmund?" I let out a small laugh. "Well, it was nice knowing you."

"I happen to be a good chess player," he said with mock chagrin. "And he is an interesting fellow. Do you know how many wars he's lived through?"

Maybe I should have said "Poor Desmund." Nate loved anything that had to do with wars and military, and he'd grill the warrior until Desmund went back into hiding.

"All right, I'll talk to you later." I hung up the phone and checked the clock by my bed. It was three o'clock, and I expected Eldeorin any minute for our daily training. Aine had returned to Faerie last week, saying that my training with her was complete. I'd been sad to see her go because we'd grown close the last few months. And because now that I had more free time, Eldeorin had stepped up his training. I'd lost count of the number of vampires and other nasty things I'd taken out in the last three weeks.

One of the worst was the incubus who had been stalking women in New York. Incubi could choose not to kill the women they fed off, but this one had relished draining the life from his victims. He'd been a real piece of work, and I shuddered every time I remembered the way he'd practically devoured me with his eyes as I lured him outside of that night club. I'd showered for thirty minutes after I got home and swore I'd never go within ten feet of another incubus. Next time I had to go after one of those bastards, I was taking him out with a crossbow.

"Why the sour expression?"

I spun to face Eldeorin who stood in the doorway to my bedroom. I should have been used to him sneaking up on me by now. "Thinking about New York."

He nodded and walked over to join me at the railing. "Ah, the incubus. That was a clean kill, Cousin. You should be proud of it."

I made a face. "Well, I didn't feel very clean after. Please tell me we aren't going after another one of those."

"Actually, I was thinking we would do something different today." His blue eyes sparkled, and I wasn't sure whether to be nervous or excited. "Are you ready to go?"

"Ready as I'll ever be."

He took my hand, and I felt the familiar void swallow us. When we arrived at our destination, I had to blink a few times to be sure what I was seeing was real. I turned slowly, taking in the sight of the pale yellow kitchen as my ears picked up the faint clang of a buoy out on the ocean. I ran to the window over the sink and stared at the snow-covered waterfront and the wide bay I'd thought about so many times since I'd left here all those months ago.

"I overheard you talking to your uncle, and I thought you might like to visit this place for a little while."

A golf ball sized lump lodged in my throat. "Thank you." I drank in the view outside the window for a few minutes before I turned away to walk through the apartment. Except for a few things that Tristan had collected for Nate like his computer and clothes, the downstairs looked just like we had left it. I stood in the doorway to Nate's office, remembering him sitting behind his desk working on his books.

My legs carried me up the stairs as if they had a will of their own, and I looked around the empty loft that used to be my bedroom. The floor creaked as I walked around the open space, my footsteps echoing in the silence.

I sat on the old couch and sank back into the cushions. "Roland loved this old thing. When he used to sleep over, he never wanted to get up in the morning."

"You are very close to the werewolf," Eldeorin said from where he stood at the top of the stairs.

"He's my best friend. I love him." I stared at the floor as it hit me that I'd never actually told Roland how much I cared about him. I knew that he knew I cared, but I still should have said the words. If I'd learned anything in my eighteen years it was that happiness was fragile, and those you loved could be taken from you in a heartbeat. With everything we'd been through in the last six months and all the turmoil in our world now, I should have said something to him. Like I should have told Remy before it was too late, and Nate before I almost lost him. Like I should say something to Nikolas.

"You look sad. I thought coming here would make you happy."

"I'm not sad. I'm thinking about how lucky I am to have so many people I care about." I looked at Eldeorin. "Can I ask you something? Have you ever been in love?"

"Many times." His eyes sparkled with laughter. "Though not the kind of love you have for your warrior."

"Do faeries ever fall in love and settle down with one person?"

"Not often, but it does happen. I have not met one person in my thousand years who enticed me to 'settle down', as you put it."

"I can't imagine living alone that long."

He laughed. "You should know by now, Cousin, that I am rarely alone."

I shook my head. I'd heard more about his "relationships" than I ever cared to know. Faeries loved freely and frequently, and they also liked to share stories. So much for not kissing and telling. That concept did not exist in their world.

Eldeorin walked to the center of the loft and looked around. "This is a very drab room. You liked living here?"

I smiled, imagining how the place looked to a faerie who was used to every comfort. "In the summer you can open the windows and get a cool breeze right off the ocean. And in the winter when there's a good storm, the whole building creaks and you can hear the wind howling down the chimney."

"Sounds absolutely dreadful."

"Not to me."

I headed downstairs again. Everywhere I looked brought up old memories, and I absorbed them all like a plant drinking in the sunlight. God only knew when – if ever – I'd see this place again, and I wanted to make the most of my time here.

I was in the front hallway when I heard faint scratching, and I looked around to see where it could be coming from. It didn't take long to figure out it was coming from the door. I started to ask Eldeorin what it could be when I heard a plaintive mewling.

"Oscar?" I looked at Eldeorin, who nodded that it was safe, and then I ran to open the door. A skinny gray tabby slipped inside and immediately began to rub against my legs. I locked the door again and bent to scoop the cat into my arms. "Oh, Oscar, I missed you."

He'd lost weight, which was to be expected, but otherwise he looked and felt healthy. His ears and paws were cold, and he rubbed his head against my chin as his motorboat purr filled the room.

I hugged him protectively. "I can't leave him here."

Eldeorin let out a resigned sigh. "Demons and werewolves and now stray felines. My house will never be the same after this."

"I thought faeries were supposed to be in tune with nature and animals."

"I adore animals as long as they stay in nature."

I stroked Oscar's neck as I walked around the apartment. "Not me. I want a house full of them someday."

Eldeorin made a face. "Then I pray you'll wait until you have your own house."

"Are you sure? Hellhounds make awfully good guard dogs."

His horrified expression made me laugh.

"Kidding."

The gleam that entered his eyes told me I was probably going to pay for my fun. I just hoped it wasn't another incubus.

"Are you ready to leave, Cousin?"

I wasn't, but I knew we couldn't stay much longer. "Can I have a few more minutes?"

"As you wish."

Setting Oscar on the floor, I wandered around the apartment one last time with him trailing close behind me as if he was afraid I'd leave him again. In the living room, I sat in the armchair near the cold fireplace and thought about the night I'd sat here with Nikolas. That was the first time I'd seen a side of him other than the warrior, and looking back it was easy to see how it had been a turning point in our relationship. I wondered how I would have behaved that night if I'd had any inkling where things would go between the two of us. When I'd offered him a truce, I'd had no idea that he would claim my heart as well.

Oscar meowed to get my attention and I pushed up out of the chair. My gaze fell on a cardboard box on the floor between the couch and the coffee table. There was nothing special about the box other than the fact that my name was written on the top in Nate's handwriting. Strange. I was sure I'd had all my things shipped to Westhorne last fall.

I picked up the box, which didn't weigh much, and laid it on the coffee table. Lifting the cover I peered at the contents. There were a few books, a photo album, some small framed pictures, ornaments, and a thin bundle of letters. None of it belonged to me. So why had Nate written my name on the box?

The answer came when I lifted the photo album, opened it to the first page, and saw the sepia photography of a little blond girl and a smiling blond man I knew well. Tristan. Which meant the girl was... Madeline. These were Madeline's things, the ones Nate had mentioned to me before Thanksgiving.

I let the photo album fall back into the box and replaced the lid. I wanted nothing of Madeline's, but Tristan might like to have her things. She was his daughter after all, even if she had hurt him by leaving the way she had. But then that was her M.O., wasn't it?

I was halfway across the room when I stopped and looked back at the box. As much as I disliked anything to do with Madeline, I was curious about what was in the box. Not because I wanted to get to know her, but because the more I learned about her, the more I'd understand her. In the game of hide and seek we were playing I needed every advantage to catch her.

Grabbing the box under one arm, I bent and picked up Oscar with the other. "I'm ready."

* * *

I sat cross-legged on my bed, staring so hard at the photograph in my hand that I was surprised I didn't burn holes through it. It was a picture of two smiling young women with long blond hair, sitting in a powder blue convertible. Based on their clothes and the peace signs they were flashing at the camera, the picture was taken sometime in the seventies. But that wasn't what had grabbed my attention, nor was it the fact that Madeline was one of the women. I was more interested in the identity of the other woman in the picture.

I knew that damn succubus was lying her ass off. Adele had told me she'd met Madeline a few years ago, but according to this photo, they were friends long before Madeline had met my dad. And from the looks on their faces, the two women had been close.

"What else did you lie about, Adele?"

Oscar meowed and jumped up on the bed, making a beeline for my lap. He had settled in surprisingly fast since we'd gotten back three hours ago. It turned out that dwarves had a soft spot for animals, and Heb had immediately gone about getting supplies and food, and spoiling my cat. After everything the poor little guy had been through lately, he deserved a bit of coddling.

I scratched his head as I studied the three other photographs of Madeline and Adele. I couldn't tell where they'd been taken, just that it was summer and there was an ocean in the background of one. It struck me how happy and carefree and normal the two women looked. They could have been two human friends enjoying a summer day. I couldn't help but wonder why Madeline had turned her back on her family and her people, and then befriended a succubus of all people.

I felt Nikolas's presence a few seconds before a knock came at my door. I was surprised he was here. For the last week, he'd been spending more and more time next door, and I usually got to see him at training or if I went to the command center. When he was here, he rarely came to my bedroom. Since the morning he had returned from Vancouver, he hadn't paid me any nighttime visits either. Jordan said he was probably trying not to rush me with everything else that was going on around us. I wanted to believe her, but the more time that passed, the more I questioned his feelings for me.

He entered the room and smiled at me sitting on the bed surrounded by books and papers. "Do you want to come next door with me instead of spending the evening here alone? Raoul is ordering from that Italian place you like."

"That sounds awesome." This morning Jordan had gone on her first warrior mission. It wasn't a dangerous one, just a recon job in San Francisco with Chris, but they weren't due back until tomorrow. I didn't relish the idea of spending the whole night here alone.

Oscar meowed in protest when I went to move him, and Nikolas's eyes went to the cat curled up in my lap. A frown creased his brow as he approached the bed. "Is that the cat you had back in Maine?"

"Yes, his name is Oscar."

Nikolas stopped at the foot of my bed. "How did your cat get here?"

I rubbed Oscar's head, and he kneaded my leg with his front paws. "Eldeorin took me to the apartment today and I brought Oscar back with me."

I probably should have thought about what I was saying before I spoke. Nikolas's face hardened and his eyes darkened to a steel gray. "He did what?"

I rushed to reassure him. "It was safe, Nikolas. Eldeorin was with me and I didn't go outside."

He was not appeased, and his next words came out almost as a growl. "What the hell is wrong with him? He knows New Hastings is not safe for you."

"Is any place safe for me?" I slid off the bed but didn't approach him. "Other than here where I'm surrounded by Faerie wards, is there any place I can go and be safe? It's a dangerous world for everyone now, not just me."

"Everyone else's safety is not my concern."

"And everyone else doesn't have built-in vampire radar or power like mine." I took a slow breath. Since our talk the morning he'd gotten back from Vancouver, he'd tried not to be as overbearing, but he was as protective as ever. All I wanted was for him to see me as someone who could fight at his side and not hide behind him. "I'm not defenseless, Nikolas, far from it. I've killed more vampires than most trainees do before they become warriors." *Tell him. Do it now.* "I'm not saying I'm invincible, just that I'm a lot stronger than you think I am."

"I know you're strong, Sara. *Khristu!*" He ran a hand through his hair, and I could see his internal struggle in his eyes. "But we're not talking about a few vampires looking for you. A Master wants you dead. Every time I think about that, it makes me want to forget my promise and take you far away from here."

I walked around the bed and laid my hands on his chest, feeling both of us relax a little from the physical contact. "There is always going to be some vampire or demon that wants us dead because of what we are. They've been trying for a while now, but we're still here. I have no plans to go anywhere. Do you?"

His hands came up to rest on my shoulders. "God, I wish it was that easy. Even with all the things you've seen, you still have no idea how much evil is out there and how bad it can get. And I don't want you to ever have to see that."

This was it, the opening I had been waiting for. There was never going to be a good time to tell him the truth about my training with Eldeorin, so I had to just suck it up and get it over with. I took a deep breath. "About that. There's something I've been wanting to talk to you about."

His phone rang and I nearly cried at the rotten timing of whoever was calling. He stepped back to answer it. "Nikolas here."

Someone spoke on the other end, and I watched Nikolas switch back into warrior mode in the blink of an eye. "When? No, I'll be there in five minutes. Tell Elijah to assemble his team." He hung up and I saw worry in his eyes before he could conceal it. A cold knot of dread began to form in my stomach.

"What's wrong?"

"One of our teams called in and said they ran into some trouble. I'm going to take another team to back them up. It's nothing you have to worry about."

"What team?"

"Sara, you don't have to worry about it."

The knot became a lump of ice and I gripped his arm. "What team, Nikolas?"

"Chris's team."

"Oh, God." I'd known what he was going to say, but the words still cut through my gut like a knife. "We have to help them."

"We will." He took my chin in a firm yet gentle hold and forced me to look at him. "Chris knows what he's doing and he'll keep Jordan safe. Raoul said they are pinned down but no one is hurt. They'll be okay."

I didn't ask to go with him because I knew what his answer would be. But there was no way I was staying here while Jordan and Chris were in trouble.

"Go. Do what you need to do."

He pressed a quick kiss against my mouth then strode to the door. "I'll call you when I find them."

As soon as the door closed behind him, I picked up the phone and calmly called Heb who was always in the kitchen. "Heb, please find Eldeorin. It's urgent."

By the time Eldeorin appeared twenty minutes later, I had almost worn a path in the floor of my room. "Let me guess, another rescue mission?" he said.

"Thank God. I didn't think Heb would find you." I pulled on my black leather bomber jacket that already had my knives stowed away in the pockets. "It's Chris and Jordan. They're in San Francisco and Nikolas is on his way there with a team, but it's over an hour away. Will you take me to them?"

He smiled and held out a hand to me. "Of course. You know I love to watch you in action, Cousin."

I took his hand. "You know the drill."

The drill was one we'd been through at least half a dozen times in the last few weeks. Eldeorin glamoured us so we couldn't be detected, and then whisked us over to the command center to find out exactly where Chris's team was. Nikolas had already left with Elijah's team by the time we got there, and it didn't take long to find what we were looking for.

"Well, this should be fun," Eldeorin muttered when we arrived outside a plain two-story building in the waterfront area of San Francisco. It was raining and windy so the street was pretty much deserted. Eldeorin used his magic to keep us dry and invisible.

"Are we at the right place?" There were no sign of Chris's team, and I couldn't sense a single vampire nearby. I did sense demons, but it was impossible to tell how many or where they were. My demon radar was still developing, and it was nowhere as good as my vampire radar.

"This is it. Your friends are inside and they are not alone."

"Okay, give me the rundown."

Eldeorin made a face like he had stepped in doggie do. "This place is called a *wrakk*, a demon gathering place. It is considered neutral territory among demons, and they can socialize and do business here without fear of being harmed. For the most part."

I studied the building, looking for the way in. "Kind of like a demon market?"

"Exactly."

"What are Chris and Jordan doing in a place like this?"

"I do not know, but I can tell you demons are very protective of their *wrakks*, and they do not care for outsiders."

"Gotcha. Anything else I should know before I go in?"

Eldeorin grinned. "They *really* do not like faeries."

"What else is new?" I started walking around the building, looking for the entrance. "You coming with me this time?" He usually liked to stay back and let me have all the fun unless it was a bad situation like Vancouver.

"I think I'd better observe this time. If I go in there, it's going to send every demon in the place into a frenzy."

I stopped at the bottom of a fire escape. "You were able to enter the Blue Nyx without bothering the demons there. Why is this different?"

"Adele siphons the energy from her clientele, which makes them rather placid. It is how Fae and demons are able to be there at the same time." He waved at the building. "Much like my house has Fae wards, this place is protected by demon wards, and my presence would set them off."

"Oh." I checked my weapons and stared at the bottom rung of the fire escape that was way out of my reach. "Little help here?"

He chuckled and then the ladder lowered so I could grab it. I pulled myself up until my feet were firmly planted on the bottom rung. "Wish me luck."

"Luck is for the unprepared, and I have trained you too well to rely on anything that fickle."

I began to climb. "Such words of encouragement. You should work for Hallmark."

At the top of the fire escape there was a small landing next to a narrow door. I cracked the door and peered inside at a dimly lit hallway with a few doors on either side. So far, so good. Slipping inside, I let the door close quietly behind me. I took two steps and came up against what felt like an invisible wall of jelly that gave when my hands pressed into it. It must have been one of the demon wards Eldeorin had spoken of. The question was, did it feel like this for everyone or was it reacting to my Fae side? And what was it going to do if I tried to go through it? It would really suck if I ended up trapped in this stuff and had to get Eldeorin to come in and free me.

Only one way to find out. I took a deep breath and pushed my way through the wall.

I emerged on the other side with a small pop. Suddenly, the muted demon presence that I'd felt outside was loud and clear. And it was big. There were a lot of demons in this place. I just hoped they weren't all gulak demons or something equally as awful.

What the heck are Chris and Jordan doing in a place like this? I moved silently to the end of the short hallway that ended in a T-intersection with a catwalk that appeared to circle the entire second floor of the building. A three-foot railing overlooked the lower floor. Checking to make sure there was no one around, I went to the rail to see what lay below.

"Jesus!" I uttered as I got my first look at a demon market.

The first floor was laid out like any public market, with stalls set up around the perimeter and another grouping in the center with a wide track for walking between them. On one side of the floor the stalls were filled with fruits and vegetables I recognized, while others contained things I could only assume were food. There was a baker hawking loaves of green bread that did not make me hungry for a sandwich, and a butcher selling God only knew what kind of meat. My stomach did a little roll and I was glad I hadn't eaten in the last few hours.

On the opposite wall, the stalls sold everything from human housewares, electronics, and clothing to strange medicines and magical objects. One stall specialized in protective wards and another sold glamours that would make a demon appear human. There was a book vendor, a stall selling soaps and oils, and even a place where you could buy driver's licenses and other documents.

The mix of modern and supernatural gave the whole place an

otherworldly feel that made me think I ⌣
strange as the place was, it was the people tha⌣
never seen so many different demons together in
gave myself whiplash trying to see them all. There we⌣
demons, green apelike sheroc demons, fat pasty white femal ⌣
skinned mox demons, and so many more that I had never seen.
They all moved through the market, keeping a polite distance from e⌣
other as they did their business.

What I didn't see was Chris or Jordan or any sign of a disturbance. If a
Mohiri team was pinned down here and needing backup, you'd think there
would be some kind of commotion.

As if on cue, a roar came from beneath my feet, and I made my way
around the catwalk until I could see what was making the racket. I groaned
when I saw the scene below.

It just had to be gulak demons.

Eight of them. Yep, eight of the scaly brutes were crowded into a
loading bay and making growling noises at the three Mohiri warriors they
had cornered. The gulaks were not alone either. There were two ranc
demons and a drex demon holding some kind of weapons that resembled
flame throwers. Every one of them looked like they wanted nothing more
than to rip apart the warriors who faced them with swords drawn. One of
the gulaks was holding his arm and baring his teeth at Jordan, whose sword
dripped black blood onto the concrete floor.

"I warned you what would happen if you took another step," Jordan
yelled at the angry demon. She glared at the others. "Anyone else want to
try to touch the helpless female?"

"Jordan..." Chris pinched the bridged of his nose, and I grinned at his
pained expression. At least he didn't look like someone who feared for his
life, and the three of them appeared to be okay except for the makeshift
bandage tied around the third warrior's thigh. I couldn't see the fourth team
member so I figured he was outside and the one who had called for backup.

The injured gulak leered at Jordan. "You have fire. You would bring a
high price in the slave market, but I think I will keep you for myself."

"Ew! In your dreams, lizard boy."

"No one keeps her," another gulak barked. "You know the deal. We call
the vampires and turn the hunters over to them. They will pay us enough
for a dozen slaves."

Vampires? Not good. I'd thought for a moment I could stay out of sight
and keep an eye on things until backup arrived, but it looked like I was
going to have to go down there.

If I had been really cool like Buffy or that chick from Underworld, I
would have flipped over the railing and landed right behind them before I
started kicking some demon ass. But knowing my luck, I'd only end up

...ning something. So I opted for stealth instead, using the stairs at the far end of the building to get to the first floor.

I'd hoped I could make my way to the loading bay and out of sight by walking behind the stalls, but I soon discovered they were flush against the wall of the building. *Damn it.* Straightening my jacket, I entered the traffic passing by the stairs while trying to look like I belonged there. It wasn't easy to blend in when I had to be careful not to make contact with anyone. Apart from not wanting to draw attention, the last thing I wanted to do was accidentally shock some poor mox demon out doing her grocery shopping.

"It's another one," said a voice behind me. It sounded like the speaker had a bad lisp. I didn't turn around in case he wasn't referring to me.

A second voice answered him. "Velec will be pleased when we bring him this one. He likes females."

"She is a hunter, so she will go to the vampires. You know that."

So much for not getting noticed. I turned casually toward a stall that looked like an apothecary then ducked into the space between it and the next stall. By the time the two ranc demons followed me in, I had my knife unsheathed and power coursing through my fingers. It was probably foolish to corner myself this way, but it would also draw a lot less attention.

"Drop the knife, girl, and this will go easier for you," said the one with the lisp. "You are no match for me and my brother."

The other one nodded, his catlike eyes fixed on the blade in my hand.

I debated the best way to handle the situation. I didn't need my knife to take out these two. Compared to some of the other things I'd faced, ranc demons were about as frightening as sewer rats. My real problem was getting the job done without drawing a crowd.

I dropped the knife. It hit the floor with a thud and skidded several feet away. The ranc demons, seeing my action as a sign of surrender, rushed at me.

Lispy reached me first, and I let him get a good grip on my left wrist before I gave him a healthy jolt. His body stiffened and he made a choking sound as he fell to his knees. The other demon, seemingly unaware of his brother's distress, grabbed for my right arm. He went down soundlessly, grabbing his throat like he couldn't breathe. Before either of them could recover, I put a hand on each of their shoulders and let them have enough juice to keep them down for a few hours. I probably should have killed them and done the world a favor, but I decided to give them a pass. This time.

I stepped over their prone bodies to retrieve my knife, and when I straightened up, I discovered I had a little audience. Two vrell children, who couldn't have been more than five or six, were peeking around the corner of the stall, their black eyes wide with fear and excitement. They were as cute as buttons with their chubby faces and tiny horns peeking through their brown curls. I smiled at them and put my finger to my lips. I could hear their giggles as they ran away.

"Later, guys," I said to the unconscious ranc demons. Then I stepped out from between the stalls. I just hoped no one found them and raised an alarm before I reached Chris and Jordan.

I still hadn't figured out how I was going to handle all those gulak demons. None of them was as big as the one I'd killed in Minneapolis, but even the smaller ones were tough. It wasn't like I had a choice. If they called in vampires, God only knew how many blood suckers would descend upon this place.

Childish laughter alerted me to the two little demons on my tail. I stopped walking and groaned silently. *Where the heck are their parents?* All I needed was for them to get caught up in the fight that was going to happen when I reached my friends.

As if she had heard my thoughts, a vrell female ran over and took both children by the arm. She kept a wary eye on me as she spoke softly to them. One of them whispered in her ear, and she looked behind them at the place where I'd knocked out the ranc demons. Her eyes were fearful when they met mine again, and she grabbed the children's hands and hurried away with them.

No one else tried to intercept me, although a lot of demons stared at me and whispered. My only concern was getting to Jordan and Chris, and as long as no one got in my way, I didn't care what they said about me.

When I finally reached the wall of gulak demons I stared at them in consternation. Now that I was here, I had no idea how I was going to take on eight of them at once. Not to mention the drex demon with its poisonous barbs and those weapons the ranc demons held. Something told me they weren't going to let me fight them one at a time.

Maybe I can create a diversion to lead some of them away and —

"What's this?" rumbled someone behind me. "You're too little to be a hunter."

I spun to face the gulak demon that had sneaked up on me. My heart banged against my ribs and I cursed my stupidity. I'd been so distracted by how I was going to handle the gulaks that I hadn't noticed one of them was missing.

The gulak grinned as he rushed at me. Instead of running, I let him catch me. As he reached for me, I grabbed one of his arms and twisted my body. Using his larger height and weight to my advantage, I pulled him forward and over my shoulder. The back of his head cracked against the concrete floor, and I wasted no time punching him in the throat. I didn't have the strength of a warrior, but my strike was no less damaging. He made a strangled sound as I introduced him to my Fae side, and then his head lolled to one side with his mouth slack and his forked tongue hanging out.

A shuffling sound made me whip my head up to look at the other gulak demons who were all staring at their fallen friend.

Correction. They were all staring at me.

Three of them growled and started toward me.

I backed up, looking for an escape route. If I could lead them away, maybe I could use the divide-and-conquer strategy.

My plan might have worked if one of the ranc demons hadn't decided to join the fun. He advanced on me, his weapon spewing small white flames. The look on his face told me he was hoping I'd give him an excuse to use the weapon on me. My power was deadly to demons, but it wasn't any protection from fire.

My back thumped against something hard and cold. I looked over my shoulder at the large glass tank full of dark murky water. Something moved in the water and a black tentacle slapped the other side of the glass. I shuddered, not wanting to know what was swimming in the water.

Water?

There was no time to think. I turned and grabbed the top of the tank that sat on a metal stand and pulled with all my strength. Someone, probably the vendor, shouted for me to stop.

The tank wobbled precariously for a second then crashed to the floor, sending a small wave of water at my pursuers.

The ranc demon was at the front, and he dropped his weapon as a black... thing latched onto his thigh. The creature looked like a mix between a squid and an eel, and it obviously liked the taste of demon if the ranc demon's screeches were any indication.

The gulaks stopped in surprise and then stepped over the rest of the flopping creatures and came at me.

I dropped and stuck my hands in the inch of water at my feet, ignoring the slimy texture as I summoned the water's magic. Golden streaks shot from my hands, moving through the water like burning trails of gunpowder. One streak hit each of the four demons. They screamed as my Fae magic, magnified by the water, enveloped them. The ranc demon collapsed first, but the gulaks soon followed. The four of them lay twitching in the water and gasping for air.

I wasted no time. Whipping out one of my throwing knives, I aimed for the remaining ranc demon who still held a weapon on my friends. The blade sank into his shoulder, and he yelped as he lost his grip on the weapon.

I stepped back and pulled out two more throwing knives as the drex demon growled and came at me. His legs were short, but that didn't slow him down. He bared his teeth and raised his hands, which were covered in venom-filled barbs. If I hadn't fought one of his kind before, I might have been scared witless at the sight of his towering reptilian form.

Sounds of fighting broke out in the loading bay, but I was too focused on my own fight to worry about my friends. My first knife found its mark in the stomach of the advancing demon and he let out a roar. He yanked it out, but thankfully he didn't have the opposable thumbs necessary to throw it back at me.

I waited until he took another step toward me before I threw my second knife.

The drex demon made a gurgling sound and reached for the knife embedded in his thick neck.

I used his distraction to strike out at him. My first drex kill in New Orleans hadn't been a pretty one because I hadn't known their hearts were located near their stomach instead of in their chest. I knew better this time, and I slammed my palm into his bleeding stomach, sending a powerful jolt into his heart. The demon went down in a heap of scales and claws, and I knew he wasn't getting up again.

Good riddance.

"Jordan, I think he's dead."

I looked at the warriors who had taken out the remaining gulak demons. Jordan stood over the one that had wanted to keep her for himself, her sword buried in his chest. From the numerous wounds on his stomach and groin, she had worked out her aggression over the slave insult.

Whispers drew my attention to the crowd that had amassed behind me. It looked like every demon in the place had come to watch the fight, and none of them looked upset over the dead demons in the loading bay. When I turned fully to face them, fear spread across their faces and, as one, they backed up.

I let out a slow breath and pulled my power back into my core until my hands stopped glowing. I held them up for the crowd to see. "I came only to help my friends over there, and I have no beef with any of you."

"You... killed them all," squeaked a sheroc demon wearing a baker's apron. "What kind of demon are you?"

A vrell demon spoke up bravely. "We did not harm your friends. No one gets involved in gulak affairs."

"Please, don't hurt us," whispered another demon.

I sighed heavily. This wasn't going how I'd hoped it would. "Listen, I'm not going to hurt any of you. Got it?"

No one spoke.

I looked up at the second floor and found Eldeorin leaning against the railing watching me with an amused expression. "Little help here?"

He grinned and the demons stared at me as my glamour lifted.

"*Talael esledur,*" said a feminine voice from somewhere in the crowd.

A flurry of whispers spread through the demons, and I heard the same phrase whispered over and over. Whatever it meant, it eased their fears, and they began to look at me with curiosity and reverence. *Great, now what?*

A thin gray-skinned demon pushed to the front of the crowd. She wore a long blue dress and there was an unusual black tattoo on the left side of her face.

"Hey, I know you." She was one of the two mox demons I'd freed from Draegan back in Los Angeles.

She smiled timidly. "It is good to see you again, warrior."

"How are you and your friend doing?"

"She is my sister and she is well. We are very happy here."

"That's good." I glanced at the other demons that were still watching me like they were waiting for something to happen. "Hey, do you know why everyone is staring at me like that?"

"They cannot believe you are here. They have heard of the *talael esledur*, but none of them expected to ever see you in the flesh."

My brows drew together. "The *talael esledur?*" I repeated, my tongue tripping over the demon words.

She nodded. "In demon tongue it means 'kind warrior.'"

I looked from her to the other demon faces. "I'm sorry, but I think you guys have confused me with someone else."

"We are not mistaken," the mox demon replied, and the others shook their heads. "You saved my sister and me just as you have saved many others of our kind. Your deeds are known to all of us."

"Those gulaks showed up here two months ago, hurting people and forcing us to pay them half our profits," said a vrell male. "We are in your debt, warrior."

"As am I. That is the second time you've saved my ass."

Taking a deep breath, I turned slowly to face Chris who stood behind me wearing a smile. But not a hint of recognition. What the...? *Eldeorin!*

Chris held out a hand. "I don't know who you are or why you keep coming to our aid, but thank you."

I grasped his hand and squeezed it. "Anytime, Cousin."

"Excuse me?"

"Show him," I called to Eldeorin.

Chris's eyes widened, and his mouth worked like a fish out of water. Behind him the injured warrior stared at me in shock, while Jordan smiled like the Cheshire cat.

"Jesus Christ! Sara?"

I smiled at Chris. "Hi."

"How is this possible?" He blinked as if he couldn't believe what he was seeing. "It's... it's been you all along? How did you...? The faerie."

I nodded and he muttered something under his breath. "All those vampire kills, the demons." He paled. "Vancouver? That was *you?*"

"Yes."

Chris let out a string of swear words, something I'd never heard him do. He looked at Jordan, who gave him an innocent smile. "You knew about this, didn't you?"

"Yes, and I am behind it one hundred percent."

"Of course you are." He rubbed the back of his neck. "I knew the two of you were trouble together."

I laid a hand on his arm. "Jordan knew about this, but she wasn't involved. It was all me."

"Somehow, I'm not surprised. Do you want to tell me how you came up with this crazy scheme?"

I explained how it had started out as training, but after a while it became something more. "I couldn't stand to see our people getting hurt, not when I could do something about it."

"You shouldn't have risked your life like that.'"

I folded my arms across my chest. "Now you sound just like Nikolas."

"That's because I..." He stared at me. "Nikolas. Jesus, he's on his way here right now."

"I know."

Chris groaned like a man in pain. "He is going to flip. You know that, right? Are you sure this is the right place to tell him something like this?"

I didn't think any place was the right one to tell Nikolas what I'd been up to, but it was time to come clean to him. I'd been trying for weeks to get up the nerve to tell him the truth, and I wasn't going to stall anymore.

"Maybe you should wait until you –"

A door slammed open, and I gave Chris a small smile. "Too late."

CHAPTER 19

SURROUNDED BY DEMONS, I couldn't see Nikolas when he entered the building, but I felt his presence through the bond. If I could sense him, then he was sensing me too, and he was probably as confused as hell. That was going to end in about ten seconds.

A dark raw energy filled the air, and the crowd parted like the Red Sea as Nikolas stalked toward us. Chris suddenly moved in front of me, blocking me from Nikolas's view before he reached us.

"Chris, what the hell is going on here? And why do I feel –?"

I stepped out from behind Chris. For one endless moment, Nikolas stared at me like I was an apparition. And then his eyes darkened and his nostrils flared dangerously. I could feel the fury rolling off him, and I wasn't the only one. Every demon in the room began to put distance between them and us.

Chris put an arm in front of me. "Take it easy, Nikolas. She's unharmed."

I was about to ask my cousin if he had a death wish when Nikolas growled, "Move, Chris."

"Shit," Chris muttered as he faced his best friend, who was a few breaths away from going into a rage. The last thing I wanted was for either of them to get hurt, so I pushed Chris's arm down and moved in front of him. I didn't flinch as I met Nikolas's thunderous stare. He might get loud and scary, but he would never hurt me.

"Nikolas."

He held out a hand. "Come here."

I blinked at him. "Listen, I know you're upset, but you don't get to order me around."

"Sara, I'm trying very hard not to lose it," he ground out. "I need to..."

Understanding filled me and wordlessly I went to him, finding myself enfolded in his tight embrace. He wasn't shaking like the last time I'd seen him in a rage, so I knew he was in control of his Mori at least.

"What the hell are you doing here?" he demanded in a low voice.

I took a deep breath, which was hard to do with my body pressed against his. "I came to help Chris and Jordan."

"Help them?"

"I didn't think you'd get here in time. I had to come."

Easing his hold, he looked at me. "How did you get here?" He looked around, and I knew he was searching for Eldeorin, who was probably hidden behind a glamour. "I'll kill him."

"No, you won't."

"The hell I won't." A muscle ticked in his jaw. "He's supposed to be teaching you, not putting you in danger."

I pushed against him and he let me go, but I had a feeling he wouldn't allow me to go far. "I asked him to bring me."

"And he should have said no. You could have been killed."

"Look around, Nikolas. Most of the demons on the floor were put there by me. The team was in more danger of being killed than I was."

I saw the disbelief in his eyes as they flicked to the dead demons, and it hurt. "*You* did this?"

"Yes." My own anger rose. "And it's not the first time."

"What do you mean?"

"I mean I've killed a lot of demons and vampires." A storm brewed in his eyes, but I refused to look away. "All over the country."

It took several seconds for my words to sink in. Nikolas's face grew stony as he stared at the dead demons again then looked at Chris and finally me. "*Iisus Khristos!* Please, tell me you're joking."

"I wouldn't joke about that."

A string of Russian curses exploded from him, and the air around us seemed to thicken with his anger. I felt Chris move closer to my back as demons scattered, some hiding in stalls and most running flat out for the exits.

Nikolas closed the distance between us and grabbed my arms in a strong but painless grip. "What in God's name were you thinking? Do you have any idea what could have happened to you out there?"

"I wasn't alone. Eldeorin was with me every time," I tried to explain.

"And that makes it okay?" Fury blazed in his eyes. "You've barely begun your training. You have no business being in any of those places."

"You had no problem with Jordan coming here."

"Jordan's been training since she could hold a sword, and she can –"

"Can what? Defend herself?" I shouted as heat suffused my body. I'd expected him to be angry, but his lack of faith in me cut deeply. "I'm never going to be like Jordan or any other warrior no matter how much I train,

Nikolas. But I'm strong, a lot stronger than you give me credit for. You saw what I did in Vancouver. Eldeorin was with me, but over half of those kills were mine."

He let out another expletive. "That was you in the backyard?"

"Yes."

"All this time." His jaw clenched. "Why didn't you tell me?"

"Because I knew you'd react this way. Eldeorin told me I had to learn to use my power as a weapon, and he was right. I needed this. I've been trying for weeks to tell you the truth, but I didn't know how. I almost told you today, but you got the call to come here."

When he didn't respond, I continued. "It started out as training, but then I realized I could make a real difference."

He let go of my arms. I'd expected him to be furious, but the look of betrayal on his face sent a sharp pain through my chest. "I can't believe this. How could you keep this from me?"

"I didn't want to. I hated not telling you."

He made an angry sound and turned away from me.

"Nikolas?"

"I need a minute, Sara," he said in a hard voice.

I felt a rift forming between us as if it had been carved with a blade, the same one that was piercing my heart. I swallowed painfully and watched him walk away from me. I'd done this. It didn't matter that I'd hated keeping a secret from him, or that I'd had no choice in whether or not to participate in Eldeorin's training. I should have had the guts to tell Nikolas when this all started. He would have been angry, but at least I would have been honest with him.

I flinched when the door slammed behind him.

No one spoke.

After a few minutes, Jordan came to stand beside me. "He'll be back. He just needs to blow off some steam."

I let out a shaky breath. "I should go and give him some time to cool down." I looked up at Eldeorin who, for once, wasn't wearing his cocky smile. "Will you take me home?"

He nodded, and I turned to the stairs.

Chris put up a hand to stop me. "You should stay. He'll be back, and he'll expect you to be here."

"I'm the last person he wants to see right now."

Chris shook his head. "Trust me, Sara. You are the only person Nikolas will want to see when he calms down."

I felt Nikolas return before the door opened. Chris quietly stepped aside as Nikolas drew near. His face was still hard and his eyes were impossible to read.

"Just tell me you're done with this."

"Done?"

"No more rogue... vigilante ... or whatever."

I hadn't thought about what would happen once my secret was out. Eldeorin and I hadn't talked about how long he would train me or what would happen when he was done. At the same time, I thought of all the people out there who needed my help. "What if this is what I'm supposed to do, just like you're supposed to be a warrior?"

"It's too dangerous."

"It'll always be dangerous, Nikolas. I was there in Vancouver, remember? You and Chris put your lives in danger all the time. Soon Jordan will be a warrior and she will too. Are you going to hold her back and tell her it's too dangerous for her?"

He swore again and raked his hands through his wet hair. "I don't want to hold you back, but every instinct I have is telling me I need to keep you safe."

Instinct, not feelings. That's what this all came down to. I had no doubt that Nikolas cared for me, but his emotions, his actions, were driven by the bond, not something deeper. I'd suspected it for weeks, but I hadn't wanted to admit it to myself. Maybe that was the real reason I hadn't told him the truth. I'd been avoiding this confrontation and having to come to terms with reality.

"I understand." I took a step back, noticing for the first time how quiet the place was. So quiet that I was sure everyone could hear my heart breaking. I wondered numbly if faeries had a cure for heartache.

"Where are you going?" Nikolas asked when I turned toward the stairs again.

The pain in my chest threatened to suffocate me, and I needed to get away before I broke down. "I'm going home. I can't do this anymore."

"Can't do what?" he asked, his voice harsh.

"Love you," I said so softly it was little more than a breath.

A hand closed over mine and tugged me around to face him. I stared at his chest as I blinked away the tears that threatened.

Nikolas's other hand lifted my chin and forced me to look at him. His eyes locked with mine, and my breath caught at the raw longing and hope swirling in their gray depths.

"You love me?" he asked hoarsely.

Two hot tears ran down my face. "Yes."

His mouth claimed mine with a fierce tenderness that made my heart want to explode in my chest. Nothing else existed for me in that moment but him, and my hands slid behind his head, pulling him closer. I let down the wall in my mind and my Mori crept forward, its joy melding with my own. *Mine*, it whispered possessively.

My knees threatened to buckle by the time he finally pulled out of the kiss. His thumbs wiped away the wetness on my cheeks. *"Ya lyublyu tebya."* Before I could ask what the words meant, he framed my face with his hands and gave me a smile that was as devastating as the kiss. "I love you."

"I love you, too."

He kissed me again, his lips gently possessing mine until I felt drugged from the essence of him. When it ended, he crushed me to him as if he feared I might disappear. I wrapped my arms around his waist to let him know I was going nowhere.

"I wasn't sure if you..." My voice broke.

"And I didn't think you were ready to hear it," he replied huskily. "I was waiting for you to say something, to let me know you felt the same way."

Nikolas loved me. My heart expanded as it absorbed this wondrous knowledge. "How... long?"

He loosened his embrace, and I tilted my face up to look at him.

His fingers grazed my cheek. "I was lost the first moment I saw you at that club in Portland. I just didn't know it yet. Before I even knew who or what you were, I was drawn to you. At first, I told myself it was my responsibility to protect you. But the more time I spent with you, even when we were arguing, the more I knew what I felt for you was anything but duty." His smile dimmed. "I don't think I knew how deep my feelings were until that day you traded yourself for Nate. That ride from Portland was the longest of my life."

I had trouble forming words. "I'm sorry I put you through that."

"I know." He touched the hair at the side of my face. "Your courage is one of the first things I came to love about you, and I should have known you'd do anything to protect Nate and your friends."

"And you."

His arm tightened around me and neither of us spoke for a long moment, until I remembered that we were in a room full of people. Heat rose in my face at the thought of having an audience for such a deeply personal moment.

"They left," he said.

"What?"

"Chris and the others. They went outside."

"Oh," I breathed.

He released me and led me to a bench in the now empty building. I sat at one end, and he surprised me when he lifted me into his lap and wrapped his arms around me. I rested my cheek against his shoulder as he stroked my hair.

"I was so busy trying to push you away that I refused to admit I felt anything for you at first." My fingers toyed with the front of his shirt. "I didn't know for sure that I loved you until Thanksgiving, but I think I started to fall for you at my apartment the night of the storm."

"Was it my mad cooking skills?"

I laughed softly. "It was the first time I saw a different side of you, and you weren't bossing me around for once."

"We've come a long way since that night."

"Yes, but you're still trying to boss me around."

"And you still make me want to tie your ass to a chair to keep you out of trouble."

"Ha, you can try."

He sighed deeply. "Sara, I hate the idea of you out there fighting, and I doubt I'll ever be okay with it. I don't think any male would be okay with the woman he loves putting herself in danger."

The woman he loves. Heat pooled in my stomach and I wanted to kiss him again. Instead I said, "Do you know what it's like for me when you go away on a job, especially with the way things are now? I don't sleep, and I spend every minute praying we don't get word that you're in trouble – or worse. It's torture. That night we heard you were under attack in Vancouver, I almost lost it. I almost lost you. Seeing you in danger kills me."

"I never thought about how hard that was for you," he admitted. "I've spent my whole life being a warrior and not much else. Before you, I didn't have someone waiting for me when the job was done or worrying about my safety."

"This is new for both of us, and we're going to have to learn to deal with it."

"Something tells me you're going to cope with this a lot better than I will," he grumbled.

I reached up and touched his jaw, and when he looked down, I smiled at him. "We'll figure it out together. Knowing us, it won't be easy, but I'll try if you will."

"I'll try, but I can't promise to have any civil words for the faerie."

I'd forgotten all about Eldeorin, and I had a feeling he'd left with the others.

"I've had a few choice words for him myself. At first I didn't like his idea of training because he pushed me out of my comfort zone. He always had more faith in my abilities than I had, and he kept pushing until I believed in myself too. He's been a good mentor and a friend to me, and he always has my back."

"You like spending time with him."

I smiled at the note of jealousy in his voice. "Sometimes, but I like being with you more."

He tilted my face up and kissed me again. "Good answer."

I glanced around the market, my eyes landing on the dead demons and the empty stalls. As much as I wanted to stay there in Nikolas's arms, we needed to let the vendors get back to their businesses. "I guess we should get this mess cleaned up."

He set me on my feet. "I'm sure Chris has already called for a cleanup crew. We should probably put one on speed dial for you."

Before I could make a retort, Jordan's voice rang through the building. "Hey, is it safe to come in now? We're freezing our butts off out here."

"All good," I called back.

"Thank God!" She sauntered into the building and grinned at us. "Well, you two look disgustingly happy. And it's about damn time."

"Amen." Chris came up behind her, smiling. "I called in a crew to help with this mess." His gaze flicked to me. "I told them they might need extra guys."

Nikolas chuckled, and I rolled my eyes as I left him to check out the damage. There were eleven dead demons, plus the two ranc demons I'd knocked out. There was also a lot of water, broken glass, and six of the black creatures that had been in the tank. Surprisingly, the creatures were still flopping around on the wet concrete. Resilient little buggers, whatever they were. I was going to have to reimburse the owner for destroying his tank. I hoped he wasn't too ticked off by the mess I'd made.

Demons began to trickle back into the building, most of them vendors who had to see to their businesses. I went around and talked to some of them, assuring them we were going to take care of the damage we'd done to their market. I found the fish vendor, a droopy-eyed sheroc demon, who was only a little put out by the loss of his tank. He said it was worth it to get rid of the gulaks.

"Maybe we'll get a few months of peace before the next ones come along," said the apothecary, a short demon with pale skin, a long furred face, and large orange eyes. He gave a sigh of resignation. "There are always more gulak thugs waiting to move in."

"Just tell them your *talael...* or whatever... is keeping an eye on things here," Jordan said as she walked up and laid an arm across my shoulders. "She is one fricking badass warrior."

The vendors nodded fervently.

I asked the apothecary for a piece of paper on which I wrote a number. "Call this if you guys have any more trouble with gulaks. The Mohiri will gladly help you with them."

He held up his hands when I tried to give him the paper. "The Mohiri do not help our kind."

"Have you ever asked them for help?"

His orange eyes blinked in confusion. "No."

I smiled and shoved the paper into his hand. "Maybe you should."

His furred hand gripped mine. "Thank you, *talael esledur.*"

"You can just call me Sara. I..." I stared down at our clasped hands. "Hey, you're touching me!"

He yanked his hand away. "I am sorry. I did not know it was forbidden."

"No, it's not that. It's just that I can't touch demons without hurting them." I studied his face. "Are you a demon?" I whispered.

He drew me away from the others. "I am a quellar demon, and my people are not affected by your magic."

"You know what I am?"

He shook his head. "I am not sure. I can sense the Mori demon in you, but I saw you use Fae magic to kill those other demons. And you came here with another Fae."

I glanced around at the other demons who were watching us curiously. "Um, do you think we could keep that between us for now?"

He smiled. "My people are also known for our discretion."

Chris raised an eyebrow at me when Jordan and I joined him and Nikolas near the loading bay. "Giving out your number, Sara? He doesn't seem like your type."

"He's not." I looked at Nikolas, and the warmth in his eyes made my pulse quicken.

"You ready to get out of here?" he asked.

"Yes." I glanced at the spot where Eldeorin had been standing when Nikolas arrived. "It looks like my ride left, so you're stuck with me."

Jordan snickered. "Something tells me he doesn't mind one bit."

The four of us went outside to one of the SUVs parked in front of the building. At the door of the building, the three of them stared at me when I slowed to push my way through the thick jelly-like demon ward.

On the other side, I wrinkled my nose. "Demon wards and Fae blood don't mix."

I was happy to let Chris and Jordan take the front seat of the SUV, and I climbed into the back with Nikolas. As soon as we were buckled in, his hand found mine, lacing our fingers together and sending a warm tingle up my arm.

Conversation centered mostly around what had happened at the demon market, with Chris and Jordan telling us how the gulaks had cornered them.

"What were you guys doing in a demon market in the first place?" I asked them.

"We discovered Adele has been sending letters to someone there," Chris said. "We thought it was worth checking out."

"People still send letters?"

Nikolas nodded. "People who suspect their electronic communications are being monitored."

"And who have something to hide," Chris added.

I met Chris's eyes in the rearview mirror. "Did you find anything?"

"We found the demon she was sending them to. He said he was paid to drop them in a mailbox. Inside the envelope was another envelope with an address and postage. Unfortunately, every time he tries to remember the address he draws a blank."

"Some kind of memory spell?"

"Looks like it. Adele is proving to be more covert than we gave her credit for."

I scowled at the seat in front of me. "So I'm learning. And I bet it's Madeline she's writing to. Turns out they have been friends for a lot longer than she let on to us."

"How do you know that?" Nikolas asked.

"I brought a box of Madeline's things back with me from New Hastings today and –"

"Whoa! Hold up." Jordan turned in her seat to stare at me. "You went to Maine? Today? How the hell did that happen, and why is Nikolas not freaking out about it?"

"Eldeorin took me there and we didn't stay long. I found a box of things belonging to Madeline that Nate had mentioned last fall. I was going to give them to Tristan, but I wanted to look through them first."

"And you were okay with her going there?" Jordan asked Nikolas.

He shook his head. "I didn't know until after she got back."

"We were in the middle of discussing it when he got the call that you guys were in trouble."

Jordan looked from Nikolas to me. "Discussing it. Riiight."

"What did you find in the box, Sara?" Chris asked.

"Pictures of Madeline and Adele that were taken back in the seventies, and they look pretty chummy in them."

Nikolas looked thoughtful for a moment. "That would have been just a few years after Madeline left Westhorne."

Chris nodded. "Looks like we need to pay Adele another visit, Nikolas."

"Not without me." No way was I staying behind for this one.

"Or me," Jordan added.

Nikolas looked at me, and I begged him with my eyes not to start that old argument again. Finally, he said, "We'll go see her tomorrow."

I smiled at him and mouthed, "Thank you."

Dinner that night was a whole new experience for me. Sitting across the table from the man you love and knowing he loves you back, makes everything… better. I could have been eating plain bread and water and I don't think I would have noticed. Jordan and Chris joined us, and there was more than one teasing comment when one of them had to repeat something they'd said to Nikolas or me. Normally, I'd be embarrassed, but I was too happy to care.

After dinner, I expected Nikolas to say he had to go to the command center. He surprised me by asking me to go for a walk instead. It was a clear night, and the moon cast a silvery glow across the grounds and reflected in the lake as we strolled around it. When we reached the gazebo, the little structure suddenly illuminated with thousands of tiny faerie lights, and I smiled to myself because I knew it had to be Eldeorin's doing. My faerie friend might shy away from love, but he was a romantic at heart.

"Wow, it's beautiful here." I sighed happily as I stood by the rail and looked across the moon-kissed lake.

Nikolas wrapped his arms around me and tucked my head under his chin. "Are you warm enough?"

"Yes." It was a chilly night, but between his body heat and the warmth coursing through me, I didn't feel the cold. I was still trying to believe this was real, that we were here together and that Nikolas loved me. He had loved me all along. How blind the both of us had been. How many times one of us could have said the words, but we'd held back. We were quite the pair.

"What do you think would have happened if someone else had found me in Maine? Or if I'd been found when I was little?"

"What do you mean?"

"I mean, who knows when we would have met? I would have been just another orphan, and you might never have noticed me." We could have gone decades without ever knowing what we were to each other.

Laughter rumbled in his chest and he pulled me closer, if that was possible. "I'm pretty sure I would have noticed you."

His husky words and his warm breath against my temple sent a new kind of heat through me, and I began to think about where we would go from here. Nikolas and I loved each other, and there would never be anyone else for me but him. The thought of sex still made me more than a little nervous, but I wanted to take the next step in our relationship, to complete our bond and make him mine forever. Would it happen tonight? My stomach did a series of flips as an image of Nikolas and me together in that way filled my mind.

"Tsk tsk, Cousin. Such naughty thoughts."

I gasped softly as Eldeorin appeared outside the gazebo, wearing a sly grin. My hands covered Nikolas's arms, and I waited for him to start yelling at the faerie for his part in my vigilante activities.

"He's in what we call a waking dream," Eldeorin said. "He doesn't know I'm here."

"What kind of dream?" Aine had put the hellhounds in a waking dream once, and she'd said it felt exactly like real life.

Eldeorin's eyes gleamed. "A very good one. Not quite as interesting as what you were thinking about a minute ago, but he won't complain as long as you're with him."

My face flamed. I didn't know if it was from imagining what Nikolas was doing in his dream, or because Eldeorin had guessed my thoughts when he arrived. "How do you know what I was thinking?"

His soft laugh floated toward me. "I didn't, but I do now."

I sighed in frustration. "Did you come here just to toy with Nikolas? He's pretty angry at you."

"Right now your warrior is feeling *something*, but it's definitely not anger."

"Eldeorin!"

He chuckled and stepped forward until he was directly below me. "Love suits you, Cousin."

My ire faded. "I know."

"I'm happy for you. You are good together, and I can see how much he loves you." He laid his hand on the railing. "I came to tell you I must leave for a week or two, but I will return to continue our training."

"Is everything okay?"

"I have been called home to assist nymph triplets who are experiencing a difficult *liannan*." He smiled suggestively. "It is a messy job, but someone has to do it."

I scoffed. "Yes, I'm sure it's such a burden."

Eldeorin laughed and backed away from the gazebo. "I'll see you soon, Cousin."

"Sara? What just happened?"

I turned in Nikolas's arms so I was facing him. Confusion was etched across his face as he stared down at me. "Eldeorin paid us a visit. He put you in some kind of dream state."

Nikolas swore under his breath. "I really don't like that faerie."

"Eldeorin's a bit outrageous, but he does have a good heart." I reached up to smooth the scowl from his face. "You'll be happy to know that he's gone to Faerie for a few weeks."

"This must be my lucky day."

"Best day ever."

He lowered his head and kissed me until my head was spinning and my legs had turned to rubber. When he pulled back and smiled at me, my stomach dipped at the heat in his gaze.

And then his phone rang.

I was *really* starting to hate that damn phone.

He actually groaned as he pulled the phone from his pocket. "Nikolas here." He gave me an apologetic smile as he listened to the person on the other end for a minute. "I'll be there in twenty minutes."

"Duty calls," I said as he hung up.

"Sorry. One of our teams reported in with some intel and I need to be there. I wasn't expecting to hear from them today."

I was disappointed, but I understood the importance of his work. "You don't need to apologize. It's your job."

We left the gazebo and started back to the house. When the lights of the mansion came into view, I sighed quietly, knowing our night had come to an end.

"Do you want to come to the command center with me?" Nikolas asked when we neared the house.

"Yes," I said eagerly. I wasn't ready to let him out of my sight just yet.

He smiled as we skirted the house to head next door. Our alone time might have been cut short, but the promise in his eyes told me we were going to pick up where we'd left off. Maybe not tonight, but it *was* going to happen.

Soon, whispered the voice in the back of my mind. *Mine.*

I smiled to myself. *Soon.*

*   *   *

"This place looks so different from our last visit," Jordan said as we walked into Blue Nyx with Nikolas and Chris the next day. Except for the two huge bouncers and a few cleaning staff, the place was deserted. It could have passed for a normal club without all the nonhuman patrons filling the dance floor.

Chris shook his head. "I can't believe you were here that night and I didn't see you."

Jordan's laugh echoed through the empty room. "Oh, you saw her alright. We walked right past you at the door."

Understanding dawned in his eyes. "The faerie glamoured you."

"Sara was the hottest nymph I've ever seen," Jordan said slyly. "They don't wear much, do they?"

Nikolas's head whipped toward us, and Chris smiled sheepishly. "I, uh..." He looked at Nikolas. "She didn't look like herself, so it really wasn't her body I saw..."

"Jordan, stop messing with Chris," I scolded loudly. "It looked *nothing* like me. And I could have gone a long time without bringing that up."

"Me too," Nikolas and Chris muttered at the same time.

On the second floor, Nikolas nodded to the guard outside Adele's door before he knocked. The fact that the guard recognized him made an irrational knot of jealousy burn in my gut. Nikolas had already told me he knew Adele because she sometimes provided the Mohiri with information. There was absolutely *no* reason to be jealous of a gorgeous, sultry succubus who lived off the sexual energy of men.

When Adele's husky voice called for us to come in, I moved next to Nikolas so I entered right behind him.

The blond succubus was lounging on her couch, wearing a long red dress and a sensual smile. "Nikolas, what a pleasant surprise! How can I be of service to you tonight?"

Adele's tone left little doubt about what services she wanted to provide. My Mori growled so loudly that for a second I feared the sound had come from my throat. I clenched my hands at my sides as I stepped out from behind Nikolas and stood beside him.

Adele's violet eyes could not hide her shock. "And Eldeorin's little cousin? This *is* a surprise."

"Hello, Adele," I said with forced politeness.

A door at the other end of the office opened and a tall man with long black hair came out holding a brown leather satchel. "Adele, do you have – ?" He stopped when he saw she was not alone, and his brown eyes narrowed immediately on me. "You!"

"Nice to see you again, Orias."

He hugged the satchel to his chest, and I knew it held his demon. "Because of you, I have no home and no business, and every vampire in New Mexico wants me dead. You are a menace!"

"Maybe you should be more careful about the people you do business with," I retorted.

Jordan came forward. "Yeah, and you shouldn't have tied us up either."

Nikolas stiffened beside me, and I laid a hand on his arm. "He was going to turn us over to Tristan for the reward money."

Orias sat on the other couch, clutching his satchel. "And you upset my demon so much that it took me a week to get him to calm down. I wish I'd never laid eyes on you."

Adele, who had been listening to our exchange, spoke up. "*This* is the girl who killed Stefan Price? You didn't tell me she was Fae."

"She's not Fae. She's Mohiri." Orias huffed in irritation. "And I couldn't tell you because *she* put a gag on me."

Nikolas gave me a questioning look, and I shrugged.

Adele's eyes came back to me. "But that means you are not Fae as you and Eldeorin led me to believe. What game are you playing?"

"This is not a game to me," I replied.

Her eyes narrowed. "Why did you lie to me?"

"I could ask you the same question." I pulled three photos from my pocket and tossed them on the coffee table.

Adele picked them up, her slender fingers almost caressing the edges. "Where did you get these?"

"From a box of things my mother left behind."

"Your mother? What would your mother be doing with...?" Her gasp was almost inaudible. "You are Madeline's daughter."

"Yes."

Adele recovered quickly. "You look nothing like her."

"I know."

She sank back against her cushions, still holding the photos. "Madeline's daughter. Pardon me for staring, but in all the years I've known her, she never once spoke of a daughter. I knew she was married to a human for a few years, but not that there was a child."

"I'm not a child anymore."

Her eyes flicked from me to Nikolas, and she gave a knowing nod. "So it would seem."

Nikolas pointed to the photos in her hands. "Tell us about your history with Madeline."

It wasn't a request. Adele looked down at the photos for a long moment. "The story I told you about Madeline saving my life from a vampire was true. That happened years after we met."

She smiled as if she was reliving the memories. "It was nineteen seventy-one and I was living in San Diego when I met Madeline at a party. We were the only nonhumans there, and we were drawn to each other's company. We hit it off immediately and spent the next few months partying and having fun. It was the best summer of my life.

"When I moved here, she came with me and stayed for a few years, but then she said she wanted to travel. She said she'd spent all her life in a stronghold and she wanted to see the world. She travelled for years, and she came back here between trips.

"She surprised me when she said she was enrolling in college in Maine of all places. Madeline was more adventurous than academic, and she liked warm sunny places. It was around that time that I lost touch with her for a few years. She sent a few letters, but she stopped visiting altogether for about four years. One day she reappeared and told me she'd gotten married but it hadn't worked out. She never said his name."

I swallowed the bitterness that welled up inside me. My dad had loved Madeline until the day he died, had kept her picture on his dresser and his wedding ring in his nightstand. She hadn't even bothered to tell her best friend his name.

Adele went to a sideboard and poured herself a glass of wine. She offered us a drink and we declined.

"Madeline was different after that, quieter. Sometimes she got a sad look in her eyes, but when I questioned her she never wanted to talk about it. I figured she still cared for her human ex-husband and I left it at that. She continued to travel and return here three or four times a year, until about ten years ago. I barely see her these days."

"What did she tell you about the Master she was running from?" I asked.

Adele's fingers tightened almost imperceptibly on her wine glass. "Madeline told me she'd had a run-in with a Master, but she didn't say more than that."

I turned to Orias. "Were you selling Madeline glamours to hide her from the vampires?"

He nodded arrogantly. "My glamours are the best – only Fae magic is better."

Nikolas crossed his arms over his chest. "Our sources tell us that Madeline was on her way here to Los Angeles in December, around the time Sara paid you a visit."

"She came to see me at my home that same night," Adele admitted. "I told her there was a faerie youngling asking after her on behalf of her daughter, and she asked me if I was joking. She left the next morning, and I haven't seen or heard from her since."

She was lying. I was tempted to go over and force the truth out of her, but I stayed where I was. She and Orias thought I was full Mohiri and I wanted to keep it that way. There was no telling what either of them would do with the information if they discovered what I really was.

Adele set her glass down on the coffee table. "This has been lovely, but I'm afraid I must beg you to excuse me. I have a lot of work to do before the club opens in a few hours."

She knew a lot more than she was saying, and I didn't want to leave until I knew what it was. Before I could say anything, Nikolas thanked her for her help and steered me toward the door.

"What are you doing?" I protested after the door shut behind us. "She knows exactly where Madeline is."

"Yes, and we are the last people she is going to tell. It's clear she and Madeline are very close, and she is not going to betray her friend."

"But she's our only connection to Madeline."

Nikolas gave me an infuriatingly enigmatic smile as we descended the stairs. "I didn't say we were giving up."

We emerged from the club into the cool evening air and I sighed in frustration. "Adele's probably on the phone with Madeline right now, warning her about us."

"And that is exactly what we want her to do," Nikolas said as we approached one of the three SUVs sitting across the street. The other two held Elijah's team, who were along as backup. Nikolas opened the SUV door for me. Once we were all inside he said, "Are we good, Chris?"

Chris pulled a smart phone from his pocket and turned it on. A smile spread across his face. "We're in."

I looked over his shoulder at the phone screen where some kind of app was displaying signal bars lit up in green. At the top right corner of the screen, a blue dot appeared followed by a red one. "What is that?"

"That is the signal from the transmitter I left in Adele's office," he answered smugly.

Jordan frowned. "Wait. Didn't you guys say you couldn't bug her place because she uses warlock magic to detect them and short them out?"

Nikolas started the vehicle. "These aren't normal transmitters. Raj loaned us one of his prototypes to test out." He looked at the phone in Chris's hands. "So far it appears to be working."

I leaned in closer to Chris. "How do you know?"

Chris pointed to the signal bars. "Green means the transmitter is working and the signal is good."

"What do the dots mean?"

"That blue dot tells us that someone is using the land line in Adele's office. The red dot means that my receiver is recording it."

I sucked in a sharp breath. "Recording it?"

Chris grinned and waved the phone at me. "Why don't we see who the lovely Adele was in such a hurry to call?"

CHAPTER 20

"YOU ARE A genius!" I threw my arms around the headrest to hug Chris.

"I have my moments." He pressed a button on the phone and Adele's voice came over the speaker.

"Orias, would you be a dear and make sure our Mohiri friends didn't leave a little gift for me?"

"Your wards should take care of that."

She chuckled softly. "It never hurts to be thorough."

Static filled the line and I held my breath. A few seconds later it cleared and Orias's voice came to us as clear as day. "If they did leave something, it's no longer working."

We heard the sound of a receiver lifting and someone dialing a number. "Darling, you will never believe who just left my office," Adele gushed. "Nikolas Danshov. And your daughter."

There was a short pause. "Yes, your daughter, Sara. Why did you never tell me you had a child?"

Another pause. "I understand wanting to leave the past behind, but you could have told your oldest friend. God knows we've shared everything else."

Madeline said something I couldn't hear and Adele laughed. "She doesn't look like you, but she certainly has your fire. And she is an inquisitive little thing. She wanted to know all about my friendship with you." Adele sighed. "I didn't have much choice. She showed up with pictures of us from that summer in San Diego. I could hardly lie about them." Pause. "Of course, I didn't tell them about that. How can you even ask?"

Tell us about what? What did Adele know about Madeline that she wasn't telling us?

"No, I think you should stay where you are for now. No one knows I own that place, and they'd never expect you to go there."

"Where?" I wanted to yell at the phone.

"Orias's glamour is good for another month at least. Here, talk to him yourself."

There was a rustling sound and the warlock spoke. "Madeline, stop worrying. None but a faerie could see through my magic."

Jordan and I exchanged glances, and she smirked at me.

"Haven't my glamours kept you hidden all these years?" He listened to something she said, and I wished we could hear her. "As I've told you many times, no one's magic is strong enough to undo that. I'm the strongest warlock I know, and I've been trying for years. No, I'm not giving up. I'll let you know if I come up with anything."

There were more background noises and the sound of a door closing. Adele spoke again. "Stop worrying, darling. Orias and I have your back as always. Now I have to go and open the club. I'll catch up with you in a few days. Night."

Adele hung up the phone and there was a minute of silence before she sighed heavily. She picked up the phone again and dialed. "Roc, make sure we have enough Glaen in stock. We almost ran out last night and the faeries won't drink anything else."

When she started to talk about liquor inventory, Chris turned off the recording and looked at Nikolas. "What do you think?"

Nikolas put the SUV in drive and pulled away from the club. "I think we need to take a closer look into Adele's real estate holdings."

I chewed my lip as I replayed Adele's conversation in my head. There had to be a clue there somewhere. Would it have killed her to say the name of the city at least? "Why would Adele say that no one would expect Madeline to be wherever she is? Is there a place Madeline would not want to go?"

"Wherever the Master is would be my first guess," Jordan said.

Chris stuck the phone in his coat pocket. "Madeline wouldn't be foolish enough to hide near the Master. She's evaded him this long by being smarter than that."

"She doesn't want us to find her either, so maybe she's hiding near one of our strongholds," Jordan suggested. "Hell, maybe she's in Boise."

Nikolas nodded. "That is a possibility. We should narrow our search to places near our compounds; see if Adele has property in any of them."

Chris pulled out a different cell phone and called Raoul. I half listened to his conversation because I was still going over what we'd heard. When Chris hung up, I took out my phone and called David. Jordan gave me a questioning look, and I held up a finger as David answered.

"Sara? Everything okay?"

"So far, so good." We caught up for a minute before I got to the reason for my call. "Listen, how much did you and Kelvan dig up on Adele? Do you know if she owns any property outside of LA?"

"Yeah, we found a couple, actually."

My pulse quickened. "Really? Where?"

"Let's see." He tapped his keyboard. "There are three that we know of. She owns a night club in New York, another one in San Diego, and a warehouse in Miami."

"What about houses?"

"Yes, she has a large house in San Diego."

I repeated what he'd told me to the others. "Anything else?"

"No, that's it. Why the sudden interest in her holdings?"

"We think Madeline is hiding out in one of Adele's places, and it's a property no one knows about."

David sighed. "That doesn't give us much to go on."

"Would it help if I said I have absolute faith in your abilities?"

This time he laughed. "I work for peanuts and flattery. Let me check with Kelvan and call you back."

"Okay. Talk to you soon."

I hung up and told them what David was doing. We had two very resourceful groups searching for Madeline, and I allowed myself to hope that one of them would turn up a solid lead. My loyalty was with the Mohiri, but if I'd had to bet, I would have put my money on David and Kelvan.

Chris tapped his fingers on the center console. "Something else I'd like to know is what Orias has been trying to undo for years for Madeline."

"I'd like to know that myself," Nikolas replied. "Orias is a powerful warlock. If he can't undo something, it must be very strong magic." He looked at me. "By the way, what was he talking about back there when he said you put a gag on him? And what did you do to his demon?"

"Oh, that." I gnawed on my lower lip. "I might have made him take a binding oath that prevented him from telling anyone we were there."

"What kind of oath?"

"You ever hear of the White Oath?"

Nikolas and Chris shook their heads, and I explained the oath to them. "It's something I learned from Remy."

Both of them looked at me with new respect, and Nikolas said, "And what did you do to upset his demon?"

Jordan scoffed. "That bastard had the rest of us tied up, so Sara took his demon hostage until he let us go."

Chris turned in his seat. "You took an upper demon hostage? This I have to hear."

"It wasn't like I actually saw the demon. Orias already had it trapped in a lamp. I took the lamp and shook it up a little. Demons really don't like Fae magic."

"No, I would guess not." Nikolas kept his eyes on the road, so it was hard to tell what he was thinking.

"How do you fit a demon in a lamp anyway?" Jordan asked. It was something I had wondered myself.

"It takes a spell cast by a very crafty and powerful warlock," Nikolas told her.

"If Madeline is using his glamours, how was Sara's friend David able to get that picture of her in Vancouver?" Chris said almost to himself.

"Orias told us his spells only last a month because they are so strong. Maybe we were able to catch her as one was wearing off." That also explained how Madeline kept disappearing and they'd lose her trail for a few weeks.

Chris nodded. "Makes sense. Let's hope she is between glamours when we find her or we'll never be able to recognize her."

"No problem. I can see through his magic."

Nikolas looked over his shoulder at me. "You can?"

"I can see through all glamours. I thought you knew that."

He cocked an eyebrow. "You forgot to share that piece of information with us."

Oops.

Jordan leaned forward. "She saw right through the glamour Orias had on his place in New Mexico. The rest of us couldn't see a thing, and we thought she was nuts when she said there was a building there."

Nikolas shook his head. "Sara, when we get home, we're going to have a long talk about all the things you've *forgotten* to mention."

Jordan and I shared a look. She smirked at me and mouthed the words *pillow talk,* which made us both laugh. Up front I heard Chris say, "Don't look at me. You're the one who told Tristan it was okay for the two of them to stay together."

We were still laughing when my phone rang.

"Tell me you have something."

"It might not be anything," David replied. "Kelvan's doing some more digging."

"And it might be everything." I looked at the others who were watching me. "David, can I put you on speaker? It's just the four of us here."

He hesitated for a moment. "Uh, okay. So here is what we found. In the last year, Adele has flown to Las Vegas twice by private charter. She stayed there for three days on one trip and five on another."

"Maybe she just likes to gamble," Jordan said.

"Maybe," he agreed. "What I do know is she didn't stay at any of the big hotels during her trips, and she doesn't strike me as a person who would charter a jet only to stay in a cheap hotel."

"She's not." I tried to contain my excitement. "Where do you think she stayed?"

"We think she has a residence there. If anyone can find it, Kelvan can. You can't hide much from him once he's on your trail."

Chris spoke up. "How long do you think it will take?"

David let out a whoop. "I think this is a new record for him."

I could barely breathe. "He found something?"

David spent the next ten seconds typing before he answered. "Adele owns a luxury condo in Las Vegas, overlooking the Strip. She bought it three years ago under the name Elizabeth Cummings."

"What makes you think this woman and Adele are the same person?" Nikolas asked.

"Elizabeth Cummings is one of the identities Adele used before she took her current one. Succubi have to create a new identity every few decades, especially if they are a businesswoman like Adele. She went by Elizabeth Cummings back in the forties."

"How the hell did you find that?" Chris cut in. "Even our records on her don't go back that far."

David chuckled. "Yours don't, but demons have their own archives."

"You guys are scary sometimes, you know that?" I said. "I'm *really* glad you're on my side."

I could tell David was grinning when he replied. "We decided it was more fun to use our power for good instead of evil."

Jordan was practically jumping on her seat. "So, are we going to Vegas?"

Nikolas and Chris looked at each other, and some kind of silent communication passed between them. Chris shrugged and Nikolas sighed. He adjusted the rearview mirror so he could see me.

"Sara, if I asked you to stay at the faerie's place while we check this out, would you?"

He could not be serious. "What do you think?"

He scowled at me, and I smiled back. At least I was honest about it.

"Chris, call and get the jet to pick us up at LAX," Nikolas said in a not-so-happy voice.

"We could drive to Vegas before the jet gets here." Now that we had a solid lead on Madeline, I didn't want to sit around waiting.

"There is no way I am taking you to Las Vegas without an easy means of escape." Nikolas's tone brooked no argument. But he wasn't beating his chest and ordering me to stay behind, which was progress for us.

David's voice came out of my phone speaker. "Now that you have that settled, I'll be off. I'll text you the address for the condo."

"Thanks, David. You're the best."

"Yeah, I hear that a lot," he joked before he said goodbye and hung up.

* * *

Four hours later, we flew into Las Vegas, and my mouth fell open when I got my first look at the sea of lights below us. "It's so bright."

Nikolas leaned in to peer out the window over my shoulder, and a little tremor ran through me. Ever since last night at the gazebo, butterflies had taken up residence in my stomach. All it took was the slightest touch from him to set them off.

"And dangerous," he said in a low voice, his warm breath caressing my cheek. "I must be out of my mind for agreeing to bring you here."

I turned my face and met his eyes inches from mine. On impulse, I gave him a quick kiss on the lips. "Thank you for not trying to make me stay behind."

His eyes turned that smoky gray color that always melted my insides. At least I wasn't the only one affected by our nearness.

"Okay, you lovebirds, no making out in the jet," Jordan said from across the aisle. "We've got work to do and all you two can do is make eyes at each other."

The pilot came over the intercom and told us to prepare for landing. My stomach dipped, but it had nothing to do with Nikolas or the plane's descent. After months of searching and almost giving up hope, I was finally going to confront Madeline and get the answers I was looking for. After she told us who the Master was, the Council would send their forces after him. That vampire had wrought so much pain and grief in my life, and a part of me wanted to be there to see his fall. But a larger part of me had no wish to ever lay eyes on him. I just wanted him gone from our lives forever.

We landed at McCarran Airport and taxied up to a private hangar where several large SUVs waited for us. When we disembarked, a black Mohiri male with a shaved head came over to greet us. His name was Geoffrey and his unit was one of two that had been here for the past year. Apparently, there was enough vampire activity in Vegas to warrant a larger Mohiri presence. Maybe that was what Adele had meant when she said no one would expect Madeleine to be there.

The warriors were all business. Before I knew it, I was in a vehicle with Nikolas, Chris, Jordan, and Geoffrey. The four warriors who had flown with us climbed into the other vehicles with Geoffrey's team.

Geoffrey drove, easily navigating the busy streets. "We scouted the address you gave us and saw a female there, but she doesn't look like Madeline."

"Madeline is using a warlock glamour to mask her identity," Nikolas told him.

"Which warlock?"

"Orias."

Geoffrey let out a whistle, and I began to wonder if there was anyone who hadn't heard of Orias. "It's no surprise no one can find her. How are you going to know for sure if it's her?"

"We have a way to see through her glamour," Nikolas answered vaguely. Despite what had happened at Westhorne last fall, few Mohiri knew about my Fae heritage. The rest were on a need-to-know basis.

"You got the warlock tied up back there?" Geoffrey joked lightly. "Ah, here we are."

My breathing fogged the window as I leaned close to it to stare at the glass building that was so tall it appeared to disappear into the Vegas sky. Somewhere up there behind one of those windows was my mother. Not that I was looking for a mother-daughter reunion. But it was surreal to know that in a few minutes, I might actually talk to her for the first time.

"Are you ready?" Nikolas's eyes were dark with worry.

"I've been ready for this for a long time."

Armed and alert, Nikolas, Jordan, Chris, and I entered the marble lobby along with two of the warriors from the California team. The rest took up positions outside in case there was trouble.

I barely noticed our surroundings as we waited for the elevator to arrive, and by the time we stepped off the elevator on the forty-second floor, my heart was pounding. Nikolas's warm hand captured mine and squeezed it gently, and I gave him a small smile.

We stopped in front of door 4220, and everyone but Nikolas and I moved away from the door. We'd decided on the plane that the two of us would talk to Madeline while the rest waited outside. Too many visitors might spook her and make her less inclined to talk. She knew Nikolas well and I was her daughter, so she might open up to us. In any case, she wasn't running this time – unless she sprouted wings.

Nikolas rang the doorbell and I could hear the faint chimes ringing through the condo. I pictured Madeline walking quietly to the door and peering at us through the peephole. Her eyes would grow round in shock when she saw who was on the other side of the door, and she'd pretend no one was home and hope we would leave.

Several long minutes passed. Nikolas knocked this time. "Madeline, we've had our people watching this place, so we know you're in there. We just want to talk."

Silence.

I moved in front of him. "An hour of your time, and we'll be out of your life forever. You owe me that much... *Mom.*" Okay, maybe I put more than a little sarcasm into that word, but really, who could blame me?

The deadbolt clicked and the door opened as far as the metal security guard would allow it. A blue eye peered out at me warily, and I sucked in a sharp breath. "I'm sorry but you have the wrong address. My name is Claire and I have no children."

"Now that really hurts," I replied dryly.

"I don't know who you are, but I'm calling the police if you don't leave."

I leaned closer to her and spoke softly. "Before you do that, I think you should know I can see through glamours... even Orias's."

Shock and recognition flashed in her eyes before she could hide it. Her lips clamped together, and the door slammed shut. It wouldn't do her any good. We weren't going anywhere, and neither was she.

Seconds later, the door opened and I stood face-to-face with my mother.

The photos I'd seen of her had not done her justice. Madeline had a good five inches on me, and her figure was svelte in the blue pants and cream top she wore. Her platinum blond hair was pulled back into a simple chignon that flattered her delicate features and sapphire blue eyes. I could see why any man, including my father, would fall for her.

When I'd met Tristan, I'd thought it was strange having a grandfather who looked only a few years my senior. That was nothing compared to having a mother who looked like she could have been in my senior class. I should have kept the money I'd given Roland and Peter. I'd need it to pay for therapy when all of this was over.

"Come in." Madeline's rich voice was laced with anger and resignation as she stepped back to wave us inside.

I went first and Nikolas followed me closely. My mother or not, he wasn't taking any chances. Normally, I'd tell him he was being overprotective, but I let it pass because just bringing me here was a big step for him.

Madeline locked the door and led us into the living room that was tastefully done in browns and creams, with floor-to-ceiling windows that provided an amazing view of the Strip. She seated herself in a leather chair, and Nikolas and I sat on the matching couch. I looked at her and wondered what I should be feeling, being in the same room with the woman who had given birth to me and abandoned me when I was just a baby. She was Tristan's daughter and the woman my dad had loved. Yet all I saw was a beautiful stranger. All I felt was cold detachment.

"You look like Daniel." It was said in a very matter-of-fact way, no emotion coloring her tone.

"I know."

We stared at each other for a long moment. She looked away first. "It's been a long time, Nikolas."

"It has. I'd say you look well, but I can't see past the glamour."

Madeline's brows drew together and she swung her gaze back to me. "And how is it that you can? Did Orias give you something to see past it?

Did he tell you where I was? I know Adele would never betray me."

A small smile touched my lips. "Orias and I are not exactly on the best of terms, and Adele didn't give you up. She is amazingly loyal to you."

"Then how did you find me? How can you see me now?"

"Some very resourceful friends of mine found you for me. As for how I can see you, that's irrelevant." I saw no reason to beat around the bush, and I got right to the reason for our visit. "You know the identity of a Master and we want to know who he is."

She started to shake her head, and I said, "He had my dad killed. *Your* husband. He's spent the last six months trying to kill me and everyone I love. I know family means nothing to you, but you must have felt something for my dad once upon a time."

Madeline recoiled as if I'd slapped her. "You know nothing about what I felt for him."

"You're right. I don't." Anger slipped into my voice. "I don't know how you can love someone and hurt them so completely. I don't know how you can stand back while they are murdered and let the one responsible walk free so he can destroy other families. I have no idea what a person who does something like that is feeling. So why don't you enlighten me?"

"I know you are angry because I left you –"

I couldn't stop the harsh laugh that burst from me. "I don't even remember you. My dad gave me all the love I needed until *they* took him from me. You have the information I need to find them, and that is the *only* reason I'm here now."

Silence fell over the room, broken by the soft patter of raindrops against the windows. I looked at the sky and watched dark clouds roll in.

"I loved him."

I turned back to Madeline. "What?"

"Your father." Her hands entwined on her lap. "I met him in college. I knew he was human and it could never work between us, but he was... He had a way of making you feel like you were the only person in his world."

I didn't know why she was telling me this, but I knew what she meant about my dad. His life had revolved around me, and he'd always made sure I knew how much he loved me. I'd been his world, just like he'd been mine.

"I should not have married him, but I was in love, and I couldn't think of leaving him. I knew it wouldn't be long before he realized I was different, so a month before our wedding, I told him what I was."

Shock rippled through me. "He knew what you were?"

"I told him I was Mohiri, but not about my Mori because I didn't think he could cope with that. It was a struggle for him to learn about the real world, but he said what I was didn't matter to him." Her eyes and voice grew soft. "Even when I said I would not age, he wanted me to stay. So we got married. Those two years were the happiest of my life."

I didn't need to ask what had ended her blissful state. I was born in the third year of their marriage.

Madeline looked almost apologetic when she spoke again. "I was content with just the two of us, but Daniel wanted a child. He talked about how wonderful it would be, and I loved him so much that I let myself believe it was what I wanted, too. The day you were born, he was the happiest I'd ever seen him. I thought that would be enough for me to be happy too, but I was wrong. I loved my daughter – you, but being a mother wasn't something I had ever wanted. I did it for two years, and then I couldn't handle it anymore."

"You left your child with a human who had no idea what would happen to her when her Mori emerged," Nikolas said in a hard voice.

"I could sense no Mori in her," Madeline replied defensively. "I thought she was human like her father." She looked at me. "I came back sometimes to see how the two of you were doing, but neither of you knew it. If I'd seen a sign that you were different, I would have gone to your father. You looked happy together."

"We were happy. Until he was killed."

Pain flashed in her eyes. "I went to him and warned him he might be in danger. He didn't believe me. The last thing I wanted was for him to get hurt."

Bitterness welled in me. "He'd didn't get hurt, Madeline. He got murdered."

She flinched and got up to walk over to the window where rain was running down in rivulets now. "Part of me died that day. No matter what had happened between us, Daniel was the only man I ever loved."

"Did you even care about what happened to your daughter after he died?" Nikolas asked harshly.

Madeline turned away from the window. "Of course I did," she snapped. "Sara disappeared after her father died, and there was no trace of her. I thought she had died, too, at first. I don't know why I forgot about Daniel's brother, Nate, but it was years later when I remembered him."

I knew why she hadn't remembered Nate. Aine had hidden me so the vampires could not find me. She'd made everyone forget that Nate even existed. It surprised me to hear Madeline had looked for me, but it didn't change how I felt about her.

Nikolas leaned forward, resting his elbows on his knees. "Tell us about the Master."

The agitation on Madeline's face immediately turned to fear. "I-I can't."

"Yes, you can." I had to force myself not to yell at her. "Why are you protecting him?"

"I'm not protecting him. You don't understand." She began to pace in front of the window. "I can't tell you because I don't know who he is."

"You're lying. A day before my dad was killed, you went to visit a friend of yours in Portland and you told him you knew about the Master."

She stopped pacing to stare at me. "Jiro Ito? How do you know about him?"

"His son, David, was there and he overheard you talking to his father. You said you knew the identity of a Master, and you needed the money he was holding for you so you could disappear."

"Jiro's son was there?" She shook her head. "He misunderstood what I said. I told Jiro that a Master was after me because I'd seen him, but that I didn't know who he was."

I folded my arms across my chest. "That makes no sense. If you saw him, you can describe him. And how did you come to see him in the first place or even know he was a Master?"

Madeline looked almost terrified when she returned to her chair. "I was in New York to see Adele, who was opening a new night club there, and I ended up at a party on the Upper East Side. I –" She swallowed and her hands clenched the arms of her chair. "Something happened to me at the party. One minute I was having a drink and the next I woke up in a cage in the basement of a place I didn't know. There were vampires everywhere, but none of them talked to me until one named Eli came in. He taunted me about being his Master's new toy. When I heard the word 'Master' I knew I was dead."

"*Khristu*," Nikolas breathed.

"A few hours later, they took me upstairs to meet the Master. I remember walking into a room and seeing him sitting by the fireplace. I remember every minute I was tortured by him for two days. I remember wishing to die. But I can't remember anything about him."

The fear in her voice was real as she relived the ordeal. "I'm sorry." No matter what my feelings were for her, no one deserved to go through that. "Did they drug you to make you forget?"

"He compelled me to forget him."

My eyes jerked from her to Nikolas. "But we can't be compelled by vampires. Can we?"

"A Master is not a normal vampire," Nikolas replied.

"He made sure I remembered everything about my time there, except him." Madeline's voice shook. "He said he was going to enjoy playing with me for a long time."

The air in the room was charged with her fear, and it made the hair on the back of my neck stand up. At that moment, lightning zigzagged across the sky, and I jumped.

"How did you escape?" Nikolas asked her.

"I didn't. He released me."

My mouth fell open. "He let you go?"

"Something happened. I don't know what. I was chained in his sitting room and I heard voices outside. Then he came in and said something that made me go to sleep. I woke up in Central Park filled with an overwhelming urge to run." She swiped a finger under her eye. "The first thing I did was go to Portland to warn Daniel. I've been running ever since."

Nikolas shook his head. "Madeline, why didn't you go home? Tristan would do anything to keep you safe."

She sniffed delicately. "Whatever *he* did to me made me afraid to trust anyone, especially the Mohiri. Adele is my closest friend, and I can't even trust her completely. He stole that from me. He released me from my chains, but he still robbed me of my freedom. Until I can get rid of this compulsion, I'll never be free."

Orias's conversation with Madeline suddenly made sense to me. "Orias is trying to find a way to break the Master's compulsion, isn't he?"

"He's been working on it for ten years, but nothing can break it."

"The only thing that can break a Master's compulsion is his death," Nikolas explained.

The weight of his words hit me. "She can't tell us where he is unless she can break the compulsion, but in order to break it he has to die?"

"Yes."

Despair settled over me, crushing every hope I'd pinned on finding Madeline. She was supposed to have the answers, to lead us to the Master, but she was as confused as the rest of us. Where did that leave us?

"Are you okay?"

I tried to smile at Nikolas and failed miserably.

"We'll find him. It'll just take a little longer than we thought."

Madeline straightened her perfect chignon. "So you are Mohiri after all. I'm glad you found our people, Sara."

"Actually, it was Nikolas who found me." I laid my hand on the couch between us and he covered it with his. The action did not go unnoticed by Madeline, and her lips parted in surprise. Neither Nikolas nor I bothered to answer the question in her eyes. As far as I was concerned, she'd lost the right to know about my life the moment she'd deserted my dad and me.

"What will you do now?" she asked, and I could almost hear the "with me" at the end of the question.

"We'll keep looking," Nikolas answered. "Keep fighting."

"We found you. We'll find him, too." I let go of Nikolas's hand and we both stood at the same time. "We should be going."

Madeline walked us to the door. "Sara, for what it's worth, I really did love your father. And I loved you, too. I still do."

I held out my hand and she hesitated before she took it. "Thank you for talking to us. I hope Orias can find a way to help you."

Her eyes glistened and she held my hand a few seconds longer than was necessary. "Thank you."

"Goodbye, Madeline."

Nikolas opened the door and I gave my mother one last look before I walked through it.

CHAPTER 21

MY WHOLE BODY sagged the moment the door shut behind us. Talking to Madeline about the past had been harder than I'd expected. Add to that my disappointment that she couldn't help us, and I was feeling like I'd been put through an emotional wringer.

Jordan ran up to us. "What did she say?"

"Not here," Nikolas said. "We'll talk outside."

Rain was coming down in torrents when we left the building, and we made a mad dash for the vehicles. As soon as we settled into our SUV, the others looked at us expectantly. I sat back during the drive to the airport and let Nikolas tell them about our conversation with Madeline.

We were all subdued by the time we piled out of the vehicles at the airport hangar. Nikolas went to speak to the pilot, and I found a seat at the back of the small jet. I reclined my seat and closed my eyes, hoping that would discourage anyone from trying to talk to me. It had been a long day, capped off by a huge setback, and I needed a little time to process it all.

"Sara?" I opened my eyes as Nikolas settled into the seat next to mine. His expression told me there was more bad news.

"We've got some bad electrical storms moving through the area, so we're grounded for a few hours, at least. Geoffrey's team has a safe house nearby, and we're going to wait out the storm there. It's more comfortable than an airport hangar."

"Okay."

He reached over and brushed a strand of damp hair out of my face. "You did well tonight. I know that was harder for you than you're letting on."

"It was," I admitted quietly.

He nodded perceptively, and I knew he wasn't going to press me until I was ready to talk about it. I followed him out of the jet and back into the

SUV where Geffrey, Jordan, and Chris waited for us.

The drive to the safe house took less than ten minutes despite the heavy rain that was causing traffic backups. Geoffrey pulled into the two-car garage, and one of the other SUVs parked beside us. The last one had to park in the driveway. I hoped the house was bigger than it had looked from the street because it was going to be crowded with all of us. All I needed was a quiet corner where I could stay out of everyone's way until it was time to leave.

The house turned out to be a lot bigger than I'd expected, with five bedrooms, three bathrooms, and a finished basement where the warriors kept their computer equipment. In every room we walked through, there were weapons and gear that made Jordan's eyes go round with envy. She asked the warriors a ton of questions about their operation, and they all sounded happy to answer. I left her talking to one of them about swords to explore alone.

On the main floor I found a small den with a black leather couch, which was just what I was looking for. I left the light off and the door open, took off my jacket, and curled up on the couch with a sigh, drawing comfort from Nikolas's presence in another part of the house. The rain pelting the window drowned out most of the voices and sounds from the rest of the house, leaving me alone with my thoughts.

A chapter in my life had ended tonight, but I didn't feel the closure I'd thought I would get after confronting Madeline. I didn't understand how she could have loved my dad as much as she obviously had and still walked away from him. I would do anything to hold onto the people I loved. I'd give up my life for Nikolas, and I'd fight any person or thing that tried to take him from me. She should have made my dad listen to her when she went back to warn him. She should have done anything to protect us. There wasn't a compulsion strong enough to override the love I had for Nikolas.

I turned on my side so I could watch the rain running down the window. I'd always loved storms. There was something about their raw power that made me feel more alive and bolstered me when I was down. Maybe it was the undine in me. I wished this storm would help ease the weight that had settled in my chest since I'd left Madeline. I had been so sure finding her would give us what we needed to free us from the Master forever. But we were no closer to finding him now than we ever had been. For months my main goal had been to find Madeleine, and I didn't know what to do anymore.

I felt Nikolas coming closer and I knew he was searching for me. I was about to call out to him when he appeared in the doorway. He entered the room and crouched in front of me.

"Why are you hiding in here alone?"

I summoned a smile. "If I was hiding, I'd be behind the couch."

"You'd never hide behind a couch."

"True. There is no dignity in lying in dust bunnies."

His smile was barely visible in the light from the window. "Want some company?"

"Behind the couch?"

"Wherever you want."

The huskiness in his voice made my stomach dip. "Yes," I said shyly, moving to sit up.

He surprised me by moving to stretch out behind me with his arm under my head. The couch wasn't that deep, and he pulled me against his delicious warmth with his free arm wrapped around my waist. Heat shot straight to my belly, and I tensed nervously before I relaxed against him.

"Comfortable?" he asked softly, his warm breath caressing my ear.

"Yes." Comfortable wasn't exactly the word I'd use to describe how it felt having Nikolas pressed against the length of me. Every nerve ending in my body thrummed with electricity, and my lungs seemed to have forgotten how to work. At the same time, I felt completely safe and loved. It was a heady mix of emotions.

"Do you want to talk about her?"

I was quiet for a moment while I gathered my thoughts. "She wasn't what I expected. I pity her. Except for Adele, she has no one, and she spends her life running and afraid and regretting the love she gave up. I think of her and I realize how lucky I am to have you and everyone else in my life."

His arm squeezed me. "That's not luck. You have so many people who love you because you're a good person. Madeline was always selfish. She proved that when she left home the way she did, and with her behavior since then. I'm not saying she deserves the things that have happened to her, but I do believe she brought most of them on herself. That you can feel sad for her after all you've been through shows how kind you are."

I thought about his words. He always knew just what to say or do to make me feel better. It was as if he could read my mind sometimes.

"Can I ask you something?"

"Anything."

"How do you always know when I need you?"

"When you're hurting, I feel it," he said gruffly.

"You do?"

"Yes." He kissed my temple. "So don't ever try to hide your pain from me."

"Why can't I do the same with you?"

"You will, someday." *When the bond is complete.* He didn't have to say the words for me to know what he meant. What would it be like to know someone on such an intimate level? To know *him* that way? The thought brought a smile to my lips, and I snuggled closer to him.

"I love you, Nikolas."

He turned my face toward him until he could press his lips to mine. "I love you too, *moy malen'kiy voin.*"

Lightning flashed and a peal of thunder shook the house as if Mother Nature was giving her approval. Or it was more likely that she was saying, "It's about damn time."

All too soon, the world crept into my little cocoon of happiness. I sighed when I thought about starting over in our search for the Master. We were no closer to finding him than we'd been months ago. "What do we do now?"

"I don't know, but we'll figure it out together. Like you told Madeline, you found her when no one else could. We'll go back to California and come up with a plan for what to do next."

I suddenly felt so world weary, and all I wanted was to see Nate and Tristan and to walk in the woods with Hugo and Woolf. "I don't want to go back to California," I said hoarsely.

"Where do you want to go?"

I shifted until I was on my back, looking up at him. "Can we go home?"

The smile that spread across his face stole my breath away. "I thought you'd never ask."

*　　*　　*

I awoke with a gasp as ice filled my chest and made it hard to breathe. "Oh God!" I rolled off the couch and stumbled to the door of the dark room. Down the hallway I heard voices, and I ran toward them.

"Vampires!" I cried as I burst into the living room.

Nikolas was standing by the fireplace with Chris and Geoffrey, and the three of them spun toward me at once. Geoffrey looked confused, but Nikolas and Chris leapt into action. Nikolas was at my side in a heartbeat.

"Where? How many?"

"Everywhere," I choked out. "At least fifteen."

Geoffrey ran over to us. "How does she know that?"

"No time to explain. Get ready." Nikolas grabbed the first sword he saw. "Chris?"

Chris stood by the living room window, peering through the closed blinds with a sword in his hand. "Nothing yet."

"What's going on?" Jordan ran down the stairs as six warriors spilled from the basement. The moment she saw my face, she snatched a katana from the wall over the fireplace. "Where?"

Nikolas took charge. "We have at least fifteen hostiles incoming. Jordan and Abigail, you're with Chris. Elijah, you, Joseph, and Noah cover upstairs. Travis and Oliver take the kitchen. Geoffrey and I will cover the back."

"What about me?" I asked as everyone ran to take up defensive positions.

Geoffrey ran up to me, carrying two swords, one of which he held out to me. "Can you fight?"

I held up my hands. "Not with that thing."

"Sara, you stay with me." Nikolas's eyes were dark with worry. "Do not leave my sight."

"She needs a weapon."

Geoffrey had a long silver dagger in a sheath on his leg. I grabbed it just as a crash sounded from the den. At the same time, a window broke upstairs and another broke in the kitchen.

My heart pounded as I raced after Nikolas and Geoffrey to the den just as two male vampires flew through the broken window. Rain blew into the room and glass covered the couch where I'd been sleeping a few minutes before.

Nikolas was on the first vampire before he knew what was coming. His sword carried a ghostly gleam as it swung in an upward arc, eviscerating the vampire before it had time to attack. He brought the sword back down and sliced cleanly through the vampire's neck.

Beside him, Geoffrey was still fighting his opponent when two more vampires leapt through the window. I watched helplessly as Nikolas glanced over his shoulder at me then moved to intercept the new vampires. I wanted to help him, but I was afraid to distract him by joining the fight. Instead, I backed out into the hallway to give him and Geoffrey room to fight without worrying about me getting caught in the fray.

From all over the house came shouts and screams and the sounds of battle. Over my head, heavy footsteps pounded, followed by loud thumps like something hitting a wall. A moment later, a vampire's screech was abruptly cut short.

I heard Jordan yell and Chris swear as a door crashed open. Shouts and sounds of struggle filled the hallway, and I knew my friends were in trouble. I couldn't just stand here while everyone else fought for their lives.

I met my first vampire in the hallway. He came up short as if he was surprised to see me, and then he smiled, revealing his long fangs. I could tell by the gleam in his eyes that he thought I was easy pickings. I dropped into a half crouch and smiled as I crooked my finger at him. *Come and get me.*

He didn't say a word as he sped toward me. He was fast but not mature, and he had obviously never fought a warrior. He went for my throat. I dropped to one knee and brought the dagger up into his ribs. It wasn't close enough to pierce his heart, but he screamed as the silver burned him. He flew over my head and crashed into the wall. Before he could recover, I was on him, shoving my blade home. His eyes grew wide with shock and his body went limp.

I jumped to my feet and gasped as pain lanced through my shoulder. I winced at the bloody tears in my shirt, and my first thought was I'd better cover them before Nikolas saw them. He was already going to be pissed that I'd left his sight. Shaking my head, I turned to the living room. We were in the middle of a battle for our lives, and I was worried about his feelings.

I pushed all thoughts of Nikolas aside as I ran into the living room. Three dead vampires lay on the floor, and two more vampires were trying to attack Jordan and Abigail. My eyes flew to the missing window, and I spotted movement outside. On the front lawn, Chris battled four vampires and they were gaining the upper hand. Apparently, they didn't know the rules of fair play.

I vaulted through the window and landed three feet from the fight. Two of the vampires spun to face me, and Chris stared at me with a mixture of shock and worry. He opened his mouth to yell at me, but I was already moving. I dropped my dagger as I released my real weapon. In the words of my mentor: it was time to go all Fae on their demon asses.

"Get back, Chris!" I backed away from him as electricity crackled over my skin. I was pretty good at focusing my magic now, but I didn't want to take the chance of him being caught up in it.

Instead of throwing my power at the vampires circling me, I raised my arms and threw it up into the air, calling to the magic in the water falling from the sky. Fat raindrops froze into thousands of sharp needles of ice that swirled around me to rip through the vampires' clothes and skin. Screams tore from their throats, and they raised their arms to protect themselves.

"Sara!" Nikolas roared from somewhere in the house. His voice startled me, and I lost my concentration. Ice turned back to water.

The vampires turned their ravaged faces toward me, their mouths twisted into snarls. But turning water to ice was only one of the tricks I'd picked up in the last few months.

I feinted toward one of them, then dropped and kicked the legs out from under another. I landed in a puddle of water, which was exactly where I wanted to be. With one hand I grabbed the ankle of the downed vampire while my other hand flew up to meet the chest of another vampire as it pounced on me.

The blast lit up the lawn like lightning. Screams tore at my eardrums before the two vampires stiffened and collapsed on the grass in smoking heaps.

Above me, a sword flashed through the air and decapitated one of the two remaining vampires. The last one, sensing the battle was lost, turned to run, but Chris cut him down before he reached the edge of the lawn.

I sat up and rolled to my feet, ready to take on the next threat, but Chris and I were alone on the lawn. That was when it struck me that all I could hear was rain and thunder. Turning toward the house, I looked up at the window I'd come through and found Jordan and several of the other warriors staring at me like I was the main attraction at a circus sideshow.

"What the hell just happened?" someone asked.

Before anyone could answer, a furious male bellow came from inside the house. Seconds later, the people in the window parted as Nikolas leapt through it. His eyes swept over the bodies on the lawn as he strode toward me. I couldn't tell how close he was to a rage, but something told me it wouldn't take much to push him over the edge.

Ignoring our audience, he pulled me into his arms, and the tremors moving through him told me he was on the verge of losing it. My arms went around his neck, and I pulled his face down to mine. "I love you," I whispered against his lips before I kissed him.

His body was rigid, and for a moment I thought he wasn't going to respond. But then his mouth moved over mine and he made a sound deep in his chest as he pulled me closer. At first the kiss was urgent, desperate, but it soon became soft and exploring as the rage drained out of him.

He broke the kiss and let out a ragged breath. "You were supposed to stay with me."

I smiled at him, barely aware of the rain drenching us. "You didn't need my help, and someone had to save Chris's ass. Again."

He looked like he was about to argue, but he groaned and rested his forehead against mine. "Now I know why Nate's going gray. At this rate, I'll be white before him."

"Well, there's always *Clairol for Men*."

The exasperated look in his eyes made laughter bubble from me. I hugged him tightly, pressing my face into his neck and breathing in the scent that could only be Nikolas.

"Damn, are they always like that?" I heard Abigail ask.

Jordan snickered. "Pretty much."

Chris chuckled behind me. "Do you two want us to give you some privacy?"

I started to retort until I realized the reason for his comment. Heat flooded my face, as well as a few other places, when I looked down at my legs wrapped around Nikolas's waist like a monkey. I lifted my eyes to his and caught him smiling like a man who was very pleased with himself. His hands slid down my back to cradle my bottom, their heat seeping through my wet jeans. My body grew so warm despite my wet clothes that I was sure there had to be steam coming off me.

His chest rumbled. "On second thought, this might be worth a few gray hairs."

I scowled at him as I dropped my legs and let them dangle until he saw fit to lower me to the ground. He kissed the tip of my nose before he released me, making it impossible to keep a smile from creeping across my face.

Nikolas looked over my head at Geoffrey, who had joined us on the lawn. "How many?"

"Fifteen." Geoffrey ran a hand over his shaved head. "Jesus! If you and your team hadn't been here, it would have been a massacre."

"Or maybe they came *because* we were here," Chris said meaningfully.

Geoffrey's gaze fell on me "How did you know? You said fifteen were coming. How could you possibly guess that?"

"I wasn't guessing." I broke off as I realized the coldness hadn't completely disappeared from my chest. "I was wrong. There were sixteen. There's still one here."

"The house is clear," Elijah called from the doorway.

I moved away from them, trying to let my radar do its thing. It was a little out of whack after being hit with so many vampires at one time, and I needed to make sure I wasn't just being paranoid.

"Chris, can you and Elijah do a sweep out here to be safe?" I heard Nikolas ask as I walked toward the front door. He was right behind me when I stepped into the house.

Water ran off me to pool on the hardwood floor as I stood in the living room, trying to locate the remaining vampire. "There." I pointed to the basement door.

"There's no way for anyone to get in down there," Geoffrey said. "The basement windows are all too small.

"Then one tried to go out that way and got trapped, because there is a vampire in that basement."

Geoffrey still looked doubtful. "We'll have to flush him out. Abigail and I will go down, and the rest of you keep an eye on this door in case he comes through it."

"We need to find out how they found this place and if they knew who was here," Nikolas said. "Unless you're in immediate danger, do not kill him." Everyone nodded, and he turned to me. "I don't suppose it would do any good to ask you to let the others handle this one."

"I've done enough killing for one night. This one is all yours." I didn't add that my shoulder was starting to hurt like hell. I'd covered it with my hair so he wouldn't get upset, but I had to get it looked at. Something told me there was gunna paste in my immediate future.

I walked to the other side of the living room to stay out of the way while the others faced the door. Geoffrey opened the basement door, and he and Abigail went silently down the stairs. I held my breath along with everyone else in the room as we waited for something to happen.

A girl's scream cut through the silence, followed by a few thumps and what sounded like a computer monitor hitting the floor. I thought I heard the rattle of chains before a screech of pain came from below. What the hell were they doing down there?

"We have her," Geoffrey called.

Everyone relaxed and a few warriors looked in my direction. They were wondering how I'd known there was a vampire in the basement, but no one voiced the question.

"What will they do with her?" I asked Nikolas, who had come to stand beside me.

"They'll confine her and wait until she gets hungry to see if she'll talk."

I thought about Nate's short time as a vampire. Tristan had planned to do the same to him to get him to talk. Other techniques didn't work on vampires. Hunger drove them insane.

An SUV pulled into the driveway, its lights splashing across the carnage on the lawn. The other Vegas team had gone out on patrol before the attack, and it looked like someone had called them back. The four warriors filed into the house and surveyed the damage to their place.

"Goddamn!" said a burly brunette with short cropped hair. "We missed all the action."

A blond warrior pushed past him and headed for the stairs. "Fuck the action," he growled. "If my *Martin* has a scratch on it, I'm going to find some vampire ass to kick."

I looked at one of the others. "His *Martin*?"

The brunette chuckled. "His guitar. Elvis gave it to him. Jackson loves that thing."

"He knew Elvis? For real?"

"Yep. Even used to jam with him."

As I was trying to wrap my mind around that tidbit, the warriors started cleaning up and securing the place. Nikolas told me they'd pack up and move to a new location tomorrow because this place was compromised.

Jordan stood in the middle of the living room looking at the vampire bodies. "Shouldn't we call for a cleanup crew?"

Jackson bounded down the stairs. "We *are* the cleanup crew. The van's out back."

I grimaced at the grisly task ahead of us. "What will you do with all the bodies?"

"We'll take them out to the desert and burn them." He looked at the bodies in the living room. "With this many it's going to take at least two trips."

Someone brought the van around to the front of the house, and the warriors quickly loaded bodies into it. They got rid of the bodies on the lawn first and then the ones in the living room. Jackson had been right. It was definitely going to take two trips.

After that, some of the warriors pinned a tarp over the living room window to keep out the wind and rain. Not that it would help much. The room was pretty much trashed. And cold. I went over to one of the warriors who lived in the house. "Hey, do you guys have something dry Jordan and I can borrow?" Not that their clothes would fit me, but anything was better than being wet and cold.

"We had a female warrior staying here two months ago, and she left some stuff behind. Upstairs, first door on the right. Bottom drawer in the dresser."

"Thanks."

We found two pairs of jeans and several tank tops. They were a good fit for Jordan, but I had to roll up the bottoms of the jeans. I also grabbed a sweater and a pair of the guy's socks to replace my damp ones. My boots weren't too bad, so I pulled them on again.

Jordan found a first aid kit and cleaned and bandaged the scratches on my shoulder. They weren't too deep and the bleeding had already stopped. Of course, no Mohiri first aid kit is complete without gunna paste. This time, I didn't complain as I took the awful stuff.

Nikolas found us a few minutes later. "The storm is letting up, and the pilot says we can take off in an hour or so. I'm going to call Tristan, and then we'll head over to the airport."

"Okay." I rubbed my chest where a small knot of ice lingered despite my warm clothes. I was so ready to put some distance between me and that vampire.

The vampire had other ideas.

I was in the kitchen grabbing a bottle of water from the fridge when a girl's scream came from the basement. Seconds later, something small and fast sped up the stairs, coming to a halt when it saw the warriors blocking its way.

The vampire, who had been a teenage girl before she was changed, stared in panic before she darted for the nearest opening. Warriors shouted as they moved to intercept her. She wasn't as fast as some of them, but her size and agility made up for that. And like most people I'd encountered, she went for what looked like the easiest target in the room. Me.

There was no time to think. I grabbed a dagger that one of the warriors had left on the island, and threw it as the vampire flew through the kitchen doorway. She screamed, clawing at the silver hilt protruding from her abdomen as she staggered toward me.

In that moment, I was struck by how young she looked, and I felt a pang of sadness for the girl whose life had been stolen from her. She could have been any one of the girls from my old school. Her speed before I'd stopped her told me she'd been a vampire for at least a few decades. Did she have a family who missed her and still grieved the loss of their daughter or sister? She was going to die here and they would never know what had become of her.

She ripped out the dagger and leapt at me, her fangs and claws bared.

I twisted to one side and brought my fist up against her throat in a strike that might have crushed her windpipe had she been human. It was enough to surprise her, and that was all I needed. I wrapped one arm around her throat in a choke hold and pulled her back against me with my other hand squarely over her heart. Her body twitched as I gave her just enough of a jolt to incapacitate her.

Every instinct in me screamed for me to end her, but I stopped myself before I could do that. We needed her alive so we could find out how the vampires had found this place. The Mohiri were very good at keeping their safe house locations a secret, but somehow the vampires had found us tonight. If our warriors were going to remain safe, we had to know how we had been compromised.

The vampire sagged against me as one very aggravated Mohiri male pushed past the warriors crowding the wide kitchen doorway. "Damn it, Sara. There are a dozen warriors here. You couldn't let one of them handle this?"

I scowled at him over her head. "Look at her, Nikolas. She's even smaller than I am. Do you think I can't handle one little vampire?"

"Don't answer that, my man," Jackson said, shaking his head. "It's a trap."

Nikolas glowered at the blond warrior who seemed totally unfazed. He must have been the first person I hadn't seen shrink from one of Nikolas's scowls.

Jordan had wormed her way to the front of the crowd. She grinned and gave me two thumbs up.

The vampire moaned and Nikolas took a step forward. "We need to get her secured again before she comes to. How the hell did she escape in the first place?"

Geoffrey came forward. "She picked the lock on the shackles. I don't know how she did it. Most vampires can't handle silver that long."

"Desperation will make you do a lot of things you couldn't do before," I said. If she hadn't been a blood-sucking monster, I might have been impressed by her survival instinct.

Geoffrey and one of the other warriors came forward. "Good job, Sara. We'll take her now."

The vampire woke up as I was handing her off to Geoffrey. She stared at the two warriors reaching for her then looked up at me. Terror filled her eyes, and she snarled and began to twist in my grasp. I zapped her again and she went limp.

"That's some trick," Geoffrey said.

"You should see me pull a rabbit from a hat."

He smiled as he and the other warrior took the vampire by the arms. "We'll make sure this one doesn't get loose again. Not sure if she's worth keeping, though."

"Why?"

"Some vampires break. Most don't. After a while you can tell the ones that will."

"Then why waste your time with her?" Jordan asked.

"Because they can't take the chance of not getting information out of her," Nikolas said as the two warriors started to drag the vampire from the kitchen.

"Wait." An idea came to me, one that Nikolas was not going to like. "Maybe I can get something out of her."

Geoffrey stopped and looked back at me. "How?"

Nikolas shook his head. "No."

"Nikolas, you said they need information. And it's not like she can hurt me."

He laid his hands on my shoulders, his eyes troubled. "You don't have the stomach for torture, and that's what it will take."

"Maybe not." I bit my lip because I knew how he was going to react to my next sentence. "I could connect with the demon."

Anger flashed in his eyes. "Absolutely not. Do I need to remind you what happened the last time you did that?"

"No, but I'm a *lot* stronger than I was that time, and I know what to expect now."

"No."

I placed my hands on his chest. "I know you're worried, but I've come so far since that thing with Nate. I've spent months working with Aine and Eldeorin, and I know what I can do."

"What are they talking about?" Jackson asked. No one answered him.

Nikolas stared at me for a long moment. Then he let out a pained sigh and lowered his forehead to mine. "Promise me you'll be careful."

"I promise."

"I mean it, Sara," he growled softly. He pulled back so I could see the worry in his eyes. "If I have to sit by a hospital bed for another two days, I really will lock you up."

I gave him a reassuring smile. "That won't happen. Trust me."

He released my shoulders. "What do we need to do?"

"Just lay her here on the floor, and I'll do the rest."

Geoffrey and the other warrior looked surprised when Nikolas asked them to put the vampire on the kitchen floor, but they did it without question. After my display on the lawn tonight, they all knew I was different, and they looked curious to see what I was going to do next.

"I need some room to do this. Can you all move to the living room?"

Once the kitchen was empty except for me and the vampire, I knelt beside her prone body and laid my hands on her chest. I didn't even have to call my power forth. It rushed to my hands as soon as it sensed a demon close by, and I had to hold it back to keep from killing the vampire outright.

The vampire's eyes opened and her mouth twisted in a scream as I pushed my power slowly into her chest. My aim was to make contact with the vamhir demon, not kill it like I had done with Nate. It didn't take me long to find the gelatinous membrane surrounding the heart, and I touched it to let it know I was there. The demon trembled and shrank away from me, but there was nowhere it could go.

I remembered every detail of my experience with Nate as if it had happened yesterday. Drawing on that knowledge, I let my power envelop the demon and called on the same force I had tapped into the first time I'd done this. The demon convulsed, and I could feel its scream inside my skull.

No! screeched an alien voice that was not my own.

You want it to stop? Tell me how you knew about this house.

It fell silent for a long moment and I began to think I'd imagined the voice. I gave the demon another jab.

Hurts! it howled.

It's going to get a lot worse. I poked it again to make my point.

Stop!

Not until you tell me what I want to know. How did you find us?

Silence.

I zapped it again. The demon screamed and a shudder went through it.

Stop.

Answer my question. I felt no empathy for this creature, and I was willing to keep this up as long as I had to.

The demon finally realized that, too. *Followed hunters.*

You followed us from where?

Not you. Followed hunters from casino.

When?

Days.

How many days ago? I asked.

Two.

Two days ago? That meant they had been planning this attack all along, and they'd had no idea the rest of us would be here. Geoffrey was not going to be happy to learn that his team had been followed right back to their safe house.

Stop now! the demon cried.

Fine. I loosened my hold, but immediately tightened it again. The demon howled, and I waited for it to stop to ask my next question.

Who is the Master?

Have no Master.

Liar. All vampires have a master.

Not true. Many do not.

I applied more pressure and it struggled uselessly. *But you've met a Master, haven't you? I want to know his name.*

He has no name. Stop. Hurts.

Then tell me where he is. Tell me something.

Can't.

I zapped it again and the membrane started to harden. *I can do this as long as I need to.*

The demon's scream filled my head. Then a picture formed in my mind of a stately stone house with turrets that made me think of a castle. Excitement rippled through me. But then the image disappeared before it could come completely into focus.

Where was that? Show it again.

Can't. Hurts.

Show me!

The demon began to scream and shake until I thought it was going to explode. I realized then that I was getting nothing else out of it and I pulled back.

From out of nowhere, another image floated into my mind, faded and grainy like an old photograph. For a second, I thought the demon was trying to show me something else. I looked at the image and saw a dark-haired couple sitting on a beach with a little girl between them who couldn't be more than ten. The three of them were laughing and the girl was pointing at the person whose memory I was seeing. The girl looked vaguely familiar...

I knew the human remained after the vamhir took control of the body; my experience with Nate had proven that. But aside from Nate, I'd never thought about the human souls trapped inside of vampires. Nate remembered most of his short time as a vampire except for the things he had been compelled to forget. He still struggled with the memories. It had to be a special kind of hell to be trapped like that inside your own body, knowing death was the only way you would be free.

I looked at the memory again, and this time I could feel the pain and longing that clung to it. The demon had taken the girl from her family a long time ago, and she still grieved for them and the life stolen from her.

My chest tightened, and I felt a tear run down my face. *What is wrong with me? Am I actually crying for a* vampire?

No, not for the vampire. My heart ached for the teenage girl who had suffered so much. I wished I could help her, but the kindest thing I could do was to end her horrible existence.

Another memory floated toward me. I didn't want to look. I didn't want to feel more of the girl's pain. But then a familiar voice filled my mind, and I cringed from my own memories of it. *Hello, sweet thing.* I forced myself to look at the memory she was trying to show me, and a shard of fear pierced my heart when I saw Eli's dark eyes and charming smile. The vampire who had tried to kill me was the same one who had taken this girl.

I felt it then, the delicate connection forging between me and the nameless girl who had been taken years before I was born. The vampire and I were mortal enemies, but the girl and I shared something that went beyond that. Our lives had been changed forever by the same monster. But I was free and she still suffered.

Suddenly, I understood what I needed to do. Whether it worked or not didn't matter. I had the power in me to set this tormented soul free, and I couldn't refuse her that. I wasn't sure if I believed in fate, but it felt like some greater power had brought this vampire to me.

The demon trembled violently and the heart stuttered as I gathered my power.

No! it screamed. *You said you'd stop.*

I changed my mind, I said without remorse.

Then I struck.

CHAPTER 22

"GODDAMNIT, SARA, DO not do this to me again."

Disoriented, I opened my eyes and looked up into Nikolas's distressed ones. "Why am I on the floor?"

He crushed me against his chest. "Fifty years. I'm locking you up for the next fifty goddamn years."

"Can't breathe," I gasped, and he eased me back down to the floor.

"How do you feel?"

"Great." I was still trying to figure out what I was doing down there, and why he was looking at me that way. "My butt is cold."

Relief flashed in his eyes and a smile touched his mouth. "We can't have that." In the next instant, he was sitting on the floor with me cradled in his lap. "Better?"

"Much better." I leaned my head against his chest, suddenly tired. God, what a night. First, I met the mother I hadn't seen in sixteen years. If that wasn't enough, we were ambushed by vampires. And then –

My head jerked up. The vampire girl!

Someone was sobbing, and it was the most heartwrenching sound I had ever heard. I twisted in Nikolas's arms until I could see behind him. In the corner, curled into a tight ball, was the vampire. Only she wasn't a vampire anymore. The absence of cold in my chest told me I'd done it again.

I tried to go to her, but Nikolas held me back. "It's not safe."

"Yes, it is." I met his worried gaze. "Trust me. She won't hurt anyone else."

It was another minute before he reluctantly released me. I crawled over to the girl who cowered and cried even harder. "Shhh, it's okay," I crooned softly. "You're safe now and no one is going to hurt you."

Her entire body shook from her sobs, and the agony in her voice was almost too much to bear. I couldn't imagine what she was going through or how terrifying this was for her. All I could do was try to help her through it.

A sound drew my attention to the kitchen doorway where a dozen warriors watched us in shocked silence. Except for Nikolas, Chris, and Jordan, no one here knew what I could do. In their eyes, I was offering comfort to a vampire. This was going to require some serious explaining. Right now though, I had more important things to take care of.

I laid a hand on the girl's shoulder, and she cringed away from me. I kept my hand in place as I spoke to her. "My name is Sara. I know you're scared and confused, and I swear I won't let anything hurt you. I'm just going to sit here with you until you're feeling a little better."

I sat on the floor by her head with my back against the cupboard doors. She was still crying, but she didn't try to move away from me. After a few minutes, I touched her back soothingly. It was too bad my calming ability didn't work on humans because I really could have used it now.

"Sara?" Nikolas spoke in a low voice. He was sitting where I'd left him and looking ready to come to my rescue if he sensed a hint of danger.

"We're good." A breeze blew in through the broken window and I shivered. At the same time, I felt the girl tense up under my hand. "Can I get a blanket for her?"

Several minutes later, Jordan came into the kitchen carrying two thick blankets. She approached me slowly and draped one of the blankets over the girl who was crying more softly now. Jordan smiled at me and wrapped the second blanket around my shoulders.

You okay? she mouthed.

I nodded and she shook her head and said, *showoff,* before she backed away, leaving me alone with the girl again.

Out in the living room, people were starting to talk softly, and I heard more than one ask what was going on. I looked over at Nikolas and inclined my head toward the other room. He shook his head, and I knew he wasn't going anywhere until he was sure the girl posed no threat to me.

The girl made a mewling sound, and I rubbed her back gently.

"Shhh. It's going to be okay."

In response, she scooted closer to me. Taking heart from that, I shifted until her head was on my lap. I began to smooth down her long dark hair, and she let out a shuddering breath and wrapped her arms tightly around my waist. A lump formed in my throat as I tucked the blanket around her shoulders. I was so not qualified to deal with the trauma this girl must have been going through, but I was all she had right now.

It took over an hour for the girl to cry herself to sleep. Her arms went slack around my waist, and I could hear her deep even breaths. My backside and legs ached from sitting on the hard floor, and I wanted to move, but I was afraid of disturbing her.

Nikolas took the decision from me. He gently picked up the sleeping girl, blanket and all, and placed her on the love seat, which was the only couch in the living room that hadn't suffered damage. As soon as he released her, she curled up into a ball again, but she didn't awaken. The poor thing had to be exhausted.

The warriors stared at the girl, which wasn't surprising since she'd been a vampire an hour ago. They were also giving me a wide berth. I guessed making a vampire human again was right up there with raising someone from the dead. It just wasn't done.

"Is she really human again?"

I glanced sideways at Geoffrey who had come to stand beside Nikolas and me. The warrior's normally dark skin was ashen and he had the look of a man who had witnessed a miracle.

"Yes."

"That's... not possible."

I was too tired to explain. I gave Nikolas a pleading look and he nodded.

"Geoffrey, let's talk in the kitchen so we don't disturb the girl."

"We can go downstairs if you don't want to be overheard."

"The kitchen will do." Nikolas's gaze met mine as he and Geoffrey moved past me. I had a feeling he wasn't going to let me out of his sight until we got home again. I was more than okay with that.

The other warriors resumed their work, packing up the equipment and preparing to move to another location. They kept throwing curious glances at me whenever they passed by, but I was used to being stared at.

Unsure of what to do next, I sat at the foot of the loveseat. The girl might sleep for hours, but I was afraid to leave her in case she awoke. Exhaustion washed over me, and I leaned back and closed my eyes.

"You okay, Sara?"

I opened my eyes and gave Chris a weak smile. "Pretty good, considering."

He studied the sleeping girl. "You've had a busy night."

"You could say that."

"Why did you do it?" He crouched by the loveseat so he was at eye level. "Why this one?"

"I wasn't going to." I began to remember more details of my experience with the vampire. "But then I saw a memory of her family, and..." My voice cracked. "It was Eli who changed her. I actually heard his voice, Chris. I felt her pain. I couldn't... I had to..."

He laid a hand on my arm. "It's okay. You did the right thing."

My gaze shifted to the girl who whimpered in her sleep.

"Did I?" She was a teenager who had suffered horrors I didn't want to imagine. Her family and her old life were gone. There was no going back to them. She hadn't uttered a word yet so we had no idea what her mental state was. If a Mori could drive a person insane, what was there to say that a vamhir demon couldn't do the same?

"Maybe it would have been kinder if I'd…"

"I don't believe that and neither do you." His warm green eyes held mine. "You've grown into an amazing warrior since I met you, and I'm proud to fight beside you. But you have a healer's soul. You could not have killed that vampire, knowing you could save the girl. If I know anything about you by now, it's that." He looked at her and let out a slow breath. "She has a rough time ahead of her, but she's alive and human again thanks to you."

"Thanks, Chris," I whispered.

He smiled again. "Now, please don't cry because I really don't want Nikolas to come over and kick my ass."

My lips twitched. "He wouldn't do that. You're his best friend."

"When it comes to you, all bets are off."

I looked at Nikolas and Geoffrey in the kitchen. Nikolas was talking to the other warrior, but he was watching me. I smiled to let him know I was okay. He said something to Geoffrey, and then the two of them walked over to us.

"How is she?" Nikolas asked me.

"Still asleep."

"Do you think she'll be able to talk to us when she wakes up?" Geoffrey asked.

I looked at the sleeping girl. "I have no idea."

He rubbed his chin. "We'll have to question her. There's no telling what information she can give us about the attack tonight."

"I can tell you that your warriors were followed here from a casino two days ago. The vampires had no idea the rest of us would be here when they attacked this place."

Geoffrey inhaled sharply. "She told you that?"

I hesitated. If I told him I'd spoken to the vamhir demon, he was not going to believe me. I could tell by his wary expression that he was still struggling with whatever Nikolas had shared with him. I was too tired to try to explain something I was still trying to understand.

"Yes. That's all she said."

"Son of a bitch." He looked around for his team and called to the brunette who'd spoken to me earlier. "Evan, weren't you guys at the Mirage two days ago?"

"No, that was Tyler's team. Why?"

Geoffrey swore then apologized to me. "I need to contact Tyler. His team is out on a job right now. Excuse me."

"I think we should move her somewhere quieter," I said to Nikolas and Chris. "She'll be scared if she wakes up and sees all these strange people."

Nikolas nodded and I could tell he'd already realized we were not flying out of Las Vegas tonight. "We'll take her to the new safe house. You need to rest, too."

"We all do." It had been a long day and night for all of us. I'd rest when I knew the girl was taken care of.

Hours later, I sat in a chair in one of the bedrooms in the new safe house and watched the sleeping girl. She hadn't awakened once during the drive to Henderson or when Chris had carried her into the house earlier. Every now and then she made a frightened sound, and I wondered what horrors she was dreaming about.

Jordan walked into the room. "I'll sit with her for a while. You need to lie down before you fall over."

"I'm okay." I stifled a yawn.

She pulled me out of my chair and pushed me to the door. "Sorry, but those are Nikolas's orders. You can take the room next door so you'll be close, and I'll let you know if she wakes up."

I was too tired to argue. I gave her a grateful smile and went into the dark room, not even bothering to turn on the light or pull back the comforter on the bed. During the night, Nikolas came to check on me, and I sleepily tugged him down to lie beside me. It was the only time I woke up until the next morning.

A girl's scream jerked me from my sleep, and I almost fell out of bed. I burst into the room next door and found the girl cowering in the corner with her long dark hair hanging wildly around her face.

Near the door, Jordan stood holding a plate of food and a glass of orange juice. "I just went to grab some breakfast. I didn't think she would wake up yet."

"That's okay. I've got it."

Nikolas arrived with Chris on his heels. "Sara?"

I put my finger to my lips and backed them out of the room. "She's awake, and she's terrified. I'm going to try to talk to her."

I approached the girl slowly with my hands at my sides. "Don't be afraid. Do you remember me? I'm Sara, and I talked to you last night. You remember my voice, don't you? I promised you I'd stay with you. I'm still here and I won't let anyone hurt you."

I spoke to her like that for at least thirty minutes before she lifted her head and looked at me for the first time. Through the veil of her dark hair I could see her pale cheeks, frightened brown eyes, and trembling lips. Her gaze flicked past me to Nikolas, Chris, and Jordan standing in the hallway.

"They won't hurt you. They're here to help keep you safe." I sat on the bed, facing her, and tried to look as unthreatening as possible. "I'm Sara. Do you remember me?"

She stared at me for a long moment before she nodded.

I gave her a warm smile. "Good. Do you want to tell me your name?"

"E-Emma."

I swallowed painfully. "It's nice to meet you, Emma. I bet you must be pretty confused and scared right now, huh?"

"I-I saw you."

"Saw me where?" I asked gently.

She swallowed and her eyes darted around the room. "You were th-there. You... talked to it."

"Yes."

"You killed it?"

"Yes."

She let out a ragged sob and sagged against the wall. "This is... not real. Is it?"

The trace of hope in her small voice was almost my undoing, but I had to be strong for her. "All of this is real. I killed it and now you're safe."

"Safe?"

"Yes."

She put her head down and didn't speak for several minutes. Finally, she stared at me and said, "It's really gone?"

"It's as dead as it can be. It's not coming back."

"Thank you." She closed her eyes and tears spilled down her cheeks. "Thank you."

I sat there helplessly as she cried. I wanted to go to her, but I was afraid of startling her and undoing the progress we'd made. After several minutes, she used her sleeves to wipe her face and looked at me with less fear in her eyes.

My stomach chose that moment to rumble, and I laughed softly. "I'm starving. I'm going to ask one of my friends to bring me some breakfast. Would you like to join me?"

Her eyes immediately went to the tray of cold food Jordan had left on the nightstand. She stared at it helplessly, and I realized she hadn't eaten food in many years.

She smiled tremulously, and my chest constricted. Jordan had once called me a waif, but Emma fit that description perfectly. She was at least two inches shorter than me and slender, and her complexion was pale because it hadn't seen the sun in many years. But even as her sad brown eyes tugged at my heart, I could see strength in her. The fact that she was smiling and speaking to me coherently after the trauma she'd been through was evidence of that.

Jordan came in with another tray bearing two plates of scrambled eggs, sausage, and toast, which she placed on the bed beside me. I shifted to make room then patted the bed in invitation. Emma waited until Jordan had left the room again before she timidly joined me on the bed. Her trust in me after all she'd been through was humbling.

At first, she toyed with her eggs, but after a few minutes she began to nibble on a wedge of toast. By the time I was finished she had eaten two pieces of toast, a good start for someone who hadn't eaten in a very long time.

Neither of us spoke while we ate, but I could sense her becoming more at ease with me. Sometime during the meal, the others left us alone and Emma looked relaxed for the first time. When we were done, I placed the tray on a small table in the hallway and went back to sit with her.

After a lengthy silence she whispered, "I never wanted to hurt anyone."

"You didn't do those things, Emma. The demon did."

"It was my hands, my body."

I reached over and took one of her cold hands in mind. She flinched but didn't pull away. "The demon took control of your body. You are not responsible for anything it did. My uncle went through this too and he felt guilty even though he knows none of it was his fault."

"Your uncle?" Hope filled her eyes and her voice. "There are others like me?"

"Just you and him so far. I'm still new at this."

"Why? Why me?"

I let out a slow breath, trying to think of the best way to answer. "I wasn't going to," I said honestly. "I was trying to get the demon to tell me how it knew where we were. But then you showed me some memories and I wanted to help you."

She stared at our joined hands. "My family, I can't go back."

"No." It was best not to give her false hope when it came to them. Emma could never go back to her old life.

Her breath hitched. "Where will I go?"

"You can stay with me." I squeezed her hand. "Once you feel better you can decide what you want to do. I'll help you."

"Thank you."

"You don't have to thank me, Emma. I have a feeling you and I are going to be great friends."

She fell silent again, and I wondered for the hundredth time what was going through her mind. She had to be dealing with so much emotionally – things I couldn't even fathom.

"Are you tired? Would you like me to leave you alone for a while?"

Her fingers gripped mine. "No, don't go. Please."

"Okay. I'll stay."

She released my hand and began tracing a seam in the comforter with her finger. Minutes passed before she spoke again. "The night it happened, I wasn't even supposed to go out. There was a boy I liked and he had a band. I wanted to go with my friends to hear them play, but my parents said I couldn't go. So I snuck out." She sniffled and swiped a finger under her eye.

As she described the night she'd met Eli, I remembered my own encounter with him in Portland. The similarities between Emma's experience and mine were eerie, and proved that Eli had definitely had a favorite type. We were both young brunettes and had a similar build. He'd stalked both of us at a club where we'd gone with friends to hear a band. Nikolas and my friends had saved me from a fate worse than death. Emma had not been so lucky.

Once Emma started to tell her story, it flowed out of her in a torrent of words and tears. Eli had played with her for a week before he had finally changed her. He'd chosen her because she was young and innocent-looking, and she would be the perfect lure for other teenagers. Even after she'd become a vampire, he'd used her for months until he finally tired of her. She didn't go into graphic detail, thankfully, but I heard enough to imagine the horrors she'd gone through.

Eli had been her maker and he'd been strong, so he'd controlled Emma completely. It wasn't until his death that she had been free to go where she wanted. So she'd come to Las Vegas because there were a lot of other vampires here.

"Did you ever meet Eli's master? I asked the demon, but it wouldn't or couldn't say."

"I know I must have because Eli took me everywhere with him, but I don't remember him. Eli told me his master was afraid of the Mohiri torturing the information out of a vampire. So he compelled everyone to forget him. Except Eli." She sighed heavily. "I'm sorry. I wish I could be more help after all you've done for me."

"Don't worry about it. It was a long shot anyway."

Emma got off the bed and went to look out the window. "I had a little sister, Marie. She was ten when I disappeared. I guess that would make her thirty-one." She leaned her forehead against the glass and I saw her shoulders shake. "My baby sister is almost twice my age now. She's probably married with children and I'm still seventeen."

"I'm sorry, Emma. I wish..."

"I know," she said softly. "You gave me back my life. I should be happy with that."

"It's okay to not be happy right now. But someday you will be. And if you want, we can find out where your sister is and how she's doing. Your parents too."

She came back to sit on the bed. "You can do that?"

I let out a small laugh. "Not me, but I have a few friends who can find almost anyone."

"I'd like that." Her eyes took on a faraway look, and I knew she was thinking about her family and her old life.

"Do you want to talk about them?"

She nodded sadly.

We talked for hours. She told me about her family and friends and growing up in Raleigh, North Carolina. I told her about my dad and Nate and my friends. When I described New Hastings she got a wistful look in her eyes and said she'd always wanted to live near the ocean. Every summer her family would rent a house for two weeks in Virginia Beach, and it had been her favorite place to go.

We had more than our love of the ocean in common. Emma's favorite hobby had been painting, and she'd even hoped to study art in college. I'd dabbled in painting at one point, but drawing was my thing, even though I hadn't done much of it lately. I found a pencil and a notepad and drew her as we talked about everything from art supplies to our favorite subjects. I mostly did drawings of people I knew and creatures I'd met. She preferred landscapes, especially the coast.

At noon Jordan arrived with sandwiches. For dinner, she brought us plates of chicken and pasta. After each meal, I stacked the plates on the table in the hall, and Emma and I continued talking.

By nine o'clock that night, Emma began to show signs of fatigue. I convinced her to try to get some sleep, and told her I'd be close by if she needed me. I left her room, rubbing my tired eyes, and found Nikolas in the hall waiting for me. Wordlessly, I walked into his arms and hugged him tightly. All day I'd been strong for Emma, but with Nikolas, I could let my guard down and show the toll today had taken on me. He held me and rubbed my back as I cried quietly into his shirt.

The next morning, Emma was in better shape, emotionally and physically. Jordan went out with Chris to buy a few changes of clothes for us, and Emma was more comfortable once she'd cleaned up and put on fresh clothing.

After lunch, she agreed to talk to Chris about her knowledge of the vampire comings and goings in Las Vegas. I'd asked Chris to talk to her because he was more easygoing and less intimidating than the other warriors. I sat with them as he questioned her about vampire numbers and locations of nests. At first she was hesitant until we assured her that none of the things she'd done as a vampire would make us think less of her. She did not remember who the Master was, but she knew a lot about the vampire activity here, and she shared it all with us.

When the interview was over, Chris gave her a warm smile. "Thank you, Emma. I know that had to be very difficult for you. The information you gave us will help save a lot of lives."

"I'm glad," she replied timidly, looking like a tiny bit of the guilt she carried had been lifted from her shoulders.

That evening Nikolas took me aside and told me we were leaving Las

Vegas in the morning. The Mohiri were sending more teams into the city in a coordinated attack on the vampires, based on the information we'd gotten from Emma. Nikolas didn't want me or Jordan anywhere near the city when that happened.

"What about Emma? We have to take her with us."

"I talked to Tristan about her, and he said she is welcome at Westhorne if she wants to come with us."

I hugged him so hard he laughed. When I asked about Oscar and our things in California, he said Raoul was taking care of everything.

I went to tell Emma the news. She wasn't as excited as I was, and I knew it was because she was afraid of being around that many Mohiri after spending the last two decades as our mortal enemy. It took a lot of persuasion to get her to agree to give it a shot since I couldn't tell her exactly where we were going until we got there. I told her how beautiful and safe it was there, and that she could leave whenever she wanted. I made sure she knew it was her choice and whatever she decided, I'd still help her. Finally, she gave me a small smile and said she would go with us.

When we boarded the Mohiri jet the next day, I was so excited about going home I could barely sit still. The four warriors who had come from California with us were staying on in Vegas, so it was just me, Nikolas, Jordan, Chris, and Emma on the plane. Even when the pilot told us there would be a short delay because of air traffic, it couldn't dampen my mood. In a few hours I'd see Nate, Tristan, and Desmund. I couldn't wait to see Sahir and hug Hugo and Woolf.

Chris laughed as I left Jordan in the front row and moved down to sit with Emma in the middle. "Are we going to have to tie you to your seat so we can take off?" he teased.

"When the pilot says we're leaving, I'll be the first one buckled in."

A minute later, the pilot's voice came over the intercom to tell us to take our seats.

Emma was quiet beside me. I knew she was still nervous about Westhorne, so I buckled in next to her to keep her company during the flight. Once we were in the air, I pulled out the notepad and pencil I'd taken from the house and doodled on it as we talked about Westhorne.

"Is that where we're going?" she asked.

I looked at the outline of a building I'd been sketching. It was a large house and made of stone. I was halfway through adding what looked like a turret.

"It looks sort of like a castle," Emma commented.

"It does, doesn't it?" My brow furrowed as I studied the partial drawing. Where had I seen this house before? I dredged through my memories and came up blank. Strange. I'd obviously seen it somewhere. Why else would I draw it?

I put my pencil to the page and continued to finish the turret. Soon, my hand was flying over the page until the finished picture lay before me. There were four turrets in all, and the front of the building had ten windows and a large door that I'd drawn in detail down to the carved door knocker.

Emma picked it up for a better look. "This is really good. I don't know why, but it kind of gives me the willies."

"Yeah, me too." I stared at the drawing. The longer I looked at it, the more I felt like tearing the page from the notepad and crumpling it up. Something tickled the edge of my memory, but every time I tried to focus on it, it slipped away.

"You know" – Emma held the drawing away from her to study it from a different angle – "for some reason, I feel like I've seen this place before."

Her words were like a key unlocking a memory that I hadn't known was there. Suddenly, an image of the house appeared in my mind. Only it wasn't my memory I was looking at. It belonged to the vamhir demon I'd pulled it from two days ago. The same demon that used to live inside Emma. The same demon that had gone with its maker, Eli, to see his master.

"It can't be." I took the notepad from Emma with shaking hands.

"What's wrong?" Nikolas appeared beside me. His eyes immediately went to Emma who shrank away from him.

"This." I held the drawing up for him to see. My initial shock was passing and excitement was building in my chest. "This is his house."

Nikolas frowned in confusion. "Whose house?"

"The Master's."

Emma gasped. Chris and Jordan crowded in behind Nikolas.

"What are you talking about?" Nikolas took the notepad from me. He peered at the drawing then looked at me and Emma. "Did she tell you that?"

"No. I drew it from memory, from a memory I took from the vamhir demon before I killed it."

"You took the demon's memory?" Jordan asked, wide-eyed.

"I asked it about the Master and it showed me this house. I forgot about it with everything else that happened."

Nikolas handed the notepad to Chris who studied it closely. "How do you know this is the Master's house?"

"I don't for sure, but something feels off about it. Emma feels it, too."

Emma nodded. "It gives me the creeps, and it seems familiar."

"I told you what Emma said about the Master being so paranoid that he compels other vampires to forget him. Eli took her with him when he visited the Master and she was compelled to forget. But no one can erase your mind that completely, and I think I found a memory he missed."

Chris exhaled loudly. "Jesus, if that's true..."

"We need to get this to our guys as soon as possible," Nikolas said.

"Already on it." Chris whipped out his phone and snapped a photo of the drawing then fired off an email to someone.

I took a photo of the drawing with my phone as well. "I'm sending this to David. If anyone can find this house, it's him and Kelvan."

No one argued, so I texted David, asking him if he could locate the house for me. He replied with a smiley face and asked if I was joking. I told him not to worry, that the Mohiri were on it. His last text said he'd get back to me soon.

When the pilot announced our approach into Boise my pulse picked up. We were almost home.

"Boise? That's where you live?" Emma asked.

"Not quite. It's about an hour away."

I grinned when I saw the two red-haired warriors waiting for us when we left the plane. It seemed fitting somehow that Seamus and Niall were the ones to drive Jordan and me home, after the way we'd left Westhorne. The little smirk on Jordan's face told me she was having similar thoughts.

The twins took the front seats, and Nikolas and Chris took the middle. That left the last row of the large SUV for me, Jordan, and Emma. Within minutes we were on the road toward home.

Jordan and I told Emma about Westhorne while the four warriors talked among themselves. It started to snow, and Emma said she didn't have boots or a coat, or anything else for that matter. I laughed when I saw a familiar gleam in Jordan's eye. Poor Emma. Jordan had just found a new dress-up doll. I really hoped my new friend liked shopping.

"You'll like Terrence and Josh." Jordan moved on to the subject of boys. "They're pretty cool."

I missed her next words as cold bloomed in my chest. "Vampires!"

Nikolas and Chris turned around at the same time to stare at me just as something slammed into us from behind. We jerked forward violently in our seats. Shouts filled the SUV as it swerved toward the edge of the icy road before Seamus got it under control.

My stomach and chest hurt from the seat belt, but I twisted in the seat to look behind us as a large white van with tinted windows and a crumpled grill came at us again. Emma let out a terrified scream, and I pulled her against me to shield her as much as I could. Jordan covered Emma's other side, and the three of us clung to each other as the other vehicle plowed into us.

"Jesus Christ!" one of the twins yelled as we skidded across the shoulder and flipped down the embankment.

CHAPTER 23

THE SUV ROLLED over twice and landed hard against a large tree at the bottom of the ten-foot drop. It was lying on the passenger side, and I found myself hanging by my seat belt over Emma and Jordan.

"Sara?" Nikolas released himself from his seat belt and reached for me. "Are you hurt?"

My whole body ached, but I didn't think anything was broken. "No."

"Stay with Emma," he said as he helped Chris to his feet. Then he pulled up the seat he'd been sitting on and the two of them grabbed swords. Seamus and Niall were already jumping through the front driver's window with swords in hand. Within seconds, Nikolas and Chris were out of the vehicle and speeding up the embankment.

A scream tore through the air.

Jordan climbed over the seat and withdrew a sword from the weapons stash. "Help Emma," she said before she followed the others.

More screams. Shouts.

"Emma, can you move?"

"Yes." There was a click and she fell against the side window. She moved into the cargo area to give me room.

I braced my feet against the seat in front of me as I reached for my seat belt buckle. It wasn't enough to hold me, and I tumbled to the other side. Groaning, I climbed into the back with Emma, who stared at me with eyes glazed over from shock.

"Sara," she gripped my arm tightly and cried over the sounds of fighting above us on the road. "Please, don't let them take me again."

"I won't." I silently prayed I could keep that promise.

We were sitting ducks in the overturned SUV. If I was going to defend us, we had to get out of this thing. I tried to push open the cargo door, but it was wedged against a tree.

Scrambling into the back seat, I grabbed a dagger from the remaining weapons and slammed the hilt into the passenger side window. The window shattered on the fourth blow and glass sprayed over the snow, leaving about eighteen inches of space between the door and the ground.

"Follow me." I squeezed through the opening. Emma came behind me and we pushed through the snow and trees. Snow fell thickly around us.

I came up short when I heard another vehicle approaching. Tires screeched. More shouts filled the air. I shoved Emma behind a clump of snow-covered underbrush. "Stay down."

A figure appeared at the top of the embankment, and his eyes narrowed on me. His lips curled to reveal long fangs.

The vampire came at me like a mountain lion pouncing on its prey. He hit me before I could react, and I flew backward into the snow with him on top of me. My head banged against a tree, and the weight of him knocked the wind from me. I struggled to breathe as he rose up with a triumphant gleam in his eyes. Instead of attacking, he jumped to his feet and slung me over his shoulder. I was too dazed to fight him or call out before he plunged into the trees.

He was old, and he moved fast. We were a half-mile away from the SUV before I was able to catch my breath and summon enough power to bring him to his knees.

He dropped me, and I rolled a few feet in the snow. I rose up on my hands and knees, but he was on me again before I could stand. The blow to my face stunned me, and I was helpless when he pressed me facedown into the snow. I choked on the fresh powder, and panic filled me as I fought for air. I struggled to throw him off me as blackness closed in.

"Not so strong now, are you?" he spat, his claws digging into my back through my jacket.

My body grew heavy. Soon I'd be unconscious and completely at his mercy. In desperation I let power flood my body and heard his hiss of pain.

Suddenly, the weight was gone from my back. I tried to move, but my body refused to cooperate. I heard the sounds of fighting as if they came from a long tunnel. A vampire screeched.

Someone rolled me over. I coughed as I sucked air into my starved lungs.

"Sara!" The fear in Nikolas's voice made my eyes fly open.

"Nikolas," I rasped.

He stood, lifting me into his arms while still holding his sword. "It's an ambush. I have to get you out of here."

"What about the others?"

"It's you they want."

"But Emma —"

The words died on my lips as five vampires materialized in front of us.

Nikolas lowered me to my feet and pulled me behind him. There was no way he could fight off five mature vampires and protect me at the same time. Power flowed to my hands until they glowed, casting an eerie white light over the small clearing we were in. Five pairs of eyes turned to me.

Nikolas blurred and one of the vampires screeched when his severed arm landed in the snow. Four of the vampires began to circle Nikolas. The fifth one came at me.

The vampire hit me so fast I was momentarily stunned. Claws raked my throat, and I spun off balance. He grabbed for me again, and as soon as his hand closed over my arm, I turned my body into his and brought my other hand up to his throat. He bellowed at the power in my touch, and backhanded me so hard my head snapped back and I saw stars. He could have killed me with one blow, but he struck only hard enough to stun me. The knowledge that he wanted me alive drove my fear to an even greater height, and I screamed as I lunged for him again. This time my hand slammed into his chest. He let out a strangled cry and fell face-first into the snow.

I moved in to finish him and Nikolas shouted, "Sara, look out!"

I spun to find two more vampires standing ten feet away from me. The female reached into her coat and pulled out a gun. *A vampire with a gun?* I thought a second before she pointed it at me and fired.

For one heart-stopping moment I waited for a bullet to pierce my chest, and I knew with unwavering certainty that I was going to die. All I could think of in that moment was Nikolas.

Instead of agonizing pain, all I felt was a sharp sting in my right shoulder. I stared down in shock at the tiny dart sticking out of my coat. Had they tried to use a tranquillizer on me? They could not know that most drugs didn't work on the Mohiri because of our accelerated metabolism and healing. Or maybe they thought it would work on me because I was only half Mohiri.

The two vampires began walking toward me. Either they were confident they could take me or they expected the drug to knock me out at any second. I wasn't going without a fight. I summoned my power.

Nothing happened.

I reached down inside for my power. I could see it swirling at my core, I could feel its heat, but it refused to come. It was as if an invisible wall had sprung up between me and my magic, cutting me off from it.

Blood pounded in my ears as I lifted my eyes to the female vampire who wore a knowing smile. What had she done to me? I backed away, though I knew there was no escape.

Behind me, I could hear Nikolas battling the other vampires. I almost cried out his name, but it froze on my tongue. If I distracted him, he could die. Terror threatened to smother me. I had no weapons, and I was helpless against two vampires without my power.

Nikolas made a sound somewhere between a growl and a shout as the vampires stalked me. They halted and turned wary eyes toward him. I didn't need to see him to know he had gone into a full-blown rage. It might be the only thing that saved him.

God, please keep him safe, I prayed.

Without my power, there was no wall between me and my Mori and I felt its fear for Nikolas acutely. *Come*, I told it. We joined and its strength filled me. I didn't know if it was enough to fight off two vampires, but I would do anything to keep them from taking me from Nikolas. He and I would survive together or we would die together.

Another growl filled the woods and it swiftly turned into a roar. The trees shook and snow fell off them in clumps as a dark shape zoomed over the tops of them.

My mind barely had time to register the scaled body and leathery wings before the wyvern dove at the two vampires who had stopped to stare at him in shock. Their surprise quickly turned to terror, but they had waited too long to flee. The female screamed as flames engulfed her.

The male turned to run, but the wyvern snatched him up and tore him apart with his teeth and claws. Blood sprayed across the snow and hot drops splattered against my cold face.

Bloody pieces of vampire hit the ground as Alex circled the clearing. His crocodile eyes swept over the battle below as if he was choosing his next target. I looked at Nikolas who was in the thick of the fight with the two remaining vampires, and so vulnerable to an attack from above.

"Alex," I shouted hoarsely, and his head swung in my direction. The last time I'd seen him he'd been chasing vampires away from Westhorne after he'd saved my life. I hoped he remembered that and wasn't just out hunting anything that moved.

I didn't sense the new vampire until he was only a few feet away. Alex dove toward us and I lunged to the side to give him a clear path to the vampire. A scream ripped from my lips when I felt clawed feet close around my waist instead. I struggled for several seconds until my feet left the ground. My stomach dropped as quickly as the ground as we rose into the air. I caught a glimpse of Nikolas swinging his sword and at least seven bodies on the ground before we flew over the tops of the trees and the clearing disappeared from sight.

Over the wind and the flapping of Alex's wings, I heard Nikolas shout my name.

"Oh God!" My stomach churned as I stared at the snow-covered trees rushing by beneath me. I didn't want to think about where Alex was taking me or what he would do when we got there. He'd saved my life before, but I didn't know if that had been intentional or because he liked the taste of vampires more. The image of him ripping apart the vampire played over and over in my head. I had to fight the panic building inside me and the urge to struggle. If he dropped me from this height I was dead.

Miles of forest passed below us. Alex flew leisurely over rivers and around hills until I lost all sense of direction. I kept my chin tucked against my chest to try to protect my face from the stinging snow and wind, but my cheeks quickly grew numb from the cold. I tried to use my Mori's power to warm me as Nikolas's Mori did for him, but we'd never done that before and it lasted only a few minutes.

I wasn't sure how long we were in the air – maybe twenty or thirty minutes – before we began to descend toward a river winding through the trees. Alex dipped until my feet were almost touching the rushing water, and I could feel the spray on my face. I held my breath, afraid he was going to drop me into the river. Without my power, the water would kill me. I was a good swimmer, but even if I made it to shore, I'd freeze to death.

He followed the river for a few minutes before he circled a large rock formation along one of the banks. I tried to brace myself for the landing, but my legs were cold and unsteady after being in the air. I stumbled and sank painfully to my knees on the icy rock.

Alex circled me and landed a few feet away, settling down into a watchful crouch. His breath sent huge puffs of steam into the frigid air and small tendrils of smoke curled from his nostrils. I huddled in a ball and watched him out of the corner of my eye, afraid to move. His flames had at least a three-foot reach, and I'd seen what they could do.

We sat like that for at least an hour. Every now and then Alex's head swung in my direction, but he made no move toward me. With every minute that passed, my body got colder until I began to fear dying from exposure more than Alex. The sky began to darken and the snow thickened until I could barely see the other side of the river. I knew I had to move soon or I would die on this rock.

Something moved in the trees below us, and Alex's head tilted as his slit eyes turned in that direction. A few seconds later, he lifted off and sped toward the trees. I watched breathlessly, terrified that a vampire had followed us. A small reddish shape darted across the snow then spun and fled when it saw the wyvern coming toward it. I released a slow breath when Alex began chasing the fox through the trees. I hoped the animal escaped, but at the same time, I was grateful Alex was hunting something besides me.

My body was cramped and my hands and feet were almost numb, making the climb down from the rock painful and difficult. It was almost dark by the time I reached the ground, and I rested for a minute in the shelter of the rock, stamping my feet and tucking my hands under my arms to warm them.

I searched my pockets for my phone and almost cried when I came up empty. It could be anywhere between here and the SUV. I wasn't sure if I could even get a signal out here, but it would have been a small comfort to have a phone with me.

I quickly made a decision. It was a long shot that this was the same river that ran through Butler Falls, but it had to lead somewhere. I was in the middle of nowhere with no hope of finding my way back to the road. Nikolas would be looking for me – I refused to believe he was unable to – but if I stayed here until help came, I would die.

Trekking along the river in the dark was slow and treacherous. I had to feel my way around rocks and trees and be careful not to step too close to the edge of the bank. The snow changed to freezing rain and within an hour I was drenched to the skin. My body shivered so hard it hurt, and I grew tired and sluggish. I refused to stop. To stop moving meant death, and I would not die out here. I had survived too much to just lie down in the snow and give up.

I stopped to go around a boulder and heard the sound of wings above the roar of the river. Alex had been following me since I set out. He made no move to attack me, and I knew now that he was watching over me. I was comforted by his quiet presence and to know that I wasn't alone out here.

But Alex's presence could not protect me from the elements. It became increasingly difficult to lift my feet, and my whole body felt numb. A few times when I stopped to catch my breath, I found myself jerking awake a few minutes later. My body was shutting down, even if my mind refused to surrender.

I came to another bend in the river and my body sagged hopelessly at the sight of more trees, more water. "Stop that," I scolded myself, but the words were slurred, almost unintelligible to my own ears.

Alex made a sound halfway between a growl and a snort, and I looked up, straining to see him through the darkness and sleet. As I scanned the area, my eyes moved over a dark shadow several hundred yards up the river. *Just more rocks*. A choked sob escaped me, and I fought down the tears that wanted to come. This place might break my body, but it would not break me.

I forced my feet to move, and I thought about Nikolas. In my mind I saw his face, his warm gray eyes and his beautiful smile as he told me he loved me. I imagined him beside me, ordering me to keep going like he did in training. My imaginings grew so vivid I felt the faint fluttering at the back of my mind that meant he was near. It felt so real that I called out his name. I even stopped and listened for him, but all I could hear was the river.

Alex growled again and flew in lower circles around me. Fear shot through my delirium. Without my power I had no way of knowing if a vampire was nearby. I tried to run, but my feet caught on a branch and I collapsed in the snow. *Get up,* my mind cried, but my body could no longer obey.

Hands grabbed me and rolled me over. "Sara, wake up," a voice ordered harshly as the hands felt my face and throat. "Stay with me."

"Nikolas." His name came out as incoherent babble.

"Sara, oh God." Nikolas gathered me in his arms and pressed his face to mine. I was too cold to feel his heat, and my arms couldn't move to hug him back, but none of that mattered. He was here.

He pulled away. "Are you hurt?" When I didn't respond fast enough he demanded, "Sara, talk to me."

"C-cold."

"*Khristu,* you're soaked through." He stood, lifting me effortlessly. "I've got you. You need to stay awake for me."

The desperation in his voice frightened me, and all I wanted to do was make it go away. "Okay," I mumbled.

I felt him moving swiftly over the ground. He stopped, and I heard the snap of metal, a clank, and a creaking sound. A door closed, and the wind and rain disappeared.

He set me down on something soft. I opened my eyes but saw only darkness.

"Nikolas?"

"I'm here."

A match flared. Seconds later, an oil lantern cast a soft glow across the room, dispelling the darkness. Nikolas left the lantern on the table and went to the stone fireplace on the far side of the small room. Within a minute, he had a small blaze going. He added some small logs and stoked the fire until the wood lit.

He came back to me. Without a word he unzipped my coat and removed it. I was too numb to care when he grasped the hem of my wet top and pulled it over my head. My boots came off next, followed by my jeans.

"Jesus, your skin is like ice." Standing, he yanked off his coat and shirt then pulled me to my feet and pressed my cold body to his warmer one. He rubbed my arms and back vigorously for several minutes until my skin felt like it was thawing. He sat me on the bed again and opened a large wooden chest, pulling out a folded quilt, which he wrapped around me. Then he picked me up and carried me over to set me on the small rug in front of the fireplace.

"It will warm up in here soon," he said, laying another log on the fire.

I watched quietly as he moved around the small cabin. He went outside and brought in several large armloads of wood. Then he locked the door. Based on the fishing gear and traps hanging on one wall, we were in a hunting cabin. There was a small table with two chairs, two single beds, and some cupboards. The cabin was small and sparse, but cared for.

Storm shutters covered the two windows, but the glass still rattled when the storm shook the small building. Sleet pelted the roof and the wind howled in the chimney, making the flames dance. The roof creaked ominously, and I stared at the beamed ceiling.

"It's the wyvern." Nikolas fed more wood into the fire and sat back on his heels, running a hand through his wet hair. "I think it's guarding you."

I shivered and pulled the quilt tighter around me. My hands and feet no longer felt numb and my face tingled from the heat of the fire, but my core was still cold. Why wasn't he freezing wearing nothing but a pair of jeans?

Nikolas went to the cupboards and returned with a man's flannel shirt and a towel. He didn't say anything as he pushed the quilt off my shoulders and dressed me in the overlarge shirt. The sleeves swallowed my hands, and he smiled as he rolled the fabric up to my wrists. Then he secured the quilt around me again and moved behind me until I was sitting between his legs, facing the fire.

I closed my eyes when he began to gently dry my hair with the towel. Emotions crowded my chest as it finally hit me that he was here, that we were safe and together.

"When I saw the wyvern carry you away I thought I'd lost you," he confessed hoarsely as he worked the towel through my hair. "And then I saw you lying in the snow."

"How did you find me?" I asked in a choked voice.

"I killed the rest of the vampires and headed in the direction the wyvern went with you. I can cover a lot of ground on foot, but there are hundreds of square miles of forest out here, and he didn't leave a trail. It was sheer luck that I found where he landed by the river. The broken branches and footprints in the snow told me what way you'd gone."

I stared at the flames, trying not to think about what would have happened if he hadn't found me when he did. "What about the others? Do you think they're okay?"

"Yes," he said without hesitation. "Half the vampires went after you. Chris and the others would have been able to handle the rest. I'm sure Chris contacted Westhorne, and Tristan has half of the stronghold out there looking for us by now."

I thought about Emma and the terror in her eyes when she'd asked me to not let the vampires take her again. "I promised Emma I would keep her safe, and I left her there."

"You didn't leave her; you were taken. Emma will understand." He began to rub my scalp with the towel, and I sighed and leaned against him. A gust of wind shook the cabin, reminding me how remote and alone we were.

"Do you think we'll be safe here?"

"I don't think we have anything to worry about. If any vampires did survive and somehow manage to find us, they are not getting past the wyvern." As if he'd heard us, Alex walked across the roof to let us know he was still there.

Nikolas tossed the towel on the floor. "How do you feel?"

I didn't know if he was asking about my physical or emotional state, and I wasn't sure how to answer for either of them. My body was warmer, but there was an emptiness inside of me that made my heart ache. My whole life my power had been a part of me, and I felt lost without it. "One of the vampires shot me with a dart and now I can't use my power," I said in a small voice.

His body tensed. "What do you mean? It's gone?"

"It's there but I can't touch it or use it. What if...?"

He wrapped his arms around me. "We'll contact Eldeorin when we get home. It's obviously something that affects Fae magic, and he'll know what to do."

Hope flared in my chest. Nikolas was right. Eldeorin was old and a very powerful healer. If anyone could fix me, it was him. "I thought you didn't like him."

"For you, I'll tolerate him." He pressed a kiss beneath my ear, and my stomach did a flip as a different kind of heat filled my body. I was suddenly very aware of the warm male body pressed against mine and my state of undress beneath the quilt.

Nikolas released me and stood, leaving me in a state of nervous confusion. He checked the fire and added more wood then went to one of the beds. When his gaze came back to me, my stomach dipped wildly, and my eyes were drawn to the firelight playing across his hard stomach and the thin line of hair running down his navel to disappear under the waistline of his jeans. I swallowed dryly and forgot to breathe.

He lifted the mattress from the bed and laid it on the floor beside me. Opening the chest, he removed more blankets and a pillow. "It's warmer over here," he said as he quickly made up a bed on the floor. When he was done, he pulled up one corner of the blankets for me in silent invitation.

I stared at the narrow mattress and thought about the two of us sharing it, and my pulse fluttered wildly. My hands trembled as I dropped the quilt and slid into the makeshift bed. I watched quietly as he went to the door and peered outside. Then he locked it again and doused the lantern before he came back to sit on the floor beside me. Disappointment pricked my chest.

"Aren't you cold?" I asked him.

He smiled and tucked the blanket under my chin. "My Mori keeps me warm."

"Oh. I was just..."

His hand stilled on my shoulder. "What?"

I bit my lip as I gathered my courage. "We can share."

Heat flared in his eyes, making my heart lurch madly. "My jeans are wet."

"You could" – I tried to swallow but my mouth was dry – "take them off."

The words hung in the air between us, and heat crept into my face. Nikolas's lips parted slightly as his eyes darkened. "Are you sure?"

"Yes." A small part of me was scared, but I was surer of this than I'd ever been of anything.

His gaze held mine for the longest seconds of my life before he slowly got to his feet and kicked off his boots. When his hands went to the button of his jeans, my heart leapt into my throat and I tore my eyes away to stare at the fire. Every sound in the room was suddenly amplified: a zipper lowering, the rustle of clothing, the soft thump of wet jeans hitting the floor.

Cool air touched my skin when he lifted the blankets and slid beneath them. Heat emanated from his body like a furnace as he lay on his side next to me. His bare leg touched mine, and a tingle shot straight to my belly.

"Sara," he said softly.

"Yes."

His hand cupped my chin and turned my face toward him. I saw the fire reflecting in his eyes before he lowered his head and kissed me with so much tenderness I thought my heart would burst. His lips were soft and worshipful as they left mine to explore my jaw and found a sensitive spot beneath my ear.

He lifted his head. "Being a warrior is all I've ever known, all I ever wanted. I thought I didn't need anything else. And then I found you, and it was like finding the other half of me that I didn't know was missing." His fingers caressed my face as his gaze and words mesmerized me. "You make me whole, Sara."

"My warrior." I reached for the hand touching my face and laced my fingers with his. "I used to think the empty place in my heart was from losing my dad. But I was wrong. My heart was just waiting for you to come and fill it up."

He kissed me again, gently at first and then with more hunger. His hand held mine against the pillow as his tongue traced the seam of my lips, coaxing them open to claim my mouth. My other hand tangled in his hair as the need to be closer to him grew stronger. When he pulled out of the kiss, I protested softly.

I looked up at him, and there was no mistaking the desire in his eyes. "Do you want this?"

"Yes," I whispered.

His eyes searched mine. "We can wait until –"

"Nikolas." I cupped his face with my hand. "I don't want to wait. All I want is you."

He rose up on one elbow and ran his fingers along my face, over my lips, and down the column of my throat. My heart thudded against my ribs when he pushed the blankets down and touched the collar of my borrowed shirt. He paused and his gaze burned into mine as he undid the top button. His fingers barely grazed my skin as his hand moved down, releasing each button, but every soft touch sent heat spiraling through me. I gasped when his warm hand splayed across my stomach.

He looked down at his hand as it moved slowly across my skin, over my ribs, and brushed the clasp of my bra. "God, you're beautiful," he whispered reverently. Fire filled my veins when he pressed his lips to the swell of my breast and blazed a trail of kisses to my mouth.

His eyes lifted to mine again and the emotions raging in them stole my breath. "Sara Grey, you've owned my heart from the moment I met you. My body and soul are yours if you'll have them."

Tears filled my eyes. "Yes, if it means forever with you."

Nikolas groaned softly and captured my mouth again. My hands explored his hard body, shyly at first, and then with more confidence as his mouth and hands stoked the fire inside me. He whispered words of love as his body claimed mine and our souls became one. My Mori joined with me, and we rejoiced together as we forged an unbreakable bond with our mates.

Outside the tiny cabin, the storm raged and the world was cold and dangerous. But in Nikolas's arms, I found only warmth and love and peace.

CHAPTER 24

A FEATHER LIGHT touch against my lips woke me, and I smiled and stretched contentedly before I opened my eyes. Nikolas lay propped up on his elbow, watching me as his fingers caressed my face. His mouth curved into a sensual smile that sent my stomach on a rollercoaster ride.

"Morning," I said as he leaned in to kiss me.

Good morning, moy malen'kiy voin.

It took me several seconds to realize I'd heard his voice in my head. *Nikolas?* I said tentatively, earning another smile from him.

His eyes gleamed mischievously. *One of the perks of being mated.*

"Mated." The word felt strange and wonderful on my tongue.

Mine, whispered my Mori as it curled up like a cat after a bowl of milk.

Ours, I corrected it, finally understanding my demon's possessiveness toward its mate. An invisible cord stretched between Nikolas and me, and through it I felt love, a touch of humor, and desire. It filled me with a sense of completeness and intimacy I'd never known was possible.

My thoughts went to last night and heat rose in my face. It didn't help that Nikolas was grinning as if he knew exactly what I was thinking.

"Can you read my mind?" I blurted.

"No. But that blush makes me wish I could."

I hid my face against his chest, and he laughed softly as he put his mouth to my ear. "I love waking up with you in my arms."

His husky admission melted me, and I pulled his head down for a long, slow kiss. When we finally broke apart, I couldn't help being satisfied when I saw his smoldering gaze.

Nikolas growled playfully. "If you keep looking at me like that, we'll never leave this cabin. In fact, I might have to find the owner and buy it from him."

More nights alone with Nikolas in the middle of nowhere? I was totally down with that. My stomach rumbled loudly. "Can we bring food next time? I'm starving."

He laughed and rolled away from me, which was when I realized he was dressed and I was... not. A fresh blush crept up my face as I sat up and pulled the blankets around me, looking for the shirt I'd been wearing last night. It was nowhere to be seen, but I spotted my own clothes draped over a chair near the fireplace. Nikolas must have gotten up in the night to hang them to dry for me. He'd obviously tended the fire through the night as well or it would be freezing here this morning.

"Your shirt and jeans are dry, but your boots are still wet." He grabbed my things from the chair and handed them to me, and then he went to the cupboard on the other side of the room. I knew he was giving me a private moment to dress, and my heart swelled at his thoughtfulness.

He came back and sat on the mattress holding a can of tuna, a pack of saltines, and a bottle of water. "Not exactly a five-star breakfast."

"It's perfect."

He put some tuna on a cracker and gave it to me. "It'll be daylight soon. The storm's over, so we should head out as soon as it's light enough."

"How far is it to the road?"

"About fifteen miles. I won't be surprised if we run into some of our people on the way. We'll be home before you know it."

Home. That word held a whole new meaning for me now. We hadn't discussed living arrangements yet, but I knew I'd be moving out of my room in the very near future. As in the moment we got home.

He seemed to be considering his next words. "How do you feel today? Is there any change in your magic?"

His question made me realize what else was different this morning. I didn't feel as empty as I had last night. I reached for my power. The barrier was still there, but it felt weaker, and a tiny tendril of magic slipped free.

I let out a shaky laugh. "I think it's getting better. Whatever they shot me with must be wearing off."

Nikolas looked as relieved as I felt. "Good. That means we won't have to call the faerie."

"Jealous?"

"I might have been a little jealous once or twice." An arrogant smile curved his lips. "But I got the girl."

I leaned over and kissed him, not caring that I had tuna breath. "You always had the girl."

After our humble breakfast, we tidied the cabin and Nikolas put out the fire. I grimaced when I donned my wet boots and damp coat, and I reminded myself that I'd be warm and dry again in a few hours.

Nikolas opened the door, and I glanced around the cabin before I left. It looked so small and insignificant, yet our lives had changed forever in this room. I'd been half-dead when he'd carried me through the door last night, and I was leaving feeling more alive than I'd ever been.

Outside, the world was coated in a layer of glittering ice. Our breath steamed the cold air and our boots crunched over the icy crust on top of the snow. Nearby, the river roared past, heedless of the ice attempting to dam it in places.

There was no sign of Alex, but his tracks were all over the sloped roof of the small cabin. If someone had told me in November that the surly wyvern would save my life twice, I would have had a good laugh over it. But I was alive today because of him. Sure, he'd carried me off and dropped me in the middle of nowhere where I'd nearly frozen to death, but he'd rescued me from a much worse fate. I would have preferred freezing to what those vampires had in mind for me.

Nikolas tested the snow with his foot. "It's going to be rough walking with the snow iced over. Climb on my back, and I'll carry you."

"You can't carry me fifteen miles."

His grin made me forget the cold already nipping at my fingers. "Are you willing to bet on that?"

"I don't know. What will you give me if I win?"

He laughed and moved to pick me up. "Anything you –" Confusion filled his eyes, followed by horror. "Sara... run," he uttered before he collapsed to the ground.

"Nikolas!" I knelt beside him, shaking him. "What's wrong?"

"Lover boy is taking a little nap."

My head snapped up as a huge blond vampire stepped out of the woods. My heart thudded and my limbs grew weak as four more vampires appeared behind him. One of them had what looked like a tranquilizer gun trained on Nikolas. Didn't they realize he would wear off the drug in a minute? *Please, hurry and wake up, Nikolas.*

"Remember our orders," the big vampire barked at the others as they advanced on us. "We are to bring them in undamaged."

Them? I stood on trembling legs. "I'm the one you want. Leave him, and I'll go quietly."

The vampire sneered. "If we weren't under orders to bring him, he'd be dead already. And as for you..." He lifted his hand, and I saw a small gun like the one the female vampire had used on me yesterday. Before I could react, a dart hit me in the arm. "You won't be any trouble."

Fear choked me as the vampires surrounded us. One of them threw Nikolas effortlessly over his shoulder and another did the same to me. My body recoiled from his touch, and I could smell the faint stench of dead flesh that all vampires carried. Even though my power was locked away from me, I felt a tiny sliver of ice in my chest.

The ice and snow caused no impediment to the vampires who moved swiftly through the woods. Each step carried Nikolas and me farther from the cabin and the hope of being found by the warriors who were out there searching for us. Despair and terror welled inside me, but I refused to let these bastards see me break down. Instead, I focused on Nikolas. I couldn't see him, but I could feel him nearby and I clung to that like a lifeline. I could face whatever fate awaited me as long as he was okay.

The vampires ran for at least a mile before we reached a clearing where three snowmobiles were parked. My fear grew as I watched two of the vampires place Nikolas's unconscious form between them and take off down a trail. The blond vampire took the second machine, and I was forced to sit between the last two vampires on the third machine. I struggled not to hyperventilate as the vampire behind me wrapped his arms around my waist and rested his chin on my shoulder.

When I suddenly lost any sense of Nikolas, I almost went nuts. My body tensed to fight, and the vampire tightened his grip on me. A few seconds later, I felt him again as we caught up to the first snowmobile, and I nearly sobbed.

We rode for almost an hour before we came to a narrow gravel road where a white utility van was parked. The blond vampire took the driver's seat and the others got into the back with Nikolas and me. Once the doors were closed, they let go of me and I crawled over to Nikolas. I sat on the floor with his head cradled in my lap and silently pleaded with him to be okay. *I love you, Nikolas. I need you. Why aren't you waking up?*

The drive was bumpy for at least thirty minutes before we turned onto a paved road. I couldn't see where we were going, but I could tell we were on a highway, judging by our speed and the sound of other vehicles going by. An hour later, we drove into a city that had to be Boise. The van stopped at a few traffic lights, took some left and right turns, and then finally came to a complete stop.

Before the doors opened, I knew we were at the airport because I could hear planes taking off nearby. Fear and hopelessness threatened to suffocate me. Once we got on the plane that was waiting for us, they could take us anywhere in the world, and no one would ever know what had become of us. I could try to run, but I wouldn't. Even if I could manage to escape, I'd never leave Nikolas. Our fates were woven together as tightly as the bond between us.

"Finally," said a husky feminine voice that sounded vaguely familiar. "I have been waiting here all night."

"You were more than welcome to go out in the woods and find them yourself," snarled the blond vampire. "You're lucky we got to them before the hunters."

"That is not my job, Anthony."

"Wouldn't want you to break a nail, would we?" He barked a laugh.

"Well, they're all yours."

She sighed heavily. "Bring them to the plane and then you may consider your job done."

The back doors of the van opened to reveal the inside of a hanger. The blond vampire grabbed me by the arm and ripped me away from Nikolas. As he dragged me toward the small jet, I heard Nikolas being lifted out of the van and carried behind me. He should have woken up by now. What had they done to him?

The vampire forced me onto the plane ahead of him and shoved me down into one of the wide leather seats. "Stay," he barked like he was giving orders to a dog.

His companions buckled Nikolas into the seat beside me, and I grabbed Nikolas's hand, clinging to it for dear life. I rested my head against his shoulder, needing to be close to him. *I'm here, Nikolas. I'll never leave you.* I didn't know if he could hear me in his unconscious state, but I needed to say the words.

"The infamous Sara Grey. You don't look like much for all the trouble you've caused."

I looked up at the female vampire standing in the doorway of the plane. Her red hair fell in thick waves down her back and she wore a black pantsuit and high heels. I sucked in a sharp breath as recognition hit me, followed by burning hatred.

"Ava Bryant," I spat. Her name left a foul taste in my mouth.

One of her perfect eyebrows arched, and her red lips parted in surprise. "How do you know my name? I think I would remember if the two of us had met."

"If we had met before, you'd be dead." I leaned forward in my seat, and she took a step back. "You met my uncle."

Comprehension dawned in her eyes and her lips curved into a cruel smile. "Nate Grey. Now that is a week I'll never forget. Nate and I had so much fun together." She ran her tongue along her lip. "He was quite delicious."

I gripped the arms of my chair in an effort not to jump at her. With no power and no weapons I was no match for her, and we both knew it.

"Poor Nate. He had such promise. Did you kill him yourself or did your warrior do it for you?"

"I killed the demon," I said, deliberately evasive.

She sat in the seat opposite me. "Impressive. Quite the little hunter you are."

"You have no idea."

"I can see why Eli was so fascinated with you." She crossed her legs and smoothed a wrinkle in her sleeve. "He was a foolish male and his weakness was pretty little brunettes." Her eyes moved to Nikolas. "I should actually be thanking your warrior for taking care of Eli. I never understood why that loser was our Master's favorite."

My hands grew clammy at the mention of the Master, but I swallowed back my fear. I was proud of how steady my voice was when I said, "I killed Eli."

Ava's eyes widened and then she clapped her hands in delight. "Oh my, this just keeps getting better! I wish I could have seen his face. What went through his mind when he realized a little Mohiri orphan had bested him?"

I leaned back in my seat and took Nikolas's larger hand in both of mine. "You can ask him that yourself when I send you to be with him in hell."

The smile bled from her lips. "Your killing days are over, little hunter. When the Master gets through with you, you'll be begging me to kill you."

"Don't underestimate me, *vampire*." I said the word as if it was something nasty stuck to the bottom of my boot. "I'm not done with you yet."

She got up from her seat and stood over me. I didn't see the syringe in her hand until she plunged it into my arm. "Oh, you're done. Nighty night."

*　　*　　*

I opened my eyes slowly and blinked several times until the dirty wooden beams above me came into focus. My head pounded, and my stomach churned. I rolled over onto my side and fell off the small stone platform I was lying on. My knees smacked against the stone floor, and I moaned as pain shot through them. I pulled my body up onto my hands and knees, fighting the urge to retch as I took in the damp stone walls and the iron bars that made up one wall of the small cell.

Panic washed over me in waves and I struggled to stand, fighting off the effects of whatever drug the vampire had given me. I didn't need to look around the cell to know I was alone.

"Nikolas?" I grasped the bars and strained to see past the circle of light provided by the single bare light bulb outside my cell. "Nikolas!"

"He's not here," said a small voice on the other side of the cell wall.

"Who are you?" I demanded hoarsely as I rubbed my arms. My coat and boots were gone, and I shivered in the cold dank air. "Do you know where he is?"

A slender arm waved, and I moved to the end of the bars. "I'm Grace," the girl replied tearfully. "They didn't bring a man, just you."

Oh God, Nikolas. Pain stabbed me in the chest. I stood very still, feeling for him, and I stifled a sob when I sensed him faintly. He was here somewhere and still alive. *Nikolas, can you hear me?* I called to him.

Silence.

"I'm Sara." I stuck my hand through the bars until my fingers touched her cold ones. "Grace, do you know how long I was out?"

"A few hours. Anna and I were afraid you wouldn't wake up."

I drew my hand back and closed my eyes against the throbbing pain in my head. "Who is Anna?"

Grace sniffled. "She's the other girl down here with us. There was a girl named Jen, but she never came back when they took her yesterday."

Neither of us spoke for a long moment because we both knew why Jen had not returned. I fought the mounting terror. *Be strong. Losing it is not going to help you.* I needed to stay calm and clearheaded if I had any hope of getting us out of this alive.

"Where is Anna now?" I asked with a calmness that belied the fear churning inside me.

"One of those things took her right after they brought you in. What if she doesn't –?"

Grace fell silent as a door at the end of the hallway opened and footsteps came toward us. I could hear a girl weeping as the door of the cell on the other side of me opened and slammed shut.

"Sleep tight, beautiful," taunted a male voice. The vampire sauntered over to leer at me and Grace. "Don't worry ladies; you'll get your turn soon enough." He snickered and left, and I heard a key turning in a lock.

"Anna, is that you?" Grace called softly.

The crying paused. "Y-yes."

God, she sounded so young. She couldn't be more than fifteen or sixteen. Grace didn't sound much older than that. I rubbed my temples. I'd thought I only had to worry about getting Nikolas and me out of here, but I couldn't leave these girls behind in this hellhole.

I hung my head helplessly. I had no weapons and my power was still blocked from me. Without my special radar I couldn't tell if there was one or a hundred vampires in this place. How was I going to protect myself, let alone two teenage girls?

"Anna, this is Sara. She's the girl they brought in today."

"Hi," Anna said weakly.

"Hi, Anna," I called back. "How long have you girls been here?"

Grace let out a shuddering breath. "I think I've been here for three days."

"Me too," Anna said. Then she started crying softly again. "I want to go home."

I walked to the other end of the bars to be closer to her. "We're going to get out of here. Just hang in there."

"No, we're not." Her voice rose then fell off again. "They're monsters. They did... things to me. They hurt me."

I closed my eyes, but I couldn't stop imagining the vile things this girl had suffered. I could hear Grace crying softly, and it was all I could do to keep myself together.

I cleared my throat. "Where are you girls from? I'm from Maine."

"I'm from Scarsdale," Grace replied.

"Mount Vernon," Anna said.

I bit my lip. Both of those places were in New York. Did that mean we were in New York too? "Do you know how you got here, or were you drugged like me?"

Anna answered first. "I-I think they drugged me. I don't remember."

"Me too," said Grace. "Sara, do you really think we'll get out of here?"

"Yes." It was better to give them hope than to admit how dire our circumstances were. Hope could be the difference between life and death in this place.

The sound of the door opening sent my heart pounding, and I stood in the middle of my cell to face whatever was coming. Instead of a vampire, a short humanoid demon with pale skin, a long furred face, and orange eyes appeared carrying a tray of food. Both girls made frightened sounds as the quellar demon slid a plate beneath the doors of their cells. I had met a lot scarier looking creatures, but he must have appeared so alien to Grace and Anna. All I saw was a quiet demon with scared eyes that flicked back and forth as if he expected someone to jump him.

The demon stood outside my cell, and we stared at each other for a long moment. He was probably curious about the new addition, or the fact that I didn't shrink from him like the others. The sound of Anna pulling her plate across the stone floor startled him, and he hurried away like a large frightened mouse.

I looked down suspiciously at the sandwich and small bottle of water. Why would the vampires feed us if they planned to kill us? Maybe killing someone who was half-starved was no fun for them. I thought about not eating it, but all I'd had in the last twenty-four hours was some tuna and crackers. If I was going to get out of here, I had to keep up my strength.

While we ate, I asked Grace and Anna questions about their families, their friends, and school – anything to take their minds off our situation. Grace was seventeen and Anna was fifteen, and they both had two siblings. Grace was in the band at school and Anna was a science geek. They'd had such normal, happy lives before they were ripped away from everything they knew. At least I had known what was out there before I was taken. Not that it helped me much now.

After our meal, Anna said she was tired and I heard her lie down. Grace whispered that they got sleepy after they came back from upstairs. I asked her about the Master, and she said she had seen a red-haired female and a dark-haired male. She closed off when I tried to ask what had happened to her upstairs, and I didn't push. Soon she went to sleep as well, leaving me alone with my thoughts.

All I could think about was Nikolas. Where was he? What were they doing to him? A thought came unbidden to my mind of Ava Bryant touching him, drinking from him, and my vision clouded as blood roared in my ears. My body trembled and I gripped the iron bars so hard they creaked. *Solmi*, my Mori growled.

We'll find him, I promised my agitated demon. *And if that bitch lays a finger on him I'll rip it off her.* Ava Bryant was already going to die for what she'd done to Nate. If she hurt Nikolas in any way, I'd make sure her death was not a quick one.

I lost track of time. I lay down on the hard slab that was supposed to be a bed, but I couldn't sleep not knowing what was happening to Nikolas. I paced the small cell and thought about last night. No matter what the vampires did to us, they could never take that away. If I died tomorrow, I would die knowing what it was to love and be loved completely.

When the door opened again, I fought to keep my breathing under control. This was it. I was finally going to meet the vampire who had terrorized my family for so long. I thought about my Dad and Nate. *Be strong.*

The vampire who had brought Anna in earlier appeared. He flashed his fangs at me as he went to Grace's cell and unlocked it.

"No," she whimpered when he pulled her from the cell.

He dragged her past my cell, and I got a glimpse of a girl with short dark hair in jeans and a T-shirt. When he opened Anna's door, she began sobbing. "Please."

The door closed behind them, and I clenched the bars of my cell as fear and rage and helplessness assailed me. A few minutes later, the unmistakable sound of a girl's scream reached me. I clamped my hands over my ears and tears scorched my face as I dropped to my knees with the scream echoing in my head.

Why was he torturing them when he finally had me? He'd gone through so much trouble to get his hands on me. What was he waiting for?

The sound of my cell opening woke me from where I'd fallen asleep on the floor. I scurried backward as Ava Bryant appeared behind the quellar demon that had brought us our meal. My eyes went to the syringe in the demon's furry hand, and I shook my head.

The vampire smiled coldly. "Time for your medicine, little hunter, and Grigor has a special batch he cooked up just for you. Don't you, Grigor?"

The demon gave a jerky nod and held up the syringe that contained a murky yellowish liquid. He was trembling, and he fumbled, almost dropping the syringe.

Ava snatched it away from him. "You clumsy idiot. Do you know how hard it is to make this stuff?" She threw back her head and laughed. "Of course, you do."

She looked at me as I got to my feet. "In case you didn't know it, Grigor here is a quellar demon, and his kind are very talented at chemistry. With the right motivation they can be very inventive." She rolled the syringe between her long fingers. "Did you know quellar demons are the only ones in existence that are immune to Fae magic? No? Neither did we until recently. It seems they figured out years ago how to block the effects of Fae magic, and they immunize their young from an early age. Quite brilliant, really. Unfortunately, their drug doesn't work on other demon races yet, but I'm confident Grigor will work it out."

I swallowed dryly. "What does that have to do with me?"

"We couldn't exactly bring you to the Master with all that Fae magic shooting out of you, could we? We wondered what would happen if we shot you with the quellar drug since you are half demon and half Fae. The results were better than we expected. The darts they used in the woods had the original drug and we weren't sure how fast your Mohiri system would burn it off. But Grigor's been busy making a newer version of the drug that will last indefinitely."

"Why do you care how long it lasts? You're going to kill me anyway."

Her smile made a pit open in my stomach. "My Master has plans for you. You won't die anytime soon. You'll just wish you were dead."

She moved before I could blink, and I felt the bite of a needle in my arm. She injected the whole syringe and let me go.

At first I felt nothing. Then a burning sensation began to grow in my chest and spread through my body. Dizziness struck next, and I had to brace my hands against the wall to keep from falling.

"That should do it. Sleep tight tonight, little hunter. Tomorrow is a big day." Ava handed the empty syringe to Grigor and walked out of the cell with the demon trailing meekly behind her. She locked the cell and turned to go, but stopped to look back at me. "Oh, I thought you'd like to know I've been getting to know your warrior *really* well. He's even more delicious than –"

I hit the bars so fast pieces of mortar fell from the ceiling. "I'll take you apart piece-by-piece if you touch him, you bloodsucking bitch."

She jumped back. "Temper, temper. You should know that those bars are reinforced to hold back a mature warrior. So don't waste your strength. You're going to need it."

I waited until they left before I sank to the floor and let the despair finally take me. I cried for Nikolas and the suffering he was going through because of me. I cried for the life we should have had together, and for waiting so long to tell him I loved him. I cried for the two young girls who would never see their families again and for all the people I was leaving behind. I cried until there were no tears left in me and I didn't have the strength to get up off the floor.

Sometime during the night, I awoke to the sound of Anna being led back to her cell. I waited hours for them to bring Grace, but they never did.

I was sitting on the stone platform waiting for them when they finally came for me. After I'd cried myself out last night, a strange calm had settled over me. It was not acceptance of my fate, but acknowledgement that there was nothing I could do to change it sitting in this cell. If there was one thing I'd learned from my life it was that nothing was certain, and you never knew how your circumstances could change from one minute to the next.

Ava Bryant and the other vampire from yesterday approached me, and I didn't say a word when the male unlocked my cell and ordered me to come out. As we passed Anna's cell I saw a small shape curled into a ball in the far corner, and my heart hurt for her. Grace was gone, and I had a feeling Anna wouldn't last much longer in this hell.

We went through the door and down a hallway before we came to a set of stairs. Ava took my arm and the male vampire walked ahead of us as we ascended the stairs. When we came out into a large kitchen, I had to put a hand over my eyes to shield them from the brightness after my day in the dimly lit cell.

Sara?

I almost cried out when Nikolas's voice spoke in my mind. It was faint, but real, and I turned automatically toward it. *I'm here, Nikolas. I'm coming to you.*

No, you have to run, he said weakly as the vampires led me through the large house. I was so focused on him I barely noticed my surroundings. *The Master...* His voice faded away and I felt real fear for the first time since the vampires had come to get me.

Nikolas?

Silence.

Nikolas!

We approached a set of open French doors. Beyond them I could see a large room with a lot of windows. Cold spread through my chest. There were vampires in that room, a lot of them. And Nikolas was in there with them.

I tore my arm away from Ava, and she let me go. I ran through the doorway and searched the room frantically. Vampires sat on chairs and couches or stood in small groups talking, all looking like they were assembled for a social gathering. When I entered the room, they stared at me with an air of excitement.

"Nikolas!" I pushed past vampires to get to the man shackled and chained on his knees in the center of the room. His shirt was gone and his head hung forward so I couldn't see his face. I fell to my knees in front of him and lifted his head. His eyelids flickered and he mumbled incoherently.

"I'm here." I kissed his lips and pulled him into my arms without a thought for the vampires surrounding us. *I love you, Nikolas. Stay with me.*

"Sara," he murmured weakly.

I pulled away to look at his face. His eyes opened and a sob caught in my throat at the agony in them. Something sticky touched my hand, and I looked down in horror at the two weeping puncture wounds in his throat. *What have they done to you?*

"How very touching," drawled a male voice.

I looked behind me at a vampire with black hair and a small goatee, sitting in a high backed chair that resembled a throne. His hair was tied back in a ponytail and he wore an expensive suit. In his hand was a crystal glass of deep red liquid, and I shuddered at the thought of what it was. His dark eyes moved over me appreciatively, making me feel like I'd never be clean again.

I let go of Nikolas and stood to face the vampire who had caused me so much grief and pain. I met his cold gaze unflinchingly, and I was struck suddenly by how unremarkable he was. There was no air of power that I'd expect from a Master, and without his expensive clothes, he'd look like any other vampire in the room.

"Sebastian, how many times have I asked you not to sit in my chair?"

A hush fell over the room. The vampire stood and bowed his head in deference. I turned slowly, recognition and disbelief clawing at my chest. Chains rattled and Nikolas's cold hand grasped mine as I came around to face my true nemesis.

"We meet at last, Sara Grey," said the voice of the girl I had comforted from my cell only hours ago. *Anna?*

Straight blond hair framed a heart-shaped face, and the blue eyes that watched me were cold and alien, yet achingly familiar at the same time. She smiled, showing perfect white teeth and two dainty fangs.

"Or maybe I should say, *niece.*"

CHAPTER 25

"ELENA, PLEASE," NIKOLAS pleaded hoarsely. I wrapped both of my hands around his, needing his strength as much as giving him mine.

"Please what, Nikolas?" asked the vampire who used to be the girl he'd loved as a sister. She circled us to sit in the throne chair that dwarfed her delicate frame. "I've waited a long time to hear you beg, so make it good."

"This is between you and me. Let her go and I'll do whatever you want."

"No!" I tightened my grip on his hand.

Elena scoffed. "She's such a loyal little thing, isn't she? How loyal do you think she'll be when she hears how you abandoned me and left me in the hands of a monster?"

"He didn't abandon you," I shot back. "He and Tristan looked everywhere for you. They thought you died."

"They didn't look hard enough!" she snarled, her blue eyes turning dark. "For weeks I prayed you would come for me, Nikolas, but you never did. Week after week, month after month, the Master used me, tortured me, and drank from me until I was almost dry. He was a sadistic animal, and for two years he kept me chained in his chambers, two years of living hell while my loving brother and friend lived their happy little lives."

I felt my face blanch at the images her words conjured. My stomach rolled and bile rose in my throat.

"One day the Master got bored and decided I'd be a more fun plaything if I was a vampire. Only I already had a demon inside of me." Elena's hands gripped the arms of her chair, and I watched her nails turn into claws. "Do you know what it feels like to have two demons fighting to the death inside your body? Do you know how agonizing it is when your Mori dies, Nikolas?"

"Elena..." Nikolas's voice was raw with pain.

She moved faster than anything I'd ever seen. Her small hands wrapped around Nikolas's throat as she lifted him like he weighed nothing. "You talk when I say you can talk."

"Stop! You're killing him." My outburst earned me a numbing backhand to my cheek that sent me sprawling across the floor. Black spots swam before my eyes, and all I could do was lie there for precious seconds as she strangled the person I loved more than my own life.

She released him, and he fell backward, coughing. I crawled over to him and pulled his head into my lap, wishing I could shield him from Elena's wrath. Nikolas had always been the strong one, and seeing him so vulnerable was almost more than I could bear.

Elena began walking around us in slow circles, her pale blue dress swirling around her knees. "The Master was so pleased with himself because he was able to change a Mohiri into a vampire. I was his favorite pet and his prized possession, and he showed me off every chance he got. He liked to dress me up in pretty clothes and pamper me. I was a life-sized doll he could take out and play with whenever he wanted. He loved how small and weak I was, and he told me every day that I belonged to him forever."

She stopped and crouched in front of us so she and I were at eye level. "But he was wrong. I was a lot stronger than I let him see, and I was biding my time, waiting years for the perfect moment. That arrogant bastard was so sure of his superiority that he got complacent. One night he didn't bother to lock me up after he'd finished playing with me, and that was the opportunity I'd been waiting for. I killed him while he slept and drank him dry. Did you know that is the only way to become a Master? His children, his wealth, and power all became mine. After years of being a slave I was free and powerful, and it felt incredible. My old family had deserted me, so I began to create a new one."

She moved forward until she was close enough to pick up a lock of my hair and curl it around her finger. I recoiled inwardly but kept very still. Deep inside me, I felt my power react to being in such close proximity to a Master vampire as it strained against the invisible barrier holding it back.

"I spent months searching for the perfect human to become my first born. Eli was special." She leaned in to speak softly in my ear. "You will pay for his death a thousand times over."

Her smile when she pulled away was almost angelic, but I was close enough to see the madness in her blue eyes. I hugged Nikolas closer to me and his hand came up to cover mine.

Be brave, moy malen'kiy voin.

She's insane, Nikolas. I'm scared.

No matter what happens, I'm here with you. A wave of calming energy flowed through our bond into me, and I could almost feel his strong arms around me. It gave me the strength to ask the questions I'd been seeking answers to my whole life.

"Why did you send Eli to kill my father? He was nothing to you."

For a brief moment I saw fear in her eyes. "Your father *was* nothing to me, but he meant something to my dear niece, Madeline."

Anger burned through me, but I kept it in check. "You killed him to get to Madeline?"

Elena stood and went back to her chair. "I killed him, not because she loved him, but because of the child she could have with him. It wasn't until ten years later that I learned I had been too late and a child already existed."

"But why?" My need for answers outweighed my fear of her. "Why did you care so much if they had a child?" There was no way Elena could have known my parents would have a half Fae, half Mohiri child. My dad had been human, as had generations of his ancestors. And even the faeries had admitted they had no idea what kind of powers I would have.

Elena studied her pink fingernails as if she was deciding whether or not to tell me. But I saw past her smooth veneer now, and I could see she was dying to share that little tidbit. That way she could gloat over the fact that she'd won.

"I was having a party and Madeline was my guest of honor. You should have seen her face when she realized who I was. Priceless. Of course, I compelled her to forget me before I let her go." She giggled. "I even made her think I was a male."

I stared at her. "You let her go?"

"Nothing like a little hunt to spice up a party." She made a pouty face. "Madeline proved to be more evasive than I gave her credit for."

"One of my guests was a warlock named Azar who was known for his gift of sight. Azar stupidly waited until after Madeline had gone to tell me he'd had a vision when he saw her. He told me that Madeline's half-blood daughter would destroy me."

I sucked in a sharp breath, and I felt Nikolas's start of surprise. All of this because a warlock had seen something in a vision?

"Needless to say, I was quite upset Azar hadn't shared that piece of information *before* I released Madeline. I discovered aged warlock is a very fine drink." She let out a girlish laugh and some of the other vampires joined in. "We managed to pick up Madeline's trail and followed her to Portland, which is how we found her human husband. Oddly, Eli saw no sign of a child even though he went to the house you lived in. It wasn't until Eli found you in Portland last fall that we learned what you really were. I had no idea someone like you could even exist. But here you are."

She stood again and smoothed down the front of her dress. "I am bored with this chatter. I think it's time we get the festivities underway. Ava?"

The red-haired vampire hurried to her side.

"Has everything been prepared as I asked?"

"Yes, Master."

"Wonderful." Elena smiled sweetly down at Nikolas and me. "Today is a very special day for me, and it wouldn't be possible without the two of you."

Nikolas, I said fearfully.

Be strong. He struggled to sit up and I moved to help him. "What are you planning, Elena?" he asked, sounding a lot braver than I felt.

She walked over and leaned down to run a finger across his jaw. My nostrils flared and my hands clenched at my sides. I had to fight not to jump at her.

"Why, today is my wedding day. All I needed was my groom."

"What?" I started to get up but Nikolas held me back. Fury seethed in my chest and my power clawed to get out.

"I have been waiting for you for a long time, Nikolas. For months, my children have tried to bring you to me. I had to find Sara because of Azar's pesky prediction. But *you* are my real prize." Elena's fingers moved intimately through Nikolas's hair, but he didn't react to her touch. I, on the other hand, was boiling with bloodlust.

"You are a magnificent warrior," she crooned softly. "And you will make an even more magnificent vampire and a fitting mate for me."

"No!" I lunged at Elena, only to find myself restrained by two vampires. "You can't have him," I shouted at her as Nikolas sent more calming energy through the bond.

She smiled, unperturbed by my outburst. "Sara, what you don't understand is that Nikolas and I were always destined to be together. He loved me, and we would have been mated if I hadn't been taken from him. Is that right, my love?"

Nikolas met her gaze sadly. "I loved you, Elena, but as a sister. I grieved your death as a brother grieves his sibling."

Her face hardened. "That's not true. We were perfect together. If we'd had more time together, the bond would have grown." He didn't respond, and she kept talking as if she hadn't noticed. "That's all in the past. Today we'll start over and create a new bond."

I twisted in the vampires' iron grip. "Nikolas will never bond with you. He's mine."

Elena's eyes glittered like chips of ice when she turned toward me. "Just because he is your protector, does not mean he belongs to you, you silly child."

"He's not my protector. He's my mate."

"No!" Elena stood and stomped her foot. "You're mine, Nikolas, not this half breed's. When you become a vampire your Mori will die and the bond with her will be severed. Then we will be together forever." She walked over to look down at me. "My wedding gift to you will be her. You will be very thirsty after the change. Her blood will be our wedding drink."

I saw the horror in Nikolas's eyes. *Sara, you need to get out of here. Use your power,* he said desperately.

I can't. They drugged me again. I would never leave him even if my power was intact.

Elena flicked her hand at me. "Take her out of my sight until the ceremony. Everyone leave us. I wish to be alone with my groom."

"Nikolas," I cried as they dragged me away from him.

Fight, Sara. Try to use your power. You're stronger than they are.

I screamed and fought all the way back to my cell. The vampires threw me inside and left without a backward glance. Alone in my stone prison, thoughts of what Elena was doing to Nikolas tortured me more than any physical pain. I couldn't hear him down here, and the sudden loss of his calming presence in my mind added to my torment.

His parting words to me rang in my mind. *Fight, Sara.* I would fight for him until there was nothing left in this body to fight with. I beat against the wall between me and my power, and I felt my power trying to reach me from the other side. A few threads escaped, and I hugged them to me, gaining strength from their familiar warmth. Hours passed. I pummeled the barrier relentlessly and felt it weaken around the edges.

The door opened and two vampires appeared. "No," I almost cried. I needed more time.

I didn't struggle as they led me up to the main floor. When we entered the kitchen, Ava Bryant was waiting to take me from them. She led me down a hallway and up another flight of stairs to a guest room. Laid out on the bed were an emerald green dress and a pair of matching shoes.

"The Master wants you to look nice for the ceremony."

The laugh that burst from me was almost hysterical. "You want me to dress up?"

Ignoring my question, she pointed to the attached bathroom. "Clean up in there. You smell."

I stared at her incredulously and she shoved me hard. "Do it or I will do it for you."

My movements were robotic as I stripped out of my clothes. I showered and dried my hair in a daze. This couldn't be real. I wasn't getting dressed up for my own death. I felt numb as I donned the soft dress that fell in flowing waves to my knees. The shoes were a size too big, but I was too out of it to care.

"You'll do." Ava opened the door and shoved me out into the hallway where I almost ran into Grigor. The demon stared at me with his big orange eyes until Ava barked at him. "Grigor, what are you doing up here? Get back to the lab."

Instead of leaving, he bowed his head to me. *"Talael esledur."*

I gasped and stared at the demon as Ava yelled at him for disobeying her. Movement caught my eye, and I looked down at his hands where he flashed a glass vial filled with yellowish-brown liquid.

A myriad of emotions assailed me as I realized what he was showing me and why. In the next instant the vial was gone, and he raised his eyes to mine again. *"Talael esledur,"* he said again then turned and walked away.

"Idiot demon," Ava spat as she shoved me toward the stairs.

My head spun from the magnitude of Grigor's revelation, and I barely saw where I was going as we descended the stairs. Had he known that I'd recognize troll bile or was he sending me another message? He was a chemist so he had to know the potency of troll bile, that it could counteract any poison. Was he trying to tell me he'd mixed troll bile with the drug they had given me last night? Was that why the barrier blocking my power was weakening?

Nikolas? Filled with new hope, I called to him as we approached the French doors.

Sara, he answered, his voice full of agony and regret. *I don't want you to see this.*

I sent him my love through the bond. *Whatever happens, we'll face it together.*

We passed through the doors into an empty room. I looked around in confusion as Ava led me to the wide glass doors on the other side of the room that led to a large snow-covered courtyard. A blast of frigid air hit me when she opened the door and pushed me outside. I rubbed my arms and tried not to trip in the too-large shoes.

Night had fallen and dozens of gaslights had been lit to illuminate the courtyard. I could sense Nikolas, but I couldn't see him because dozens of vampires blocked my view. Cold blossomed slowly in my chest until I could barely breathe. I struggled to maintain my composure. If my radar was working, then my power was coming back. *Please, don't let me be too late,* I prayed as the vampires parted to let us through.

"Oh, God." My knees weakened when we emerged from the crowd.

A raised stone platform sat in the center of the courtyard, and on top of it lay Nikolas, unshackled and dressed in a black tuxedo. A female vampire stood on either end holding his legs and arms down. Standing beside the platform and facing me was Elena, dressed in a white bridal gown and veil that made her look like a little girl playing dress up.

Nikolas turned his head to look at me as we approached, and I could see blood staining the collar of his white shirt. His eyes had a glazed, pained look, but they softened when they met mine. "My beautiful little warrior," he rasped as, if speaking was painful for him. *Look away, Sara. Please.*

Elena clapped her hands sharply. "My children, we are gathered here for a very happy event. Tonight, I will take a mate." Applause erupted from the vampires surrounding us until she raised a hand to silence them. "The transformation has begun, and in a few hours my mate will be born."

Begun? I shook my head as I saw the horrible truth in Nikolas's eyes. A scream tore from my throat. "No."

Nikolas's face twisted in pain and shudders wracked his body. I struggled in Ava's grip and she released me, allowing me to run to him. I took his cold face in my hands and crooned softly to him. "I'm here, Nikolas. I won't leave you." *Fight it. Your Mori is strong. You can defeat this thing.*

Sweat broke out on his brow as another wave of pain hit him. I wiped it away and my touch eased him. Through the bond I felt some of his pain, and I realized he was blocking me from the worst of it. Even now, he was trying to protect me. *Listen to me, Nikolas. I've seen vamhir demons, and they're weak. They control through pain. Fight the pain, and you'll beat it.*

He grew still and his eyes opened. "I'll fight until my last breath for you. But if this thing takes my body, I want you to remember that my soul belongs to you. No matter what the demon does or says, I love you. I will always love only you."

"I'll fight too. I promise." I tested the barrier, and my pulse leapt when more power slipped past it. It wasn't enough to use as a weapon, but it meant the barrier was failing. We just needed a little more time. *Nikolas, my power is coming back. Just hold on a little longer, and I'll be strong enough for both of us.*

You can't save me and fight Elena. Use your power to get away from here.

No. I won't leave you.

His eyes pleaded with me. *Get out of here, Sara. Get help and come back for me.*

I shook my head. "It'll be too late."

Elena's hand gripped my shoulder painfully. "You two have had plenty of time to say your goodbyes. It's time to get on with my wedding."

"Wait, Elena, please." Nikolas begged and her grip loosened.

"Yes, my love?" she asked sweetly. I could hear in her tone that she liked hearing him beg.

"One kiss before you take her."

Elena snarled, and I was glad I couldn't see her face. "You're *my* groom, Nikolas. You don't kiss another girl on your wedding day."

"Just a goodbye kiss. You will have all the rest."

"Oh." She let out a girlish giggle that made me grit my teeth. "Very well. One kiss."

"My arms?" He gave her a beseeching look.

She huffed then ordered the vampire to release his hands. "Fine. Get on with it."

"Nikolas, what are you doing?" I whispered. He'd said he would fight, but he sounded like he was giving up.

I nearly wept when his arms wrapped around me. He smiled tenderly as he brushed aside the hair that had fallen on my face.

The first brush of his lips against mine was so achingly sweet I couldn't stop the whimper that rose in my throat. It felt like weeks instead of days since the last time he'd kissed me, and I pressed close, needing more. His mouth parted under mine and he deepened the kiss, drawing me in until I forgot everything but him. For one blissful moment, there was only Sara and Nikolas, and there was no world outside of his arms. The bond between us expanded as we opened ourselves completely to each other and shared our love and fear.

I didn't realize I was crying until I tasted my tears on my lips. Nikolas kissed the tears away and whispered that everything would be okay. I buried my face against his throat and wept.

"Time's up," Elena snapped.

I lifted my head, but Nikolas tightened his arms around me. "Be strong, Sara," he said against my ear. "Live – for me."

I gasped when a tidal wave of energy surged through the bond, overwhelming me in its intensity as it coursed through my body. Never with my own Mori had I experienced such raw power or felt the kind of strength that was saturating every cell of my body.

Nikolas's arms fell away and I staggered back from him. "What have you done?"

His face was gray and clammy, and his eyes were clouded when they met mine briefly before they closed. A violent tremor shook his body, and the vampires had to restrain him to keep him from falling off the platform. The episode passed and his head lolled to one side.

My Mori wailed. Every part of me froze, incapable of accepting what I was seeing and feeling. *Solmi!* my Mori cried, freeing me from my paralysis. The bond was still there, but already I could feel it weakening. I threw my arms around him and pushed the strength he'd given me back into his body. "You promised you'd fight!" I screamed. "You said you wouldn't leave me."

Nothing.

I beat on his chest. Beneath my fists something moved, and my power surged around the weakening barrier to get to the vamhir demon growing inside him. I pushed desperately into his chest, but I already knew it was too late.

I sagged against him and stared down at his lifeless face. "No. No, no, no, no."

"Nikolas?" Elena ripped me away from him, and I fell to my knees in the snow, gasping for breath.

He wouldn't leave me. He's not gone. He's not gone. He's not gone.

Elena's scream of rage penetrated my shock and sent vampires running from the courtyard. "You killed him."

Her words sent a shockwave through my body, and I felt something fracture deep inside of me. Out of the fissure poured grief unlike any I had known before, and it burned through me, consuming me until I knew there would be nothing left but an empty shell. My Mori roared its own agony, and I called to it. It joined with me and our pain became one. I hung my head and let the grief take us.

When Elena's hands wrapped around my throat and squeezed the air from my lungs, I didn't fight her. When she threw me across the courtyard and I lay in a heap in the snow, I didn't try to get up. When she screamed all the ways she was going to torture me, I didn't flinch. She had taken the only thing that mattered to me. There was nothing else she could do to hurt me.

Then Elena stalked over to the platform and picked up Nikolas's body.

My head lifted from the ground. My vision tunneled on the vampire holding the most precious thing in my life.

Blood roared in my ears. I trembled as the demon's energy suffused my body until I didn't know where I ended and it began. I stood and the snow crunched beneath my bare feet.

A growl rumbled up from my chest and echoed through the courtyard.

Elena turned and shock crossed her face before she snarled. "Ava, I need to tend to my mate. Deal with that until I'm ready for her."

"Yes, Master."

Ava blurred across the courtyard and grabbed my arm. "Let's go."

Blue static erupted across my skin, and she hissed and dropped my arm. "That's not possible," she uttered as my body began to glow and my hair crackled and lifted off my shoulders. She took a step back.

I captured her wrist. She screeched in pain and tried to pull away, but my hand was fused to her. A jolt of power took her to her knees.

"Ava Bryant," my Mori and I said in one voice. "You hurt our mate."

Her eyes rounded and she shook her head. "I didn't. She wouldn't let me touch him."

I tilted my head to one side and studied the fear in her eyes. Her fear turned to shock when my hand blurred and punched straight through her ribcage. She made a wet choking sound as my hand reappeared holding her demon-encased heart. I squeezed and they both turned to dust.

"Piece-by-piece," I said as she toppled into the snow.

I turned to face Elena as she laid Nikolas on the ground. Seeing him lying at her feet intensified my rage until there was room for nothing else inside me.

The world slowed down. Elena moved, and I raced forward to meet her attack. We collided and she grabbed for my throat while I went for her chest. My strike was not enough to disable a Master, but it tore her away from me and sent her flying backward. She landed easily on her feet and came at me again. Her claws scored my chest before I struck again. This time she stumbled when she landed.

Hands grabbed my arms from behind. Elena sneered triumphantly as two vampires held me for her.

Flames erupted on either side of me. Screams tore at my eardrums before the two vampires exploded. Burning gore spread across the snow and splattered Elena's white wedding dress. She shrieked and smacked at the fire licking at her skirt. At the same time, an explosion came from inside the house, followed by screams. It sounded like Grigor's lab had blown up.

Elena stared hard at me. "I think, niece, that it is time to end this little tantrum of yours. Now, stop this and come to me."

I felt a soft push against my mind, and I batted it away as if it was an annoying gnat. "Your weak little mind has no effect on me."

She started to circle me, visibly agitated by the discovery that I wasn't such easy prey after all. "I can't believe Nikolas took a half breed for a mate," she sneered. "Look where it got him."

Pain lanced through me, but it was quickly consumed by my rage. "Don't say his name."

"It's your fault he's dead, you know. He gave you his strength through the bond, didn't he? He would have survived the change if not for you." She shook her head. "How does it feel to know you killed your own mate?"

I knew she was baiting me, but the truth in her words flayed open my soul. Nikolas had sacrificed himself for me. He was dead because of me. I would carry that with me for the rest of my life.

Her words served their purpose. I didn't react fast enough when she flew at me, and she was able to pin me to the ground.

"Looks like old Azar was wrong about you," she gloated as her fangs extended.

Shouts from inside the house tore her attention from me, and I sent another powerful blast into her. She flew backward and landed a dozen feet away. Smoked curled from the ends of her blond hair, and her fair skin had taken on a slightly gray pallor. Her movements were slower when she got to her feet this time to face off with me.

"Oh dear God. Elena!"

The two of us turned our heads to look at the blond warrior standing near the door. Tristan's face was etched in shock and pain as he stared at the sister he'd lost many years ago. Behind him stood Chris and Desmund. I should have felt joy at seeing them, but all I felt was anguish and rage. They were too late.

"Tristan," Elena simpered, giving him an angelic smile.

Her brother stood frozen as a dozen warriors spilled into the courtyard and fanned out around us. Chris and Desmund moved toward Elena with their swords raised.

My voice resonated through the courtyard. "She's mine."

"Sara," Chris began.

The grief tried to surface again, but the rage smothered it. "She killed him. She is mine."

Chris looked past me to the body lying in the snow. Sorrow filled his eyes, but he didn't speak. He nodded and stepped back.

Desmund hesitated then did the same.

Elena let out a girlish laugh. "It's like a family reunion. My beloved brother and cousin, and of course my darling niece. If you'd only arrived a little earlier, Tristan, you could have given me away at my wedding."

Everyone stared at her, but I knew what she was doing. She was stalling, trying to throw them off while she recovered from my last attack. When Elena's eyes shifted to me, I saw her real intent. My body buzzed with electricity as I coiled to attack.

In a blur, she was gone, leaving behind nothing but a trail in the snow beyond the courtyard.

A roar of pure rage scorched my throat and blackness filled my eyesight. A second later, I was standing in the middle of a frozen lake that lay behind the house. I threw up my hands as Elena came out of the darkness, her eyes rounded in disbelief. The blast lit up the night, and chunks of ice flew from the surface of the lake when her body slammed into it.

I ignored the shouts from the shore as I stalked toward the vampire who was already getting to her feet. Her arrogant sneer was gone now, replaced by fear and pain. She feinted to her left and then sped to the right. Instead of giving chase, my bare feet planted on the ice, and I called to the magic in the lake. Elena skidded to a stop as a jagged wall of ice erupted in her path. She whirled in the other direction, but the wall moved faster. Within seconds, the two of us were enclosed inside a dome of solid ice.

Panic showed on her face and she tried to use her vampire strength to punch through the ice. Every molecule of frozen water around us was connected to me, and the moment her hand touched the ice, magic coiled around her wrist. She screamed as it snaked up her arm, branding her skin.

I released her, and she stumbled back, clutching her arm to her chest. Her expression was a mix of fear and hatred when she turned to face me.

"Impressive display, niece. Too bad you couldn't use your magic to save dear, sweet Nikolas."

My body trembled as my Mori fought to take over, to destroy the thing that had killed our mate. I held it back and watched Elena as she walked along the wall of ice, looking for an escape.

"Do you want to hear about our time together while you were locked up in my cell, what his sweet blood tasted like on my tongue? Maybe you'd prefer to hear about how my hands ran over his naked body as I forced him to take my blood into him. The change is never easy, but it is agonizing for a Mohiri. Do you know he called out for you when the pain tore through his body?"

A scream welled up from deep within me, and my fragile hold on my sanity threatened to shatter as the demon pushed to the surface. The ice groaned beneath my feet. The walls shook, and shards of ice fell around us as the entire dome threatened to drop onto our heads.

Elena smiled. That was exactly what she wanted.

I smiled back. "I met a powerful Hale witch who could also see the future. He told me the ones hunting me would give me the power to become the thing they fear the most. I thought he meant you would fear me because I could make you human again, but I was wrong. I finally get what he was telling me.

"You hunted me, and you hurt the people I love. You did everything in your power to destroy me. You took my power and held me prisoner. You won, but that wasn't enough for you. You had to take *him* from me."

My laugh sounded mad to my own ears. "And now look at me. You brought me here. *You* made me into this. It looks like Azar was right after all. Madeline's half-blood daughter will destroy you. I guess Azar forgot to tell you that *you* would be the one to make his vision come true."

I walked toward her and she ran for the other side of the small space we occupied. A smile curved my lips, and the walls began to move, closing in on us. Grief poked around the edges of the rage, and I knew I would not be able to keep it at bay much longer. It was time to end this.

When Elena realized there was nowhere else to run, she faced me in a last stand. Ice sprung from the wall behind her and encased her small body despite her attempts to break it. She was no match for the magic of the whole lake that had come to do my bidding.

Standing over her with so much power coursing through me, I had never felt so alive, yet dead and empty inside at the same time.

A shard of ice flew into my outstretched hand. I ran my other hand along the ice, and a long thin blade formed under my fingers. It was blue with golden threads running through it, and the hilt was an exact replica of the one on Nikolas's sword.

My eyes met Elena's. I wanted to make her suffering go on forever because that was how long mine would last. Instead, I raised my weapon as I'd seen Nikolas do countless times.

"He was mine," I said as the razor sharp blade sliced through her throat.

The sword slipped from my fingers and shattered, and the dome of ice crumbled around me. On the other side, Chris, Tristan, and Desmund stood transfixed as I walked toward them. Tristan reached for me, but I pulled away from him. Chris's hand touched my arm as I passed, but he didn't try to stop me as I walked back to the shore.

Warriors stared at me as I entered the courtyard and went to where Nikolas's body still lay in the snow. Sitting on the ground, I pulled his head and shoulders into my lap. My hands trembled as I stroked his face and ran my fingers through his soft hair. He liked to touch my hair whenever he held me, and I'd always found it so soothing. I touched the still lips and remembered his smiles and the beautiful gray eyes that had looked at me with love such a short time ago. I could still feel the bond that connected us, but it was empty like a phantom limb. It was a jagged hole inside of me that would never be filled.

My rage faded and I rocked back and forth as waves of grief crashed down on me. *Why did you make me love you and then leave me?*

Tristan knelt beside me. "Sara, we have to –"

"No." I hugged Nikolas tighter, prepared to fight anyone who tried to separate us. "Leave us alone."

"No one is going to take him from you," Tristan said gently. "Let us move you both somewhere warmer."

"Nikolas doesn't get cold." And I would never be warm again.

Chris sat on his haunches on my other side. "Nikolas would want you to take care of yourself. You can't stay out here."

I shook off the hand he laid on my shoulder. "He needs me. I won't leave him."

"Here, little one." Desmund wrapped a thick blanket around my shoulders. I grabbed the edges and pulled it over Nikolas and me, blocking out the rest of the world. *I'm here, Nikolas. I won't let them take you from me.*

My Mori shifted restlessly, making me aware that we were still joined. After everything we'd been through, we had finally become one. *You would have been so proud of me, Nikolas.*

It was strange sharing my mind with another consciousness, trying to filter out its emotions from my own. It moved again as it tried to settle in, and a host of emotions and sensations washed over me. One sensation reminded me of Nikolas so acutely it was like a knife in my chest.

Stop, I said. *Don't do that thing you used to do when he –*

Butterfly wings caressed my mind so softly they were like a memory.

Now I'm going crazy. Please, don't do this to me.

The demon quieted.

I let out a long, ragged sigh. Maybe going crazy was better than never feeling him again. I stroked the planes of his face, as familiar to me as my own. *I don't know if I can bear this. I'm not as strong as you thought I was, Nikolas. I'm so lost without you.*

A memory of him holding me filled my mind. I could feel the warmth of his arms, his love wrapping around me.

Oh, Nikolas.

Sara.

Solmi? my Mori cried.

My hands stilled and I forgot to breathe. *Nikolas?*

I'm here, Sara.

Oh God, I am going crazy.

I felt another soft caress against my mind. *Feel my face, Sara.*

I laid my palm against his cheek and felt... warmth. *Please.* I bent over him until my mouth hovered about his. A second later, I felt a shallow breath against my lips.

I sat up and shouted frantically. "He's alive!"

Tristan and Chris were beside me in an instant. "No, Sara, he's gone," Tristan said hoarsely.

I grabbed his hand and held it above Nikolas's mouth.

"Jesus Christ, he's breathing."

Chris shot to his feet. "Get the healers," he shouted. He looked down at me. "We need to move him inside."

I nodded, and he lifted Nikolas easily. I ran beside him as he carried Nikolas into the house. The place was trashed, and there were vampire bodies everywhere. Chris found what looked like a guestroom on the main floor and laid Nikolas on the bed.

I'm here, Nikolas.

Two healers I recognized from Westhorne ran into the room, carrying medical bags. I had to move aside to give them room, and my heart thundered in my chest as they worked on him. I listened to them discussing his vital signs and debating the best treatment. Finally, I couldn't take it anymore.

"Just help him, goddammit!" I screamed at them. I was not going to lose him a second time. My heart couldn't survive it.

I'm not going anywhere, Sara.

If you do, I'll never forgive you.

One of the healers produced a syringe, which she inserted into Nikolas's chest. I held my breath as she checked his pulse and breathing. She looked at me and smiled, and my legs almost gave out.

"He's suffered some trauma around his heart, but nothing that won't heal," she explained kindly. "He should wake up soon. He's very strong."

My heart was close to bursting. "Yes, he is."

Tristan and the healers stepped out of the room to talk. Chris brought in fresh blankets to place over Nikolas, and his smile was so big his dimples showed. "You two are definitely meant for each other. I don't know which one of you is more stubborn."

"Him." I sat on the edge of the bed and held Nikolas's warm hand. My emotions were such a mess I didn't know whether to laugh or cry. My body decided for me, and hot tears spilled down my face.

Shhh, don't cry. A gentle wave of warm energy came through the bond at the same time that Nikolas's fingers closed around mine.

Then you better hurry up and get better, because I'm a bit of a basket case right now.

His lips twitched slightly at one corner. *I'd heal a lot faster if I could hold my mate.*

He didn't have to ask me twice. I climbed in beside him and curled against his side with my cheek resting above his heart so I could hear every precious beat. "Is this real? Because if I'm dreaming, I never want to wake up."

It's real. I'm here, moy malen'kiy voin.

"How is this possible?" My throat closed off until I could barely speak. "I felt you die."

You killed the vamhir demon. My Mori just needed time to recover. You brought me back.

A sob escaped me and I pressed my face against his chest. "Please, don't leave me again."

His arm moved slowly to wrap around me. "Never."

CHAPTER 26

"I STILL CAN'T believe that all this time, Tristan's little sister was the Master."

"You're not the only one."

Roland shook his head. "That's messed up... and really creepy when you think about it."

A shiver ran through me. "You're telling me." I'd spent the last two weeks trying to put those nightmarish days behind me. I still woke every night in a cold sweat with Nikolas holding me and whispering that we were safe and together. He had fully recovered from his physical injuries, but our spiritual wounds would take a lot longer to heal. Every day it got a little easier, and one day we'd be able to put our ordeal behind us.

You okay? Nikolas's hand covered mine on my lap. It still amazed me how good he was at reading my emotions and knowing exactly what I needed. Like this trip to New Hastings.

Yes. I looked at the people sitting around the living room of the apartment. Roland and Peter were there, of course. I couldn't have a homecoming without them. Jordan had come with us to "see where it all started" as she put it. Chris was here for old times' sake.

"So how is Tristan handling all of it?" Peter asked.

"Good, considering," Chris said quietly. "He arranged for her burial, and he had to tell my mother and their parents about her. They're taking it hard, as expected."

My chest tightened when I thought about Tristan. He'd been devastated about Elena, and racked with guilt over what she had done to Nikolas and me. I'd told him he was no more responsible for what she had done than he was for what had happened to her. One day he would see I was right, but for now he was grieving his sister all over again. After the burial, he'd immersed himself in work. He spoke very little except to Desmund, who was a good friend and a confidante, just as Tristan had been for him for so many years.

It was through Desmund that I'd learned Madeline had finally contacted Tristan two days ago. The Master's death had freed Madeline from her compulsion and she no longer had to live in fear. According to Desmund, Tristan and Madeline had talked for a long time, and Tristan had looked happy for the first time in weeks. Maybe rebuilding his relationship with his daughter would help him through his grief.

I had no plans to build anything with Madeline, but even I couldn't stay mad at someone forever. Maybe, someday. For now, I was glad she had reached out to her father.

Roland exhaled loudly. "Tristan's a good guy. Hate to hear he's having such a rough time."

"Me too," Peter said.

Jordan looked at me and her expression said she'd had enough of the sad talk. "This is a nice place, Sara, but it's small and so quiet. How did you stand it?"

Nikolas and Chris laughed. "It wasn't this quiet the last time we were here," Nikolas told her.

Chris made a face. "I seem to recall taking a vacation after my time in Maine." He looked at Nikolas. "How many vampire nests did we clean out on that trip to Vegas?"

Roland shot me a sly grin. "When the pack heard you were coming for a few days, a couple of them went to visit family out of town."

I rolled my eyes at them. "Funny, guys. And to answer your question, Jordan, I loved it here. We used to find plenty of things to keep us occupied when we were kids. I don't think I was ever bored."

Roland grinned. "If our parents knew half the stuff we used to get into..." He leaned forward to rest his elbows on his knees. "Is Nate moving back now that it's safe?"

"I think there are too many bad memories here for him to ever come back." The last time Nate had been in this apartment, he was a vampire. He was still trying to forget that part of his life.

"What's he going to do with the place if he doesn't come back?" Peter asked.

"He was talking about selling it, so Nikolas bought it for me." I turned my head to smile at Nikolas, and he leaned in for a quick kiss.

Jordan snorted. "Yeah, they're like that *all* the time now since they mated."

She and I shared a secret smile. Jordan had been positively giddy when I told her that Nikolas and I had finally completed the bond. She'd tried to pry the details out of me, but some things are just too intimate to share, even with your best female friend. I'd given her the "when" and "where" but that was pretty much it. She'd replied that the dreamy look on my face told her all she needed to know. Plus, we *were* talking about Nikolas.

"So I guess that means we'll be seeing more of you guys," Roland said hopefully.

"Until we leave for our trip," Nikolas told him.

"In June we're going to spend the summer in Russia." I couldn't keep the excitement out of my voice. Nikolas had told me so much about his homeland that I couldn't wait to explore it with him. I was nervous about meeting his parents, but eager to learn more about his early life. I'd already spoken to his mother on the phone, and she was as excited as I was for our visit.

Chris's lips twitched. "Perhaps we should tell Miroslav Fortress to be on alert this summer."

I picked up a small pillow and threw it at him. "You're going to miss me. Admit it."

He caught the pillow and flashed his dimples. "I don't know how I'll get by without you, Cousin."

Roland's mouth turned down. "Well, we'll miss you. This place is not the same with you gone. School sucks even more now."

"That reminds me; how is all the extra schoolwork coming along?"

Roland and Peter groaned together. Once they'd returned to school, the teachers had piled a bunch of assignments on them to make up for the month they'd missed. They had to complete it all if they didn't want to repeat their senior year.

"I'll graduate this year if it kills me," Roland declared. "Or if Uncle Max doesn't do it first."

"Is he still mad about you two taking off?"

Peter grimaced. "He's over that. I think. Now he's all about us learning our pack responsibilities. Hunting, patrolling, stuff like that."

"That doesn't sound so bad," Chris said.

"That part's okay. It's the other stuff I dread." Roland clenched his hands. "We have to start attending pack gatherings."

His eyes met mine, and I understood the real reason for his anxiety. Pack gatherings meant a lot of female werewolves looking for a mate, and the last thing my best friend wanted was to settle down. Roland wanted freedom to come and go as he pleased, and to enjoy the classic Mustang GT he and his cousin were rebuilding for him.

I looked from Roland to Peter. "I thought Maxwell didn't make you go to those."

Peter seemed resigned, but Roland looked ready to bolt. "Not the whole thing, but we're expected to go to some of the meetings once we turn eighteen. There's no getting out of it." Roland smiled grimly. "I don't suppose there's any chance of a vampire invasion to get us out of it, is there?"

"Maybe not here, but there are always lots of baddies out there to kill, especially for us *warriors*." Jordan smiled smugly. Last week, she had officially become a warrior. It shouldn't have happened for another six months, but her field experience put her far ahead of other trainees. She had more kills under her belt than any new warrior, and people were already calling her the next Nikolas.

Not that anyone could ever be as good as *my* warrior.

"Wish I could help you guys out, but I'll be in LA. That's where I'm going when I leave here." Jordan's face flushed with excitement. "They still have a lot of vampires there, and I can't wait to do a little hunting." That and she'd heard the foreign warriors were still in California. She planned on getting better acquainted with one surly Egyptian male in particular.

Chris winked at me. "If anyone can attract a horde of vampires, it's Sara. Maybe she can help you out."

I made a face at him. "Sorry, guys, but my schedule is kind of full right now. Eldeorin wants to start training me again, and we decided it was a good idea."

Nikolas made a low sound that was suspiciously like a snort. He was grateful for everything Eldeorin had done for me, but he couldn't bring himself to like the faerie. Eldeorin didn't help, taking any opportunity to annoy Nikolas.

"Eldeorin was pretty excited when he found out I transported like he does. It was only that one time, but he thinks we've barely tapped into my powers. I might even be able to do glamours by this time next year."

"Cool!" Roland and Peter said together.

"And I'm working with David on a new project."

"David, your hacker friend?" Peter asked.

"Yep. After he found Elena's place, Tristan offered him a job working for us. We got word that some gulaks are running an international slavery ring. David and Kelvan are going to track them down, and then I'm going to kick some demon ass."

"*We* are going to kick some demon ass," Nikolas corrected me.

Roland laughed. "So I guess that means you're done with combat training."

I made a face. "I wish."

Jordan picked up her bottle of water from the coffee table. "Oh, that's right! Have you seen that new trainer who just arrived from Greece?" She fanned herself. "Makes me almost wish I was a trainee again."

I nodded. "I hear he's wicked good with a crossbow, too."

Nikolas made a sound in his throat just loud enough for me to hear.

Down boy, I teased, earning a playful scowl. Completing our bond had eased his possessive male instincts, but it hadn't eliminated them. I was a lot more understanding of them now because I had my moments, too. And being fully joined with my Mori meant getting used to a lot of emotions and urges I hadn't had to deal with before. One thing I'd learned was that demons were *very* temperamental and possessive of their mates.

Jordan snickered and took a mouthful of water – and promptly began to choke on it. Peter slapped her on the back as she gaped at something past the living room archway.

I leaned over to see what she was staring at, and my breath caught in my throat.

Letting go of Nikolas's hand, I launched myself at the thin pale gray creature standing in the hallway. He let out a gravelly laugh and hugged me back as I cried into his shaggy gray-brown hair. Behind me I heard Jordan wheezing and Chris say, "Still think it's boring here, Jordan?"

I pulled back and met Remy's wide violet eyes. "I can't believe you're here."

He grinned, showing off his short sharp teeth. "I ward house to keep it safe for you. It tell me when you come home."

"But won't the elders be angry?" I held his hands, afraid he'd disappear again.

"Elders say it okay to be friends again. I miss my friend."

I wiped my eyes with my sleeve. "I missed you, too."

Remy looked behind me, and I glanced over my shoulder at Nikolas standing in the doorway. "You remember Nikolas and my friends."

He gave a slight nod. "Warrior."

I turned toward the living room, still holding one of his hands. "I guess you've met everyone here except Jordan. Jordan, this is my friend Remy, who I told you about."

"Hello," she croaked.

Grinning, I faced him again. "Let's go to into the kitchen so we can sit." I had so many things to tell him that I didn't know where to start. My life had changed drastically since the last time we'd seen each other, and I was sure he had things to share with me, too.

Roland came out of the living room. "We're going to show Jordan around and give you guys some time to talk." He leaned toward me. "I think she could use some air."

Jordan smacked the back of his head as she walked by. "I heard that, Wolf Boy. Come on. But no peeing on fire hydrants."

Roland and Peter scowled and the others laughed as they filed out, leaving Remy and me alone in the hallway.

We sat at the kitchen table, and for a long moment we just stared at each other as if neither of us could believe we were here together.

"I thought the elders would never allow you to see me again. What changed their minds?"

"Eldeorin come to visit. He make elders change minds."

I gawked at him. "Eldeorin? He never told me he knew you."

"Trolls and faeries cousins. You know that."

A long ago memory surfaced of when we first became friends, and he'd told me about his people and how they were related to the Fae. How could I have forgotten that? "Wait. Does this mean I'm your cousin, too?"

He nodded, and I almost jumped out of my chair. "Why didn't you ever tell me?"

"I not know you Fae then. You go through *liannan* and now I see."

After all I'd been through I'd thought nothing else could shock me, but Remy had managed to blow my mind. Cousins. It was going to take a while for that one to sink in.

It also explained why the elders had decided to allow us to be friends again. I owed Eldeorin a huge hug when I saw him – just not when Nikolas was around.

Remy's eyes grew serious. "Eldeorin say you kill many vampires and vampire Master. He say you very strong now."

"That's true." I let out a deep breath. "I have so much to tell you."

For a long time we talked about what had happened in our lives since the last time we'd seen each other. He asked questions about some of the things I'd seen, and it felt odd to be educating him when he had always been my teacher. It just showed me again how much I had changed.

"Warrior is good mate for you," he said with approval, and my heart expanded as it did every time someone called Nikolas my mate. "It good to see you happy."

"I was happy before."

"You laugh, but you always have pain here." He placed a hand over his heart. "No more sadness in your eyes."

It didn't surprise me that Remy had seen the pain I'd carried inside me for so many years. My troll friend had always been wise beyond his age.

And he was right. I had never stopped grieving for my dad. My grief, my bitterness toward Madeline, and my hatred and fear of those who'd taken my dad from me, had festered inside me for so many years. I no longer carried around those dark emotions. I would always miss my dad, but I'd finally laid my grief to rest.

Meeting Madeline had closed that chapter in my life, and instead of bitterness, I felt pity for the woman who would always regret giving up the man she loved.

I would always hate the evil things in the world, but I no longer feared them. Maybe it was because of my new strength, or because nothing seemed as frightening as my ordeal with the Master. Or maybe it was because of the warrior who'd been beside me through it all, offering his strength when I needed it and giving his love selflessly.

"No more sadness," I agreed. "And now I have you back, too."

He smiled. "Will you come often?"

"Yes. I'll get Eldeorin to bring me here every chance I get." Something occurred to me. "You can transport like he does, can't you?"

"Yes."

"Then you can come visit me, too."

He grinned, as if the thought had never occurred to him. "I like that."

Eventually, Remy said he had to go. I was sad when he hugged me goodbye, but at least this time I knew we'd see each other again soon.

After he left, I wandered around the apartment, thinking how blessed I was. Most people would not say that with all I'd been through. But I knew those experiences and the suffering had made me who I was, and I had gained so much from them. I had found a home among the Mohiri and the Fae, something no one had believed possible. I had friends and family who loved me unconditionally. And I had Nikolas and the kind of love most people only dreamed of.

I stood in the middle of my old room, wondering what I'd do with the building. Judith had offered to continue taking care of it for me, but it seemed a shame to let it sit empty most of the year.

Looking around the brightly lit loft, it struck me that this would make the perfect studio for someone who loved to paint. Someone like Emma. She and I had become good friends over the last two weeks. I loved having her at Westhorne, but she felt out of place there. She was still recovering from her ordeal, but I knew she would leave when she was strong enough. I'd told her I would help her with whatever she decided to do. She kept saying she wanted a simple, quiet life. What better place to start over than New Hastings?

I was making a mental list of art supplies and furniture when I felt Nikolas returning. The door opened as I ran down the stairs, and their laughter filled the apartment.

"I'm starving," Roland complained, bringing a smile to my lips because he and Peter were always hungry. "I say we pick up some beer and order Gino's."

"Gino's?" Chris asked, and both boys stared at him.

"Dude, you were here for what, a month?" Roland asked incredulously. "How could you not have had Gino's pizza?"

"It's only the best pizza ever," I said as I reached the main floor.

Nikolas's eyes found mine. *I like seeing you this happy.*

I like seeing you. I gave him a little smile that made his eyes change to that smoky gray color I loved.

"Okay, Gino's it is," Roland declared. "Does everyone like lots of meat on their pizza?"

"Duh," Jordan and I said together.

Nikolas came over to me as the others discussed pizza toppings and beer. "Want to take a walk with me before dinner? I hear the wharves are empty this time of day."

We both smiled at his reference to our first walk together. I grabbed my coat, scarf, and gloves because March weather in Maine is no joke. Telling the others we'd be back in time for dinner, we set out.

It was close to sunset and the air was frosty on the quiet waterfront. I hooked my arm through Nikolas's as we walked toward the wharves. Memories of my old life surrounded me. I had a new home now, but this place would always hold a special place in my heart.

An icy wind buffeted us when we reached the wharf, and Nikolas wrapped an arm around me. "Are you cold? We can go back."

"I'm good."

We didn't talk much as we walked the length of the wharf, just like when he joined me at Westhorne for my daily walks with Hugo and Woolf. Sometimes, just being together was enough and no words were needed between us.

At the end of the wharf, we stopped and he drew me back against him so he was blocking the wind. He wrapped his arms around me, and we watched the sun set the bay on fire as it sank below the horizon.

I leaned into his warmth. "Remember the last time we stood in this spot?"

He pressed his lips against my hair. "I'll never forget that day. You looked so lost after our talk, and I didn't know how to make it easier for you. I wondered if I should have sent someone else to talk to you. I had no experience with orphans before you."

"So I've heard. If it makes you feel better, no one could have broken that news to me in any way that I would have accepted it easier." I hugged his arms. "I'm glad it was you."

"You say that now."

I laughed softly. "Would you really have sent another warrior to talk to me?"

"No. I couldn't let anyone else come to you, not when I knew what you were to me. In Portland, you didn't show any sign that you felt anything between us. I needed to see you again to be sure of the bond." He pulled me closer. "When I pushed against the bond, I felt your Mori respond, and I could see it in your eyes."

I turned in his arms and gazed up at him. "My poor warrior. I didn't make it easy for you, did I?"

He kissed my forehead. "I laid some heavy things on you all at once, so I knew it was going to take some time for you to accept it. I could have handled it better, too."

"Tell the truth. I was a total brat."

"Well, if you really want me to be honest..."

I smacked his chest and he smiled. "You have no idea how hard it was to ride away from you that day when you refused to leave. My Mori wasn't happy either. It wanted me to throw you over my shoulder and make you come with us."

I raised an eyebrow at the image that conjured. "And what did you want?"

His eyes sparkled with laughter. "I wanted to find the nearest bar and drink until I forgot a certain orphan with bewitching green eyes. I kept telling myself it was my Mori who wanted you, but the truth was, I noticed you before my demon did, and I wanted to see you again."

Warmth pooled in my stomach. "Would you do it differently now?"

"Yes."

"What would you do?"

"I'd do this."

I squealed as he swung me up over his shoulder and started striding back toward the waterfront. "Nikolas, put me down, you big lug!" I yelled through my laughter.

He patted my backside. "This time my Mori and I are in complete agreement."

"You do know I can zap your warrior ass, right?" I squirmed and he held me tighter.

His deep laugh warmed me to my toes. "But you won't."

"How do you know?"

"Because you like me... *a lot*."

I stopped wriggling and started grinning like a fool. What could I say? He was right.

~ The End ~

ABOUT THE AUTHOR

When she is not at her job as a computer programmer, Karen Lynch can be found writing, reading and baking. A native of Newfoundland, Canada, she currently lives in Charlotte, North Carolina with her cats and two crazy lovable German Shepherds: Rudy and Sophie.

Made in the USA
Columbia, SC
06 February 2019